ISBN 978-1-914301-19-3

Published 2021

Published by Black Velvet Seductions Publishing

All Gone Copyright 2021 S.K. White
Cover design Copyright 2021 Jessica Greeley

Dedication

I would like to dedicate All Gone to the romance and sci-fi lovers out there who inspire me to create new worlds and endless adventures for all my characters. In addition, I want to thank my family and friends for their never-ending patience, support and encouragement.

Chapter One

6-20-2024

Freelance investigative reporter, Paige Martin, glimpsed down at her tablet and clicked on a video entitled *Amazing Crop Circles*. She watched as a crop circle magically carved its way into the landscape. Paige tossed back her head, removed several loose strands of her honey blonde hair out of the way and drew her blue eyes closer to the screen.

"Holy shit!" She pushed pause, leaned back in her chair and stared at the provocative image. "This can't be real?" Paige stuck her fingers in the ceramic bowl and fumbled through a mass of elastic hairbands, clamps, paperclips, barrettes and hair clips. She pulled out a hair clip and secured her wayward strands. After clipping the shoulder-length offenders, she hit play and finished the video.

Other links from around the world popped up, so she clicked on each link, and the same crop circle appeared in different countries. She scrolled back to each previous clip. "They all appeared today." She glanced at the repetitive date displayed around the circle. "Huh? 4-20-25 Very odd."

Paige grabbed a Post-it, wrote the date and time, and underlined the numbers four, twenty and twenty-five. Then she wrinkled her forehead, clicked on the videos and viewed them several more times. "It looks real. Better make sure the last one was a hoax."

She jerked as her phone vibrated then swiped the call icon. "Kent."

"Hey, girl. I'm headed to examine the second sighting several miles outside of LA." Kent drew in a deep breath. "No time to talk now. Paige, this could be it."

Paige pressed the phone closer to her lips. "Call me if the sighting is confirmed."

"Will do." Kent hung up.

Paige bit her bottom lip. "Damn. If Kent's going, they must be real. He's the expert on UFOs."

She heated the teakettle and retrieved a pastry from the kitchen counter. As her English Breakfast tea steeped, Paige bit into her glazed donut and scanned the files on her tablet. Then she licked the glaze off her fingertips, clicked on a file she'd saved on crop circles and tapped the record button to dictate. She replayed the videos of the old crop circles and compared them to the newest ones.

"No similarities. The old ones vary like snowflakes, but the new ones are identical in shape, size, and content." She zoomed in on New York and LA. "One large circle and a smaller circle in the center. Stick figures huddled inside the small circle." Paige bent forward. "All of them pointing to the sky." She leaned back, focused on the outer edge of the large circle and the series of numbers repeating 4-20-25. "Damn! In between each series of numbers are several primitive or antiquated-looking symbols." Paige zoomed in on each of the ciphers. "They look like the ancient symbols I've found in archeology books that were painted or carved on rock walls or pyramids. Must be a reference to a religion or several ancient cultures. Maybe 4-20-25 refers to a very specific date. Perhaps the stick figures pointing up toward the sky are instructions to view the heavens on that date."

Paige's phone beeped. Kent had sent a text.

>Check your email.

He'd forwarded several links from work contacts. Paige clicked on the new links and viewed several images from Europe, Asia, Africa, South America, Mexico, and Australia. Kent had included several pictures he'd taken in New York and a few pics from members of MUFON—the Mutual UFO Network.

>After I finish in LA, I'm headed to Asia. I'll send you any information I collect.

Paige selected a happy emoji and pushed send.

Paige stared at the symbols on her tablet. "If anyone can decipher these symbols, it's Andrea."

She snatched her phone and swiped Andrea's phone number. Andrea answered, and Paige enlarged the symbols on the crop circle. "Andrea, besides the fact that the date coincides with Easter, do you have any idea what the other symbols represent?"

"I noticed Easter too. Provocative isn't it." Andrea cleared her throat. "I've consulted with several colleagues from different universities, and we've all reached a consensus about the symbols. I'll email the groups' analysis to you now. Take a look and call me back if you have any questions. Paige, this is seismic."

Paige scrolled through the ancient symbols from Christianity, Islam, Native American, Bahá'í, and several eastern religions. "Damn! Andrea's symbols match those found in the new crop circles."

She reviewed the rest of the information from Andrea and emailed her.

Thanks, Andrea, I promise to send a copy of my article when I finish.

Paige incorporated Kent's pictures and information from New York and LA into with Andrea's findings and wrote an article on the new crop circles. Two days later, she sold her article, lifted a glass of Merlot and emailed a copy to Kent and Andrea.

Within four days, every evangelical preacher and religious leader had weighed in on the meaning of the symbols. Paige hit the play button on her tablet and turned up the volume.

Followers, this is the end of the world. It is the second coming. Prepare!

Paige selected videos from several other televangelists and radio talk show hosts that were dominating the internet and the airwaves, and they all echoed the same sentiment—prepare for the second coming.

By the end of the week, UFO enthusiasts joined in and appeared on talk shows. Paige grabbed her teacup, propped her legs on the coffee table and took a sip. The host turned to one of his guests and asked, "What do you make of this?"

The man sat up straight. "This looks like it may be an opportunity for first contact with extraterrestrials. I believe they will arrive on April twentieth, 2025. The numbers coincide with Easter. Perhaps this represents the dawning of a new beginning. I acknowledge its importance by the way the numbers are displayed repetitively. It is also clear to me that something will appear in the sky on that date, and, logically, that could happen at the locations of the first crop circles. However, all of us, whether as science enthusiasts or religious scholars, must remain skeptical at this time. We must ask ourselves, is this real or an elaborate hoax? Or could this be a huge conspiracy?"

Paige clicked off the television. "Real or hoax? If this is a conspiracy, it's a damn good one."

The next day, Paige seized the remote and pressed the on button. A charismatic evangelical preacher filled the screen. She snatched her notepad out of her backpack and wrote down his name, the local church he was affiliated with, and the cable station he preached from. Just before five, she called and set up an interview for the following week with Reverend Paul Stevens. Then she hung up her smartphone, set it down on the coffee table and headed to her bedroom to get ready to meet Logan for dinner.

After her shower, Paige dressed in her favorite crimson wrap dress with the low neckline then reached down in the closet, grabbed her black stiletto heels and carried them into her living room. She threw her shoes down next to the coffee table and reached for the phone. Logan's picture appeared with a text message. Paige read it then tossed her phone down on the table.

"Dinner canceled again. The ER's shorthanded! He's always covering for the other doctors."

She stormed over to the wine rack, opened a bottle of red wine and poured a glass. She fixed a chicken salad sandwich, grabbed her wine and headed back to the coffee table. She tapped DVR, chose a chick flick from the menu and nibbled on chicken salad and rye bread.

Around midnight, Paige opened her eyes to a home shopping commercial blasting the latest must-have crap. She fumbled for the empty bottle of Merlot and kissed it.

"You're the only thing that's cuddling me tonight. Logan and I have been together for three years, but according to him, we're in no hurry to get married. Hell, no. We bought our dream house, and he decided to remodel it first. So, with our wedding on hold until the house is finished, and Logan staying there to oversee its progress and me here at the apartment, we never see each other." Paige hugged the bottle. "I thought if I stayed here I might see him more with all the late on-calls in the ER, but no… what does he do? He stays at that damn hospital instead. Oh yeah, I'm supposed to join him at the dream house on Thursdays, but when I go, he's never there." She lifted her bottle. "What's a girl to do? Huh? Screw it, I'm going to bed."

Paige turned off the TV and tossed the bottle in the trash. She pulled off her dress, tripped over the skirt and stumbled into bed.

In the early morning hours, Paige opened one eye as Logan crept in and crawled into bed beside her. She mumbled, "Glad you could join me."

Logan nuzzled. "What's that, babe?"

"Nothing. Goodnight. See you in the morning."

***

A week later, Paige ambled into the reverend's elaborate megachurch. Marble stairs led up to the podium, with two beautiful statues of angels standing on both sides. Stained glass windows depicting the second coming served as a background behind the podium for the Sunday sermons.

Reverend Stevens walked up behind Paige. "Ms. Martin?"

Paige spun around. "Yes. What a beautiful church you have."

The reverend held out his hand. "Welcome. Please come into my office." He motioned to a room off to the side, and the two entered his elaborate oak-trimmed office.

Once inside, he pointed to a chair in the front of his desk. "Please make yourself comfortable."

Paige sat down, retrieved her tablet from her handbag and opened it up. She inspected the reverend's eyes to size up his motives, searching his steely dark irises for clues to the windows of his soul and attempting to get a read on the good reverend's intentions. She squinted her eyes and typed.

First impressions. Oh yeah, this good reverend and his elaborate church is out to score mega money from the many souls that fill his pews. I'll bet the collection plates he passes around every Sunday and the tithings gathered monthly from the faithful contribute to the cause. The collections from his cable show that airs every Wednesday night and the cash deposits on his bank statements every month are definitely motivators for this goodly preacher to reach as many souls as possible.

Paige lifted her head, hit record and studied his plastic smile as he rambled on. Images of old ladies sending in their last savings to ensure their salvation invaded her thoughts.

The reverend coughed. "So, you have questions for me, I presume?"

"Yes. I was interested in your interpretation of the meaning of the crop circles. I have been researching and writing articles about the varying opinions on their meaning. I would like to hear your personal perception."

The reverend drew in a breath. "Well, the religious symbols lead me to believe the message is for the believers, and the image pointing to the skies tell me to be watchful."

Paige adjusted her tablet and held her stare. "What will you be watching for?"

The reverend shot her a half-smile. "You want me to tell you if I think it is the second coming of Christ, don't you?"

"You did say that on your TV show."

"Yes, I did." The reverend raised his eyebrows and bent forward. "I think we should be prepared for it, don't you?"

Paige peered up from her tablet. "So, you believe this is the first sign of the apocalypse?"

"I have looked at the state of the world these last few years, and I believe all the signs are already here." The reverend raised his hands in the air. "We are just waiting for Christ's triumphant return."

"So, you believe Jesus is coming on April twentieth, 2025?"

"I believe we should be ready. That's Easter Sunday, and I intend to help my parishioners get prepared for his arrival." The reverend narrowed his eyes. "What about you, Ms. Martin? Will you be ready?"

Paige paused and lifted her fingers from the tablet. "Either way, I will."

"If I can help, let me know." The reverend stood, leaned over his desk and held out his hand.

Realizing the interview had just ended, Paige stopped, bit her lip, put her tablet in her bag, stood up and shook his hand. "Thank you for your time."

The reverend squeezed her hand, then put his left hand over hers and patted it. "I'm glad I could help."

His cold, dark eyes pierced her. She shivered, released her hand from his grasp and muttered, "Thanks again."

He bobbed his head in response and held up his hand. "Please send me a copy of your article when you're finished."

"Happy to do that, Reverend," Paige said and walked out of the room.

She wiped her hand on her slacks, balanced her bag over her shoulder and scanned the rows and rows of pews. *These must hold thousands. I wonder if the good reverend fills every pew on his Sunday sermons. There's no doubt that as the date of the sighting draws closer, this church will be standing room only.*

A month later, Paige finished her two-page article on Reverend Paul Stevens and his megachurch and sent him a copy, but she never heard back from him.

***

On November 5, after three grueling months of interviewing experts and writing articles on crop circles, Paige typed the last word on her latest article and hit send. She grasped her glass of Merlot and sighed.

"Finally finished. Now it's just you and me." She took a sip and swirled its contents. "So, my friend, you dark, rich red beauty, the debate continues, and each group declares its own side. The religious are convinced it's the second coming, and the UFO enthusiasts draw large crowds ready to meet a first contact. Whether for a religious reason or a close encounter, the results will be the same—people will gather by the thousands where the crop circles appeared last year." She swigged the remains of the scarlet liquid. "Another article done, my friend, and it's time to bid you goodnight. Tomorrow James and I head to Rio and beyond."

The next morning, Paige set out on her journey for answers. Chasing the story of a lifetime, Paige and James, her longtime photographer, flew to Rio, Cairo, Israel, Islamabad, Beijing, and Moscow to cover the gatherings.

On March 20, 2025, Kent joined Paige and James in London, and the three went on to Rome near the Vatican. Once at the Vatican, they mingled among a large crowd of the faithful. Paige stood shoulder to shoulder with a sea of people waiting for words of comfort from the Pope. He walked out onto the balcony dressed in a long white robe and raised his hands in the air. The crowd fell silent. He waved his hands.

"We must prepare and accept a second coming or, if God willing, the unknown." Heads bowed in prayer and tears ran down the people's faces. James snapped pictures of the faithful's response to the Pope's words. After the Pope left, many followers stayed behind and knelt in prayer.

The faithful returned for several more days in search of solace, but as the date drew closer, Paige noticed more and more people were leaving the Vatican and congregating at the original crop circle in a farmer's field just outside of Rome. Paige stared out over the congregation. "It's time to go home."

On April 18, Paige, James and Kent headed back to New York to witness the final viewing.

Chapter Two

Due Date 4-20-2025

Paige and James gathered their camera equipment and met Kent at a farmer's field in the Hudson Valley, several miles outside of New York City. Thousands made their way to the area where the first crop circle had appeared a year earlier. Paige, James, and Kent pushed their way through the crowd but could not get close to the target area. They headed back to a cluster of condominiums they'd passed by earlier that bordered the farmer's field.

Light flashed from a rooftop. Kent pointed to a group of people perched on top of one of the buildings. The small group had positioned themselves on the roof of the condominium with several pairs of binoculars and long-range camera lenses. After a few friendly greetings, Paige, Kent and James joined them on the roof. James put his lens in place and began shooting pictures of the people. Paige grabbed the video camera and shot footage, alternating cameras with James. Kent scanned the huge crowd and took close-ups with his telescopic lens. He turned to Paige.

"It isn't possible to see the crop circle itself from here, but we can snap pictures of the people that surround the area. There must be at least forty thousand people out there. Most expect to see something miraculous, but some are UFO enthusiasts hoping for a first contact."

The sun dropped over the horizon, white fluffy clouds multiplied over the twilight, and a whirling bright light broke through the clouds like a projector. A face took shape among the clouds, and the people pointed and screamed in unison. Some dropped down to their knees in prayer. The sky vibrated at a pitch that sounded similar to a distant trumpet. As the timbre deepened, Paige's body pulsated in a steady beat like she was standing in the front of speakers at a rock concert.

James struggled to hold the video camera on the image that appeared in the clouds. His camera shook and shuddered. Kent kept his finger on the camera button nonstop, taking pictures of the same image in the sky. The trumpets grew louder and louder until people covered their ears. The blinding blue light flashed ever brighter and forced viewers to avert their eyes.

Suddenly, a shock wave knocked everyone to the ground and stunned them for several minutes. A green light surrounded the area. Then, without warning, all the light retracted from the sky. An empty pitch black remained behind. The black hole robbed every particle of light from the sky and from the neighborhood homes in the area.

The people slowly climbed back up from the ground and called out for each other, trying to gather their missing loved ones in a sea of darkness.

Paige sat up, rubbed her eyes, and tried to recover from her blindness. She choked. "James." Her ears rang. She screamed, "Kent."

Muffled voices echoed in the background.

Kent struggled to find his voice and eventually answered back. Paige fingered and flailed around for James and once again called out. "James!" Dead silence. Her hands landed on his camera.

Kent took out a solar pen light on his key chain and shone it on the rooftop. No James. His narrow light counted three people. Out of nine souls, there were only four of them left on the rooftop. Kent pointed his solar pen light down toward the empty ground. He swallowed hard. "They've vanished."

Voices in the distance cried out for friends and family. Paige sat back on the rough tar shingles and cleared her scratchy throat. "Something happened, Kent. What's going on here?"

Kent gathered up all the equipment. "I have no idea, but let's get the hell out of here before we're next."

The four made their way off the roof, using Kent's narrow beam. Kent tried to persuade the other two to leave, but they insisted on staying until their friends returned. Kent shook his head and seized Paige's hand. The two scanned the area with the penlight once more but had no luck.

Kent squeezed Paige's hand. "James is gone." He dragged her back to their car and attempted to start the engine.

"Shit, the engine's dead." He searched for a car or house lights in the area. "This isn't possible. There's not one car light or house light visible. This is a fucking city." He grabbed the gear, then Paige, and used his small penlight. They walked among several other people, and the only sound were whispered voices in the night. Everyone kept quiet so as not to awaken the giant or any other unknown retribution that might await them. Each shared the silent night together, limiting their use of solar flashlights or penlights and restricting themselves to the safety of the road.

Paige whispered, "What happened, Kent?"

Kent leaned in. "I don't know yet."

"They're gone," Paige screeched. "They've vanished."

Kent put his arm around her. "It appears so."

"James. My God, James is gone." Paige stopped and turned. "He was right beside me."

"I know." Kent adjusted his equipment. "It seems like several people are gone by the sounds of the screams."

"Is this the rapture?"

"No, James was an atheist." Kent stifled a grin. "I don't think you get to go if you are an atheist. It doesn't work that way."

"Yeah. What the hell?"

"Hell. Let's hope not," Kent said. "I don't like the idea of being left behind in hell."

The two walked away from the carnage and spotted a house lit by candlelight. They knocked, and the owner opened the door. Kent dipped his chin. "Could we please have a drink of water?"

The owner, a young man, pointed to the kitchen. His dead eyes stared down at the floor.

Kent filled two glasses. "At least the faucet works." He eyed a phone on the wall. "Landline." He lifted the phone to his ear. "Of course, that would be too easy," he snarked. "No ringtone."

Paige nodded at Kent and turned toward the owner. "Did you see what happened?"

The young man gazed up. "My wife and two sons disappeared. I was holding my son."

"I lost a very good friend named James." Paige kneeled down in front of him. She took his hand and rubbed it. "It will be all right."

Kent knitted his brow and handed Paige her water. "Did you see them go?"

"No, I was knocked down and lost my son right out of my arms."

Kent sipped his water. "Were you inside or outside?"

"Outside looking at the sky. I saw him." The owner shuffled from side to side. "I did, I saw him."

Kent cocked his head. "The face?"

"Yeah, God's face," the owner said. "He took them to heaven and left me here."

Kent sat his glass down on the counter. "I'm sure you'll be with them when it is your time."

The owner's eyes grew wide. "You think so?"

"I'm sure. He just needed them right now." Kent grabbed his gear, eyeballed Paige and motioned to the door. Paige placed her glass on the counter, and the two left.

On the road, Paige rubbed Kent's arm. "Kent, that was really nice of you. The poor man looked shellshocked."

Kent slipped his backpack over his shoulder. "Hope is all he has now."

Paige pointed to lights from a subdivision. Lanterns and candlelight lit the night, surrounded by dark streets. Kent pulled out his smartphone and tried it again, but it was still dead. They passed the last house of the subdivision, and Paige stopped.

"Listen, someone yelled over here." They answered back and headed toward the voice.

A man manually lifted his garage door all the way up and smacked the back of his Ford truck. "Just trying to fix Old Faithful here." Gas fumes and the roar of a generator revealed working lights and tools spread out over the concrete.

A German Shepherd stood at attention as his owner walked toward them. The man turned around. "Bo, go lie down." Then he pointed to his truck with the extended cab. "I think I can get the old Ford working again by morning." He held out his hand. "Nick Landon." He shook their hands. "Do you folks know what the hell is going on around here?"

Kent tossed his backpack on the concrete. "I don't know, but we're trying to get back to the city to find out."

Nick, a thirty-year-old mechanical engineer, opened the door to the utility room. "No sense stumbling around out there in the dark. Mind as well stay the night. I'll give you a ride to the city in the morning, provided I can get Old Faithful working again. Come on in."

Kent stepped inside. "Do you know what caused all the electrical problems in the area?"

"I think it may have something to do with a strong magnetic field disruption." Nick stopped and leaned up against the washer. "It's like nothing I've ever seen."

Paige filed in behind them with Bo in tow, begging for attention. Nick grabbed Bo's collar and led him into the kitchen. "Thirsty, boy?" He twisted the cap on a bottle of water and poured it into Bo's dish.

Kent sat on a barstool at the counter. "Were you watching the sky when it happened?"

"I was in the house when I saw the flash out my window and ran outside." Nick held up a bottle of water. "Like one?" Paige and Kent nodded. Nick handed them a bottle and took another for himself. "Strange, though, by the time I made it outside, all I could see was light being sucked out of the night sky into a dark cloud, like a swirling black hole. I thought the flash and shockwave were a meteor exploding or solar flare, but now I'm not so sure." He shook his head, popped the cap off, threw it in the trash and took a sip. "What were you folks doing in our area?"

Paige plopped her bottle on the counter. "We were here to write a story on crop circles, take photos of the gathering and do research."

"I see. Are you two reporters?"

Paige folded her arms. "I'm a reporter; Kent is a writer and photographer."

"I won't hold it against you." Nick flashed a sly grin and pulled out lunch meat, bread, mayo, cheddar cheese and mustard from the fridge. "I'll bet you're both hungry." The two nodded.

After dinner, Nick grabbed two pillows and blankets from the closet and sat them on his couch. "The couch is a hide-a-bed. Please make yourself at home. With any luck, we'll get the Ford working and find the answers you and I seek." He pointed to the garage. "Better get back to work on the truck." Bo and Kent followed Nick to the garage, and Paige cuddled up with a blanket on the couch and fell asleep.

The morning sun drew Paige to the window. Daylight revealed groups of people from the sighting filing by the house headed to the city. Most had waited until the light of day to migrate back to their homes. The pain on their faces unveiled a story of loss and confusion—the same empty feeling Paige suffered inside with the loss of her friend James and the uncertainty of the future.

Paige ambled to the garage. "Have you two worked all night?"

Kent poked his head up from the hood and stuck his thumb up. Nick jumped in Old Faithful and turned the starter. The engine spit and sputtered. He struck the steering wheel with his palm.

"Come on sweet girl, give it to me."

The engine engaged with a roar, and Nick eased the gas. "That's my girl."

Paige pet Bo and sat beside the contented dog. Bo flopped his head in her lap and closed his eyes.

Nick stuck his head out the window. "Looks like Bo found a friend."

Paige peeked up, lifted the corners of her mouth and winked. Nick held his stare and flashed a crooked smile until Kent slammed the hood. Nick jerked.

"Okay then. Better let Old Faithful idle to charge her battery. We don't need a stall on the road."

The group packed up the tools, food and Nick's clothes. Nick loaded a spare alternator, two tires, and his porta-potty and said, "Mustn't forget the crapper." He shot Kent a wink and a wide grin as he threw in ziplock storage bags and empty plastic grocery bags. "To bag my business."

He took his shotgun and two rifles and placed them on his gun rack behind his seat. He placed two pistols under his seat with several boxes of ammo stored in a metal case. Then he grabbed his guitar case and all his camping gear, which included a tent, a Coleman cook stove, four sleeping bags, and his backpack with rain gear. Next, he seized a truck battery off the shelf.

"Better put this where we can get right to it."

Kent and Nick stored the gear in the back of the truck, leaving room for Bo. They covered the gear with a tarp and tied it down with bungee cords. Last of all, Nick threw a huge bag of dog food and Bo's bed in the back. He pointed to the truck. "Bo, come."

A wide-eyed Bo jerked his head up, rushed over to the truck, barked, jumped in and plopped down on his bed. Nick shut the tailgate. "Ready, boy?" Bo barked, and Nick hit the side of his truck. "Okay, Bo, we're off to see the wizard."

After they'd driven several miles dodging stalled vehicles on the back roads, Kent dozed off and Paige turned to Nick. "Did you see an image in the clouds?"

Nick wrinkled his forehead. "What image?"

"Kent and I saw a face in the clouds. Didn't he tell you?"

Nick furrowed his brow. "No, not a word. I just saw the light getting sucked away."

"There was definitely a face. We all saw it."

"I guess we'd better find some answers." Nick glanced over at Kent. "He sure snores."

An hour later, Kent snorted and opened his eyes. "The guy I told you about lives a few miles down the road, just before you get to Yonkers."

"Your old colleague?" Nick yawned. "The physics professor at the university?"

"Yeah, Levi." Kent sat up and stretched. "His specialty is in applied physics."

"Good, because I'm about spent." Nick jerked the wheel and swerved suddenly to avoid another stalled vehicle. "Sorry, folks. I'm glad we're stopping soon."

Forty minutes later, they pulled into Levi's driveway. Nick glanced over at Kent. "Just a few miles down the road, huh?"

Kent smirked. "Oh, you know, give or take a mile here or there. Besides, it's not my fault the roads are jammed with stalled cars."

A spark of light from a battery-operated lantern emanated from the living room. Voices from a radio blasted a two-way conversation from a radio host's interview.

Kent knocked on the door. Levi cracked the door open and threw his arms around Kent.

"My God, Kent, I'm so glad to see you. This is a real shit storm."

Kent motioned for the others to come and he introduced Nick and Paige. Levi invited them in. Nick collected Bo from the truck and released him in the backyard. The four sat around the table and exchanged experiences.

Levi lifted up his tablet. "I replaced the batteries in the tablet and radio, but there are no working cell towers, TV, or internet sites available. I can view saved files on my tablet and get one station on the radio—everything else is dark." Levi shook his head. "First there was a shock wave. Then, after the wave, we lost power and all electronics. It looks like the power grid is compromised. All the electronics need to be replaced." Levi tapped the top of his tablet with his fingers. "I worked on it most of the day using spare parts from old models. I've accessed most of my files but have limited battery life. The same is true for my CB radio. I listened to the radio most of the day but had to be sparing."

Nick leaned back in the chair. "Was this a solar flare?"

"Don't know, but something blew out all the electronics," Levi said. "Word on the CB radio is that something knocked out orbiting satellites, GPS, and everything electric just before the shock wave hit."

Nick bent forward and raised his hands. "Terrorists?"

Kent and Levi stared at each other, and Kent said, "Something malicious." Levi nodded in agreement.

Nick rubbed the stubble on his chin. "What's next?"

"We find out the damage. Get as much information as possible and as fast as we can." Kent slapped his thighs and stood. "We need to be prepared for what comes next."

"There's more?" Paige's eyes grew wider.

Kent shook his head. "Bet on it."

Paige glanced over at Levi. "Levi, did people disappear in the city?"

"I heard that." Levi squinted. "Several people reported loved ones missing. Why?"

"James vanished right before our eyes." Paige lowered her voice and clasped her hands together. "A terrorist can't do that."

"Vanished?" Levi sat up straight. "Like poof?"

"Yes!" Paige scowled. "Like poof."

"Kent, this looks like it's in your area of expertise, or the Pope's." Levi fluttered his fingers in the air. "Do, do, do, do. *Twilight Zone*, bro."

"Time will tell. At some point they, or it, will reveal itself," Kent said. "Either way, we need to prepare."

Bo peeked in the sliding glass door and barked at his master. Nick slid opened the door and snapped his fingers. "Lay down." Bo flopped down on the wooden deck, wielding droopy eyes and a somber whimper. Nick strolled out to the truck, filled Bo's water and food dish and sat it next to him. "Okay, boy. We'll soon be on our way."

Levi gathered a few files from his file cabinet, his tablet, the CB radio and all of his non-perishable food. They siphoned gas from Levi's tank, Nick loaded Bo and the four headed to Kent's in Columbus, Ohio.

People wandered along the sides of the roads past abandoned cars destined for home. Levi and Kent had to spring out of Old Faithful's king cab to put deserted vehicles in neutral and move them out of the way to clear a path. Around the twentieth time, Nick shrugged. "Sorry, guys. I tried to stick to low traffic areas, but there don't seem to be any."

Kent smirked. "Yeah, yeah, yeah."

After a quick stop for dinner, Nick and the group hit the road. After a short drive, he spotted a bottleneck up ahead. Nick shifted down, cautiously advanced a few car lengths and stopped the truck. "Shit, a roadblock. This can't be good."

"Shit is right." Kent growled. "We're only halfway to Columbus."

A line of cars stacked bumper to bumper packed the roadway. Nick turned the truck around, but high-centered. Kent, Paige, and Levi pushed the truck, but the tires spun round and round in the mud without movement. A crowd gathered.

Nick reached under his seat, pulled out his .45 and put it between his legs. He stuck his head out the window. "We're the only working truck in the area."

Kent eased up to the window.

Nick pointed between his legs. "Just in case."

Kent nodded.

One of the men from the crowd yelled, "How did you get it working?"

Levi shouted, "Replaced the alternator, battery, and some electrical."

Two men from the group joined Paige, Kent, and Levi and pushed the truck back on the road. One of the young men walked up to the side of the truck. "Can you drop us off at the local auto parts store down the road?"

Nick covered up his gun with his shirt. "Sure. Thanks for the help. What's with the roadblock?"

The young guy moved in closer to the window and shuffled from side to side. "We thought it might be a good idea after what happened. Didn't want to get surprised by the unexpected. There's some crazy shit going on."

"Yes, there is. Climb in the back with Bo. He won't bite."

"Thanks." The young man pointed to Levi. "The guy back there told us what to get."

"Good; it should work." Kent, Paige and Levi climbed inside, and the two men crawled in the back of the truck with a suspicious German Shepherd. But after a friendly pet, Bo settled.

Levi pointed the way to the auto store after receiving instructions from the weary inquirer, and Nick picked up a couple of batteries, gas cans, and an alternator for his Ford. He removed his debit card, scoffed and slipped it back in his wallet. "That won't work." He pulled out all his cash. After his purchase, he stored the items in the truck and dropped off the two men back home.

On the way to Kent's, Nick plucked out a quarter from his pocket. "This is the last of my cash. Debit cards won't work anymore. Anybody have any?"

Paige snatched the quarter from Nick's hand. Everyone emptied their pockets and counted out the rest of their cash.

"Five hundred. We'd better make it last." She inserted the coins in a sock, rolled up the bills and zipped them in a secret compartment inside her backpack.

Just outside town, Paige spotted smoke in the distance. "What's going on over there?" As they got closer to the source, smoldering trails of black revealed a demolished jet engine among burned debris. "It must have crashed a while ago. Nothing could survive that. Look at the scavengers picking through the rubble."

Kent put his hand on Paige's shoulder. "I'm sorry, Paige, but we'll probably see evidence of more crashed airplanes along the way."

Levi grasped the edge of her seat and leaned forward. "If the autos suddenly stopped, so did the planes in the air." Paige turned her eyes to focus on the road ahead. Nick glanced over at Paige, reached over and gently touched her knee. She turned towards him. He shot her a sympathetic grin, shifted gears and pushed his foot down on the gas.

After a long night of dodging and siphoning gas from abandoned vehicles, they pulled into Kent's around one-thirty in the morning. By candlelight and lanterns, Kent rounded up sleeping gear, and the group claimed a resting place for the night.

At sunrise, using light from open windows, Kent laid out all his files on MUFON, and his books on alien contacts and past abductions. The four scanned the materials, looking for similar reports of shock waves and disabled electronics. They sorted and gathered anything they thought might help answer their questions.

Later, Kent gathered food from the pantry, his clothes, and any essentials that could help. He scrounged up three hundred dollars in cash and a jar full of coins. He handed them to Paige. "Add this to the kitty."

She unzipped her backpack. "Every little bit helps. We might even have a thousand now."

The group gathered around the kitchen table by candlelight. Nick pulled out the map and they highlighted a route to Paige's in Colorado.

The next day, Nick pulled the cover off Kent's car.

"Oh yeah, a 1969 cherry red Mustang. You're beautiful." He jumped in the driver's seat, stroked the leather interior, rubbed the steering wheel and put his hand on the original gearshift knob. He peered in the rearview mirror, shook his head and licked his chapped lips. "Wish we could take you, sweet thing." He opened the car door and rubbed his hand along her side. "Guess I should get this over with."

He seized his gas can and plastic hose and siphoned the remaining gas. He patted her shiny crimson rear. "Thanks, Red." Nick grabbed the canvas cover, covered her back up, leaned down and gave her a kiss on the hood. "I would have loved to take you for a spin, sweetness, but another day, another time. It's getting late and we need to hit the road."

After dinner, the group loaded all Kent's gear and departed to Denver. Each one took a turn at the wheel to relieve Nick.

Around midnight, Paige woke up in the back of Nick's extended cab, ready to take her shift at navigation. Levi stopped on a deserted road to relieve himself. Paige needed to do the same, so she quietly leaned over the seat, opened the driver's door and let herself out.

Levi squealed, jumped, and quickly zipped up his pants. Paige giggled, walked down a few feet and disappeared into the darkness. She unfastened her jeans and relieved herself.

After she'd finished, Paige embraced the night sky and took a deep breath. The northern lights flickered through the expanse in blue and green waves. She leaned her head back. "The stars are so much brighter in the country." She stood in the starlight, with the waves of the aurora gifting a light show and soaked in a moment of peace.

For the first time in days, there are no planes crashing or cars burning, just a quiet space filled with only nature's gift. Under a lonely sky, empty of any evidence of man and surrounded by the serenade of crickets, it feels like a trip back in time.

With only beautiful stars, suns, and planets sharing the night, Paige inhaled and drew in the serenity of the moment. After a few minutes of deep breathing, she opened her eyes and returned to reality. She gazed out over the vacant landscape and thought about Levi's last words after witnessing the 747 crash site.

Everything manmade, flying in the sky or orbiting out in space, disappeared or came down that dreadful day.

Paige exhaled and adjusted her pants. "Better get to it. Time for the night shift."

She got on the driver's side and Kent nodded. "Let's hit the road."

A few hours later, Paige passed a Kansas City mileage sign and noticed a turn arrow pointing to Perry Lake. "I could use a dip." She glanced over at Kent sleeping on the passenger side and the others in back snoring away.

After driving a few miles, she checked in her rearview mirror and noticed Bo up on the rail in the back of the truck with his nose raised high in the air. *You noticed the change in scenery and smells, didn't you, Bo?* Paige pulled into a secluded spot within eyesight of the lake. She climbed out, snuck her hand in the open window and retrieved her backpack from the back. Then she crept around the back of the pickup and whispered, "Come, Bo."

The two proceeded to the water's edge. Paige peeled off all of her clothes, grabbed her body soap and waded into the cold water, waist-deep. She dropped below the surface, popped back up and rushed back towards the shore. She stopped knee-deep, squeezed out a dollop of body wash in her hand and washed her hair and body. Bo creeped towards her but stopped and barked. Paige pressed her fingers to her lips and walked toward him.

"Shush, boy, don't give us away. You'll wake them up." She stopped and stared at the truck. "Good, they're still asleep."

Paige waded ashore, snatched up her panties and bra and headed back to the depths. She squirted body soap on her undies and scrubbed. Once clean, she attempted to rinse them out, but Bo snapped at them in play. Paige laughed, raised them above her head and waded deeper. She dipped down in the water and rinsed them off. The depth of the water hampered Bo's determined attempts, but he gave it all he had.

Nick plucked a piece of grass from his mouth and threw it on the beach. "How's the water?"

Paige ducked down. "How long have you been standing there?"

"Long enough," he said with a sheepish smile. "Cold, isn't it?" Nick kneeled down, submerged his fingers in the icy water. "Little icy." He stripped off his shirt and pants, and revealed his chiseled abs with a fit, six-foot-three-inch frame. Last, without a stitch of clothing, Nick smirked at Paige and, with an irreverent swagger, strutted into the water.

He went a short distance, stopped, spun around and eyed Bo running on the sand with a stick in his mouth.

Paige noticed several interesting tattoos all over his back, chest, and arms. *I'll bet there's a story behind each one of them.*

Nick called out for Bo. His German Shepherd ran up to him with his stick. He grabbed the stick and pushed back in play.

Paige clumsily put on her bra and panties under the water. Nick trod deeper and deeper towards her with Bo following. His biceps bulged and his firm chest muscles jutted as he held on firmly to the stick and pushed back against Bo and the water. His brown hair and scruffy stubble exposed their plight after days on the road. Paige eyed the ruggedly attractive man. *Even scruffy, he's good-looking.*

Nick drew closer and closer, his light willow-green eyes twinkled in the sunlight. He leaned in and sniffed her freshly washed hair. "You smell like a woman." He growled lightly and circled back around. "Nice body too."

"Thanks," Paige said. "Sneak."

"I'm a bad boy." Nick planted his hands on her waist, lifted her up out of the water, and slowly let her down until they were face to face. He moved in to kiss her, but she turned her head.

"Not happening." She pushed him away. "Bad boy."

"Too bad." Nick leered and dove into the water.

Paige headed for the shore, got dressed and sat on the beach.

Nick slipped his pants on, tossed the stick for Bo and sat beside Paige. "Are you taken?"

"Taken? What is this, the Middle Ages?"

Nick chewed on his bottom lip. "Okay, spoken for?"

"Yes, I have a boyfriend back home."

Nick frowned. "Lucky guy."

Paige tilted her head, collected her blonde hair with her hands and squeezed the water from it. "Anyone waiting for you?"

"No one currently," he said. "A very nasty breakup a few months ago."

"Been there before." She tussled her head and fingered her hair to dry it.

Nick lowered his head. "Haven't we all." Bo raced back with the stick, flopped down and chewed on it. Nick snatched it from Bo's mouth and threw it once again. Paige shivered and drew her legs up. Nick seized his shirt off the rocks and wrapped it around her.

She glanced up. "Thank you. It is a bit chilly."

Kent and Levi joined the couple on the beach. Nick's stomach growled, so he hiked back to his truck. He rummaged through his camping gear and removed a pan, a coffee pot, and his cook stove. He opened four cans of chili with the can opener on his pocketknife and dumped the contents into his pan. Then he poured bottled water into the coffee pot and took out his hand grinder and a bag of coffee beans. Nick scooped the beans into the grinder and ground his stash. He shoved the fresh grounds right up to his nose and drew in the sweet aroma.

"I'm going to savor every drop. It's been days." He placed the precious grind in the proper basket, secured the lid, and turned on the gas.

Nick stirred the beans and gazed at Paige petting Bo. "Just my luck. She has a boyfriend."

Bubbling chili and coffee percolating enticed the rest of the group from the beach. They lined up with tin cups and plates to sample Nick's culinary delights. Then, after finishing breakfast and the last drop of coffee, they packed up and headed for Denver.

Paige and Kent slumbered in the extended cab, and Nick drove, with Levi riding shotgun. After four hours of driving, Nick slowed the truck down and stopped. Two semi-trucks blocked the road. An open trailer on one of the semis revealed several cases of beer. Levi got out, peeked inside and peered back at Nick.

"No one here."

Kent woke up and jumped out. Levi and Kent circled around both trailers, then Levi returned to the truck and leaned in.

"Anyone want beer and donuts? The second trailer is filled to the brim with baked goods. Some cases of beer are missing, but most of the contents are undisturbed."

Nick nodded. "Okay, we'll grab a few cases of beer and a few cakes."

Paige woke up. "What's happening?"

Nick turned around. "The boys are gathering a few supplies. So far, Levi's loaded four cases of beer and gone back to help Kent."

After fifteen minutes, Nick glanced back at Paige. "Something's wrong. They should be back." Nick tapped the steering wheel with his hands. "Paige, wait in the truck."

He grabbed his .45, seized the keys and walked towards the semis. He turned around and caught a glimpse of someone walking towards the passenger side of Old Faithful with a gun in their hand. He ducked down, crept back to his truck and slipped behind the tailgate.

The man approached the truck and checked inside. "Where's the keys?"

Paige pointed at the empty ignition. "Kent is getting beer. He has the keys."

The man flashed her a glare. "I searched his pockets. There were no keys."

Paige stared straight ahead. "I have no idea where the keys are."

The man opened the truck door and rifled through the glove compartment. He fumbled with his gun, put it on the dash and continued looking.

Nick slowly snuck up behind him, pressed his .45 against his head, pulled back the hammer until he heard the click, and said, "Put your hands on your head and back out slowly."

The man gradually raised his hands, placed them on his head, and backed up. Nick pressed the barrel hard against his skull. "Get on your knees and keep your hands on your head. Eyes closed."

The man bent down, kept his shaking hands on the top of his head and closed his eyes. Nick held his stare on the intruder. "You move, I shoot." He motioned to Paige to get the gun off the dashboard. Paige crawled over the seat and grabbed the gun. Nick raised his voice. "Open your eyes. Where are the two men who are with me?"

The marauder opened his eyes. "Locked in the back of the trailer."

"Anyone with you?"

The man stiffened. "No."

Nick glimpsed over at Paige. "Paige, is the gun loaded?" Paige nodded. "Good. Take the gun, stay in my line of sight, and get Levi and Kent."

Paige freed Kent and Levi, and the three searched the semis and the abandoned cars, but found no one else. An undeterred Kent loaded up his packages of chips, donuts, and cupcakes.

Nick glared at the man and waved his gun in the air. "Stand up and start walking."

The man walked down the road in the opposite direction. Once he was out of sight, Nick slipped his .45 in the waistband of the back of his jeans and stood beside Paige. He clutched the marauder's gun, unloaded the clip, emptied the chamber and gave both pieces back to her. He eyed her hands and noticed they were shaking. He put both of his hands on her shoulders.

"I don't scare easily, Paige. I never bolt when I'm under the gun." He lifted Paige's chin and peered directly into her eyes. "I'm not leaving you. You're safe with me."

Her gaze froze. "Okay."

Nick lifted the corner of his mouth and squeezed her shoulders. "Time to saddle up, babe."

Paige cracked a smile, climbed in the truck, and put the gun and clip under her seat in the extended cab. She leaned back on the headrest, closed her eyes and murmured, "Better get some shuteye before my shift."

Relentless flashbacks of the marauder invaded her mind. Her jaw clenched and her shoulders knotted. She rolled each shoulder and stretched out her arm. She opened her mouth wide and puckered her lips to relieve the spasm in her jaw. She drew in a deep breath through her nose and let it out slowly. Her palm protested, so she opened her eyes, released her closed fist and rubbed four little indentations from the impact of her fingernails.

Paige glimpsed over at the ruggedly handsome man behind the wheel. Nick chuckled and teased Levi about his snort when he laughed. She sighed. *He's completely unshaken by the day's events. So confident.*

Nick flashed his mischievous grin followed by his signature charming cackle. Paige grinned, pressed her head back against the headrest, shut her eyes and conjured up his steely image. Nick's words—*You're safe with me*—played over and over in her head. *I'm so glad we found him.* Her body relaxed and her eyes grew heavy.

Later, Kent took the wheel and Paige navigated. Her heavy eyelids drooped and blinked several times until they closed for good. Kent reached for a slab of jerky and threw it at Nick's head. Nick jerked and opened his eyes. Kent pointed his finger at Paige. "Let her sleep." Nick gently removed the map from her hands and navigated.

Paige woke up and glanced over at Nick driving. She wrinkled her forehead. "What happened?"

Nick cracked a smile. "You fell asleep, and we let you."

"Pull over and let me drive."

Nick glanced over at her. "You sure?"

"Yes, I'm good now," Paige said. "Levi can navigate."

"Let's let Levi sleep another hour. I'll do it."

"I'm sorry I messed this up." Paige bit her lip. "There is no excuse. We're all tired."

"Yesterday was a bad day. I get it."

"You've dealt with guns before, haven't you?" Paige doubled her fists. "You showed no fear back there."

"Served several tours in the military," Nick said. "A person learns quickly when they're behind enemy lines."

"What enemy lines?"

Nick turned slowly. "Middle East and others."

"Thanks."

Nick furrowed his brow. "What for?"

"I don't know! Your service." Paige threw her hands up in the air. "Saving me. The truck. That asshole would have taken it and maybe shot me."

"Okay," Nick said. "You're welcome."

Paige gazed out the window. The sun faded as the clouds and fog rolled in and hid the evidence of downed planes and abandoned vehicles. She focused on memories of past assignments during better times. A gentle rain followed the rolling fog, leaving droplets congealing on the glass. She traced her finger across the trails and scrolled her name in the mist that her hot breath left behind. The rain had temporarily cleansed the trauma and confusion from the previous day. As the fog cleared, Paige embraced the beauty of a rainbow and briefly escaped their new world of unknown realities.

Suddenly, the daydream ended. Nick pulled into a gas station parking lot and turned his head toward Paige. "Ready to switch?"

During the exchange, Paige met Nick in front of the truck but stopped. She caught something moving out of the corner of her eye. She squinted through the spotty haze, spied a dark figure and shouted, "Looters."

Nick motioned to hurry, and Paige rushed to the wheel and shifted the gear. Nick opened the passenger door, hopped in but stumbled and dragged his boot on the pavement as Paige hit the gas. She squeezed the wheel, checked the rearview mirror and spotted a man with a bat lagging behind. "It's not safe to even stop anymore."

"Nope." Nick lifted his boot and rubbed a deep gouge on the sole. "We need to get gas soon."

Paige bowed in response. "Next isolated abandoned car."

A few miles down the road, Paige pulled up to the side of an SUV. Nick grabbed his tube out of the back, opened the gas cap on both of the vehicles, stuck the tube in the gas tank of the SUV and sucked on the end of the tube. The gas surged up the tube, so Nick swiftly stuck it in the Ford's gas tank and siphoned out every drop.

Paige glanced down at the gas gauge, and the tank registered three-quarters full. She drove on a few more miles and stopped at the next abandoned car. They topped off the tank and filled two of the empty gas cans stored in the back of the truck.

With a full tank of gas and the clouds clearing, Paige continued with her new navigator, Levi. She bit into a slice of jerky. "I'm still good for a few more hours. We just crossed into Colorado and it has given me a second wind. Home sweet home, here I come."

Later, Paige passed a sign that read *Denver 50 miles*. She glanced over at Levi. "Your turn, Levi. I need a couple of hours of sleep before we get to Denver. Who knows what we'll find."

Levi took the wheel, and Paige traded places with Kent and slept next to Nick in the extended cab.

A few more miles down the road, a refreshed Nick took over driving with Paige navigating. They traveled unimpeded until they were stopped by a National Guard roadblock. Nick handed the guardsman his registration and driver's license.

"We're all headed to Denver." The guardsmen checked their supplies in the back and let them go.

Chapter Three

Denver

Just outside of Denver, soldiers and emergency personnel were clearing the highways of abandoned vehicles.

Paige spotted a supply station. "I'm so glad to see evidence of a working civilization again. It looks like The Guard and other branches of the military have managed to get food, water, and other supplies to the city."

Kent pulled over at the supply site, and the guys loaded bottled water and MREs—Meals Ready-to-eat. Paige cornered an officer. "Does the military know what's going on?" The officer shook his head. She scrunched her forehead. "How did the shock wave affect your operations?"

"No one knows what happened. It affected all the vehicles, planes and computers. Virtually everything electrical is compromised." The guardsman stood firm. "The whole electrical infrastructure remains wiped out. The other officers in the unit believe the damage is global." He raised his brow and tilted his head. "We were grounded for days. Some areas are still chaotic."

Paige thanked the officer and climbed in Old Faithful. They drove another thirty minutes and pulled up to her apartment. She cracked open the unlocked door. Photos, pens and papers littered the wooden floor. Open kitchen cupboards revealed empty shelves while broken dishes lurked scattered across the tile.

Paige turned to the guys. "Everything of value is gone."

She wandered to her bedroom, packed the remaining clothes and grabbed her old backpack off the top shelf. She gathered bathroom products and stuffed them into her backpack. Paige picked up several old photographs and put them back in their boxes. She removed Logan's photo out of the broken picture frame and put it in her pocket. Paige lifted a pocket-size notebook, a couple of pens and pencils off her desk, and stuck them in her backpack.

Kent, Levi, and Nick straightened up the items they'd salvaged from the destruction and stored them properly in drawers, cupboards, containers, and boxes. After the cleanup, Paige locked her house.

"It looks like Logan hasn't been here in days. The house in the country is better shelter anyway. It's far enough away from the city; there will be fewer looters. The remodel is nearly finished. We should go there and regroup." They siphoned gas from her SUV in the garage and headed to the hospital.

Law enforcement and guardsmen lined the entrance to the hospital and stood vigil on every floor. The receptionist pointed to the ER. Paige peeked through a slit in the curtain and spotted Logan attending to a patient. He caught sight of her and mouthed the words, "Thank God." He rushed over, hugged her and whispered, "I thought you were gone."

Paige kissed him. "It is not that easy to get rid of me."

"Wait right here. I need to finish stitching my patient," he said. Paige agreed.

Logan joined her afterward. "Where have you been? It's been crazy around here."

"I was stuck on the east coast." Paige touched his cheek. "No way to send word."

Logan grasped her hand. "I have been here for days in this chaos."

Paige scoffed. "My place was completely trashed."

"I haven't had time to check on it, Paige. I'm not surprised. There were several homes burgled before the National Guard arrived. We lost electronics after the images appeared during the sightings and people panicked in the streets. Many people immediately believed it was the second coming and still do." Logan stared straight ahead and lowered his tone. "The believers think they have been left behind. The military and police have been finding several suicides in homes across the US and the world. The churches are packed with converts."

Paige detailed the events of her days on the road and asked Logan if the group could stay at his house. Logan smiled. "You're all welcome, but I haven't been able to go home yet. Wyatt's checked the property and so far, it's been fine." Logan took Paige's hand and checked out of the hospital. The group headed out to Logan's.

Once at Logan's, Levi started the gas generator and for the first time the group had electricity and civilization. Levi grinned and pointed to the bathroom. "Ladies first."

Paige bowed in response. "You'll get no argument from me."

She stood in the shower, briefly turned on the water, then soaped every inch of her naked body. She lathered up the shampoo on her hair and again turned on the shower for a short while, careful to reserve every precious drop of warm water. Paige rinsed off, snatched her clean towel, slowly sniffed and patted herself dry. She squeezed out her jasmine-scented lotion and rubbed it into her neglected body. She stared in the mirror and wiped a tear from her cheek.

"I feel like a woman again, a civilized human, able to use a real toilet instead of the crapper or the cold hard ground." She combed her squeaky-clean hair, put on deodorant and slathered on lip gloss. Paige stepped into a clean pair of underwear, dried with dryer sheets, and snapped on a bra that wasn't stiff from bar soap and washed in water from a fishy lake. Last of all, she slipped on a fresh shirt and a pair of jeans. "It feels so good to be clean and have fresh running water from the tap, instead of using wipes or creek water."

Logan knocked and peeked in. Paige curled her finger. "Come in."

Logan kissed her softly on the lips and gently moved down her neck. He drew his dark brown eyes back up to her, shot his all-too-familiar-look and slowly disrobed her. He turned her around, pressed his lips on the back of her neck and tactically removed his jeans, never missing a beat. Logan stripped his t-shirt off, dropped it on the floor and the two embraced. He lifted her up on the counter and positioned himself between her legs. He put his hands on her round bottom, pulled her toward him and entered her. Paige replied, meeting his thrusts in perfect rhythm. She closed her eyes and let the wave of pleasure overtake her. The image of willow green eyes flashed before her as her climax hit. She opened her eyes wide to confirm her accomplice and muttered, "Logan."

Logan's intensity grew and released. He grunted, kissed Paige's neck and put his lips up to her ear. "I'm glad you're home safe."

Paige gazed into his brown eyes. "You have no idea."

"I'm sure I don't."

Paige kissed him. "I'm just glad to be home."

"Me too," he said. "Rough few weeks?"

"Rough, but I couldn't have asked for a better group of guys to get stuck with."

"I need to thank them for taking care of my girl."

"Truth be known, I had to take care of them." Paige giggled. "If you want something done right, get a girl to do it."

"They were lucky to have you."

Paige slid her jeans on. "Someday I'll have a hell of a story to tell."

Logan tucked in his shirt. "Don't we all."

"It isn't over yet." Paige said. "I'm afraid it is just beginning."

Logan slid out of the bathroom, and Paige pointed at her reflection in the mirror. "Really? You see Nick's face in the middle of an orgasm? What's wrong with you?" She reapplied her lip gloss, smacked her lips together and joined the others in the living room.

The group filled Logan in on everything they knew so far. Afterward, Paige sighed. "I want to go to the church and talk to the people who have congregated there." She glimpsed over at Nick. "And Logan needs to get back to the hospital. Can you take us, Nick?"

Nick stood. "Sure, that will give me a chance to pick up some gas."

Kent elected to go and help Nick. Levi volunteered to stay and watch the place. They loaded containers to hold gas for storage, put Bo in the back, and headed for town.

Nick dropped Logan off at the hospital and let Paige off at the Catholic Church.

Paige spun around and stuck her head in the driver's window. "Nick, I'll walk to the hospital when I'm finished. Pick me up there." Nick saluted and drove off.

Paige entered the building. With every available space occupied, she stayed in the doorway and listened to the priest give a final evening prayer by candlelight. After he finished, no one moved. They all remained in place with their heads bowed. Paige scooted up to a man standing against the wall. "Why aren't they moving?"

The man leaned in. "There waiting. They have been like this for days."

"What do they think will happen?"

The man adjusted his glasses. "To be taken or forgiven."

"Were people taken in Denver?"

"Some were." The man lowered his head.

"So, it wasn't just at the sightings?"

"No." The man wiped under his eye. "Here too."

Paige bowed. "I'm so sorry."

He bobbed his head in response. Paige buttoned her jacket, quietly exited, and walked to the hospital in the moonlight.

She cornered Logan in the ER. "Has anyone claimed there were people missing?

"Several Reports," Logan said. "At the hospital too." He leaned up against the counter. "There's something else that's very, very odd. Since the sightings, all the new blood tests have been Rh negative. The most common blood type is Rh positive. Seeing only Rh-negative blood types is very unusual." He frowned and crossed his arms. "After I saw this strange pattern, I went back and inspected all the personnel files at the hospital and discovered that all those left behind were Rh negative. All the missing personnel were Rh positive." He shook his head and lowered his voice. "I also checked the medical files of anyone reported missing in the Denver area and found the same results. Paige, both of us are Rh negative—you're A negative and I'm AB negative."

Paige leaned into Logan and whispered, "What do you think all this means?"

He put his arm around her. "I don't know yet, but it's very, very strange."

Nick, Kent and Bo picked Paige up at the hospital. Paige jumped in. "Logan needs to stay. He has too many patients left on the docket." Paige explained to Nick about the strange blood test results and tapped him on the shoulder. "Nick, what is your blood type?"

Nick shrugged. "Type O, but I don't know if it's negative."

Paige glanced at Kent. "What about you?"

Kent twisted his mouth. "B negative." They pulled into Logan's, and Levi confirmed his Rh-negative status.

Levi shook his head. "A ticket to heaven doesn't include an Rh-positive blood type."

Kent furrowed his brow. "Or exclude an Rh negative one."

Paige rubbed her hands together. "We're not looking at a second coming." She thrust her hands forward. "And terrorists aren't this advanced."

"We're the most advanced country in the world." Levi lifted his index finger. "But even we couldn't pull this off."

"Looks more and more like outside forces," Nick said. "Something tells me they aren't done."

***

The next day, Nick searched the area for older vehicles that didn't have computer systems. He eyed a refurbished 1987 Ford four-wheel-drive pickup in great condition and a 1989 Oldsmobile. He hooked them up to his truck and pulled them one at a time to Logan's.

For the next month, he collected parts from abandoned vehicles and old salvage yards. He stopped at a few auto parts stores that had managed to stay open and paid cash for the necessary parts he was unable to salvage.

On one of the trips, Nick passed by an abandoned music store and stopped. He grabbed his .45 off the seat, tucked it behind his back in the waistband of his button-fly jeans and concealed it underneath his long sleeve shirt. He broke the lock and entered the deserted and dimly lit building.

Several guitars and other stringed instruments lined the walls. Nick glanced at the upstairs and viewed drum sets and wind instruments. He spied a supply rack near the counter by the guitars. He reached over, picked up extra picks and strings for his acoustic guitar off the rack and spotted a grand piano in the back room. Nick stuffed picks and extra strings in his pocket, walked into the back room and sat down on the piano bench.

He opened the lid, stroked the keys, and remembered piano lessons with his father. "So many hours teaching me how to play the piano, and several other instruments. After Mom's death, we filled the empty space with music until cancer took you. Thanks, Dad. This one's for you."

Nick peered down at the keys, smiled, shook his head, and played that very expensive and exquisite piano.

After an hour at the keyboard, Nick shut the lid. "Grand, you're coming home with me." He stood up, ready to leave, but noticed a Gibson custom electric guitar on the side wall in the main room. He pulled it off the brackets. Memories of late-night jamming sessions in college flooded back.

"Ours was not as good, *but* we sure had fun. I'll have fun with you." He leaned the custom guitar against the wall and grabbed a guitar stand off the lower shelf.

Suddenly, he heard the front door close. Nick turned to see a young man holding a 40-caliber Beretta pointed at him.

The young man waved his gun. "You own the truck outside?"

Nick cocked his head. "Yes."

The young man thrust the gun forward. "I don't want to hurt anybody. Just give me the keys."

"I'm not giving you the keys to my truck."

The young man shuffled from side to side. "Just give me the keys!"

"You'd kill for a truck?" Nick scowled. The young man nodded, walked closer and pointed the gun right at Nick's chest.

Nick raised his hands. "Okay, then. Take it easy. I'm going to get the keys out of my pocket." With one hand, Nick slowly reached into his pocket and pulled out his key ring. The young man held his hand out, but Nick quickly tossed the keys in a far corner. The surprised young man turned and glanced over at the keys on the floor.

In a flash, Nick pulled his .45 out from the back of his jeans and pointed it at the young man's head.

"Okay, now you have a choice to make. I have this aimed right between your eyes and if you move, I'll take you out." Nick stared straight at the young man. "I can see that you don't know that much about weapons because your safety is still on. I'm an excellent shot. I won't miss, so listen closely. Take your finger off the trigger and slowly lay the weapon down on the ground."

The wide-eyed young man nodded, took his finger off the trigger and laid his Beretta down on the floor.

Nick said, "Raise your hands, slowly stand up and take three steps back." The young man raised his hands palms up and complied. Nick picked up the young man's Beretta, lowered his Glock and tucked it in the front of his pants. He removed the clip from the Beretta and cleared the chamber. He furrowed his brow.

"Your chamber is empty and your clip has one bullet. What the fuck are you thinking?"

The young man gazed down at the floor. "I just need to get home."

Nick put the Beretta in the back of his pants and the clip in his front pocket. He pulled his .45 out of his pants and collected his keys. "What's your name?"

"Declan White."

"Where are you from, Declan?"

"Portland," Declan said. "I just want to get home."

"Why so urgent?"

"I need to make sure my parents and little brother are okay." His nostrils flared and his voice cracked. "I'm a college student and play hockey for the University of Denver. During the summer, I work on a painting crew in their maintenance department."

"What do you study at the university?"

"A BS in Computer Engineering." Declan clasped his hands together.

Nick grinned. "Rethinking that, are we?"

Declan worked up a smile. "Yeah, I'm shut out now." His smiled faded. "Just needed to find a way home."

"Why me? Why now?

"I saw you drive up to the music store," he said. "It took me a while to work up the courage to come in."

Nick exhaled and pursed his lips together. "Where did you find the gun?"

Declan paused and cast his eyes back downward. "I took it from an abandoned house. I found it under the mattress." Declan pointed at the gun. "Looters must have found all the extra ammo."

Nick plopped down on the piano bench and motioned for Declan to sit on the floor. He folded his arms.

"Trying to take a man's truck away at gun point is very dangerous and foolish. Especially foolhardy, when you know nothing about weapons and with no prior experience with guns." Nick stared intently at Declan. "Pointing a gun is easy but pulling the trigger and taking a man's life is not. Even harder is living with it after the fact."

Nick held his stare. "Declan, taking a life for a truck is flat wrong. There is always a better way." He studied Declan's reaction and distress.

I hope his distress is out of guilt and shame and not a foiled plan, Nick thought. He eyeballed Declan from head to toe. His clothes hung loose, he was bone thin and clearly malnourished. After Nick finished his assessment, he bit his lower lip.

"This is a sticky wicket." Declan peered up and the fear suddenly drained from his face. He cracked a smile at Nick and nodded. Nick took a deep breath, slowly exhaled, and threw his hands up in the air. "Declan, you're coming home with me. We'll find and fix up a truck, so you can head west to join your family. You'll stay with me until you're stronger and have gathered enough supplies to make the journey." He bent forward and put his hands on his knees. "You'll need to find others to travel with. It's too dangerous alone."

Declan peeked up at Nick, rubbed his watery eyes and wiped his runny nose on his jacket sleeve. "I would appreciate the help, sir."

Nick tucked the .45 in the front of his pants and helped Declan up. "You've got it."

Nick pointed to all the supplies he'd put aside. "Let's load this stuff." They placed the electric guitar and stand in his king cab. Then Nick selected a half stack vintage amplifier, a Marshall and small combo amplifier, and the two loaded them in the back of his truck.

Just as Nick was ready to leave, he stopped and stood at the door of the music store. He glanced over at Declan in the truck.

"What the hell. Looters will just destroy everything in this place." He turned, went back inside and took a bass guitar, a Gibson double-neck electric guitar, two acoustic guitars, and four stands. They put each guitar in a guitar case and loaded them in his king cab. Nick grabbed music sheets, two music and microphones stands, and all the remaining guitar picks off the shelf. The two loaded a very expensive drum set from upstairs, and then at the last minute added a flute, a violin, an electric keyboard, and several drumsticks.

After they finished loading the goods, they shut and locked the front door and drove to Logan's. Nick introduced Declan to everyone and filled them in on Declan's circumstances. Nick glimpsed over at the group.

"I promised we'd help Declan go west. Sound good?" Everybody agreed and Nick and Declan stored the amplifiers, keyboard and drums out back in Logan's shop. . Nick took the acoustic guitars, violin, and flute and stuffed them in his bedroom closet. Last of all, Nick put both electric guitars on their stands and proudly displayed them in his bedroom. After he finished admiring his prizes, Nick rushed downstairs.

Kent slapped him on the knee. "How are you going to play with your new electric toys? Last I looked, there's no electricity." The group snickered. Nick pursed his lips tight. Kent pushed on his knee. "Guess you'll be playing *air guitar*."

Nick moved his head from side to side. "You guys just don't appreciate music at all. Hell, those instruments are art."

The group shared a hearty meal and after dinner, Declan relayed stories of survival under very chaotic circumstances. At bedtime, Nick handed Declan a sleeping bag and a pillow and pointed to the floor. "You'll need to sleep on the floor next to me until the group trusts you. I'm in charge of you for a while, and that means I have to watch you."

Declan shrugged his shoulders. "No problem, I deserve it." Declan laid out his sleeping bag, crawled inside and closed his eyes.

Nick smiled. *He's learning. It could've been much, much worse. The dumb ass could be dead.*

The next day, Nick hooked up a flatbed trailer to the Ford, grabbed Kent, Levi, and Declan, and the four retrieved the grand piano, its bench filled with sheet music, and took it to Logan's. The group shuffled furniture around until they found the perfect place for Nick's grand discovery.

Later that night, Nick and Declan retold their story, but this time Nick added a bit of humor to lighten the mood. Then after shared war stories from the group and their indiscretions of youth, Nick sat at the new grand piano and played.

Afterward, Kent squeezed Nick's shoulders. "Who needs television and expensive sound systems, we have Nick."

A few days later, Nick and Declan pulled up to an abandoned 1982 Chevy truck and opened the hood. Nick checked the engine, fluids and wiring and said, "This one's in good condition." He slammed the hood shut and flashed a Cheshire cat smile. "It won't take much to get her purring."

They towed it to Logan's and, over a few days, fixed it up. Nick drug Declan out to his makeshift shooting range and taught him how to use a rifle and pistol.

By the end of the month, Declan had gained weight, vitality and the confidence to make the long journey. He recruited two of his friends from the university, and they loaded up all the supplies they collected. The three stood next to the Chevy, folded their arms and waited.

Nick scanned their bounty. "Looks good, but you're going to need protection." He lifted Declan's Beretta from his waistband and handed it to him. Then he retrieved a rifle and a box of ammo from the porch and eyeballed both friends.

"Either of you two have experience with weapons?" Both declared that they were hunters and demonstrated how to operate Declan's rifle and pistol. Nick held up his hand. "Wait one minute."

He sprinted inside the house and retrieved another gun. Nick jogged back out to the truck, caught his breath and handed the boys another pistol. "Now it's good enough."

After they finished storing the weapons, Declan hugged Nick. "You saved my life." He pointed to his friends. "I will never forget what you did for me, for all of us. Thank you."

Nick smiled and whispered, "You made the right choice."

Declan grinned. "You are very convincing at gunpoint." The two laughed, and Declan got into the Chevy.

Nick closed the truck door. "Watch your six."

Declan pointed and said, "Ah-ha! I knew you were military."

Nick gave a sly grin. "Be safe out there."

Declan leaned out the window. "Yes, Dad."

Nick smirked and dismissively waved his hand in the air. Declan drove off and blasted his horn until they disappeared from view.

***

A few days later, Paige creeped out to the backyard to help Nick with one of his restoration projects. She handed him a bottle of filtered water, three pieces of jerky and a package of cupcakes. "You miss Declan?"

Nick took the food and water and placed them on the roof of the Ford. He stood behind Paige, put his hands on her shoulders and whispered, "Yeah, it's good to have projects. Declan was a good one." Then he put his lips right up to Paige's ear. "Thanks for the goodies."

Paige stuttered. "The-the food supplies are running low."

Nick held Paige's shoulders tightly, moved to her other ear, gingerly brushed her earlobe with his lips and in a low baritone voice said, "After I finish with the motorcycle, we'll make a trip to the supply station."

Paige closed her eyes. A shiver raced through her body. She nodded, squirmed out of Nick's embrace and sat at a safe distance. He flashed Paige a devious grin, bit off a hunk of jerky and chewed slowly. After the last bite of his cupcake, he wiped the crumbs on his dirty jeans and resumed installing a new battery.

Once he'd finished the install, Nick jumped on the bike and started the engine. Feeling satisfied, he hopped off the bike, secured his makeshift wooden ramp and loaded the motorcycle. Last of all, he threw Logan's helmet in the back, and glanced at Paige in her safe corner.

"Ready?" Paige climbed in the truck and hugged the passenger door. He glimpsed over at her. "Don't lean too hard, you might fall out."

Paige shot him a look. "You wish."

"It might be funny," Nick said. "But no, Paige. I'm far too fond of you for that." He leaned over, grabbed Paige's seat belt, stopped inches from her face, and gazed deep into her pale blue eyes. "Beautiful."

Paige flushed crimson and stared at the floorboard.

Nick fastened her seat belt. "Now, you're safe and sound." He touched her cheek. "Relax, I'll stop giving you a hard time, even if you are sooooo cute when you turn red."

Paige gazed out the window. "Good."

Nick stuffed a tie wrap in his mouth and stifled the urge to snicker at his accomplishments. He clicked his seatbelt, put the truck in gear and hit the gas.

After a twenty-minute drive, Paige and Nick picked up supplies at a National Guard supply tent and headed to the hospital. They unloaded Logan's motorcycle, so he could travel back and forth and save fuel. Nick chained the motorcycle in a secure area and gave Logan the key.

Logan dipped his chin in response. "This should help. I'll try to get home more."

On the way home, Nick stopped at the market. The deserted store housed several empty shelves. Paige spotted packages of seeds and seized a handful. One clerk and two armed guards occupied the deserted space.

The clerk procured the cash from Paige and smiled. "Take as many packages as you need." Paige returned to the section, grabbed two of each and held up her stack. The clerk waved. "That's fine."

Paige climbed in the truck and lifted her packages. "We need to plant these next year, but right now, we need to hit a few garden stores for supplies and prepare for next spring planting so we can get them in the ground as soon as possible." She exhaled. "I hope we can collect enough existing food for the winter. I know Levi's been tending Rosie's abandoned garden this summer. He added several plants from container gardens he scrounged up from the neighborhood and placed them in her garden. I hope it's enough." She fastened her seat belt. "Next year we'll be in better shape."

Nick bobbed his head. "Sounds good. Better get supplies before they're gone." He raised his index finger. "I know the perfect spot for a spring garden. Besides, Levi wants to move Rosie's greenhouse over after we harvest it. I think we can expand on it before next summer. I also want to rig the sprinkler system with solar power so we don't have to do it manually."

Paige cracked a smile. "That's a great idea. Solar-powered sprinklers. Who knew?"

Nick scrunched his face. "Who else?"

Paige pointed her finger at him. "Yeah, who else."

The next morning, Nick and Paige staked out their garden area and included a space to place Rosie's greenhouse. Levi used Rosie's rototiller and prepared Paige's staked ground for planting. Levi planted spinach and arugula seeds. Then he transplanted slightly wilted peas, green beans, cucumbers and cherry tomato plants he had collected from abandoned gardens in the area.

Kent hammered the last nail into the bins he built to house the apples, squash, pumpkins, potatoes and carrots they planned to harvest from Rosie's garden. He glanced over at the group and smacked the top. "All-righty. Now this fall, we'll fill them with Rosie's goodies."

Just after sundown, the group admired the fruits of their labor and cracked open a cold-filtered beer and MREs around Levi's makeshift campfire, constructed from rocks he gathered. Levi tossed another log on the fire and said, "Now we need to get wood for the winter."

Nick raised his beer. "Here's to a prosperous garden and a future trip to the mountains."

Logan drove up on his motorcycle. Paige handed him a beer. "I'm glad you finally made it home."

"Finally got away." Logan opened the beer and took a long drink. "Thank God, it's a cold one. Bet you pulled it from the creek?"

Page nodded. "We're celebrating. The garden's in." She tapped on the side of her can. "We plan to gather wood for winter soon."

"I'm sorry for missing out on all the work." He glanced over at the shed. "There's a chainsaw in the shed. I'll try to help."

"Yeah right." Paige shot him a cold stare. "We haven't seen you in days."

Feeling the tension, Kent, Levi and Nick left. Paige flung her empty beer can into the fire, opened another one and stared at the flickering flames. The two sat silently for several minutes until Logan broke the tension. "I'm sorry, what else do you want me to say? We're shorthanded."

"All right, Logan. I get it. It's hard," Paige said. "Nick fixed the damn motorcycle, so you could come home more."

"Nice of Nick. Nick can do no wrong. Seems to me like Nick does an awful lot for you, doesn't he?" Logan stood and pointed his finger. "What else does Nick do for you while I'm out saving lives?"

"Be there, something you're not," Paige said. "Nick has just been a good friend to me, nothing else. A good friend to both of us."

"All right. I'm sorry, I don't mean to sound ungrateful. I'm just tired."

Logan swigged the last drop and tossed his beer can in the fire. "I need sleep. Goodnight."

Logan stormed off. Paige sat by the campfire until the flames died down. She poured her warm beer over the smoldering embers.

Kent strolled up to Paige, scooped a handful of dirt and sprinkled it over the dying coals. He turned around. "Everything all right?"

Paige grasped the shovel and tamped out the last burning ember. "Yes."

The two headed for the house and flopped next to Levi in the living room. Nick peeked up and strummed on his acoustic guitar.

Paige sighed. "Did Logan go to bed?" Levi nodded. Paige twirled her finger. "Don't stop playing."

Nick winked at Paige and sang. After the song, Kent smacked Levi on the knee. "Better get our zees, Levi; we have a long day tomorrow." The two excused themselves and left.

Paige tilted her head. "Nick, where did you learn those two songs?"

"An old friend from the military." He placed the guitar on his lap and rubbed his fingers over the strings. "They're from a group that was popular in the seventies. They were my friend's favorite band." Nick bit his lip and looked to the left to recall an old memory. "We played both songs around the barracks waiting for deployment. Most of our deployments were in the desert, so the songs were definitely appropriate."

Paige smiled and nodded, but didn't want to push any further. Nick held his gaze, positioned his guitar at the ready and strummed a new song. Halfway through the instrumental, Paige wrinkled her brow and pursed her lips. Nick finished and gave Paige a shrewd grin. She thrust her hand in the air.

"What's that song? I know it."

He put his guitar on its stand and turned. "Logan's a fool. Wild horses couldn't drag me away from the woman I love."

Paige stared at him wide-eyed. " 'Wild Horses'! That's it, 'Wild Horses'."

He shook his head. "I think you missed the point, babe."

Nick trudged up the stairs. Paige wrinkled her forehead. "What are the lyrics to that damn song?" She hummed the familiar tune. The words *suffer* and *pain* made her head spin. The chorus spun around and around in her mind. Nick's last words, *Logan's a fool and you missed the point, babe*, replayed over and over.

Paige whispered, "Babe" and gritted her teeth. She huffed. "Who does he think he is? Just because he can play and sing, that doesn't make him judge and jury over my relationship." Paige glared at Nick's guitar, glanced up at an empty staircase and yelled, "Go to hell, Nick." A few minutes later Paige marched upstairs. Nick stood at his bedroom doorway.

Nick cocked his head to the side. "Struck a nerve, did we?"

Paige turned to him, narrowed her eyes, raised her hand and defiantly flipped him off.

Nick smirked. "Definitely struck a nerve."

Paige snuck into her bedroom and checked on a sleeping Logan. She quietly slipped into the bathroom, brushed her teeth, and dressed for bed. She pulled the sheets back but stopped and gently put them back down. Nick's piano and his soft voice wafted in the distance. *He's so infuriating. Damn him and his beautiful voice.*

Paige snuck back out to the head of the staircase and watched Nick play and sing in the candlelight. The grace of his fingers stroked the black and white keys. She sat mesmerized and lost in the melody. *So talented at the guitar, but even more accomplished at the piano.* She peeked down at this ruggedly handsome, unkempt engineer and spied his gentle touch on the keys. She shivered at his tender voice and resisted her feelings of attraction. Tonight, Nick had taken her by surprise. She closed her eyes and embraced his beautiful melody. She struggled to hear his lyrics. Paige scooted down the stairs to hear the words "I can't make you love me" fill the darkness around her. She scurried down two more steps to peer closer.

Nick scowled as his painful words washed around him. He played the song's instrumental and grew lost in the haunting rhythm of the keys. After he'd finished the song, he took a deep breath, exhaled and shut the lid. He stood shirtless and exposed his well-framed muscular physique. His faded jeans hugged his body. He leaned over, blew out the candle and broke the spell.

Paige skedaddled up the stairs, lifted her feet off the top stair and slid back out of sight. She tiptoed back to her room and stood behind her bedroom door.

Nick passed her door, turned around and spied the crack. He smirked and whispered, "Goodnight, Paige."

Paige waited a few moments and without uttering a word, shut her door. Nick opened his bedroom door and glanced back at Paige's closed door.

"Patience, my good man. Logan will blow it. Entitled men like him always do."

Paige slipped into bed and whispered, "Oh shit." Logan turned over in bed and softly moaned.

The next morning, the bright sunlight roused Paige from a deep sleep. Logan turned over, opened one eye, and put his hand up to block the light. He asked for the time, Paige peered over at their wind-up clock. "Nine."

Logan grimaced. "Forgive me for being an asshole."

"Maybe."

"Let me make it up to you." Logan pulled her close.

Paige snuggled up closer, and the two kissed. Logan removed Paige's pajamas and continued kissing down her body until he found the right spot. With slow gentle motions, Paige's hips responded with ever-increasing intensity until a wave of pleasure crested, leaving Paige completely satisfied. Logan moved up and kissed her neck and lips. Then he positioned himself inside her and began a steady rhythm until he found his own release.

In the afterglow, the two cuddled for a while. After sensing the right moment, Logan grazed Paige's cheek. "Am I forgiven?"

She kissed his forehead. "You have redeemed yourself."

Freshly ground coffee drew the couple downstairs to breakfast. Powdered eggs, Spam, and fried potatoes lined the kitchen counter.

After breakfast, Paige accompanied Levi to Rosie's to water and pick a few peas, green beans, and cherry tomatoes for dinner. At day's end, the group sat around the campfire and indulged in MREs and a cold beer taken right out of the creek. As they relaxed and sat around the fire, Nick and Levi presented ideas for an irrigation system and a solar and wind energy system to replace or aid their gas generator. After final approval from the group, Kent raised his can of cold-filtered beer. "We just might make it through the winter."

Levi held up his can. "Nick and I will start shopping or scrounging for materials."

Nick dipped his chin to Levi. "A-scrounging we will go, my good man." He eyed the group. "Do we have any hunters among us?"

Logan lifted his hand. "Did some deer and elk hunting around the area."

"Good." Nick lowered his chin in response. "We'll try to get elk, venison and turkey by November and make jerky for winter."

Kent drew his fingers to his lips and smacked. "Jerky. Hey, we could catch steelhead or salmon and smoke it. I love smoked salmon." He pointed at the shed. "We could make a modest smokehouse out of the shed and dig a cellar for food storage."

Logan nodded. "I'll help as much as I can. There's probably enough building materials around here from the remodel." He furrowed his brow and shuffled in his seat. "By the way, I discovered some strange things at the hospital and around the city. I've been looking at the medical files and talking with my brother, Wyatt. Wyatt and several soldiers have gone house-to-house to search for survivors and according to the reports it appeared that two-thirds of the population is missing." Logan bent forward and clasped his hands. "I checked a list of the missing and found a survivalist I know nicknamed Bunker. He stockpiled goods for the end-times in an underground shelter close to his house. We should take a look at his property and take his supplies if he's no longer there. Bunker bragged that he had weapons and enough food for two years at least."

Nick bobbed his head. "Logan, you better go with me in case looters have had the same idea."

Logan agreed.

The next day, Logan and Nick pulled up to Bunker's empty house. Nick broke a small window, reached inside and unlocked the door. Rotting meat permeated the house. They pulled their shirts over their nose and mouth and searched for supplies. The two collected everything useful inside and loaded their cache. Logan entered the garage to sort and pack. Nick scoped around for keys, maps, or prints of the property in Bunker's file cabinets. He retrieved a file for an emergency shelter and poured over the original prints.

Nick slipped out the back door and discovered a locked shed. He seized his bolt cutters from the back of his truck and cut the paddle lock. He entered the shed, lifted a trap door in the back and yelled, "Logan!"

Logan rushed out of the garage and climbed down the ladder. Weapons and ammo lined one side. The other side contained canned food, dried foods, toilet paper, and water. A small bed centered the shelter with a chemical toilet for waste in the back.

Logan sighed. "The survivalist was definitely set up for the apocalypse."

They headed back home with their first load and unloaded their bounty. Levi and Kent drove back with them in the 87 Ford and both trucks made numerous trips to retrieve every item that could be used. They took Bunker's shed and shelter apart and stacked the building materials next to Logan's barn.

Logan stood in front of his barn. "All this material should build a great emergency shelter." He cast his eyes over his estate. "Hell, every room in the house, shed and garage is filled to capacity. We should be good for a while."

Kent scouted Logan's basement, sprinted back upstairs and dragged the others down to the future refuge. "We can use this for our emergency shelter. Put in an extra room and additional insulation for fresh food storage."

For the next two weeks, they worked on the emergency shelter. Kent, Levi, and Nick replicated Bunker's wall of weapons on the back wall of the main section. Automatic weapons, grenades, hunting rifles, handguns and ammo lined the wall. Kent and Nick redesigned the basement bathroom to accommodate Bunker's chemical toilet, in addition to the regular toilet, sink and shower that were already there.

Nick designed a working food pantry that hid the entrance to the shelter. They used shelves to conceal the hidden door. To protect their cache, Nick installed a latch on the back of one of the shelves to unlock the secret door and gain access to their bunker.

Logan claimed one shelf of the fresh food storage in the shelter for the medications that required cool storage to preserve them. He confiscated several vials of a variety of antibiotics and medications from the pharmacy at the hospital for emergencies. He stored the rest in the main area with the rest of the first aid materials like bandages and tape.

Paige pilfered a pressure cooker for canning their future bounty. She searched abandoned houses, and kitchen and dollar stores for tongs, funnels, ladles, jars, lids and other canning necessities ready to fill with venison, fish, and vegetables from the garden.

With all the supplies ready, Paige headed to Rosie's garden and picked peas and string beans. "You beauties are ready to can." Paige separated a few for the night's dinner and placed the remaining bounty for the next day's canning.

The next morning, Paige put a towel down on the counter. On top of it she placed the jar rings, a jar lifter, a ladle, a canning funnel, a small bowl with lids, a bubble tool, canning tongs, and a rack. Then she prepared her canner and put the shelled peas and string beans out for canning. After finishing the jars and lids, she filled them with veggies, processed the jars and then let them cool overnight.

The following day, Paige checked the seals and stored the jars in a vegetable area she designated in the storage cellar. The three jars that didn't seal were placed in cool storage to be eaten that week.

Paige grabbed one of the jars of dilly beans. "You naughty jar. Too bad you didn't seal. I'll just half to make good use of you right now." She snatched a small can of tomato juice off the shelf and rummaged around for the vodka. She raised her finger to her lips. "Sssh, I'm such a sneaky girl." She poured a snifter of vodka in a tall glass, added the tomato juice and tossed in dilly beans. "Time to celebrate our early bounty with a Bloody Mary."

Paige threw open the screen door and flopped down on the porch. She withdrew a bean from the glass, munched on her creation and chased it down with a sip. "Nothing like having a cocktail after a full day's work. Tomorrow we do salsa!" She curled her lip and mouthed, "Shit… Better save tomatoes and peppers for Levi and Nick's fish." She took another sip, closed her eyes and snuggled down in the chair. "Aw… delicious."

Nick, Levi, and Kent returned at dusk with two truckloads of chopped wood and stacked them in Logan's enlarged woodshed—wood was their main source of heat now to preserve the gas for the generator and vehicles. Kent took a 50-gallon metal container and welded it to a metal perch for easy access for the vehicles and then buried a 350-gallon metal container of gas for storage. The group conserved gas, understanding that in time availability would end. Kent also confiscated a gas stove and installed it on the enclosed front porch at Logan's. He collected butane tanks from abandoned homes and campers and stored them for fuel for the winter. Currently, the group used wind and a solar panel system for their hot water, electricity for lights and refrigeration, and heat—they used fossil fuels only when necessary.

After a full day of chores, Nick sat on the front porch and waited. He set up Logan's chess set. Logan strolled in from work. Nick crossed his legs. "Care for a game?"

Logan arched an eyebrow. "I never refuse a challenge." He sat down, and the two played a heady game of chess.

Finally, heading into hour two, Nick scraped his bottom lip with his upper teeth, gave Logan a wily grin, and made his last move. Logan glanced up at Nick and shook his head. Nick stared straight at Logan. "Checkmate."

Logan threw his hands up. "Damn. Well played, mate."

Nick sat back and thumped the arms of his chair with both hands. "Thanks."

Logan stood up. "You need to play Wyatt. He's the chess player in the family."

Nick slipped down in his seat, leaned his head on the back of his chair, stretched his legs out straight and crossed one foot over the top of the other foot. "Look forward to it."

Logan smirked and went inside the house in defeat.

Nick put his hands behind his head, closed his eyes, and whispered, "No ring on Paige's finger. Watch out, Logan, game on." Nick had accomplished the first step in his very long endgame. *I just assessed the strategic ability of my opponent.*

A week later, Mr. Dawson and his son Kellan pulled into Logan's, hauling two horse trailers containing four horses. Logan's neighbors asked if he could graze his horses on his property for a few months.

Logan leered. "I'll make you a deal. I'll let them graze, if you let us use them to go hunting this fall."

Mr. Dawson nodded. "It's a deal. Kellan and I would love to join you. We can use my truck and two trailers." Logan and the group welcomed the invitation.

After father and son left, Kent reared back. "I'm sure glad they were *friendlies*. It could have worked out differently. We need to build a metal fence around the house and all our provisions." Everyone scanned over the estate and agreed.

The next day, Kent and Levi drove the truck and commandeered a flatbed trailer. That afternoon, they got the truck and trailer out and collected chain-link panels and barbwire for an electric fence.

Nick declined to go with Kent and Levi on their mission for fencing materials and instead went hunting. He grabbed his bow and arrows off his shelf, yelled for Bo, loaded him in the truck and headed out. The two trekked across the pasture and hiked up the mountain. Bo caught a few ground squirrels and other rodents as they trekked across the trail.

Nick spotted a rabbit grazing on the dwindling foliage and quieted Bo. He seized his bow, positioned an arrow from the quiver off his shoulder and took aim. Suddenly, he froze to a rustling sound emanating from the bushes. He slowly turned his head and spied babies scurrying in the underbrush. He slowly removed the arrow, put it back in his quiver and replaced the bow across his shoulder. He backed away and snapped his fingers for Bo to follow. He scanned around for landmarks to record the location in his memory. Nick returned to the house and gathered up materials to make a snare to trap the mother and babies.

The next day, both Nick and Bo returned to the same location with their traps and tempting leftover greens from the garden in hand. Nick put out the traps.

Master and German Shepard returned to collect their catch a few days later. Nick brought his bounty home and put them in a temporary cage. He patted Bo on the head. "Next, Bo, we build a rabbit hutch and see if we can capture a few more rabbits to breed for another meat source for us this winter, especially for you."

Later, Nick and Bo took a trip to farm and pet stores around the city and confiscated all the rabbit, chicken, and dog food they could find and stored it in the shed. Nick stopped in a lumber yard and loaded chicken wire to build a chicken coop. He unloaded the wire and gazed down at Bo. "After the rabbit hutch, Bo, we'll build a coop and collect abandoned chickens in the countryside and place them in their new home. But first, we need to help Levi and Kent complete the electric fence around the perimeter." He shook his head. "So much to do." Throughout the summer, Nick and Levi had fished the rivers on the weekends. After they'd returned with their catch of the day, the two had canned and smoked their bounty for the winter.

One sunny September morning, Nick, Bo and Levi loaded up the truck and started the engine. Paige rushed out to the truck dressed in outdoor gear and carrying a sack lunch. Nick eyeballed her from head to toe and bit the side of his lip.

"Jump in." Levi opened the passenger door, let her ride shotgun and jumped in the back of the king cab with Bo.

Nick glanced over at Paige and smirked. "What are we having for lunch?"

Paige lifted the sack and tapped the side. "I brought four tuna sandwiches with homemade mayo."

Nick gazed in the rearview mirror at Levi. "A feast." Levi shot Nick a wily smile.

Paige frowned and wrinkled her nose. "Had to use powdered milk for the mayo."

Nick winked and shifted into third. "Better than the two plain peanut butter sandwiches I made for Levi and me." Paige nodded, shrugged her shoulders, and gave Nick her funny, flirty grin.

When they arrived at the river, Nick and Levi retrieved their waders and fly poles out of the back and took off for the stream. Paige followed Nick. Bo and Levi trekked to Levi's favorite spot further upstream. Nick tied a fly on the end of his line and handed his pole to Paige. She stood on the bank and cast her line midstream. Nick scrutinized her form.

"Stop casting." He walked up behind her, put his hands on her waist and guided her stance. He removed the pole from her hands, put it down on the ground and grabbed her wrist. He stood behind her and showed her the proper arm movements for fly casting. Standing together, they flowed in unison until her motion came naturally. Satisfied, Nick picked up the pole, handed it to her and watched her whipping cast from a safe distance.

Paige cast her fly into the water until she established a steady rhythm. Suddenly, her pole jerked. She hooked a fish and yanked. She squealed and reeled it closer to the bank. Nick grabbed the net off the bank and waded in the water to net her thirty-two-inch catch. He tugged the net to the bank, removed the fish off the line, cleaned it, and stored it in his fishing cooler on the water's edge.

After her catch, Paige sat on the bank and eyed Nick. He waded out into the icy cold stream and cast his line. She studied every move. His line skipped across the shimmering stream in a poetic cadence that drew her into a trance. The crisp morning air left a trail behind as his breath and body kept time. She embraced his perfect rhythmic dance with nature as the sun's rays sparkled like a spotlight around him.

She jerked and blinked. Nick tugged hard; the fish was on. He yanked and reeled in his line.

Then, the tall brush behind Paige rustled. She swung her head. The branches cracked. Paige froze.

"Nick!"

He glanced over at her. "What?"

She pointed over to the stand of brush behind her.

Nick bellowed, "Just stay there."

He reeled and stepped towards the bank. A big thud blasted from the brush. Paige jumped in the freezing water and waded toward Nick. He grabbed his net out of the back of his waders and net his hooked fish. She slogged halfway to Nick but lost her footing and fell in the water. He rushed towards her with his netted fish, then shuffled his pole and net into one hand and helped her up. She seized his arm, pulled herself towards him and put both arms around his neck. He wrapped his arm around her waist and handed her his pole and net with the fish still hooked on his line. She released his neck and grasped both items. He hoisted her in his arms and waded back to the bank.

Paige glared at Nick. "No! Go the other way." She pointed to the other side of the stream and kicked her legs. "There's a bear."

Nick smiled at Paige. "Take a look at your bear. I guess it's a *cowbear.*"

A cow emerged from the brush with a calf trailing close behind. He plopped Paige down on the bank, took his hooked fish and pole from her and placed them on the ground. He waved his arms in the air and yelled. The mother and calf stormed off.

Paige plunked the empty net down and shivered from the cold. Nick helped her up and picked her up in his arms once again. She shuddered and shivered. He put her down next to the pickup and opened the passenger door for cover. "Take off those wet clothes."

Paige slipped off her sweater and handed it to Nick. He chucked the drenched sweater in the back. "Keep going."

She kicked off her shoes, socks, removed her pants and shirt.

Nick removed his hoodie and barked, "Everything off."

Paige gave him the stink eye but complied. "Can I have your boxers?"

He smiled. "Relax, I've already seen you naked, and you know I don't wear boxers. Sorry, I'm commando again."

He raised his brow, smirked and motioned for Paige's bra and panties. She scowled and handed them over. He passed her his hoodie. She slipped it on and zipped it up. Nick wrung out her bra and panties and sat them on the floor of the king cab.

Paige jumped in the passenger side of the truck. Nick climbed in the driver's side, started the engine and turned the heater on high. "I'll see if Levi has on boxers." He lowered his voice, leaned in and whispered,

"Hope there's no skid marks. Let's hope he is skid free."

Nick paused and waited for her reaction. She shook her head, mildly amused. He tried to maintain a serious face. "If we were alone, I would use our body heat to warm you up."

Paige furrowed her brow. "Body heat?"

Nick laughed. "We'd just jump in the back skin-to-skin and use our bodies to warm you." He winked. "In emergencies, you have to do what you have to do. A matter of life and death. Hypothermia you know."

Paige shivered and stuttered. "Sh-shut up, Nick."

Nick chuckled and hopped out of his truck. He took off his waders, unbuttoned his flannel shirt and removed his t-shirt. Then he opened the passenger door and put his t-shirt across her bare legs. Paige shot him a half-grin. "Thanks."

Nick smiled back, shut the door and headed upstream to find Levi. He strode up to Levi and cleared his throat. "Levi, Paige fell in and needs your dry boxers if you can spare them. She's pretty cold."

Levi shook his head. "That's our girl." He stripped off his waders and jeans, then took off his boxers and handed them to Nick.

Nick raised the boxers in the air and snickered. "Thanks. Wait ten minutes for Paige to get changed and head back to the truck. We need to get her back home."

Nick brought the boxers back to the truck and opened the truck door. He turned Levi's boxers inside out, peeked at them and handed them to Paige. "What do you know, skid free."

She peered up and giggled. "Thanks, Nick. Levi's cleaner than most of you guys."

He shrugged his shoulders and whispered, "Cleaner than most girls too."

Paige nodded. "Clean and pithy."

Nick pointed his finger at her. "You got that right." He shut the door, cleaned their fish, and loaded all his fishing gear.

Fifteen minutes later, Levi stored his fish and gear in the back and jumped in the king cab with Bo. He turned to Paige. "Paige, everything okay?"

Paige turned up the corner of her mouth. "Warmer now, thanks to your boxers."

Nick hopped in the truck, glanced back at Levi and smirked. "Levi, did you see any *cowbears*?"

Levi scrunched his forehead. "What?"

Nick turned to Paige, winked and glimpsed at Levi. "Did any cows or bears bother you while you were fishing?"

Levi shrugged his shoulders. "No."

Nick gave him an evasive grin. "Good to know."

Paige glared at Nick and whispered, "Shut up." Nick snickered, put his truck in gear and drove off.

Nick parked the truck, grabbed their fish and brought them inside. Levi ferried his catch to the smokehouse. Paige removed her clothes from the back of the truck and put them all in water to soak. She showered, dressed and walked up behind Nick, who was cleaning their fish in the kitchen sink.

Paige leaned in. "I'm sorry I ruined our fishing today."

"Nothing ruined, but next time we use our body heat." He cocked his head and leered. "It was worth it to see you naked again, Paige."

Paige smacked him on the shoulder. "Shut up, Nick."

She stood beside him and helped him clean the rest of the fish. After cleaning the fish, Paige handed him the cutting board and took out two knives from the drawer. She retrieved the cast-iron skillet from the cabinet, placed it on the gas stove and poured in vegetable oil. She picked up a fillet, stopped and turned to Nick.

"Why didn't you tell Levi about the cow?"

Nick arched a brow. "What happens between us is our business. It's private." Then he moved in closer and stared straight back at her. "I would never embarrass you like that. That's your story to tell, not mine, babe." A mystified Paige smiled back and dipped the fish in the hot oil.

After drying the rest of their catch, Nick tasted a piece of steelhead off the drying rack in the smokehouse and set out the jars and lids. Nick, Levi and Paige added small tomatoes and jalapeno peppers from the garden to the smoked fish and tasted their final masterpiece. Levi shrugged his shoulders and stuffed more jalapenos in a few selected jars and drew a star on the lid.

Afterward, they stacked their jars of fish in the cellar for the winter, and Levi tucked his special spicy brew in the back. Nick put the last jar on the shelf, stood back and admired their cache of canned vegetables and smoked fish. "Looking good." Then he eyeballed the only section in the cellar left to fill. "Now we need venison and elk." He clapped his hands. "A-hunting we will go."

On the first day of autumn, Logan's neighbors showed up at daybreak with their trucks and trailers. The Dawsons hitched one of the horse trailers to Nick's truck. Nick put the rifle in the gun rack and gathered all their camping gear. After all the gear was loaded, the Dawsons, Logan and Nick headed out for Logan's favorite hunting grounds in the Colorado Mountains. After an hour's drive, the hunting party set up camp, mounted their horses and rode out to hunt game.

The crisp, cold air echoed the cracking sound of twigs underneath their horse's hooves. The group steadied their horses, Logan sounded an elk call, and they waited behind the brush. Nick caught a quick movement out of the corner of his eye and dismounted. He spotted an elk in the distance. The elk lifted his head. Nick tied his horse up and motioned for the others to stand firm. He pointed the scope of his rifle at the elk's head and fired. The elk dropped to the ground. Father and son congratulated the pair and rode off in the opposite direction.

Logan and Nick field-dressed the elk, buried the organs and prepared it for transport. The two men cut two small trees, made a travois, secured the huge creature with a nylon rope to the travois and Nick's saddle. Nick and Logan transported the elk back to camp, hung it and bled it out.

Around sunset, Mr. Dawson and Kellan rode in with a whitetail deer and repeated the process. They built a campfire, prepared coffee and ate smoked fish and black beans. After dinner, father and son turned in for the night, and Logan and Nick sat and watched the fire die down.

Nick poured the remaining coffee into their cups and pulled out a bottle of whiskey from underneath the seat of his truck. He held it up. "Care for a snort? This will take the edge off a cold crisp night."

Logan smiled. "You bastard, you've been holding out on us."

"Saved it for special occasions."

"You bagged a big one," Logan said. "That deserves celebrating."

"Thanks to your special hunting area." Nick poured a good amount into their coffee. "Can I ask you a personal question that is none of my business?"

Logan flashed a surreptitious grin. "Okay, ask at your own risk."

Nick handed him the cup. "Why do you spend so much time at the hospital?"

"I'm a doctor," Logan said. "We're shorthanded."

"Yeah, but no one expects you to give that much, man."

Logan sipped his coffee. "Why, is Paige complaining?"

"Sometimes." Nick plopped down on his lawn chair. "You're a lucky man to have her." He clasped the cup in both hands. "My first girlfriend dumped me for a lot less. That's when I bought my first bottle of whiskey. The day she left, I bought a bottle, poured a shot glass all broken-hearted, raised my glass and said, 'Dumped and gone.' I cried like a baby and finished the bottle in two days."

He slurped his drink, bent down and lifted the whiskey bottle.

"This five-year-old bottle was different. This one was a celebration. When she left, I raised my glass and shouted, 'Dumped and gone!' That girl was crazy. She checked my emails and my cell phone, and I swear she would have inspected my underwear if I wore them. The night she left, I did a snort and thanked God I dodged that bullet. I didn't feel the need to finish the bottle."

Nick kissed the glass of the five-year-old whiskey.

"So here we are, my good man. Care for another snort?"

"Sure, but don't get any ideas about Paige, lover." Logan flashed a grin and handed Nick his empty cup.

"Paige is a loyal one, she is." Nick poured another round and put the cup to his lips.

"She already shoot you down?"

"Oh yeah, right after I met her." Nick sat back in his chair. "She told me there was someone special at home." He raised his cup. "Now here we are at home, *Mr. Special.*"

"Good to know." Logan finished his cup and headed for the tent. "Night, lover."

After he left, Nick smirked and mumbled, "This overconfident guy is going to screw it up with Paige. Just give him time." He stared at the dying embers. *You're showing your weakness, Logan. Step two in my endgame—determine your opponent's weakness.* Nick smirked, cleaned out the cups, put out the fire and piled into his sleeping bag.

The next morning, Nick and Logan woke up to a roaring campfire, coffee, and leftover fish and beans. Kellan brought out his beef jerky to add to the entrée. After breakfast and cleanup, the group loaded their horses, supplies and meat and headed back to Denver.

Once back home, Nick and Logan put plastic down in the garage, hung the elk with a nylon cord, skinned it and butchered the huge creature. By midnight, they'd separated the meat into two sections—one for canning and one for jerky.

The next day, Nick and Logan took the section for jerky, trimmed the fat and sliced it into small thin pieces. Next, they prepared the marinade using black pepper, tamari, garlic, vinegar, and parsley. Logan grabbed their largest canning pot and briefly boiled the thin slices of elk in water. Nick procured several pieces of elk for Bo and set it aside, and the rest they marinated overnight. The next day, they put the slices of elk on racks and dried them in the smokehouse. Nick put Bo's on a separate rack in the back.

After finishing the jerky, they took the rest of the meat, gathered all the canning supplies together and formed an assembly line. Then, they cut, cooked and canned the remaining elk meat for soups, stews and chili. Nick and Logan stored their pride and joy on the shelf in the meat section. Even Bo had his own section of canned goods for the winter, but his had a little extra fat added.

After the jerky had thoroughly dried, they stored the dried meat in containers and stacked them on the remaining shelves in the storage area. Nick scanned over the canned meat section and the vegetable and fruit section and pointed to the staples.

"Looks like we have plenty of beans, flour, rice and pasta." He opened the cellar door. "Plenty of potatoes, squash and apples in cool storage. Paige has organized everything for easy access." He tapped Levi on the back. "We just might make it through the winter."

Levi nodded, and the two headed up the stairs. Nick stopped.

"Go ahead, Levi, I need to check my coffee supply." He bound downstairs and rummaged through his stash. "Shit."

Nick raced back up the stairs and locked the cellar. He poked around the kitchen and pulled out two packages of coffee beans. He rushed outside, let the tailgate down on his truck, let Bo in the back, shut the tailgate, jumped in his truck and started it.

Paige ran over. "Where you headed in such a hurry?"

Nick twisted his head from side to side. "Coffee emergency." Paige giggled and climbed in on the passenger side. Nick scowled. "Bo and I are on a coffee mission."

Paige grinned. "Well then, a-hunting we will go."

They tried the National Guard supply station first and acquired two large cans. Paige skimmed their food shelves at the station and touched Nick on the shoulder. "Supplies are drying up."

The two hit abandoned houses in subdivisions and remote areas and collected bags and containers of coffee, and a few bottles of wine, vodka and scotch. On the way home, Nick pulled into the market. Broken glass littered the blacktop and empty bent shelves lined the tiled floor.

Paige exhaled. "The markets and small chains have already been looted and emptied." She shook her head. "Nick, we are truly on our own." Nick clasped her knee. She placed her hand on top of his. "You had better ration your coffee."

He chuckled. "What the hell. I drink too much anyway."

Paige smiled. "Looks like booze and coffee on special occasions only."

Nick dipped his head. "Go easy on me, Paige. At least let me taper down gradually."

"We'll see."

Nick puckered his lip. "Paige, have a heart."

"Okay, boob." She twisted her hair in a ponytail and tucked it behind her head. Nick glanced over with a wily grin.

The two headed back to the house and deposited the appropriated coffee in the cellar. When Nick left, Paige stashed two bags of course grind in a large plastic container of feminine products she'd previously collected for herself and stored in a special area of the cellar. She opened up another container and counted the packages of her birth control pills. "Five months." She closed the container. "I need to go on my own mission, a birth control mission."

That night, she cornered Logan. "Can you get birth control pills from the hospital?"

He agreed and within two days handed Paige a box filled with two years' worth of pills and several pregnancy test strips. She kissed him and flipped through the packages. "Mission accomplished. Is there anything left at the hospital?"

"Not much. The nurses stashed most of it before looters could get it." Logan pulled her closer. "Smart, huh?"

"Very."

Once things settled down on the home front, Logan spent more and more time at the hospital. Evenings tested the couple's resolve. Paige pulled the covers up and patted the empty space next to her. "Alone again."

The next morning, she grabbed her birth control pills out of the drawer, removed one from the package, popped it in her mouth and chased it down with water. "Why do I even bother?"

Later that night, she glanced over at the clock, scowled at the vacant space next to her and huffed. "After midnight and still no Logan." She tossed and turned. She fluffed her pillow and stopped to strain her ears. A guitar strummed in the distance.

She crept halfway down the stairs and spied Nick sitting in a chair with his guitar, with Bo dutifully resting next to him. Paige hid in the shadows and watched Nick's fingers skilfully produce another amazing instrumental in the candlelight. His fingers sped across the guitar strings. He tossed back his head and flipped his long walnut strands out of his eyes. It had been months since his last haircut, so the long brown strands reached past his bearded chin.

Nick sat shirtless in jeans. The muscles in his biceps and pecs strained as he plucked the strings of his guitar. The candlelight exposed tattoos on his arms and chest. A barbwire border looped around his neck, wrists and ankles.

Paige swallowed hard. *One day, Nick, I'll find out the stories behind all those tattoos.*

She studied every inch of Nick's well-defined athletic body. His jeans displayed several holes with frayed edges. Paige replayed the times in the garden she suppressed the urge to poke her finger in the tattered holes and rip them further to make him squirm. A smile crossed her face.

The candle flickered. The flame captured Nick's passion as he tapped his bare feet to the rhythm of the moment. He hugged his guitar like a lover. Paige sighed. *He's so beautiful strumming his guitar, Ella. Oh, the things Ella has shared with Nick on his travels around the world on engineering jobs and many deployments. Her scratches tell the tales.* Paige closed her eyes and swayed to Ella's soothing beat. A flash of Nick walking toward her naked at the lake and pulling her close consumed her thoughts.

Suddenly, the music stopped. Paige opened her eyes.

Nick was staring at her. "Hey, must have been some pretty sweet thoughts."

"Hi, I'm sorry to disturb you. I couldn't sleep."

"You never disturb me, Paige. I can't sleep either," Nick said. "Playing helps me relax, so I can sleep."

"That's a beautiful song." Paige folded her hands in her lap. "Please sing it for me."

"You sure?"

She bit her lip. "Of course."

"Okay." Nick played and sung the words for Paige. His sweet words flowed with Ella as he painted the air with such beautiful notes. The last verse in the song caught Paige's attention. It repeated the same message over and over—*if you really love a woman, you have to treat her right.*

After Nick finished, he smiled at Paige. She wiped a tear from her cheek. Nick laid his guitar down and sat next to her on the stair. He put his arm around her, then took his finger and moved Paige's chin towards him. He gazed in her blue eyes. "Was I really that bad?"

"It was beautiful." She smiled and sniffed. "Did you write it?"

"Thank you for believing I could, but no." He reached over and put a strand of Paige's hair behind her ear. "You know, a very wise woman once told me the secret to loving a woman. She said I must follow three rules."

Paige peered up at him. "What three rules?"

"You sure you want to know?" Nick gave Paige a sly grin.

She suspiciously raised her brow. "Yes, Mr. Mysterious, tell me your secret."

"Okay then." Nick pulled her close. "Rule number one is treat her right."

"Okay, good rule," Paige slurred. "And number two?"

"Rule number two." He slipped in a momentary pause for dramatic effect. "She must be kissed often."

"Okay, another good one." Paige shrugged her shoulders. "And three?"

"Do you really want to know number three?" Nick bit his lip and cocked his head.

"Sure."

He leaned in close to her ear. "She must be properly... fucked."

Paige snorted. "Do tell."

"No, no, this must be shown. It can't be explained." Nick snuggled close. "Be happy to show you."

Paige giggled. "You wish."

Nick stared straight at Paige. "Indeed, I do."

"You're full of shit, Nick. You made those rules up."

"Didn't make up the last rule." Nick rocked his head back and forth. "That was Zelda's rule." Nick smacked his lips. "She was a damn good teacher too."

"Really?" Paige squirmed.

"Yeah." Nick flashed a wide grin.

"Are you trouble, Nick?"

Nick narrowed his eyes and shot her his all too wily grin. "Definitely."

Paige flipped her hair out of her eyes and softly murmured, "Hum."

Nick held his gaze with his intense light willow green eyes and scooted closer. "Please promise me, Paige."

Paige paused and peered into Nick's serious green eyes. "O...kay."

"Please remember that you are not one of Logan's shiny toys that he can take off the shelf and play with any time he wants." Nick grasped her hand. "And please, please don't mistake possession for passion."

Paige wrinkled up her forehead. "What the hell does that mean?"

"You'll figure it out, babe." Nick stood up and walked up the stairs.

"Wait." She threw up her hands. "What did I promise?"

He turned around. "You'll figure it out." Nick called out for Bo, and the two toddled off to bed.

Paige sat alone on the stairs, frozen. She scrunched her forehead and replayed the last conversation. After several minutes and no resolution, she headed to bed. She stared at the ceiling until her eyes refused to stay open any longer and sleep overtook her.

His soft lips gently touched the back of her neck. Her naked body quivered as he cupped her breasts. He reached around between her legs and began gentle circular patterns with his finger. Paige threw her head back as the intensity of her arrival drew near. She reached back with one hand, grabbed his hair and pulled him close. He sucked her earlobe and softly whispered, "I'm going to fuck you now, Paige. Yes or no?"

Paige drew in a breath. "Yes." He held her firmly with one arm around her waist, spread her legs apart with his knee and leaned her forward with the other hand. She put her hands against the door for support, and he entered her slowly.

He lightly ran his fingers down her spine and kissed her back. "Soft or hard?" She paused and stuttered, so he softly continued with a few gentle strokes and instantly slammed into her with several hard thrusts then stopped.

She lifted her head up and tossed her hair out of her eyes. "Hard."

He eased his hand down her back and leaned her over once again. "Hold on tight."

Paige fumbled in the dark and grasped the doorknob with both hands. He thrust deep into her and continued with even strokes until he sensed her body start to arrive. A few more thrusts and her body exploded around her. Her knees grew weak. He held her up but cautiously persisted. The intensity built in her once again. She found her feet, resumed the stance and pleaded for another hard round. He increased intensity until they both simultaneously released and collapsed to the floor.

Paige drew in a deep breath and fell back against his chest. He moved her honey blonde hair to the side, leaned in and whispered, "Now you're properly fucked, babe." Paige swung around and gaped into his light willow green eyes. The soft light from the hallway revealed his contentment. Nick closed his eyes. Paige gently touched his long black lashes with her finger and kissed him tenderly. He moaned and murmured, "Such a sweet surrender." He cracked open his eyes, held her close and gazed deeply into her light blue eyes. "I love you, Paige."

Suddenly, Paige opened her eyes and sat up in bed. She glanced over at the empty space beside her. "It was just a dream." She rubbed her eyes and cried out for Nick, but only a closed door and vacant darkness answered back.

Chapter Four

Revelation

Kent tinkered with his camera and pushed play. The image of the sighting appeared. He plugged in his adapter, transferred the recording to Levi's tablet and zoomed in on the image. Kent clapped his hands. "Levi! Get in here."

Levi rushed in. "How the hell did you get your camera to work?"

"I smacked it." Kent chortled. "And a few more things."

"It works, that's all that matters." Levi leaned in close, and they eyed it frame by frame. Bright lights filled the screen. Kent scrolled back and paused it on something shiny before the bright lights began.

"There! It looks like an outline of something very large in the shadow of the clouds." He forwarded it, and a face emerged. Kent stopped and hit zoom.

Levi pointed and traced an outline with his finger. "Christ, is that a ship, Kent?"

Kent turned his head. "Well, it ain't Christ."

"No, it ain't."

The battery register on the tablet read two percent, so Kent sprint out to the generator and added gas. He plugged the adapter into the receptacle and recharged the battery on the tablet.

Later that evening, Kent gathered everyone around the kitchen table, and the two men showed the recording and still shots from Kent's camera. Kent closed the tablet. "The sighting was not the second coming, but a UFO incident."

Nick leaned back in his chair. "Just like a fish. All of us were lured in by that crop circle."

"What better way to attract a million people. They used salvation and curiosity," Paige said. "Just tell people to look to the sky and use symbols from every religion to get them all to come. We can't resist."

"Or, use crop circles to draw in UFO enthusiasts." Kent slapped the top of the table. "It's the perfect plan."

"The real question is why?" Nick tapped the tabletop. "And why take only the ones they chose?"

Logan bent forward. "They want people with Rh-positive blood."

Nick turned his head toward Logan. "Okay, but why take the ones with positive?"

"They definitely have a preference," Logan said. "But is it positive or negative?" He rubbed his hands together. "We need to find out."

Nick scowled. "Time to hit the medical books."

"I'll research at the hospital," Logan said. "Time to hit the lab."

"We need to check the library for medical books." Paige stood and tapped Levi and Kent on the shoulders. "Thanks, you two. Great work."

The next day, Nick, Levi, Kent and Paige entered a cold library empty of patrons. They gathered medical books, headed back home and spent the afternoon searching for anything on Rh blood factors. After rifling through several pages on old abductions, Kent stood up.

"Shit! They claimed there were a higher percentage of Rh-negative people abducted by aliens."

"No way, we're here," Levi said. "All the positives are gone."

Nick scrunched his face. "Why would they eliminate Rh-positives?"

"They don't need them." Paige grimaced. "But they need us for something."

"Hold on." Nick tapped the books with his finger. "Let's get the facts."

Everyone started reading, underlining and highlighting. Logan ambled in and flopped down in a chair. Paige placed her hand on his. "Any luck?"

"Well, Rh has a protein called Rhesus. Those with Rh-negative blood don't have that protein." Logan clasped the arms of the chair. "Rh-negative is a danger to the surface of the red blood cell, and the potential danger is to erythrocytes in those with positive Rh factor, especially Rh-positive babies."

Kent lifted his book. "According to the book, Rh-negative blood type is rare. Only fifteen percent of the population is Rh-negative. Seven percent are blood type O, six percent A, two percent B and one percent AB." He pointed his finger down at the page. "The highest rate are

European Basque from Spain and France." Kent closed the book wide-eyed. "I'm screwed. I have both."

Paige reached over and squeezed his arm. "Relax, they will take one look at your ugly mug and throw you back."

Kent grasped her hand. "Promise?"

Nick chimed in. "I think you're pretty, Kent."

Kent flashed him a middle finger. "Not nearly as pretty as you."

Nick hopped up, shuffled downstairs to the cellar and pulled out a bottle of whiskey. He snatched five shot glasses off the shelf, poured them to the brim, passed them out and lifted his shot glass. "To the screwed, glued and tattooed."

They each rose their glass. "To the screwed."

Kent interrupted and turned to Nick. "Forget the glued and tattooed. That's only you, Nick." He leaned close. "Nick, what the hell is glued?"

Nick snickered. "All your capped and veneered teeth."

Kent smiled wide and bared his teeth. "Well, all right then." He raised his glass once again. "Let's add Levi's glued toupee to the list."

Levi cackled and rubbed his bald head. "Gave that rug up years ago."

Kent snorted and raised his glass. "Okay, let's toast to the screwed, glued and tattooed then."

Everyone raised their glasses and held them up again.

Kent stood straight. "Nick, what about all those poor bastards who aren't screwed, glued or tattooed?"

"Oh yeah, those bastards, with perfect teeth and hair and not one tattoo," Nick said. "Too bad. Fuck 'em."

Kent laughed. "No, no, no. Let's toast the poor bastards anyway."

"All right, you have a point." Nick seized the bottle. "We need to show a little compassion." He refilled everyone's glass and raised his. "To the rest of the poor bastards." They raised their glasses and tipped back another shot of whiskey.

Logan stood up. "Well, I have an early morning call, so this poor bastard is headed to bed." He flashed everyone a half-wave. "Goodnight."

Paige excused herself and followed behind him.

Nick waited silently for their bedroom door to click shut and poured another round. "Well, let's get back to business and have a drink to the fartless." Nick pointed upstairs to Logan's bedroom door. "The feckless and the fartless, like Logan." Nick snorted. "Have pity on the bastards like him who are so tight they squeak when they walk." Nick lifted his glass. "Squeak, squeak." The three men laughed and held their stomachs.

After the shot of whiskey, Levi pulled out a joint from his pocket and held it up. "Care for some Colorado Gold?"

Nick shot him the stink eye. "Well, you sneaky bald bastard. Where did you get that?"

"Paige and I found this a few months ago in that private mansion on the hill." Levi sneered. "We found a large stash hidden in containers. We also hit a private stock of expensive liquor in a secret cellar." He waved the joint in the air. "Paige bagged, organized and stored most of the weed in medical supplies, but gave me a stash of my own for these aching joints and arthritis." He kissed the joint. "Yep, Nick, this Colorado Gold is indeed some of the best I've ever used."

Nick shook his head from side to side. "I can't believe she withheld that information from me."

Levi snickered and wagged his finger. "She probably thought you'd raid the stash."

Nick nodded. "She's right. I'd complain about my shoulder or some other ailment to warrant a sample and drive her crazy." Nick leaned over and kissed Levi's bald head. "Light that puppy up, my good man. Let's give it a go."

Levi lit the joint and passed it around. Nick exhaled. "This is like my college days and parties at the frat house." He shared a few stories from his college days over chuckles and ribbing.

Afterward, Nick spotted his shot glass. "One last toast, gents." He poured their last shot of Kentucky whiskey and raised his glass one last time. "To the poorest bastards of all, the fuckless." Nick swirled the dark brew. "We belong to the saddest bunch of all, *the fuckless minions.*" He pointed to Bo. "But poor, neutered Bo is in far worse shape. He was neutered before I got him at the pound. I would never have done such a terrible thing to him. Poor Bo is fuckless forever."

Nick jiggled his glass. "Hey, there is still hope for the three of us as long, as we keep our balls and can get it up." Nick raised his glass and frowned. "To the fuckless."

Everyone chortled and threw back the whiskey. Nick banged his glass down on the coffee table and stood up. "Well, gents, I bid you adieu. I must retire to my lonely boudoir and cry myself to sleep." Nick bowed to them. "For I'm the saddest feckless…est and fuckless…est of us all. For I'm in love with the woman upstairs, and she's in the arms of another man."

Kent peered over at Nick. "Fear not, my good man, for I believe there is trouble in paradise."

"Oh yeah, and I'm the trouble." Nick smirked. "Cause all I can, I will."

"Hear, hear, my goodly man," Kent tittered. "Turn on that Landon charm and give 'em hell, son. Give it the good fight."

"Hear, hear," Levi echoed.

Nick kissed a tat on his bicep. "Remember the secret to success, gents. Go full on, be all in, or..."

Nick pointed to Logan's bedroom door. "Get the fuck out of my way."

Kent pumped his fist in the air. "That's the spirit, Nick."

Nick snapped his fingers. "Come, Bo, you ball-less bastard. We must go lick our wounds and prepare for the good fight."

He waved goodnight and hobbled upstairs. He stumbled into his bedroom and shut the door. Paige was standing against the wall. Nick creased his brow. "Well, now, isn't this a surprise? What can I do for you, my lady?"

Paige stood in her bedroom boxers and a tank top draped with a knitted sweater. "Nick, lower your voice. I need to ask you a question."

"Ask away." Nick pressed his hand on the wall above her. "Hey, I'm sorry if we kept you awake." He leaned closer. "Did you hear what I said downstairs?"

"You guys didn't keep me awake. I have no idea what you said after I left." Paige chewed the side of her lip. "Logan fell asleep before I made it out of the shower. I didn't want to wake him tossing and turning so I came here." She cast her eyes down. "I wanted to ask you a question."

Nick moved in closer and put his other hand on the wall behind her. "What's so important that it's keeping you up all night?"

Paige peeked up. "Did I wake you up the other night when I called out your name?"

Nick leaned down next to her ear. "Why did you call out my name?"

She drew in a deep breath. "I had a nightmare and called for you."

"A nightmare?"

Paige scraped her teeth across her bottom lip. "Well, not really a nightmare."

"Dreaming about me, Ms. Martin?"

She shut her eyes. "Yes."

Nick stuck his finger under Paige's waistband. He brushed his fingertip below her belly button, abrading her mound of hair. She froze as an electric shock raced through her body. He pulled her boxers open, peered down the front of her shorts and softly moaned in her ear.

Paige stuttered. "I-I... just wanted to apologize if I woke you up."

Nick inhaled the aroma of jasmine shampoo, grazed her earlobe and brushed across her lips with his. He moved to her other ear and whispered in his low breathy voice. "Apology accepted. You can wake me up anytime, Paige." Then he kissed her forehead. "Can I do anything else for you, babe?"

She opened her eyes. "No, I wanted to apologize."

Nick narrowed his eyes and gave her his crooked smile. "Well, then, I'll wish you good night."

He opened the door and Paige slid past him. As she started to walk off, he grabbed her arm and pulled her close. "Babe, if I went through life always worried and afraid that I might do something wrong or make a mistake, then I would never have done all the amazing things that I did. And more importantly, I would have missed out on all the things I did right. Don't let fear paralyze you."

Paige stared into Nick's green eyes. A slow smile crossed her lips. He winked and released his grip. She strolled down the hall. Her hips swayed with each step. He closed the door and clenched his jaw.

"Damn." Nick kicked off his shoes and plopped on the bed. "Bo, come." Bo placed his head on Nick's chest. He stroked Bo's fur. "It won't be long now. I'm in her dreams." He turned his gaze toward the couple's bedroom. "Sweet dreams, babe. Dream of me." Nick adjusted the discomfort in his jeans and clasped the sides of Bo's head. "Sorry, boy, one more thing before we turn in. Gotta go rub one out in the shower." He jumped up, snapped his finger and pointed to the floor. "Stay."

The next morning, Nick joined a somber group eating breakfast. He flashed a big grin. "Hey, look at the bright side. If the only survivors are Rh-negative, then our overpopulated Earth just rid itself of over six billion people."

Kent scowled. "With our luck, only to be replaced by a few billion aliens."

Nick winked at Kent and sat down with his plate.

"We have Rh-positive blood in storage," Logan said. "We need to secure it."

Nick scooped his powdered eggs. "How much is there at the hospital?"

"It's the most popular." Logan sat his fork down.

Kent piped in. "Get all of it and put it in safe storage."

"We need refrigeration." Logan rose to fill his cup. "I need to find Wyatt."

Kent nudged Nick and whispered, "What's got you all happy?"

Nick leaned in. "Things are looking up."

Kent mouthed the word "Paige." Nick nodded. Kent dipped his chin. "Good."

Logan returned with a full cup in hand. Nick jumped up, poured a cup, and the three discussed plans for blood storage.

Later that afternoon, Kent and Logan met with Wyatt at base camp and Wyatt agreed to meet with his commanding officer and discuss storage plans for the blood.

That evening, Kent rummaged through his camera bag. He snatched the video camera that Paige used during the sightings and held it up. "Let's see if you have anything more to say."

He replaced the low batteries and pushed play. Black and white static erupted on the screen. He hit fast forward and captured an image. He rewound, stopped and zoomed in. James appeared. Kent twisted his head toward the kitchen. "Levi! I got something."

Levi loaded the video on his tablet and slowed it down frame by frame. On the last image, James vanished in a flash of light. Levi glimpsed over at Kent. "Beam me up, Scotty."

Kent shrugged his shoulders. "Maybe, but let's keep this one in our back pocket."

"Yeah," Levi said. "It's subjective at best."

Around ten at night, Wyatt introduced two of his commanding officers. Kent and Logan opened Levi's tablet and pushed play. PowerPoint slides on blood type and Kent's photographs scrolled across the screen. Kent shared his books on UFOs and materials from his files.

After their presentation, the officers agreed to provide the storage for the blood at an underground site in a secret location.

When the commanding officers left, Kent folded his arms. "We need to keep some blood for us."

Logan bent forward. "We could put a small amount in a cooler and store it in the cellar."

"Instead, I'd like to build another cellar at Bunker's house where the old emergency shelter was but make it smaller." Logan nodded. Kent slapped his hands together. "Tomorrow, Levi and I will look for materials with the flatbed."

Kent and Levi finished the frame for the blood storage unit at Bunker's the next morning and sat down for a warm bowl of soup back at Logan's. Nick slipped in from shoveling a fresh layer of snowfall off the sidewalk and ladled a bowl of soup. He slurped a spoonful. "How's construction going?" Kent reported slow progress. Nick dipped another spoonful. "Need some help?" Kent nodded.

After lunch, the three grabbed their coats, gloves and hats and headed out. The guys unloaded the lumber, and Nick and Kent climbed down the ladder. Levi handed insulation and boards down the hole for the men to use. Nick struck the last nail on one of the side walls and turned just in time to watch a stack of lumber fall. He jumped back, but one board bounced, slashed the side of his head with its jagged edge and knocked him to the ground. Blood squirted from a deep gash on his scalp. Kent retrieved a handkerchief from his pocket and held it firmly on the wound. Nick slowly stood up with Kent's help, put his hand on the handkerchief and stepped up the ladder.

Kent examined the injury in the sunlight and opened Nick's passenger door. "Get in the truck, Nick."

Levi climbed in, and the three headed to the hospital.

"Drop me off here and stop fussing. I just need a few stitches," Nick said. "I'll ride back with Logan." The guys reluctantly agreed and headed back to finish their construction project.

Nick walked into the ER holding the bloody handkerchief against his head.

"No nurse."

He headed towards the back of the ER. Logan's voice echoed from behind a closed curtain. Nick reached to pull it back but stopped. A female voice tittered. Nick stepped back, not wanting to interrupt if she was a patient.

The voice said, "I'm wearing your favorite teddy tonight." Logan's voice answered back. "I can't wait." Nick peeked between the curtain and spied Logan kissing the young woman. The two separated, and she slipped out the back.

Nick jerked the curtain open. "Logan, you're a real piece of shit."

Logan dropped his head. "I know what this looks like, but there is more to it."

Nick's nostrils flared. "I'll bet."

"You're bleeding." Logan moved toward Nick. "You need to get looked at."

Nick block Logan's arm and backed away. "Don't touch me."

Logan raised his hands in the air. "Okay, you got it." He ripped open the curtain and called on another doctor to come in.

Dr. Brody entered and removed the handkerchief. She cut the blood-soaked hair around the area, washed the wound and stuck a needle in to deaden the pain. She stitched the gash, flashed her penlight in his eyes and asked him a series of questions to check for signs of concussion. After feeling satisfied that he displayed no symptoms, Dr. Brody folded her arms.

"That should do it, but come back if anything changes."

Nick eyed the name on her coat. "Thanks, Dr. Brody." She dipped her chin, and he walked out of the partition.

He took a few steps and stopped dead in his tracks. He clenched his jaw, turned around and pulled the curtain back. Dr. Brody glanced up. Nick stared straight at her. "Don't keep Logan out too late."

Dr. Brody furrowed her brow. "You know Logan?"

"You could say that," Nick said. "Thanks again, doc." Nick turned and walked out.

Logan rushed up to Nick. "Wait, let me explain."

Nick followed Logan to a back room. Logan closed the door. "Last year, Renee lost her husband. With Paige gone all the time, we turned to each other for comfort, and Renee got pregnant." His voice broke. "Nick, we're having a child together." Logan threw his hands in the air. "I'm trying to do the right thing by Renee." He paused. "I asked Renee to give me time to break it to Paige, but I'm having a hard time. I don't want to hurt Paige."

Nick scowled. "Do you love Renee?"

"Yes," Logan said.

"Then tell Paige it's over."

"Okay." Logan cast his eyes to the floor. "I know, I know."

"Today!" Nick opened the door and started to walk out. Suddenly, he stopped and turned around. "You're still a piece of shit, Logan."

The blood rushed to Logan's head. "You want to fuck another man's leftovers, Nick?"

Nick stepped back in, closed the door and glared at Logan. Logan moved towards Nick, but in a flash, Nick clenched his fist and punched Logan's nose.

Logan fell back and grabbed his face to stop the blood. "You broke it!"

"Good!" Nick flagged his middle finger. "Fuck you, Logan." Then a red-faced Nick stormed out the door and marched to the entrance of the hospital.

Paige met him at the door. She touched his shoulder. "Nick, are you okay? Levi said you were hurt in an accident." She eyeballed the bandage. "Kent said you needed stitches, and Levi told me to take the truck so you didn't have to wait for Logan to get off shift."

She reached up to touch his forehead, but Nick grabbed her hand. "I'm okay. Let's just go home."

Paige quickly retracted her hand. "Okay, Nick, I'll be right there. I need to talk to Logan first."

Nick bobbed his head. "I'll wait in the truck."

Paige slipped in the back of the ER. Logan peered up, holding his nose. She wrinkled her forehead. "What happened?"

Logan explained everything that transpired. Then he rose from the chair. "You take the house, and I'll move my stuff out and stay with Renee at the hospital. I need to do the right thing for Renee and our child." He pointed to another wing of the hospital. "They've transformed a wing for the doctors to live in. I'm here most of the time, anyway." Logan shook his head. "Keep the house. You deserve it after all the crap I put you through."

Paige wiped her eyes. "Damn right. Goodbye, Logan."

She stopped in the bathroom and splashed cold water on her face. "I should have known."

She climbed in Nick's truck and turned toward him. "You broke his nose."

"I did, and it felt so… good." Nick started his truck.

"I know everything, Nick."

Nick cocked his head. "I'm glad Logan finally found some courage."

"He's moving out. He gave me the house."

Nick shifted gears. "That's the least he could do. I'm glad we don't have to live in the same house. Sooner or later we'd come to blows again, and I'd beat the crap out of him."

He drove on to Logan's and parked the truck, then he turned off the key and glanced over at a smiling Paige. "You are certainly calm about this."

"The truth is, Logan left me a long time ago," Paige said. "He was almost never home, and when he was, he was never really here."

"Okay." Nick grinned. "We'll leave it there."

"Good enough." Paige drew back the handle on the passenger door and marched inside her home.

Nick stared in the bathroom mirror, traced across his stitches and pulled back. "You're one scruffy looking bastard."

He grabbed the scissors and cut his hair short. He mussed his short locks and covered the bald patch from his stitches. He snipped his beard as close as the scissors would go, picked up the shaving cream and squirted a handful. He lathered his face, shaved the rest of his beard and slapped his bare face.

"It's been months since my last shave or haircut." Nick scooped up a handful of facial hair and long strands and tossed it in the waste basket. "Good riddance."

He stepped into the shower, splashed on enough water from the faucet and lathered up. He turned on the shower and rinsed off. He drew in a deep cleansing breath and slowly released all the burdens that weighed him down.

"Freedom."

Nick wrapped the towel around his waist and stood in front of the sink, brushed his teeth and gargled with water.

Paige cracked the bathroom door open. Nick turned and leaned against the sink. She raised her eyebrows. "Is that really you?"

He unfastened his towel and spread his arms wide. "In the buff."

A wily grin crossed her lips. "You clean up mighty fine, sir."

"Glad you like it." Nick grabbed Paige's hand and pulled her close to him. "Are you going to pull away from me again?"

"No, not this time. I'm not taken," Paige said. "Free as a bird."

Nick leaned in and gently pressed his lips on hers. This time, Paige didn't turn her head away like she did at the lake. She returned his kiss. Nick slow-walked her to his bedroom and shut the door. He removed her shirt and bra and threw them down on the floor. She wrapped her arms around his firm body. He reached down and unfastened her pants and slid them off. Nick lay her down on his bed and kissed her lips. He tenderly moved down her neck and breasts.

Paige's body heaved in response to his every touch. Nick slid her black lace panties off and dropped them next to the bed. In the heat of passion, she opened herself up to receive him completely, and he entered her. His intensity grew and grew with every thrust. Then all at once, there was a sudden release, and he was finally freed—a liberation of intense desire for the woman he'd loved for months and months. He emptied body and soul into her. And after all the countless times Paige resisted, she clutched the sheets and surrendered. She matched his release and unraveled underneath him.

In their afterglow, Nick cuddled up next to her and nuzzled her earlobe. "Wild horses couldn't drag me from your side."

Paige beamed. "That's our song, Nick."

"Glad you remembered."

She kissed his earlobe. "I'm glad I'm the one you love."

"Indeed you are, babe." He held her tight. "You're the only one I want."

She nuzzled next to his ear. "I think we can say you accomplished rule number three, Nick."

"Aw… are you telling me that you have been properly fucked, Ms. Martin?" Nick gave her his crooked little grin.

"Yes, Nick." She cupped his face with both hands. "A proper job, well done."

"A proper what, Paige?" Nick narrowed his determined eyes.

"You know." Paige kissed his nose. "Rule three."

"What is rule three?" Nick rolled on top of her and wiped the strands of her hair out of her eyes.

"Properly… you know." Paige teased.

"Say it Paige, properly wh… at." Nick moved in eye to eye, pinning her down.

Paige laughed and squirmed with no success. She whispered, "Properly fucked, Nick."

Nick took one hand and once again swiped away the strands of hair that had softly fallen across her face in their gentle tussle.

"Good to know," he said, still holding her in his firm grip with one hand. He kissed her cheek. "But first we must confirm there's no fuckery."

Paige laughed. "What, like kinky fuckery?"

"BS, Paige. Fakery."

Paige giggled. "Oh."

"First, we must make sure that you understand the definition of a Proper Fuck," Nick said. "To confirm, I must ask you a question."

"Shoot."

"Let's say that our tryst was a meal. Do you feel full, or were you still hungry after we finished our dinner? In other words, are you full or do you feel like you are still hungry and need more?"

Paige stared directly into Nick's eyes. "I left our table full and with the sweet taste of a full course meal, dessert included."

"Well then, I would say that you were properly fucked, Ms. Martin." Nick gave her a quick kiss and released his grip. "I intend to repeat it as much as possible."

"You'll get no arguments from me, Mr. Landon." Paige kissed him. "Is there any kinky fuckery on the menu?"

Nick grinned. "Maybe, if Ms. Martin enjoys a bit of kink, but you appear to be more vanilla than kink."

"Maybe a little kink." Paige shot him a devious smile.

"Maybe?" Nick said. "I happen to like vanilla, but a little kink is fun."

Paige lifted her finger. "Zelda kink?"

"She was a master at kink. One might say the fuck-master—definitely an expert on pain and pleasure," Nick said. "But thankfully, we had more pleasure than pain. Kinky pain is too much for my blood. I'm more of a fan of pleasure than pain."

"Do tell, Mr. Landon."

"That conversation is for another day." Nick yawned, cuddled close, and nestled his nose in her mussed-up hair.

After several minutes, the steady rhythm of Nick's breathing echoed as he drifted off. His body relaxed against her. She faced him and kissed his forehead just below his stitches. Nick tightened his hold around her and resumed his slow steady breath. He snored lightly as he slumbered. She stared at the rise and fall in his chest and closed her eyes. *I'm truly loved and safe in his arms. I trust this man with my life.*

The next morning, Bo scratched on the bedroom door. Paige stretched and kissed the top of Nick's, head avoiding his stitches. Nick kissed her back, jumped out of bed naked and opened the door for Bo. The German Shepherd flopped his head on the side of the bed, demanding a pet from Paige. She gave Bo a pat, slipped on her top and got out of bed. The two dressed and joined Levi and Kent for breakfast.

After breakfast, Paige packed up all of Logan's things and put them on the porch. Kent pointed to the boxes. "What's this?" She explained the breakup. He shook his head. "It's about time you gave him the boot."

Paige furrowed her brow. "Did you know Logan was cheating?"

Kent stared straight into her eyes. "No man stays away from home that long unless he is."

Paige crooked her finger. "Come with me, Kent."

Kent and Paige drove to the deserted mall and picked up three sets of sheets, blankets, curtains, and a rug for the bathroom and bedroom. She loaded the collected goods, shut the tailgate and glanced at Kent. "I'm replacing everything Logan touched."

Kent dipped his chin in silent response. Paige stuffed a bag of clothing for herself and Nick in the back seat and marched in the craft store. Kent followed behind.

She rolled a shopping cart down the aisles and threw in knitting and crochet needles, several colors of yarn, a pair of sewing scissors and a few squares of felt. "Making gifts this year."

Kent grinned without a word.

They stopped at an antique store that Paige spotted on their way out of town. She peeked through a small glass window in the door. "This one's abandoned. The only occupants here are the dust particles that cover the antiques."

She picked up a rock from the flower bed, broke the window, cleared the glass and opened the door. She scanned the shop. Something on the back wall caught her eye. She picked up an antique gun. "This is perfect for Nick." She skimmed through the book cabinet, snatched a book written at the turn of the century and tucked it under her arm.

Kent spotted an old desk in the corner. "You're a real beauty. Solid oak." He rubbed his hand across the scratched oak surface. "I can refinish this."

The two loaded up their items and Paige dropped Kent off at Bunker's to help Levi. Paige and Kent had put the gun, desk and books in Levi's truck, so Kent and Levi could hide the items until Christmas.

When Paige got back, Nick helped her unpack the items from the mall upstairs. "Did you leave anything at the store?"

Paige snarled. "What can I say. Out with the old, in with the new."

Nick bobbed his head. "No complaints from me." He slapped the headboard. "This is definitely going." He hauled it out of the bedroom, took it out back and leaned it up against the other trash to be recycled. Then he grabbed a shot glass and his bottle of five-year-old whiskey out of the back of his truck. He gripped the bottle and swirled the brown liquor.

"Saved the last shot of whiskey for this special day. The day Logan lost." With bottle in tow, Nick strolled back to the headboard, poured himself the last shot and raised his glass. "Here's to you, Logan. Finally gone." He drew a deep breath. "Good riddance, you feckless fuck."

He swigged the whiskey and threw the shot glass against the headboard. The glass shattered. Nick stroked his empty bottle. "I did it. It's over."

He heaved the empty bottle against the headboard, dodged incoming chards of glass and threw a fist high in the air.

"Yeah! The endgame is complete. All four steps nailed. Assess your opponent, determine his weakness, master the endgame, and the last step—take down in defeat!" Nick scanned the broken glass, smirked and strutted away from yesterday's trash. He stuffed his hands in his pocket and muttered, "Final checkmate, Logan. Broken nose and all."

Nick strolled inside the house, removed two quart jars of cooked elk off the shelf and grabbed four cans of red kidney beans and chili powder. He dumped them in the soup pot on low heat and let it simmer all afternoon.

Then Nick joined Paige upstairs and helped her make the bed. Paige lifted up the shirts she picked out for him at the mall and hung them up in the closet. She wagged a pair of men's underwear and leered.

Nick took a deep breath. "I won't wear those, Paige."

"Who said you'd keep them on very long?"

Nick arched his brow. "I'll wear those if you take them off me."

"Deal," Paige said. "Nick, close your eyes."

He closed his eyes. Paige fumbled and shuffled. Nick opened one eye for a quick peek. Paige stood without a stitch on. He snapped his eye closed, and the blood rushed to his lower extremities to prepare for detonation.

"Open your eyes, Nick," Paige purred. Her pert breasts peeked through the black-laced teddy she'd brought from the mall.

Nick gulped. "You won't have that on for long, either."

"Promise?"

Nick pulled her close and brushed his lips across her cheeks. Paige's body quaked and quivered as he ran his hand down her back. He leaned over and dispersed featherlike kisses down her neck. He kicked his shoes off and pulled the teddy over her head. Then he lay her down on the bed and gazed into her pale blue eyes.

"You are so beautiful. You have no idea what you do to me." He palmed her breasts and used his tongue to tantalize and tease her nipple. Her pulse quickened underneath him. Nick took two fingers and pulled the lace panties off her as he kissed his way down to her mound and unleashed his expert tongue.

Paige's climax built as he circled her sweet spot. Her body burst and subsequently flowed with serenity. She murmured, "Nick."

Nick slowly moved up to her ear. "I love it when you say my name, babe." Then he stripped off his shirt and pants and threw them in the corner. He pressed his lips against hers and flicked the tip of his tongue to meet hers. Nick used his foot to part her legs and entered her. He crafted slow, even strokes to build Paige's second arrival. She met his strokes with a craving that begged to be unleashed. He ejected one final thrust and their bodies erupted.

After release, they collapsed and spooned between their new pair of sheets and basked in the afterglow.

After a brief rest, Paige turned over and fingered the tattoo on Nick's upper arm next to his shoulder. It had three circular gears that connected to each other. One gear was a vertical profile, and the other faced forward. The last gear was horizontal and lay flat. Paige traced her finger across the words—*I'm an engineer*. She tapped the last letter. "What kind of engineer?"

"I got this tattoo after I graduated from college," Nick said. "I thought it was a good representation of a master's degree in mechanical engineering."

She dipped her chin. "Gears. I can see that."

"I was all of twenty-four at the time and full of BS."

Paige pushed Nick onto his stomach and continued her search. She kissed two tattoos in the middle of his upper back that covered both shoulder blades. On the right side of his back were an antique flintlock trade musket with a leather scabbard, a bow with a leather quiver filled with arrows, a tomahawk, and a sword with a scabbard. On the left side of his back were a clipper ship, an antique bearing compass, a spy glass, and the big dipper located in the upper corner.

Paige swiped her fingers across his back. "The tattoos flow together like a beautiful painting."

Nick grinned. "All the items in ink are replicas of the late seventeen and eighteen hundreds."

Paige pointed to a heart at the bottom of the tattoo. It read—*Z ur FB*. "Who is Z? The artist?"

Nick smirked. "Yes, Zelda is the ink artist. To her, she is an artist and her canvas is human skin."

"Aw, Kinky Zelda with the rules?"

Nick snickered. "Yeah, Zelda with the rules."

"What is FB?"

"Do you really want to know?" Nick flashed an intense stare of caution.

Paige stared straight back. "Yes, Nick."

"Zelda and I were very intimate."

"I know, Nick, she signed it with a heart," Paige said. "After all, she was the great teacher."

"You have to understand Zelda was a bit of a freak," he said. "It was kind of a no strings thing."

"Okay, but what is FB?" she coaxed.

Nick smiled. "You know damn well what it is."

"Say it, Nick." Paige insisted with a jeer. She crawled on top of his back and attempted to pin him down.

He flipped over on his back, sat up, got on his knees, pushed her down on the bed, and whispered, "Fuck buddy."

Paige giggled. "Zelda should have signed KFB instead."

Nick smirked. "Okay, why KFB?"

Paige chortled. "Kinky Fuck Buddy."

Nick cocked his head, bit his lip and grabbed Paige. "You're not going to let me forget it, are you, Ms. Martin?"

Paige giggled and squirmed free. "You're a bad, bad, kinky boy."

Nick rose up, grabbed her once again and held her tight. He put his lips up to Paige's ear. "I'm your bad, kinky boy now."

Paige bit her bottom lip. "How old were you?"

"I met Zelda after I finished college. I was around twenty-five." He raised his eyebrows several times. "I would see her on leave or returning from a job somewhere." Nick fell back on the bed with Paige in his arms. "I was a horny kid, and she was a freak in bed."

"Did it end well?"

"Like I said, she wanted no strings." He shrugged. "So yeah, pretty well."

Paige pointed to a tat on his chest. She kissed his muscular left pec, raised her head and asked, "Why the tin man? This has to be a very interesting story." She pointed to the oil can the tin man was holding. "Give it up."

"Tin man was a military nickname," Nick said. "I gained the reputation from the members of my team. They thought I ran a mission or operation like a well-oiled machine."

Paige pointed to the can. "Hence the oil can?"

"Yeah." He tapped the can. "The oil can also represents the tools of the trade, and the fact that I made things work. If the gears don't turn, the machines won't run."

"What kind of things?"

"Things you fly, ride, or shoot," Nick said. "Anything the military needed."

"There's more to this, Nick."

Nick squinted. "Let's just say in the land of Oz some things remain confidential."

"Confidential, huh?" She bent forward. "Like maybe if you were in the SEALs or Delta Force?"

"Maybe," he said. "My oil can and I fixed things for the military. I solved problems."

"What kind of problems?"

"Problems that required me to design, build, and create certain items." Nick wrinkled his forehead. "Often times the problems required that I had to infiltrate, examine, extract, denigrate, or destroy things."

"And tools of the trade?"

He paused. "Whatever I designed or needed."

"Did Oz include Delta or SEALs?" Paige crossed her arms.

"Maybe, but it was more like the brother of another mother," Nick said with a sly grin. "But that was a lifetime ago."

"Secret Ops?"

"Very secret." He lowered his voice. "We didn't even exist."

Paige put her finger on a heart-shaped pin on Nick's tin man tattoo. The heart was strategically located right over Nick's heart, and it had a clock with both hands pointed at twelve o'clock. She traced the second hand. "The witching hour."

Nick gave Paige a wicked grin. "My favorite hour of deployment." Then he leaned over the top of Paige and whispered, "Under the cover of darkness."

He gave Paige a quick kiss and pointed to the tattoos of piano keys and musical notes on the inside of his arm. Then he skilfully went on to the acoustic guitar on the outside of his arm and transitioned effortlessly to the electric guitar on his left chest. Nick waved his hand across them. "The reasons for these are obvious."

Paige traced back over them with her finger and examined every detail after Nick's quick tour of art. The piano keys, musical notes, and acoustic guitar started at his elbow and extended to his wrist. The electric guitar stretched across his pectoral muscle, with the cord ending at his belly button. Floating picks surrounded both guitars. Paige smiled. "Obvious, yes Nick. It is obvious that this is the work of Zelda."

"Yes, it is the work of Zelda," Nick said. "But I love playing as well."

Paige pointed to the electric guitar and traced the cord to Nick's belly button. "True, but it is very Zelda."

Nick shot Paige a shrewd smile and put his finger on the next tattoo on his other arm. It bore a close-up of a snow leopard perched on a rock, surrounded by a beautiful high mountain range in the distance. "This is the rare and illusive snow leopard," he said. "They're masters at hunting prey, always silent and deadly." He lifted her chin. "I'll let you figure that one out."

Paige raised both brows. "Something to do with your special operations?"

Nick nodded. "Something like that."

Paige read the words—*Leave no man behind*—written on a collar around the snow leopard's neck. Then she traced over the Roman numerals in *Snow Leopards. VII* was embossed on an army dog tag that dangled from the snow leopard's collar. She stopped. "What does the VII mean?"

"VII is the number of successful missions."

Paige gazed up. "No man left behind?"

"Yes." Nick pointed to the tattoo of a shot glass on the inside of his upper arm near his armpit. At the top of the shot glass were the words—*Failure Is Not an Option*. Then written below the motto in big bold letters were—*You FUCK up, then BUCK up, and get it DONE!* On

Nick's other arm, near his armpit, was another shot glass. Written at the top of it was—*The Secret to Success*. Written below it, in bold letters was—*GO full on, BE all in or get the FUCK out of my way.*

Paige smiled. "A bit of a rebel, aren't we?"

"I pushed every boundary there was, and still do," Nick said. "Most of these tats were added after active duty. It was too dangerous to have some of these during special operations. Our team added the collar and tag after active duty. I added the other military references on the other tats later, too."

She squeezed his hand. "Some of these tats didn't sit well with your commanding officers, did they?"

"Not in the beginning," Nick said. "They pushed back a bit. Zelda left the questionable ones incomplete and finished them after my active service." He turned back to the other arm and pointed to a scorpion on his upper arm near the shoulder. "This was my first freshman mistake." Nick rubbed his finger across it. "The original tattoo artist really botched it. But later, Zelda fixed it for me."

Paige pressed her finger on the tat and jerked her finger back. "Why a scorpion?"

Nick snickered at her antics and flexed his biceps. "As a freshman in college, I thought it was tough and very manly." She kissed his flexed muscle. He took a deep breath. "You missed one, babe." He pointed down to his nether regions. "Keep looking."

Paige cocked her head to the side and slurred. "O…kay." She leaned in and inspected the ink underneath Nick's hair that began at his naval and trailed to his nether regions. She pulled the hair aside and read the vertical letters that ran down his trail. On close examination, it spelled out—*Come get it babe*, with a wide arrow pointing down to another small tat of a garment tag that read—*XXL*.

Paige laughed. "Really, Nick!"

"That was my second freshman mistake," Nick said. "This is what happens when you get drunk with a bunch of frat boys and a couple of you end up at a tattoo shop."

Paige snorted. "Zelda couldn't fix the second freshman mistake?"

"She wanted to, but I knew she would have enhanced the message instead," he said. "I wouldn't let her touch it."

"Smart man," Paige said. "I'll bet you were harassed at college nonstop."

"No, Paige, you have to do a little digging to find this," Nick said. "Not too many people get to dig around down here, you know."

"Okay then," Paige said. "What did *all* the babes say?"

"I hate to disappoint you, but I haven't had that many babes crawling around down there."

"How many?" Paige tossed up five fingers.

"Only one that I care about," he said. "And she just finished excavating my jewels."

"That's why you always call me babe."

"You got it." Nick grabbed her. "You're the one I love." Then he rolled on top of her. "Come get it, babe."

Paige gave him a grin. "Extra-extra-large, huh?"

"No one has ever complained."

"I'm not complaining," Paige said. "But maybe we need a ruler." He tickled her. She squealed and squeaked out, "You pithy math experts want to be exact, you know. That's a mighty big claim."

"Some things you just know." Nick flashed a wide grin. "But if it will give me some, let the measuring begin."

"No need to measure, big man." Paige drew in a recovery breath. "I have already tested the merchandise."

"And?" Nick paused.

Paige exhaled and licked her lips. "Hum... I think I need a few more samples before I concede."

"Do you now?" Nick gave Paige a devious smile. "I'm happy to oblige, my lady."

The two cuddled and spent the rest of the afternoon doing in-depth research on the matter.

In the evening, Kent and Levi returned from a day of construction on Bunker's cellar and sat down next to Nick eating chili.

Kent sniffed. "Smells good. Where's Paige?"

"Finishing up in the bedroom. She should be down soon." Nick held up his spoon. "She said to start without her."

Kent threw Nick a wide smile. "You two together for sure now?"

Nick scooped a piece of the elk and popped it in his mouth. "Gentlemen, bagged and tagged."

Paige walked in. "What's bagged and tagged?"

Nick gave her a smile. "Oh, my elk was bagged and tagged. The boys and I were just talking about the hunt."

Paige ladled a bowl. "The hunt?"

"Oh yeah, let me tell you about the hunt," Nick said. "You are out there hunting and suddenly you spot the one. She is perfect, but far away on a ridge. So, you have to be patient and move in slowly. It's a lot of work, but when the time is right, you carefully take aim and take the shot. She falls, and you move in, bag her and tag her. Claim her. That's bagged and tagged."

Nick took his spoon, scooped up another piece of elk, kissed the piece of meat and glanced back at Paige. "She's a beauty."

Kent and Levi rubbernecked each other and chuckled.

"You know you have to get the recipe right to make good chili. That takes a bit of practice, but once you get that recipe right, it's delicious." Nick glimpsed back at Paige. "How's your chili?"

Paige gave Nick a smile. "It's really good, Nick."

Kent and Levi choked back their laughter and Nick grinned. "You know, I think I have room for one more bowl."

Nick got up, poured another bowl and sat down. All three men eyed each other and laughed, holding their stomachs.

Paige shook her head. "Real mature, gentlemen. Or should I say boys!" She picked up her bowl and stuffed the last chunk of elk in her mouth. "Who bagged and tagged who?" The guys laughed harder. She smirked, set her bowl in the sink and headed back to the bedroom to finish cleaning and organizing.

Kent slapped Nick on the back. "She's not the only one bagged and tagged."

Nick shrugged. "I'm definitely bagged and tagged."

The next morning, Nick pulled on his t-shirt and slipped on his sweatpants. He snuck into his old room, did his daily push-ups, squats, lifts and pull-ups, and snatched his hoody off the chair for his morning run.

When he finished, he unzipped his hoody and sweatpants and laid them on the dresser. He threw his stinky wet t-shirt in the laundry basket and kicked off his shoes. He stepped in the shower, brushed his teeth and crept to the foot of the bed. Then he lifted the covers and crawled over the top of Paige. She opened one eye. "What time is it?"

"Seven," Nick said and gave her a kiss.

"Your hair is wet."

Nick shook his wet hair. "Just got back from my daily workout and shower."

Paige stroked his shoulders. "All pumped up, I see."

Nick flexed his biceps. Paige giggled and politely oohed and awed. Nick rose up on his arms and did a push-up, then he kissed her on his way down.

On the third push-up, Paige squirmed out from under Nick and ran to the bathroom. She peed and flushed the toilet. Nick twisted his head to the side. "Baby, come back."

Paige slid the shower door open. "Shower first, lover."

After she dried off, Nick climbed out of bed, grabbed her, and with a huge smile on his face led her back to the bed. He lay her down and kissed her lips. Nick touched his tongue on hers and tasted the woman he loved. He continued down her body and explored all the flavors her body revealed. Then without interruption and undisturbed, they tasted, sampled, and investigated new ways to please each other.

Chapter Five

The Holidays

The week before Thanksgiving brought the usual amount of snow, leaving evidence of tracks from the much-treasured fowl. Nick sighted a few turkeys in a cluster of bushes on the hill and snowshoed back home. That night over dinner, he spooned his stew. "Any takers for turkey hunting?"

Paige dipped her bread in the stew. "Take me, oh great hunter."

Nick smiled. "Can you shoot a gun?"

"No, teach me."

Nick smirked. "Really?"

"Yes," Paige said. "It's time to shoot something besides a camera."

The next day, Nick grabbed a .22 pistol from the gun rack and put glass and plastic bottles on a log out in the field. He demonstrated the proper stance in grave detail and fired. The glass bottle shattered. Nick arched his brow and handed Paige the pistol. She raised it, aimed at the bottles and squeezed the trigger. Every bottle flew or shattered in rapid succession. Nick shrugged his shoulders. "Liar."

Paige giggled and handed him back the gun. "I'm sorry, I couldn't resist."

"We hunt tomorrow, sharp-shooter." Nick holstered his pistol. "Let's see what other surprises you have in store for me."

She exhaled. "Sounds good, but I should practice using a shotgun. I've never shot one before." Nick got the shotgun and some bird shot and set up a few tin cans. He showed her how to hold the shotgun to limit recoil, moved out of the way and let Paige practice.

The next day, at sunrise, the two raised their weapons and, on the count of three, bagged two turkeys. The remaining turkeys scattered, and Nick collected their bounty. He snowshoed back a few hundred yards to retrieve the sled, and Paige stood watch. They pulled the turkeys back to the truck and drove home. They cleaned, feathered, and hung their shoot in the smokehouse. Nick locked up the shed and slapped his hands together. "Guaranteed turkey for the holidays."

On the way back to the house, Paige dipped her head and sniffed the crisp air. "Smells like it's going to snow again tonight."

"With more snow falling every day and the roads unplowed, we'll need to have at least two snow machines for winter," Nick said. "Kent and I better see what we can find."

The next morning, the guys took both trucks and cased the neighborhood. Nick spotted a trailer and two snow machines. He pulled over, and Kent stopped behind him. They opened the front door. Musty air and stale putrefied meat hit their nostrils. Kent ambled up the stairs to check the second floor for supplies, and Nick investigated the downstairs.

Kent opened the bedroom door at the end of the hallway, seized his handkerchief and covered his mouth and nose. Three corpses rested on the top of a king-size bed. One corpse, dressed in a long pink nightgown, lay with her arms folded across her chest. Two children, one on each side, were cuddled up beside her. On a bedside table sat three empty juice glasses and an empty bottle of sleeping pills and oxy. A family picture hung behind them on the wall. Kent snatched the picture off the hook, slipped out in the hall and closed the bedroom door. He stared at the picture.

"Such a young couple with a beautiful family. The parents must have been around thirty. The boy looks to be around ten and their two daughters, about eight and five." He searched the rest of the bedrooms. "No father. The five-year-old is missing too."

Kent went back to the mother, picked up a letter placed between the woman's folded arms and stepped back into the hallway. He opened the letter and read the words:

I'm sorry. Please God forgive me. You took my husband and daughter in the rapture, and I have failed to teach my other children the right path and how to live a righteous life. Please forgive me for taking their lives. Have mercy on us.

Kent walked over to the staircase. "Nick!"

Nick jogged up, and Kent opened the bedroom door and handed him the letter. Nick viewed the bodies and read. He shook his head and drew a breath. "My God."

Nick handed the letter back to Kent, and Kent slipped it back under her crossed arms. Nick seized a gas can out of the back of his truck and poured gas on the first floor. Kent said a few words for the departed. Nick threw a match, and they both stood outside and watched the house burn down.

After the house burned, Nick turned to Kent. "Let's go find a snow machine. Feels wrong to take from the tragically departed." Kent nodded, and the two resumed their search.

After a full day of searching, they loaded up four snow machines and two trailers. A few days later, they confiscated a couple of four-wheelers and a blade to plow snow. They stopped at a sports store and grabbed five helmets. On the way home, the two picked up extra parts at an auto store and unloaded their cache. Nick clicked the paddle lock and patted Kent on the back. "We're set."

On Thanksgiving Day, Nick carved the turkey and passed it to Kent. "Courtesy of Tom Turkey. This is the one Paige and I scored on the hill."

Kent stabbed a piece of dark meat with his fork and handed the platter off to Levi. Levi chose a slice of light and dark and placed the turkey slices next to his dilly beans. Paige poured turkey gravy over her mashed potatoes and handed the gravy pitcher off to Nick. After everyone filled their plates, the four feasted and topped it off with hot apple pie and homemade vanilla ice cream. Later that night, Nick played several songs on the piano, and Kent joined in on the harmonica. Levi assisted Nick on vocals, and Paige sipped a glass of wine and enjoyed the show.

On December first, Nick grabbed the oak and cedar wood planks that he'd collected from the lumberyard and laid them out for a hope chest for Paige. He sanded each piece, put them together using wood glue, tacked them with finishing nails, tapped the nails with his tool and used wood putty to hide the nail heads. He stood back to examine it one last time before he stained it.

"Not quite."

He sanded the edges one more time and wiped it down.

"Now it's ready to stain."

He opened a can of dark stain, dipped an old rag inside and wiped it across the grain. The next morning, he put a coat of varnish on it and let it dry overnight. A day later, he put on brass handles and a locking latch. Then he stuck notebooks, typing paper, and an old typewriter inside the chest. And last of all, Nick covered the chest with a blanket from storage and hid it out of sight for Christmas.

On his way out the door, Nick spotted the set of drums he'd scored at the music store in the far corner of the shop. He walked over and properly set them up. He grabbed the stool and his drum sticks and took the position. He started off slow until his rhythm and flow returned. Thirty minutes later, the sweat was pouring off his forehead. The sun's light dipped behind the horizon and the burning embers from the cast-iron pop-belly stove faded. With darkness closing in, Nick put his drum sticks down and wiped the sweat off his face with the sleeve of his shirt.

"Damn, I scored a great drum set."

He acquired an old sheet from storage, covered his drum set, and headed inside for dinner.

The next week, Nick flopped down on the porch. The northern lights filled the night with a brilliant light show.

"There sure are a lot of you, since the sightings." Beautiful green streams pulsed like waves of water across the sky. "Not complaining, mind you."

Nick exhaled and left a crisp, cold trail behind. "Time for a midnight ride."

He put on his helmet and started the snowmobile. The snow glittered in the moonlight, and the lights from the aurora borealis reflected like a sheet of ice as he raced over the white landscape. Only the hum of the engine and his breath in the winter wonderland filled the night air.

He squeezed the throttle down and opened it up on the snow-covered roadway. Fence posts flew past him. His heart raced, and the blood rushed to his head. The high rate of speed delivered endorphins straight to the brain, he stared straight ahead and yelled, "Free and untouchable."

Then Nick spotted a subdivision in the distance and eased up on the throttle. He pulled his snow machine up to a quaint house. "I'm sure you must have Christmas ornaments," he said.

He pushed the door open and turned on his solar flashlight. The unforgettable stench of an abandoned home hit him. He leaped upstairs, pulled on the rope, climbed up the ladder and entered the attic. He wiped off a tub labeled *Christmas* and lifted the lid. Several ornaments all neatly wrapped in tissue paper lined the first section. He lifted one up, peeled off the tissue paper, and read the name. Justine. He stared at the name and imagined the face of the girl who owned it. He swallowed hard, wrapped it back up and put it back in the tub.

Nick closed the lid and pulled out another box. He chose generic ornaments, then plucked out silver and gold tinsel and a string of small lights. He grabbed a backpack off a hook on the wall, emptied it, and put in the decorations. He spied a couple of expensive fly-fishing poles with cases and snatched them. A tackle box on a table caught his eye. He opened it and discovered brand new flies and lures. He stuck them in the backpack and zipped it closed. Nick put the backpack on his back and tucked the fishing poles in their cases under his arms. He stretched a bungee cord across the snow machine's seat and tucked the cases underneath. Nick rode home, snuck in the garage and hid the backpack and poles in the back on a top shelf.

The next day, Nick grabbed an ax and some rope and started one of the snow machines. He retrieved the sled from the garage and tied it on the back of the snow machine. He cracked open the front door.

"Paige, you ready to go find a Christmas tree?"

Paige plopped her hat on, grabbed her scarf and gloves and hopped on the back of the snow machine. Nick hit the throttle. She jerked back unbalanced, smacked him on the back of the head and held on tight. He snickered and proceeded at a steady speed.

They rode to a grove of fir trees, and Paige pointed to a medium-size tree. Nick stopped, removed the ax off the sled and cut down the fir tree. They tied it to the sled, and he faced Paige and kissed her frozen lips. Light snowflakes fell on her eyelashes. He removed his gloves, touched the flakes and cupped his hands across her red cheeks. "I love you."

"I love you too."

The two headed back in the light snowfall and unloaded the tree. Nick grabbed the tree-stand he'd made from the shop and put the tree in the living room. After Paige left to shower, Nick retrieved his backpack from the garage and placed it next to the tree with the tinsel hanging out.

Paige ambled downstairs and spied the backpack. She picked it up and shrieked. "Nick!" Nick sported a Cheshire grin and helped Paige decorate her medium-sized tree.

After she'd finished, she jumped in Nick's lap, kissed his forehead and cheeks, and pinched his lips together. "Merry Christmas, Nick. Boy, have I got a gift for you."

Kent and Levi walked in, raised their eyebrows, turned around and left. Paige kissed Nick in the candlelight and strummed her fingers through his hair. "Let's turn in to claim your early gift."

Around three in the morning, Paige tossed and turned. Her head spun with sensations of spinning and flying among the clouds. The dream ended with impressions of falling to the ground.

A pinch to her arm forced her body to jerk. She opened her eyes and caught a shadow in the corner. Paige blinked to focus her eyes, but the image disappeared. She stared at the corner in an attempt to bring back the image. Nick turned over and put his arm around her naked body. Paige grabbed his arm to secure her safety but kept her gaze at the same spot. She rubbed her arm to lessen the pinch. After twenty minutes, Paige's eyes grew heavy, and she gave in.

The next day, Paige brushed her teeth and inspected her arm. She spotted three small puncture marks in the shape of a triangle. She rubbed it to see if she could wipe it away, but it remained. Paige washed it and slipped her top on. She showed Nick at breakfast.

"I found these puncture marks this morning."

Nick arched a brow. "What is it?"

"I don't know," Paige said. "But I woke up around three in the morning after a strange dream. I thought I felt a pinch."

"A spider bite?"

"No, Nick, I thought I saw a shadow in the bedroom," Paige said. "Someone there."

"Logan? Would he come back here?"

"It wasn't Logan." She grimaced. "This shadow was from someone bigger than Logan. You know, maybe it was just my dream."

"Maybe, but I'll check the house to see if anyone broke in."

Nick inspected all the windows and doors, searching for evidence of an intruder, but found nothing.

That afternoon, the guys left to do chores. In their absence, Paige took out the hats and scarfs she'd knitted for each of them. She sewed felt on the inside of two of the hats to add extra warmth. Working on the last hat, Paige pulled her needle through the felt and finished her last stitch. After tying off the thread, she grasped the scissors and made her cut. Paige drew in a deep breath and slowly let it out. She reached down, grabbed the other two hats and gave them a final inspection. Feeling satisfied, Paige put the hat and matching scarf together and wrapped them in tissue paper. She took three pieces of decorated paper and labeled one for Levi, Kent and Nick. After careful calligraphy, Paige taped the homemade card on their gift and placed them under the Christmas tree.

***

On Christmas morning, Paige snuck downstairs and placed the wrapped antique book and music sheets she'd got Nick under the tree. She tiptoed into Nick's old room, reached into the closet, and pulled out the antique rifle she'd wrapped in a sheet. She stepped lightly down the darkened stairs and sat the gun next to the book under the tree.

Boots stomped on the front steps, and Paige jerked. She slipped into the hallway and peeked around the corner. Kent and Nick hauled a chest into the house and put it next to the tree. Nick walked into the kitchen, removed the coffee pot off the stove, and filled it with water. He grabbed the coffee off the shelf and plopped three tablespoons in the basket. He turned on the gas burner then strolled back into the living room and sat next to Kent. Nick checked under the tree, furrowed his brow, cocked his head and scanned the area. Paige rushed back upstairs and climbed back in bed.

Nick proceeded upstairs and slunk into their bedroom. He eyeballed Paige lying in bed with her eyes closed and shook his head. She turned over with her back towards Nick, opened her eyes, and smiled. Nick slipped back downstairs and turned down the perking coffee. He seized two cups off the shelf and poured the piping hot coffee. The two men cooked powdered eggs and spam for breakfast.

Kent stood at the landing of the stairway and yelled, "Breakfast!" Levi and Paige came down and joined the two men. After they ate, Nick and Paige stuffed the turkey and stuck it in the oven. Levi and Kent snuck off and returned with a refinished desk and chair. They hauled it up to Nick's old room.

Paige dried off her hands from the kitchen and rushed upstairs. "What are you two up to?"

Kent grinned at Paige. "Merry Christmas. A place for you to work."

Paige wrinkled her forehead. "Work? At what?"

"That novel you always say you're going to write one day." Kent swiped his hand across the wood.

"Oh that." Paige clasped the top of the chair. "It is a beautiful desk."

"We refinished it for you and Nick," Levi said. "You write, and he's always sketching and drafting something.

"It's perfect." She poked her head out of the bedroom door and yelled, "Nick, come see what the guys made for us."

Nick sprinted up the stairs. "That's beautiful, you two. Thank you." He wrapped his arm around Paige. "We love it." He turned to Kent and Levi. "Yours is under the tree, boys."

The four marched downstairs. Levi pulled a shiny knife out of his pocket and handed it to Kent. "So you won't need to borrow mine all the time."

Kent chuckled and gave Levi a solar-powered headlamp. "For you to read by."

Paige passed out the hats she'd made to the three men. They thanked her and put them on. She presented Nick with his book, music sheets and antique gun. He reached over with his hat and scarf on and kissed her. "Thank you, babe."

Nick handed Kent and Levi their fly-fishing gifts and stopped. "Hold on a minute." He rushed upstairs, pulled out the case with the flute inside from his closet and ran back downstairs and handed it to Levi. "I heard you used to play, Levi."

Levi opened the case. "Thank you, I did. I do."

Nick patted his knee. "I look forward to hearing you play."

"Happy to," Levi said. "I'm a bit rusty."

"We'll play sometime," Nick said. "We're all rusty."

"Good," Levi said. "Love to."

Paige knelt down, rubbed the hope chest and admired the smooth grain of the wood. She opened the chest and sniffed the cedar. "This is just beautiful, Nick." She removed the notebooks, typewriter, and typing paper. She cupped the side of Nick's face and kissed him. "Thank you." She took her notebooks, paper and typewriter upstairs and positioned them on the new desk.

Nick and Kent placed the hope chest at the foot of Nick and Paige's bed. The group ate Christmas dinner and ended their evening around Nick's piano with Kent on harmonica, Levi on flute and Paige belting out Christmas carols out of tune—all over an expensive bottle of red wine.

The next day, Paige seized a piece of her typing paper and fed it into the typewriter. At the top of the page, she typed—*Chapter One*. On the second line she typed—*End or Beginning*. She scooted her chair in, placed her fingers on the keys and let go.

***

The last day of December dumped a couple feet of new snow. Paige procured a bottle of champagne from the storage cellar and plopped it on the counter. "I've been saving you especially for New Year's Eve." She ladled Nick's famous hunter's chili, cut her cornbread and the group ate dinner.

Ten minutes before midnight, they opened the bottle of champagne and poured it into four champagne glasses. Levi, Kent, Nick and Paige raised their glasses, and at one minute before midnight, Kent cleared his throat. "To 2026. May it be better than the last." The four raised their glasses. "2026."

Nick cuddled up to Paige. "2025 was the best year of my life. I met you."

Paige kissed Nick. "Me too."

"When you and Kent walked up to my door, and I got one look into those blue eyes, I was done. I knew you were the one. The only one I wanted," Nick said. "I was never giving up."

"I'm glad you didn't," Paige said. "I don't even want to think about what would have happened to me if you weren't here."

"I'll always be here, babe." Nick squeezed her tight. "Not going anywhere."

On February second, the ground hog didn't see his shadow, so the group celebrated an early spring. For Paige and Nick, love was in the air. On the fourteenth, Nick jumped on the bed with a silk rose in his hand. "Happy Valentine's Day, beautiful."

Paige opened her eyes, took the silk rose and gave Nick a kiss. "I suppose you are expecting something very special in return?"

"Well, okay. If you insist," Nick said. "Love a sweet treat."

"It will have to wait until tonight, Romeo." Paige climbed out of bed. "I haven't made your gift yet."

"You're my gift." He tried to grab her. "I'm easy."

"Patience, my good man." Paige escaped his clutch and headed for the bathroom. She peeked around the door. "Tonight." The door clicked shut.

Paige dressed and joined Nick downstairs for breakfast. After breakfast, Paige chased Nick out of the house. "Please get wood for tonight."

Nick proceeded out to the woodshed and chopped the day's supply. Paige retrieved the powdered milk, chocolate instant pudding, and everything she needed for pie dough. She made Nick his favorite chocolate pie and placed it on the porch out of sight to cool. She snatched the candlesticks, a bottle of red wine, and placed them on the table. She prepared a marinara sauce and let it simmer for the afternoon.

Kent and Levi spied the candlesticks and wine on the table. Levi smacked Kent on the arm and snickered. "Looks like we're going out for the evening."

Paige laid her teddy on the bed and the boxers she'd got for Nick earlier. Nick opened the front door and stopped. "Smells wonderful in here." He spotted the candlesticks on the table. "Wow." He sniffed his armpits. "Better hit the shower."

He leaped upstairs and noticed the teddy and boxers. "This is going to be good." He jumped in the shower and gaze down at his hard-on. "Down boy. We've got a long night." He slipped into his boxers and pants and strutted downstairs to join Paige.

Paige lit the candles, poured the red wine, served the spaghetti and topped it off with a piece of Nick's favorite chocolate pie.

After dinner, Nick blew out the candles and led Paige upstairs to their bedroom. He ogled Paige's black teddy on the bed and grinned. "The best sweet treat of all."

Paige grabbed the teddy off the bed and dressed in the bathroom. She emerged to see Nick sporting his tight boxers, smiling with his hands clasped behind his head. "Come get it babe." She crawled towards him. Nick stared at her bulging breasts protruding from her teddy. He blinked twice. "Let's free those from their bondage."

Paige posted on Nick ready to ride her steed. Nick removed her teddy and primed for a wild ride. He caressed her breasts and rose up, kissed her lips, neck and erect nipples. He used his tongue to arouse her. Then Nick lay her back and removed her panties. He fingered up and down her body, embracing every curve. He cupped her large breasts. "Babe, they're bountiful and gorgeous."

Paige pushed him back down on the bed and slowly removed his boxers. She fondled him and placed him inside her. Nick closed his eyes and stroked her nipples. He gently moved his pelvis in sync until both their passions soared and erupted.

After mutual contentment, Paige released herself and slid her body beside his. Nick opened his eyes and kissed her. "Happy Valentine's Day."

The next morning, Nick turned over in bed, pulled her close and cupped her breasts. "I'm not complaining at all. In fact, it makes me very happy, but are your boobs bigger?"

"I think so," Paige said. "The teddy was tight and my bras are tighter."

"Babe, are you pregnant?"

"No, I'm regular."

He stroked her firm nipples. "I think you should do a test and see."

Later, Paige trekked to the storage cellar, got a pregnancy test from her tub of supplies and peed on the stick. She waited several minutes and checked the stick. Paige took a deep breath and double-checked the stick again. "Thank God, negative."

Nick knocked on the bathroom door and examined the negative test. "Okay, eating right I guess."

Paige snatched the test strip out of his hand. "Maybe it's the workout you give them."

"It is good to keep them in shape," Nick said. "I'm just doing my part to keep you healthy."

Paige kissed him and pressed her bountiful breasts together. "Healthy I am."

Chapter Six

Chess Masters

On the last day of February, Wyatt and Second Lt. Justin Jones knocked on the door. Paige opened it and the two sat down. She handed them a cup of piping hot coffee and rounded up Kent and the others.

Justin rolled the cup in his hands and said, "Last week, I got a report from two soldiers in the Nevada desert who claimed they saw large crafts in the area. After the sighting, all air force aircraft were grounded and we were unable to get any aircrafts working. According to the soldiers' intelligence reports, the large crafts sighted in the desert were not from Earth."

Wyatt piped in. "They're sending in troops from several units to investigate." He glanced at Kent and Levi. "I have two spots. We need an expert in UFOs and a scientist, preferably a physicist. You two interested?"

"I'm definitely going." Kent gazed at Levi. "You in?" Levi nodded.

"Wait a minute." Paige shot up out of her chair. "I want to go."

Nick cocked his head. "She goes, I go."

"Paige, they need a physicist," Kent said. "Levi has to go."

"Damn it, Kent." Paige crossed her arms and stared at Wyatt.

"Just two spots, Paige." Wyatt shrugged. "Sorry. Next time."

She flashed Kent a glare. "Kent, you better take pictures and keep good notes." He nodded.

Wyatt stood up. "Okay, we leave in two weeks. I'll assign two soldiers to help Nick while Kent and Levi are gone. Could be some trouble ahead because of dwindling supplies." Wyatt turned to Paige. "I'm sorry about Logan. He's an ass."

Paige smiled and gave him a hug. "Be safe. Next time Wyatt, I go."

Wyatt dipped his chin and turned to Nick. "Be good to her."

"Always." Nick shook his hand and leaned in. "No worries, I've got this. She's safe with me."

Wyatt tipped his head to the side. "I can see that." Wyatt and Justin walked a few steps toward the door. Wyatt stopped, turned around and pointed to Levi and Kent. "See you in a few days. Be ready, this could get sticky."

Nick and the others sat down. Nick leaned back and put his hands behind his head. "Wyatt warned trouble ahead. I think we better secure our perimeter. Any ideas?"

"We have the fence already." Levi sipped his coffee. "Maybe some armed guards? We could each take watch, if it gets bad."

Paige flipped the hair from her eyes. "Get a few more people in our group to help out. Maybe Wyatt can assign more help after he gets back."

"We could electrify the fence using large batteries from the base," Levi said. "Or take some from the abandoned central office at the phone company." Nick nodded.

The next day, Nick and Levi loaded batteries from the phone company's warehouse and central office. A few days later, Wyatt dropped off two large generators with batteries. Nick and Levi built a shed to house the generators and hooked them up, ready to go. After they'd finished the fence, Kent finished the storage unit at Bunker's to house the blood. Nick wired a heating and cooling system using propane to control the temperature. Kent picked up their supply of Rh-positive blood from Logan at the hospital and properly stored it at Bunker's.

The night before departure to Nevada, Kent turned on his CB radio. Instead of picking up the usual chatter from the military, he got a hit from Charley Howard, a MUFON member in Nevada. Though scrambled and broken, Charley reported his location just outside of Reno and a brief UFO report of activity in the area.

Kent pushed the talk button. "Charley, can we meet in Nevada next week?"

Charley's voice cracked. "Ten-four. There are several sightings of large and small crafts in the desert. Should be worth your time." Kent confirmed that the military had made the same reports and signed off. "See you soon." Afterward, Kent tossed his bag on the bed and packed his things for an early departure to Nevada.

The next day, Levi and Kent hugged Paige and said their goodbyes.

Nick drove the two to meet Wyatt at base camp. Nick squeezed Kent and Levi. "You two stay safe." Kent and Levi put their gear in the back of the military truck and hopped in the back with Wyatt riding shotgun and Justin driving. As they drove off, Nick waved and yelled, "Give em, hell."

Justin leaned out. "Hell's a-comin'."

With a total of five military vehicles from Fort Carson and a small squadron from USAF Academy, the group set out to meet squads from Buckley AFB, Schriever AFB and Peterson AFSPC—outside of Denver. From Denver, the four groups hit the road to meet another squad from Francis E Warren AFB in Wyoming at Hill Air Force Base in Utah.

On a cold March morning, the convoy traveled nonstop from Colorado and pulled into Hill's AFB to collect more supplies, eat and rest. The commanding officer, Colonel Baker, welcomed the weary soldiers and scheduled a meeting with officers from each squadron at first light.

Kent and Levi stowed their gear and chose a bunk close together. Kent removed the camera out of his bag and clicked pictures of young, strong men in their twenties, full of piss and vinegar in the cafeteria and rec center. Hoots and chuckles drew Kent's camera lens over to a group of female officers in the far corner playing a game of pool. One officer commanded his attention. He zoomed in and snapped her photo. Her mouth widened with laughter. Then once again, with the click of a button, he captured the moment of a sweet echo of amusement. The corner of his lip turned up. *It's been so long since I heard the glee of a group of women. I've missed it so.*

Wyatt tapped Kent on the shoulder. "We meet first thing in the morning to go over the schedule. Please tell Levi."

The next morning, Kent and Levi strolled into the conference room and sat with a dozen military officers. Kent tilted his head and whispered, "Levi. It sure feels strange to be in the company of so many military officers and part of a secret mission. Can't tell you how many times I've tried to gain access to classified material."

Levi nodded. "Right? They usually guard it with their lives."

Colonel Baker of Hill's AFB pulled out maps that displayed routes highlighted for the group. He handed out reports from Nellis, Beale, and Mountain Home Air Force Base. Baker pointed to all three bases. "All three have investigated UFO sightings in northern Nevada. They all complained that the squadrons dispatched had been disabled after the sightings, and the bases were unable to send reinforcements because of loss of men and equipment. The squads warned that there was no working equipment at the three bases and that the same was true in the area past northern Winnemucca. The bases believe advanced technology is blocking their computer, electrical and mechanical systems. Every large military installation is affected. NORAD is compromised. All satellites, the space station and communication systems have been destroyed." He cleared his throat. "You depart first thing in the morning."

The next morning, the group took off with Colonel Baker and Lt. Col. Claire Turner from Hill's Air Force Base in the lead. With over a hundred men and twenty-five trucks, the convoy set out for Winnemucca, Nevada. The sunrise revealed a clear day with melting snow along the roadside.

Kent tapped Levi. "The bright sunshine is a good omen. Hope the nice weather holds until our mission is complete."

The convoy rolled at a slow and steady pace. They passed Wells, Elko and Battle Mountain and stopped outside Winnemucca. Local law enforcement met them outside town and led them to a military camp filled with the thirty remaining soldiers from Nellis, Beale and Mountain Home Air Force Base. They'd confiscated jeeps and horse trailers from citizens in the surrounding area after several of their military vehicles were stranded out in Black Rock Desert, north of Winnemucca.

The colonel ordered the troops to unpack and set up their military tents. He cornered the local sheriff and pulled him aside. The sheriff shifted his toothpick to the side of his mouth. "No vehicles work once you are about twenty miles north of Winnemucca. You'll have to take horses or mules if you plan on going into the desert to investigate." He flicked his toothpick into the grass. "You better meet with a few locals who've journeyed past the dead zone. They've got very interesting information you'll find helpful."

Colonel Baker agreed. "Let's meet in the morning in your office. I'll bring Kent and Levi with me. It's their area of expertise."

After they'd set up camp, Colonel Baker called a meeting in the officer's tent. Wyatt, Justin, Kent and Levi joined a group of officers from Nellis, Beale and Mt. Home Air Force Base. The Colonel introduced four intelligence officers to the group. "This is Major Aidan Price and First Lt. Duncan Smith from Nellis Air Force Base." The two nodded an acknowledgment. The Colonel twisted left. "Meet First Lt. Travis Mathews from Beale Air Force Base and Second Lt. Brandon Jackson from Mountain Home Air Force Base."

Colonel Baker pointed at the chairs. "Sit." Each selected a chair, and the Colonel said, "Officers Price, Smith, Mathews and Jackson arrived on March twenty-first, 2025, when a squadron from Mountain Home AFB was reported missing." The Colonel threw out his hand. "Major Price will fill us in."

Major Price turned to the Colonel. "Thank you, sir." The major moved behind the desk near the map. "This is what we know so far. On March twenty-first, the squadron scrambled to investigate reports of unidentified aircraft in northern Nevada. They suspected the squadron had crashed over the area or had been shot down. In response, three more squadrons were dispatched, one each from Mt. Home, Beale and Nellis. Their mission was to investigate, rescue, or recover the missing. Within a short time, they too were reported missing when they disappeared from radar. Ground forces were deployed to investigate both events."

Major Price pointed to Lt. Smith. "First Lt. Smith departed at daylight on the twenty-third and were on route to the area of the squadron's last sighting, when their convoy was suddenly disabled. Two-thirds of the soldiers under his command vanished. The lieutenant reported that the remaining soldiers made their way back to base camp and remained in the area waiting for reinforcements and better weather to proceed." Major Price twisted towards the Colonel. "As you know Colonel, the investigation had to be on horseback because motorized vehicles will not operate in the area. We attempted a search with vehicles in the fall, but it failed. We tried by horseback in October but had to stop because of the weather. I recommend we take a small party out in the next month by horseback." The Colonel nodded, and Major Price tapped the map. "We've observed several sightings over the last few months. It is currently active in the desert with unidentified large and small craft." Colonel Baker stood. "Major, you and the other officers select members of your squads to send." The officers rose to attention, saluted and dispersed.

The next morning, Kent, Levi and Colonel Baker met with Dalton Rose, a local rancher, and Wayne Walsh, a geologist from the local Indian reservation. Both men had witnessed sightings in the desert.

Dalton narrowed his eyes. "I rode my horse out in the desert to investigate previous sightings and in the process experienced a first contact. I was within two hundred yards of the craft and its pilot."

Dalton folded his arms and shuffled in his chair. "I took my rifle, looked through the scope and saw the pilot. The pilot stared directly at me, and told me, using no words, to drop my weapon or be gone. I understood him and instantly dropped my weapon. I got right on my horse and rode like hell."

Colonel Baker gazed over at Kent and shifted his eyes back to Dalton. "What did the craft look like?"

"It was a smaller craft," Dalton said. "The large one is saucer-shaped, but the smaller crafts are triangular."

Kent bent forward. "What did the pilot look like?"

"White, bald with large eyes." Dalton inhaled. "Very tall and slender."

Kent lifted his hand. "Human or not?"

"I got the feeling he had some human qualities, but he could speak without moving his lips."

Kent glanced at Levi. "Perhaps a hybrid."

Colonel Baker twisted his mouth and stared at Kent. "You mean part human?"

Kent arched his brow. "Possible."

The Colonel gazed at Dalton. "What did the pilot mean, you'll be gone?"

"Gone! Removed from Earth. Dead," Dalton said. "That meaning was crystal clear. I would vanish."

Levi turned to Dalton. "Vaporized?"

"Yes," Dalton said. "Or whatever they do."

Wayne nodded and cleared his throat. "The crafts I saw were small. But I watched the small crafts emerge from a larger saucer-shaped craft, then disperse out in every direction at a breakneck speed." Wayne lifted his leg and propped his boot on his knee. "After the small crafts left the area, the large craft shot directly up into the sky at an incredible speed and vanished." He tapped the side of his boot. "The large craft appears at least once a month in the same area and the smaller crafts stay in an underground base."

The Colonel grimaced. "Can you show us their base?"

"I can show you," Wayne said. "But it must be a small group."

"How small?"

"Less than ten," Wayne said. "Preferably, five."

"Why five?"

"Less threatening. People tend to disappear," Wayne said. "They'll know we're there, but they won't care if there is no threat. I work for the Borough of Land Management and go through the area several times on patrol." He stared straight at the colonel. "They leave me alone."

The colonel bobbed his head in response. "I would like you to take a scouting party of five to investigate."

Wayne nodded. "I'll get the horses and mules together with Dalton's help and meet you in three weeks to finalize plans for our departure." The colonel shook Dalton and Wayne's hand, thanked them, and the group headed back to base camp.

The next day, Colonel Baker called an officers meeting and ordered Major Price to select three men to accompany Levi and Kent on the scouting mission. Major Price selected Captain Wyatt Reynolds and Second Lt. Justin Jones at their request. Then he chose Intelligence Officer Second Lt. Brandon Jackson because he had experience working with horses and mules in the back country. The colonel ordered Major Price to take thirty men and set up a camp at the beginning of the dead zone. Colonel Baker closed his file. "You'll depart ASAP."

After finalizing their plans, Wayne met the scouting party three weeks later at Major Price's camp located at the edge of the dead zone just off an unpaved BLM road. At daybreak, the five packed up their supplies and secured them on the mules. Wayne steadied his horse. "Our destination is a total of sixty miles in the desert. We'll ride northwest at least twenty miles deep into the desert today. It should take us three days to get there and three or four days to get back, depending on weather and time spent observing."

At sunset, after a full day's ride, the scouting party dismounted and Second Lt. Brandon Jackson secured their animals. They pitched their tents, gathered a few sticks of wood and dead grass and started a fire. Captain Wyatt placed his kettle on the red coals and the six ate MREs for dinner. Kent sat next to the fire and scanned the skies for lights. Finding the night skies quiet, the scouts turned in for the night and prepared for an early morning departure.

The next morning, Wayne rekindled the coals from the night before, and the group ate MREs once again. After breakfast, the scouts packed up, mounted their horses, and put on their rain gear.

Dark clouds, blowing winds and spring showers slowed their progress. By noon, a drenched scouting party stopped for lunch. Wyatt pulled out two butane stoves and rescued the soaked scouts with warm drinks and MREs. Around two, the rain turned to a drizzle, and the group mounted and hit the trail. By four in the afternoon, blue skies erupted, and the sun-dried the weary travelers. At sunset, the scouts relaxed by the fire and embraced the last sliver of sunlight that dipped behind the horizon.

Suddenly, Lt. Justin Jones pointed to an aircraft approaching from the distance. The craft descended and flew right over their heads. The horses and mules jumped in protest. Wayne and Brandon sprang up and settled them back down. The craft circled past the campsite twice and raced off.

Wayne stroked his horse. "They know we're here."

"Shit, Wyatt," Justin yelled. "We have nothing that maneuvers like that."

Wyatt shot Justin a look across the campfire. "No, we don't."

Wayne sat down next to the fire. "They want us to know they're aware of us."

"That we are," Kent said. "They obviously don't want to hurt us or they would have."

Justin checked the last halter and sat down. "What do they want?"

"We don't know," Kent said. "But I'm sure at some point they'll tell us."

Levi raised his cup. "Sooner or later." He sipped the last drop of his coffee. "Either way, it can't be good."

Wayne smothered the fire, and the group went to bed. Justin propped himself against his saddle on first watch.

The next morning, the group packed up. Wayne jerked his reins and faced the others. "Yesterday's rain put us behind schedule. We need to press on."

Around noon, the scouts stopped to eat a bite, rest the horses and mules, and let them graze a bit of spring grass. After an hour, they resumed the mission at a steady speed until dusk. Then the group set up camp and ate dinner under clear skies and scanned the night sky.

A few hours later, three small crafts flew over them. Two darted off, but one craft stayed and hovered above them. The craft emitted a bright blue light over the group and probed them. Kent counted five distinct lights on the craft. One light was located at the top of the triangle, two in the middle and two lights in back. A bright blue light emanated from the underside of the craft. Kent pointed.

"The craft has a triangle shape. Yet the back end is curved much like the shape of a boomerang. The front is rounded off, instead of coming to a sharp point."

Levi scanned the craft. "What kind of propulsion system?"

Justin and Brandon examined the craft and its capabilities through the eyes of a pilot. The craft hovered at close range. Suddenly, the craft ascended straight up. A wide-eyed Justin groaned. "That's faster than any craft I've ever seen or flown."

Brandon stared at the empty spot left behind in the sky. "Fuck, no way."

"Believe it," Kent said. "Meet an advanced society."

Justin wrinkled his forehead. "Why the scan?"

Levi lifted his shoulders. "I imagine to size us up."

"Wait until you see the big one," Wayne said. "She's the size of a couple of football fields at least."

Wyatt twisted his mouth. "What the hell do they want?"

"I guess tomorrow we might get some idea," Wayne said. "We should get to their base by noon."

The men went off to bed. Justin closed his eyes. "Better get some sleep tonight. We're going to need it." Silence answered back. He turned over and within minutes, joined a symphony of snores from the men in his group.

The next morning, the men resumed their mission and rode west. Around noon, Wayne stopped the group a half-mile from the alien's base, and Brandon hobbled the horses and mules and tied a line to the dried vegetation. The six men grabbed their daypacks, put on their side arms, and walked to their destination.

Wayne stopped the men in the same two hundred yards that he'd stood in several months before. The group waited for signs of activity. Around sunset, the ground vibrated under their feet and the earth opened, like a zipper being unzipped. Six triangular crafts emerged from the ground and flew straight up. The ships filed in single formation and flew off.

The group peered inside the base as it closed. The underground facility had docking stations that extended as far as the eye could see. Wyatt whispered, "At least twelve aircraft."

After the facility closed, Brandon turned to Wyatt. "I need to head back and make sure the horses and mules are still secured. The aircraft might have spooked them." Wyatt sent Justin back to help Brandon and build a fire for a late dinner. The rest stayed behind to witness the aircraft's return.

About an hour later, the ships returned and once again the ground opened and the aircraft docked. The pilots exited the crafts and stood at attention.

Wyatt, Kent and Levi seized their binoculars out of their daypacks and studied the pilots. Just as Dalton had described, they were tall, slender and hairless with big eyes. Kent traded his binoculars in for a camera and zoomed in on their large eyes, small nose and lips. "Their lips are thin, but human." He shot several pictures.

Kent inspected the eyes for color. "Can't tell the eye color. Their nose is small, appears human." He shot pictures in rapid secession until the doors closed and sealed tight.

Wyatt motioned the group to head back to camp. The scouts strolled into camp and joined Justin and Brandon by their modest fire. The group stoked the embers, ate their MREs and discussed everything they witnessed and turned in.

The next morning, Levi and Kent wanted to stay and see the large ship. Wayne shook his head. "I can't leave the animals. They need proper feed. We should return in three weeks. The large ship should keep to the same schedule and routine. We can return then." Kent and Levi reluctantly agreed, and the scouts packed up and headed home.

Three days later, the group arrived back at Major Price's base camp located on the edge of the dead zone and discussed their findings. Major Price leaned back in his chair. "We also witnessed six crafts in the dead zone while you were gone." He stood and put on his hat. "Let's go brief the colonel."

After the briefing, the colonel agreed to send the group back out to gather information on the larger craft.

The next day, Kent met Dalton at a friend's house in town, and Kent developed his film in his dark room. He shared the photos with Dalton and took them to the base.

The colonel put down the last photo. "This is a real clusterfuck." He shook his head. "What the hell are we in for?"

Kent scrunched his forehead. "I don't think war is in the cards."

Wyatt scowled. "We can give them a hell of a fight."

Kent bit his lip. "You try, you're gone. Remember?"

"Fighting is not an option," Levi said. "But perhaps there is more than one way to skin a cat."

"I'm listening." The colonel folded his arms.

"We haven't figured it out yet," Levi said. "It's like a good game of chess."

Wyatt laced his fingers together. "Better hope they're not chess masters."

"Work on your game of chess, will you?" the colonel said. "Come up with a winning game, quickly."

"We need to see the large craft first and that'll be in three weeks," Levi said. "Not so quick, I'm afraid."

"Right," Colonel Baker said. "But ASAP."

Levi and Kent headed back to their tent. Kent flipped back the canvas door. "Levi, if you think we can win on brains and strategy alone, you're delusional."

Levi furrowed his brow. "Stop being so pessimistic."

Kent shook his head. "Can't wait to hear your big plan or game plan, Levi."

Chapter Seven

Grace

Denver

Staff Sergeant Seth Hayes and Airman Colt Walker knocked on the front door. Paige opened the door. The sergeant dropped his bag and removed his hat. "Wyatt sent us to help out while Levi and Kent are away." Paige waved them in and escorted them to Kent and Levi's room. The men put their gear down and joined Nick and Paige in the living room. Sergeant Hayes cast a broad smile. "Do you need us to do anything?"

Nick waved his hands in the air. "Just relax. We'll get to it in the morning." He sipped his black coffee. "Where are you two from?"

Airman Colt Walker piped up. "I'm from Seattle and Seth is from Texas."

Nick dipped his chin. "How long have you served in the Air Force?"

"We've served two years at Buckley AFB." Sergeant Hayes said. "We haven't been back home that whole time." Paige handed them a cup of coffee and a plate of homemade sugar cookies. The four chatted and emptied the plate.

The next morning, Nick snatched his rifle from the gun rack, and the airman retrieved their weapons from the jeep. The three patrolled the perimeter of the fence, checked for weaknesses, and tested the batteries and electricity. The rest of the morning, they chopped and stacked wood.

During lunch, Colt dipped his fresh bread in the vegetable soup, lifted his eyebrows as the flavors hit his taste buds. He gazed at Nick. "This is a real treat. Our chow is never this good."

Nick grinned at Paige. "She's a hell of a cook."

Colt nodded. "Thank you, ma'am." Paige lowered her chin in response. Colt placed his spoon down. "Wyatt heard there was a gang of looters causing trouble around town. He thought they were robbing easy targets and had set up at the airport." He grew wide-eyed. "I heard the police tried to monitor the area but found it difficult to break the gangs up. Their police force is small in number. The gangs are moving around and hard to pin down." Colt sipped his water. "Reports stated that the gangs were growing in numbers because supplies were dwindling in the city."

"We'd better start taking shifts watching the grounds." Nick raised his spoon. "Sooner or later the gang will make it our way."

The next day, Nick rode out on his four-wheeler to check on Kellan and his father. Kellan met him at the gate. Nick removed his helmet and warned Kellan about the gang of looters. Nick tapped the top of his helmet. "Kellan, if you run into trouble, come to Paige's."

Kellan thanked him and promised they would join them if trouble came their way. Kellan's sister, Kami, ran outside to meet Nick. Kami was a couple years younger than Kellan, but all the traumatic experiences since the sighting had matured her beyond her years. Nick shook her hand. "Glad to finally meet you. You need to come to Paige's for a visit. Paige would love to see another woman. She's surrounded by all of us good-for-nothing men."

Kami snickered. "I'll try to come sometime in the next month."

Nick started his four-wheeler. "Stop by anytime, Kami. But you bring Kellan with you." He glowered at Kellan. "Make sure you come with her. Don't let her come alone." Kellan bobbed his head. Nick punched the throttle and waved goodbye.

He drove down the road and checked the surrounding properties for signs of trouble. The closer he got to town, he spied disheveled properties with broken glass, vandalism and debris scattered from conflict. Twilight descended, so Nick turned on his headlights and headed home.

He removed his saved dinner from the antique wooden cook stove he'd installed the week before and dipped his spoon. The airmen joined him with a cup of coffee. Nick slurped his soup.

"I took a little trip into town after I checked on my neighbor and spotted some of the damage the looters have done. They're getting closer, and they don't leave much behind but destruction."

Colt scowled and rubbed his chin. "I'm not surprised. We need to be vigilant. They will challenge us at some point, but they'll pick over the easy ones first."

Nick agreed and glimpsed over at Paige on the couch. "I met Kellan's sister today. She could use a woman's touch. I think she's lonely."

Paige grew wide-eyed. "I'm going to see her. I'll bet she misses not having another woman around. She must miss her mother terribly."

Nick agreed. "Let me know when you want to go. Either I will go with you, or you take Colt or Seth."

Paige glanced at each of the guys. "I'm so lucky to have all of you in all this chaos." She sipped her drink and tapped the side of her glass as her mind wandered. *Life is so short. I'm going to enjoy life, satisfy every curiosity and experience as much as possible in my uncertain future. Live life with no regrets.*

The next night, Paige opened her dresser drawer, pulled out her scarlet scarf and two feet of rope that she'd cut the day before. She held it up to Nick. "Look like fun?"

Nick cocked his head to the side and smiled. "What's all this?"

"A little kink."

Nick slanted his eyes. "So, you want a little kinky fuckery, huh?"

"Just one shade of kink." Paige narrowed her eyes and dangled her toys. "Show me what you can do with these."

He shook his head. "I don't want to make you mad at me or hurt you."

"I won't get mad at you," Paige said. "I promise."

"I'd better get that in writing," Nick said with an intense stare.

"You have my word, Nick."

Nick pursed his lips. "You'd better tell me if you don't like it."

"I want a safe word."

"I see you have really thought about this." Nick moved in.

"A bit," Paige said. "My safe word is scarlet."

Nick arched a brow. "The color of your scarf?"

Paige giggled. "The scarlet letter."

"The forbidden," Nick said. "Feeling naughty, are we?"

"With my naughty, kinky bad boy."

Nick took a deep breath and exhaled. "Okay, if you're sure."

"Yes." Paige handed him the scarf and rope.

Nick handed the scarf back and lowered his voice. "Go put your hair in a ponytail, take all your clothes off and put the scarf on like a blindfold.

"Ooo…whee." Paige strolled into the bathroom, stripped off her clothes, fashioned her hair in a ponytail, put the scarlet blindfold on and felt her way back to Nick. "Do what you want with my body."

"You sure?"

Paige murmured. "Yes."

"Okay," Nick said. "Tell me your safe word again."

"Scarlet."

"Don't say another word. You may only say your safe word," Nick said. "Remember that your safe word stops everything. Nod if you understand." Paige nodded. "You must do everything I say," Nick said. "Nod if you agree to my terms." Paige complied.

Nick wrapped his hands around her waist and moved her close to him. "Kneel down on the floor. Close to the edge of the bed." He tapped her shoulder. "Put your arms up over your head." He tied her hands together with the rope. "Put them in your lap and do not move."

Nick retrieved a carbon feather arrow from his quiver, unscrewed the slick tip and threw it down on the dresser. He walked over to the bedroom window, opened it, snapped off a piece of icicle from the eve, popped it into a glass from the bathroom and filled the glass with water. Nick clasped the dropper out of Paige's rose petal oil, squeezed the oil out, rinsed it, and submerged it in the glass of water. He fluffed the feathers, wiped off the metal base on the arrow and returned to the bed next to Paige with his collection.

Then he grabbed Paige's ponytail and yanked it back, exposing her neck. Nick gently stroked the feathers down Paige's neck and lightly touched her nipple. Paige shivered as her erect nipple responded. Nick alternated between both nipples. Paige arched her back in response.

Nick tugged on her ponytail. "Paige. Get up, sit down on the bed and lie back with your hands over your head." She stood up and got on the bed. He squeezed the dropper, released the bulb and drew in ice-cold water. Nick seized the dropper and dropped icy water on her erect nipple. Paige gasped from the cold. Nick leaned down with his warm lips and sucked the droplets off. He repeated the same on her other nipple. It sent electric jolts throughout her body. He directed Paige to spread her legs, and she complied. Nick acquired the dropper and dropped icy water between her legs. She shuddered as a chill touched her sweet spot. He waited a few seconds and quickly licked the droplets off with his warm tongue. He kissed the insides of her thighs and lightly brushed passed her skin with his lips all the way down to her knees. Nick dropped the dropper back in the glass and grabbed the arrow. He lightly touched her nipples with the feather until she heaved in response. Then he instructed her to turn over on her stomach. He stroked the arrow's feather up and down her spine. Her body quaked. Nick retrieved the icicle from the glass and slowly ran it down the length of her spine. He leaned over and lightly kissed the back of her neck. Her body quivered. Afterward, he lightly brushed down her spine with his tongue and lips, following the same path as the ice, but only leaving a trail of his hot breath behind.

Once satisfied at her intense arousal, he pulled on Paige's ponytail. "Get up, sit on the bed, put your hands back over your head and spread your legs." Nick sat down on the floor and opened up her legs wider. He softly kissed her inner thighs again and used his tongue to bring Paige to the brink.

He stopped, glanced up at Paige to confirm her desperate craving for release, and said, "Not yet Paige!" He stood up and grabbed her ponytail. "Get on your hands and knees on the bed." She complied. He grasped the arrow's feathers, stroked them down her spine, the bottoms of her feet and inner thighs. Nick lightly brushed the skin between her legs with his fingertips. He inserted his middle finger inside and checked for proper arousal.

She's ready. Nick tossed the arrow on the floor and removed his shirt and pants. Standing naked and eager, he grasped her ponytail, pulled her head back, kissed the back of her neck and sucked on her earlobe. "I'm going to fuck you now, Paige." He pushed her head down on the bed next to her tied fists. Nick wrapped his arm around her waist, pulled her closer to the edge of the bed, slowly entered her, and teased her with a few shallow strokes and stopped. "You want me hard and fast?" Paige raised her head, turned and nodded. He ordered, "Head back down." Nick thrust hard into her several times and stopped.

A frustrated Paige about to explode said, "Don't stop. Go hard."

Nick smacked her on the butt with his bare hand. "No talking."

Paige jumped and quickly resumed her position. Nick slammed into her, increased his intensity and depth with each stroke and said, "Give it to me, Paige." He continued his thrusts until a quake rolled through her body, and she unraveled. Paige toppled forward. Nick propped her back up and initiated slow gentle shallow strokes. Paige held her position and prepared for another liberation. He increased his intensity and depth, but this time he carefully timed his own release. He watched Paige's breathing for signs of her response. Her soft moans and body contraction revealed a final build. Nick pulled her hips towards him, plunged deep inside her and increased his speed. They both erupted and Nick freed his grip. The two collapsed on top of the bed.

Nick caught his breath and removed the scarf and untied her wrists. "Had enough kinky fuckery?"

Paige blinked to adjust to the light and rubbed her freed wrists. She flaunted a side smile. "No! That was a rush."

Nick shook his head and kissed her. "Let's talk tomorrow morning and see if you can still walk."

Paige grinned. "It was worth it, but next time baby, don't hold back. I thought I would explode."

"Paige, that's the point," Nick said. "It heightens the experience."

"What did you use on me?"

Nick picked up the glass of ice water with the dropper and arrow off the floor and held it up. Paige leered. "Very creative." She put her scarf around his neck, wiped the beads of sweat off his face with the end of the scarf and kissed him.

Nick tugged at her ponytail. "My kinky, beautiful girl. If you want a hard fuck or a sweet fuck, I will do whatever you want, as long as it doesn't hurt you. You get hurt; it ends. That's my hard limit."

Paige traced her fingertip across his long eyelashes. "Baby, I trust you. I know you would never intentionally hurt me. I knew that when you saved me from the gunmen on the road to Denver. I have felt safe in your arms ever since."

Paige cleared a lock of moist sweaty hair out of his eyes and said, "Before we were together, you made it so hard to be faithful to Logan. The time at the lake when you stood close to me naked, I wanted you then. And late nights singing to me with your shirt off drove me crazy." She kissed his forehead. "There were times that you'd lean into me, and I'd feel your breath on the back of my neck. It made my body tremble and crave your touch. I wanted you so much." Paige drew in a deep breath. "At night you invaded my dreams, and you consumed my thoughts in the day. Nick Landon, you made it very hard to stay with Logan." She stared into Nick's loving eyes. "Even right now, the way you look at me, I melt. Nick, I love you, and all I can see in those beautiful green eyes is our lives together. And if I'm truly honest with myself, it's been you since the day we swam naked in the lake."

Nick pulled her close and held her tight. "My God, I'm a lucky man."

A week later, one of the soldiers from Seth's platoon appeared at the gate at four in the morning with a baby in his arms. Seth opened the gate and let the three soldiers from Wyatt's squadron inside. He glimpsed at one of the privates. "Stay and guard the gate." He raised his hand in the air. "You two, come with me."

Seth brought the two soldiers inside the house, dashed upstairs and tapped on Paige's bedroom door. Nick cracked open the door and Seth whispered, "You two better come downstairs." Nick dropped his chin and closed the door. Paige and Nick joined the three soldiers in the living room.

One of the soldiers stood at attention. "Ms. Martin, I was a very close friend of Logan's." Paige frowned and threw her hand over her mouth. The soldier scowled. "I'm so sorry, ma'am. Logan and Renee were killed tonight in a gas explosion at the hospital. We think the oxygen tanks ignited around midnight. One entire wing of the hospital was destroyed. It included the doctor's residence. Logan and Renee died immediately in the explosion." He swiped a tear from his cheek. "Somehow the baby's room was the only room that survived. It was untouched." He plucked the infant from the arms of a soldier standing beside him and shifted the baby forward. "This is their baby, Grace."

He cleared his throat and handed Paige the two-month-old infant. "I know Logan would want you to take care of Grace. Wyatt is away, but I know he would want that too. There is no one they trusted more than you."

Paige stared at Grace and gasped. "Did you bring bottles and clothes for her?"

He inhaled. "We brought everything that was in her nursery, but it wasn't much. A few diapers, some clothes and a baby blanket. That's all we could get before the rest of the wing burned down." He ordered the private to get the bag. The private retrieved the diaper bag from the truck and handed it to Nick. The soldier strolled over to the front door and turned the doorknob. "Let us know if there is anything you need." Nick nodded, shook their hands and closed the door.

Nick searched through the bag. "No bottles or formula." He glanced at the top of Paige's robe. "Your robe is wet."

Paige peered down and handed Grace to Nick. She peeked inside her nightgown and gazed up at him. "Well, now we know why they were getting bigger."

Nick squinted. "You have to be pregnant, Paige."

Paige lifted her shoulders. "I have to be." She furrowed her brows and took Grace upstairs.

Nick mumbled, "Lucky for Grace. Looks like we won't need those bottles and formula after all." He slung the diaper bag over his shoulders, sprinted upstairs and sat beside Paige struggling to get Grace to attach and nurse. He kissed her wet cheek. "Everything will be all right, Paige."

Paige fumbled with her nipple and sniffed. "How could this happen to such a sweet baby?" Grace attached tight and suckled. Paige grew a wide smile. "She's got it."

Nick drew both of them to him. "This little one is in good hands."

"I know, but it is such a tragedy to lose your parents."

Nick bit the side of his lip. "What do you think Wyatt will do?"

"He is in no position to care for an infant," Paige said. "He divorced his wife a few years ago. They had no children."

"I know his friend is right. We're her best option." Nick covered Paige's legs with a blanket, fluffed a pillow and positioned it behind her. He tucked his arm under his head and lay beside them.

The next morning after breakfast, Colt relieved Seth on watch. Seth filled his plate and plopped down at the table. Nick poured a cup of coffee. "Care to take a trip with me to get a crib and other essentials for Grace?"

Seth chewed his powdered eggs and swallowed. "I can go for you, so you can stay and help Paige. I'm very experienced preparing for and caring for a baby. Had two children of my own."

"Thanks, Seth, but we can go together after we get a few hours of sleep," Nick said. "There's no hurry. After last night, we both can use a bit of sleep."

Nick dashed upstairs and snuggled in beside Paige. An hour later, Paige crept off the bed and emptied out a drawer from her dresser. She stuffed a beach towel inside a pillow case, flattened it down tight and laid it on the bottom of the drawer. Paige changed Grace's diaper and placed a sleeping eight-week-old Grace in her temporary bed. She packed the drawer downstairs and fixed brunch with Grace close by.

After brunch, Paige headed to the storage unit, dipped into her private container and got a pregnancy test. She climbed up the stairs and stopped. A tall figure stood beside the drawer on the table. She blinked, and the figure vanished. Paige scanned the empty room, tiptoed over to the table and peeked on a sleeping Grace.

Around noon, Seth and Nick slogged downstairs and ate lunch. On their way to the mall, Nick dropped off lunch for Colt. After dinner, Seth and Nick set up the crib, a dresser and a changing table. Paige unpacked a baby carrier and placed Grace inside. She washed and dried some t-shirts and onesies and put them in Grace's new dresser.

Nick relieved Colt as watchman around eight. Paige nursed and bathed Grace in her new plastic tub. She rocked her to sleep and lay her in the crib. She removed the pregnancy test out of the package and peed on the stick. She viewed the second hand on her watch. One minute ticked by, then two minutes. After the second hand hit twelve, she snatched the stick and held it up.

Paige squinted and pulled it closer. "Negative?" She shook her head. "How can that be?" She tossed the test in the trash and peeked at Grace. She rubbed her tiny hand. "Beautiful sleeping beauty. Don't you worry. We're here for you." Paige leaned down and kissed Grace's cheek. Grace kicked her legs and suckled her fist. Paige crept to the bed and crawled under the covers.

A few hours later, Paige turned over and opened her eyes. A dark shadow hovered beside the crib. She blinked, but the shadow remained. Paige sat up. "Nick!" The shadow turned, gazed back at her and vanished. She jumped up, snatched Grace out of the crib and snuggled beside her in bed. Paige stared at the ceiling until her eyes grew heavy. She reached over, put her hand on Grace and fell fast asleep.

Two hours later, Grace kicked her legs and belted out a hungry cry. Paige changed her diaper, propped the pillow behind her, stuck her nipple in Grace's mouth and nursed. At sunrise, Nick removed Grace from Paige's arms, put her in the crib and cuddled close to Paige.

Paige blocked the sun's glare as it assaulted her eyes. She plucked Grace out of her crib, tucked her safely inside the carrier and made breakfast. Colt ate with Paige and a contented Grace sucking on a pacifier.

Nick meandered downstairs around three in the afternoon and started dinner. He turned the gas down on the stove, simmered a sauce for the pasta and spied Paige nursing Grace. "I know that look, Paige."

Paige peered up from nursing. "What look?"

"The same look you gave me when I knew I'd won your heart."

Paige grew a wide smile. "No one could resist her."

"I know that no one is going to take that child from your arms."

She stuck her index finger in Grace's hand. "She's very special." Grace clasped Paige's finger. "We'll never let go, Grace. You're stuck with us."

Nick turned his head toward the door and spotted Kellan and Kami. They rapped two more times. Nick opened the door, and they joined Paige in the living room. Nick introduced them to Paige. Kami kneeled down and squeezed Grace's tiny foot. "May I hold her?" Paige removed her from the carrier and put her in Kami's arms. Kellan and Nick slipped outside. Kami rocked Grace in her arms. "Anytime you need help with Grace, please ask."

"You need to come and visit us," Paige said. "Grace likes you."

Kami beamed. "Is next week okay?"

"Anytime, Kami. I would love the company," Paige said. "Grace and I need another woman to talk to."

Kellan and Kami stayed for Nick's special pasta. After Kami left, Paige wrapped her arms around Nick. "It was so good to have a woman around. I didn't realize how much I've missed female companionship."

A few nights later, Nick had the night shift, and Paige woke from a deep sleep. She glimpsed over at Grace's crib. The silhouette of a man stood beside the crib. Paige jerked. "I know you watch her. I feel you there, watching."

The shadow turned and glanced back at Paige. "I am her charge."

"I won't let you hurt her."

"I'm her charge," he said. "A guardian."

Paige growled. "A guardian protects."

"Indeed. They do."

Paige glared at the tall, thin silhouette until he vanished. She jumped up and raced to Grace. Paige picked her up and put baby Grace in bed next to her. She tossed and turned in the darkness and Grace squirmed. Paige rubbed her back. "The shadow says he's your charge or guardian. Does he mean in charge of you? That's what a guardian is." Paige chewed on her bottom lip. "I guess it could be good if he's looking out for you. Let's hope he's a good guardian." She exhaled. "He'll have to deal with me otherwise."

The next morning after Grace's bath, Paige caressed Grace's tiny fingers. Grace flailed her arm up and down, searching for Paige's nipple to suckle with her mouth, fussing, bobbing and bouncing until Paige fingered her nipple and Grace attached. She giggled. "You're a fighter, little one." She leaned down and sniffed Grace's freshly shampooed hair. Paige smoothed out Grace's baby fine hair with her fingers. "You have Logan's dark hair, and in time, perhaps his chocolate brown eyes." She wiped a tear from her cheek. "I can't believe Logan's dead. I'm so sorry you lost your father."

Suddenly, Paige twitched. The front door shut. Nick's voice echoed up the stairway. Paige smiled at Grace and yelled, "Up here." She leaned down and whispered, "Don't worry, little one. Nick will be a great father."

Nick dashed up the stairs and into the bedroom. He leaned over and kissed both of them. "How are my girls this morning?"

"Just fine."

Nick sat on the bed. "I saw the pregnancy test you left in the bathroom."

"I know," Paige said. "Odd, isn't it?"

"That it is," Nick said. "I'm going to shower and hit the bed."

Paige and Grace let Nick sleep and made dinner. A few hours later, Nick ate with Seth and Paige.

After sunset, Paige brought Grace upstairs, put her in the crib and crawled under the covers. Nick tiptoed in, checked on Grace and climbed in next to Paige. He kissed the back of her neck, slid his hand up her pajama top and caressed her engorged breast. Paige stirred and Nick whispered, "She's sleeping. Let's make love." He put his hand down her pajama bottoms and stroked her sweet spot in gentle circles with his finger. Paige softly moaned. Nick pulled her pajama bottoms down with his free hand, slid in close behind her, adjusted her leg, and entered her with slow, even thrusts. He maintained a steady motion and sensed Paige's arrival. The two released in unison and snuggled. Nick nuzzled her ear. "I think that kinky fuckery is going to have to wait until Grace can sleep through the night and has her own room."

Paige turned over and kissed the tattoo of the electric guitar on his chest. "Babysitters, babe."

"I guess we have a house full of those, don't we? but I'm perfectly happy with just a sweet fuck like tonight." Nick pulled Paige close, cuddled for a while and fell asleep.

A few hours later, Grace wailed, ready to nurse. A sleep-deprived Nick crawled out of bed, brought Grace back and handed her to Paige. He watched Paige nurse until his eyelids grew heavy and gradually shut.

The next morning, Colt rushed in the front door and stopped at the banister. "Nick! Seth! Better get down here." He ran back outside to resume his duty. Seth and Nick put their pants on, raced downstairs and joined Colt near the fence. Nick charged back inside, grabbed two guns and rushed to the gate. Two trucks with men in the back cased the perimeter of the fence holding semiautomatic weapons and stopped at the gate. Nick, Colt and Seth pointed their weapons at the men.

One of the men leaned out the window. "Hey."

Nick pointed his sniper rifle at him. "State your business."

The man narrowed his eyes. "Check you out."

"You've done that," Nick said. "Now move on."

"Soldiers, huh?" The man smacked the side of his truck with his palm.

"Yeah," Nick said. "We're still around."

The man pointed to the barbwire. "Nice fence."

"Hot enough to kill." Nick aimed his finger at the voltage sign.

"Huh, have to try it someday." The man motioned to leave.

Nick smirked. "It will be here waiting."

"Huh," the man said and spun out, spitting gravel.

Colt lowered his rifle as the men drove out of sight. "You think they'll be back soon?"

"Soon enough. We can count on it," Nick said. "They'll pick off the easy targets first and save us for last."

"I'm going to request more soldiers," Seth said. "Take the four-wheeler to avoid running into them."

"Okay," Nick said. "Leave as soon as you can."

"I'll leave in an hour," Seth said. "Put some distance between us."

Nick scrounged in his truck and handed Seth a walky-talky. "Just in case you run into trouble." Nick and Colt stood guard at both ends of the complex with their portable radios in hand.

Later that night, around eleven, Seth returned on the four-wheeler with six soldiers trailing behind in an old military vehicle. The soldiers pitched a tent in the back. In two days, the men built two towers at both ends of the property and posted a sniper at each. Nick fastened wooden shutters on all the windows and cut slots for sniper rifles.

After a couple of days of the soldiers camping out, Seth and Nick surveyed the property and spiked land-markers to build a bunkhouse. Nick glimpsed at the tent and snickered. "I'll bet they'll be glad to shit in a bathroom instead of a porta-potty."

Seth chuckled. "Glad they can eat something besides MREs too."

"I've drafted prints for an extra septic system with three toilets, two urinals and five shower stalls," Nick said. "It even has a kitchen area, with a table large enough to accommodate ten people. I also drew up plans to expand the compound if we need more units later."

Seth eyeballed the markers. "How long to build?"

Nick fingered the remaining markers in his hand. "With ten of us working on it, I think we can get it up fairly fast."

A couple weeks later, Grace was sitting in her carrier and giggling. Paige scrolled up Grace's legs with her fingers and tickled her tummy. "That's my girl."

Nick crept up behind Paige's chair and lifted his index finger to his lips. Grace's eyes lit up. She kicked her legs and cooed. Nick dropped his fingers close to Paige's sides and rushed in for a tickle. "Looks!... like you two are having fun."

Paige jumped. "Damn you, Nick."

Nick kissed her cheek. "I'm sorry. I just couldn't resist."

"Despite you, we were having fun."

"Sorry babe." Nick jiggled Grace's foot. "She is really smiling now. She's at a fun age."

"She'll be sleeping all night soon."

"Now, that will be nice," Nick said. "Imagine a full night's sleep."

"I know. Between Grace's feeding schedule and your night shifts, we haven't had a decent night's rest in weeks."

Nick squeezed her shoulder. "But you wouldn't change a thing, right?"

"Not with Grace," Paige said. "We could do without a night watch."

"It is better with the addition of the soldiers," Nick said. "Even if I have one tonight, but it is less often."

"I know."

Nick kissed her cheek. "You know, I love you."

"Love you more."

With Nick on night shift, Paige hugged his pillow and shut her eyes. Grace cooed and giggled. Paige opened her eyes and glanced at her crib. A tall silhouette hovered beside the crib. Paige cleared her throat. "How is she?"

The silhouette turned. "Thriving."

"What should I call you?"

"Charge." He stared directly at her. "That's what I am, in charge."

"Did you give me the shot in December so I could nurse?"

"Yes," Charge said. "It helps you produce milk and essential nutrients."

"How did you know I would get Grace?"

"That information is not available." Charge stroked Grace's cheek.

"When is it available?"

He dipped his chin. "At a later date."

"What can you tell me?"

"That she is thriving," Charge said. "And that is important to us."

"Who is us?"

"That information is not available." He tilted his head.

"Are you human?"

"In time, Paige," Charge said. "I will explain in time."

Paige squinted. *He never moves his lips when he speaks. How can we understand each other?*

Charge gazed at her and smiled. *I can read your thoughts and send my own.*

"Can you speak?"

"Yes," Charge said. "I can do both."

"Are you human?"

"In time, Paige," Charge said. "I will explain."

Charge stepped into the moonlight. Paige studied his body. His eyes were slightly bigger than a human's and his nose and lips were small. He stood over six feet, with a lean build and long fingers. Completely bald with no hair on his body or face. Similar ears, but smaller lobes. A heart-shaped face with a sharp chin. Paige zeroed in on his eyes. *His pupils are large and black. The iris, smaller and lighter.*

Charge grinned. "They are a darker shade of blue, but much like your own."

Paige smiled back. "You're part human."

"Half human," Charge said. "Plus, we have similar genes."

"You have some human genes, but your alien genes are similar?"

"Yes," Charge said. "In time, Paige."

Paige blinked her eyes in an attempt to focus, but Charge faded to black and dissipated into the darkness of night. She turned over on her back and stared at the ceiling. *Should I tell Nick about Charge?*

Chapter Eight

Comply

Nevada BLM Camp

Three weeks later, Kent and the others packed their gear to head back to the desert to get a view of the large craft. Wayne loaded the horses and mules and waited at the soldiers' camp on the BLM road. Kent's friend and MUFON member, Charley, pulled into camp with his twenty-six-year-old daughter, Amber, and two horses. Kent showed Charley and Amber the photos from the first trip to the desert and all the reports. Lt. Colonel Claire Turner joined the special operations mission and left First Lt. Travis Mathews in charge of a quick response team at the soldier's camp on the BLM road. With their first response team in place under First Lt. Mathews, and members of the special operations team selected, the colonel's team departed at morning light.

At sunrise, the group mounted their horses. Wayne, Claire and Wyatt led the team. Kent, Levi, Charley and Amber tracked close behind. Justin and Brandon brought up the rear, leading the pack mules. With clear skies, the group stopped around noon, watered the animals and filled their canteens. Munching on jerky and dried fruit, they resumed the trail and rode until sundown.

With sunlight disappearing, they pitched their tents and camped next to a grassy knoll for the horses and mules. Wayne lit a fire and heated water for coffee and MREs. After dinner, the group huddled around the fire and scanned the night skies for evidence of alien crafts.

Charley chuckled. "Have any of you heard of an event held every year called Burning Man?" Everyone nodded. Charley swallowed his coffee. "That is one hell of a good time." He placed his empty tin cup on the ground. "I attended one after a crop circle showed up near the site. The planners thought it was part of the artwork, until they saw reports the next day from around the world, and realized no one at Black Rock had organized it or ever claimed it. Once everyone realized that it wasn't a piece of art, it got crazy. The conspiracy theories ran amok. MUFON members attracted all the attention. A good time was had by all."

Charley poked his stick in the fire and stoked the embers. "The next year, 2025, I decided to go on April twentieth, but couldn't get close to the area. I had to turn around and go back to Reno. I heard from a friend who'd attended that it was complete chaos after more than half the people disappeared." He waved his hands around. "Survivors ran away as fast as they could. That day in the desert was very dangerous. I'm so glad I had to turn around. That would have been a terrible thing to witness and survive." Charley yawned, set his stick down and smacked his hands together. "Well, you all, it's time for me to turn in. These old bones need to rest."

Amber piped in. "Me too. Looks like the stars are the only thing that's going to peek through an overcast sky tonight."

A short time later, everyone but Kent and Claire turned in for the night. Kent tossed another log on the fire and stirred the embers with Charley's long stick. Claire watched the flames grow. "Why are they here?"

"I don't know," Kent said. "But no doubt sooner or later they will tell us."

Claire pursed her lips. "Perhaps sooner, because we're here."

"We're right in their face," Kent said. "They won't ignore us for long." Claire nudged the burning coals to coax a few more minutes of heat from them. He grinned. "Should I add another log?"

Claire stood. "No, but thank you for the company. Time for me to turn in as well." Kent dumped dirt on the burning embers and joined Levi in their two-man tent.

The next morning, the group headed out for another day of travel under gray skies. Claire and Amber shed their long-sleeved shirts from the morning's cool temperature. The desert sun peeked through the clouds and bared down without mercy. Feeling muggy, the guys stripped off their official uniforms down to their t-shirts. Each sported a baseball cap or cowboy hat to block the sun's glare.

Claire snatched her sunscreen from her backpack and passed it around. Justin spied Amber slathering sunscreen on her brown skin. A clip pinned back her long black hair. Loose strands escaped from their bondage and flew in the breeze. She rubbed the thick white lotion into her arms and face. Amber smoothed the goo across her lips with the tip of her finger and pressed her lips together. He imagined their sweet taste on his. Her firm body bounced in all the right places with the motion of the horse. Images of the two of them together late at night flooded his thoughts.

Brandon rode up beside him, slapped Justin on the back of his head and interrupted his daydream. Justin glared at him. "What the fuck, Brandon?"

Brandon smirked. "You wish, bro. You don't have a chance in hell. She's way out of your league."

"Out of both of our leagues," Justin said. "But a man can dream."

Making good time, the group set up camp before sunset in Wayne's favorite spot. Justin and Brandon tied off the lead line for the horses and mules. They watered, tied and hobbled them for the night. After the night's dinner, the group sat around the fire and stared at the skies.

As the group thinned down to just the male soldiers, Brandon and Justin whispered about the day's ride. Wyatt eyeballed Brandon and Justin. "Charley will kick both your asses if you two get any ideas about his daughter." The two laughed and bragged that they could take the old man.

Wyatt fired back. "I'll help the old man tune both of you up." After a quick chuckle, all three headed to bed.

The next morning, Amber spun around on her horse and glanced back at both Brandon and Justin laughing over the events of the day before. They both quickly shut up. When she turned back around, they resumed their antics. Wyatt turned and flashed them a glare. Claire gawped back at them, then quickly eyed Wyatt.

Wyatt shook his head. "I'll take care of it, Colonel."

Wyatt trotted back. "Are you done yet?"

"Yes sir," Justin said. Wyatt scowled, jerked the reins and rode away. Justin gazed over at Brandon and smiled. Brandon smiled back and jockeyed behind Justin in single file.

At sundown, the group set up camp for the night. Justin and Brandon tended to the animals. After finishing, Justin brushed his horse and bent down to check one of the hooves.

Amber sauntered up and put her hand on his horse. "Is he all right?"

Justin peered up and stumbled back. His horse rebelled and jerked. He jumped up and steadied his horse. Amber snickered. "I'm sorry I startled you."

Justin stood upright. "No Name is just fine. I was just checking his hooves."

"You call your horse No Name?"

"It's a long story," Justin said. "A friend of Kent's sings a song about a horse with no name and going into the desert." Justin patted his horse. "It seemed like a good idea. We got a kick out of it."

"Are you a pilot?" Amber stroked No Name. "My father told me you are in the Air Force and an officer."

"Yes." Justin stared into Amber's hazel eyes and gave her a wily grin.

Amber held his stare and tucked a strand of loose hair behind her ear. She licked her dry lips. "I'll let you get back to your horse." She slowly walked away. Her hips swayed back and forth, drawing Justin's gaze in a hypnotic trance.

Amber's firm backside held Justin's stare until a zipped tent took her out of view. He checked the rest of No Name's hooves and joined the rest of the group at the campfire.

Brandon handed him a cup of coffee and an MRE. Amber emerged from her tent and sat across from him. She sipped coffee and hugged her cup. In between sips, Amber tapped the side of her cup with her fingertips. After she drained the last drop, she rolled the empty tin between her hands and produced a click, click, click from a gold ring. Her father shot her a glare, reached his hand out and snatched the cup.

Amber shrugged. "Sorry, Dad." Charley dumped the remainder of his coffee out and took the tins to their tent. Amber grasped a lock of hair and twirled it. "Touchy, isn't he?"

Justin glimpsed over at her and smirked. The fire burned down and all that remained were Justin and Amber. Justin scooted closer. "What classes are you taking at the university?"

"I'm in graduate school working on my master's in psychology," Amber said. "Well, at least I was before the sighting."

"I know," Justin said. "The sightings changed everything."

Amber flipped a strand of hair from her eyes. "What about you?"

"I'm second lieutenant in the Air Force with an engineering degree in aeronautics, but all I've ever wanted to do is fly." Justin wrapped his arm around Amber and said, "The night air's grown chilly."

He pulled her closer, leaned in to kiss her, but stopped. A bright light drew closer and closer. It hovered above their heads. Amber threw her arms around Justin's waist and cuddled close. Justin whispered, "Just sit still. They've done this before."

The craft lingered above them, released a beam of blue light and scanned the two. Wyatt and the others unzipped their tents and peeked out. Justin held his fist up and signaled everyone to stop. The beam remained firmly on Amber. Justin hugged her tight. Then the blue light expanded over the entire camp and abruptly shut off. The craft shot straight up, turned west and zoomed off.

Charley ordered Amber to come to their tent. The two froze and stared at each other. Justin squeezed her shoulder. "It will be all right." He slowly rose and helped her up. Amber glared at her father, hugged Justin around the waist, kissed his cheek and thanked him. She marched off, flipped the tent flap back and climbed in to join Charley.

Wyatt nodded at Justin and popped back in his tent. Justin extinguished the fire and crawled in his sleeping bag.

The next morning, Charley marched up to Justin. "Thank you for helping my daughter."

Justin's eyes grew wide. "Glad I could help." Charley ambled off, and Justin mounted his horse. He bent down to No Name's ear and whispered, "Didn't expect that. I thought he was going to kick my ass."

After two hours on horseback, the group arrived at Wayne's border, and Brandon hobbled the horses. The airman holstered their sidearms, seized their daypacks, and everyone proceeded on foot. The group arrived at the safe boundary, grabbed the binoculars out of their pack and scoped the alien base.

At sundown, the small crafts flew in after patrol, and the base opened up. Shortly after the small crafts docked, a larger craft appeared and hovered silently above the base. The large saucer-shaped craft encompassed the area of at least two football fields and extended over the top of the group.

Wyatt and the others turned over on their backs and examined the craft. The saucer housed flashing circular lights on its perimeter with a large circular hatch in the middle that opened. The large craft lingered over the alien base. A section of the alien base opened, and a tower emerged. The hatch on the large craft unsealed and a thin, blinding beam of light shot out and hit the tower. The group averted their eyes. The beam continued for several minutes then instantly shut off. They blinked to recover focus. The hatch sealed, and the large craft shot straight up and floated high in the sky. The tower retracted back into the base, and its hatch closed.

A second large craft arrived and hovered north of the base. The craft separated into two parts. A large dome disengaged from the top of the craft and hung above the terrain. The ground opened up, the dome turned upside down, and the inverted dome lowered into the ground until it locked into place. The alien base opened again, and several aliens walked out and headed north to the inverted dome. The inverted dome opened up, and they all went inside. A few minutes later, the small crafts emerged from the alien base and flew off. Then the large second craft dropped close to the ground and in a bright beam of light teleported several aliens to the entrance of the inverted dome. The aliens entered the inverted dome, and the second large craft shut off the beam, closed the hatch, and flew straight up to join the first large craft, and the two promptly flew off. Both the inverted dome and alien base shut tight, leaving the illusion of desert ground.

Wyatt turned to Lt. Colonel Claire Turner. "The perfect camouflage."

The colonel exhaled. "Now we know."

Kent glanced over at Wyatt. "Well… now we have some idea of what we are dealing with."

A half-hour later, the group gathered their packs and stopped. The smaller crafts on patrol returned. The group scrunched down. The alien base opened, and the crafts flew back in and docked, except one. The remaining small triangular craft circled back around and hovered above the group's head. A sphere detached from the bottom of the triangular craft and stopped right in front of the group.

Justin placed his hand on his sidearm and started to retrieve it. "Justin, stop!" Wyatt said. "Put your hands in front of you, palms out." Justin did, and the sphere probed him. Wyatt eyed the sphere. "We understand."

The sphere's blue light scanned Justin's eyes, and without words relayed. "Comply or gone."

Justin nodded. "Comply."

The sphere shut off the scan, flew up to the triangular craft and attached itself, and the craft flew back to the alien base and docked.

Justin drew in a deep breath and exhaled. "Fuck."

Wyatt sat back. "You almost were fucked, Justin."

Justin eyed everyone. "Did everyone get its message, gone or comply?" Everyone bobbed their heads. Justin clenched his fists. "Gone means dead, evaporated, terminated."

"Yes," Kent said. "Just like Wayne told us."

Justin gaped at Wyatt. "Thanks, Wyatt, you saved my dumb ass."

Wyatt arched his brow. "That's why they pay me the big bucks."

"They need to give you a raise." Justin stared at the colonel. "Colonel, he deserves a raise."

"After today," the colonel said. "We all do."

Chapter Nine

Abduction

Nevada BLM Camp

First Lt. Travis Mathews pushed his sunglasses up. "Large tent looks good, soldier." He turned and scanned the area. "At least the tents in our temporary camp are good to go." The last truck loaded with soldiers pulled in. He slapped his hands together. "Looks like the gang's all here. We're ready to roll if Wyatt's team doesn't make it back on time."

Lt. Mathews wiped the sweat from his bald head and ordered the troops to unload their gear and stow them in the tents. A total of twenty-five soldiers from every branch of the service packed away their gear and reported for duty. The troops set up a mess tent and prepared the grounds. They installed portable latrines and showers and promptly set up a communications system using field radios to talk to base camp. The soldiers set up their command center in the officer's tent.

Lt. Mathews pushed back the tent flap and glimpsed the sun's last gasp before darkness ensued. He tilted his head and spied the first star emerging. "Finished just in time. BLM camp is ready for action."

On the second day, seven lights appeared in the night sky. The sergeant entered the officer's tent. "Seven lights, sir. They're here."

Lt. Mathews grabbed his binoculars and rushed outside. The lights moved closer to the camp. The lieutenant clenched his jaw. "It appears like some kind of search pattern." He spun around to the sergeant. "Alert the troops."

The troops filed in at the ready. One soldier seized a rocket launcher and assumed the position. Another used an M4 with a grenade launcher. The others drew their sniper rifles and automatic weapons and waited for orders.

The small crafts circled in formation and scanned the area with their lights. Suddenly, the lights stopped, and the crafts hovered above camp. The triangular-shaped crafts probed the troops and released a series of metallic spheres. The spheres approached the soldiers and, within seconds, stopped right in front of each soldier and scanned them from head to toe with a blue light. Six soldiers panicked and fired at the orbs. The six disappeared in a flash of blinding yellow-orange light. The spheres perused the remaining soldier's eyes.

Lt. Mathew's shouted, "Stand down. Drop your weapons and raise your hands." The lieutenant threw down his weapon and raised his hands. The other soldiers complied.

The metallic globes stopped scanning the soldiers and focused on the weapons. The spheres emitted a yellow-orange light, and each weapon vanished. Several spheres maneuvered above the trucks, scrutinized them with a red light, and shot back up to the small triangular crafts hovering above the camp. The remaining orbs used a red light to scan the entire camp, and after completion, rejoined their craft. The spheres attached, locked in place, and the triangular crafts flew off.

Lt. Mathews assessed the damage. "Sergeant, do a roll call."

The sergeant returned. "Sir, six missing. All the weapons are missing as well."

Lt. Mathews growled. "Test the vehicles." The soldiers tested the vehicles, and they were completely disabled. They opened the hood. The wires, circuits and fuses were either missing or destroyed. The radios no longer worked, and everything that had a battery or bulbs was unable to function.

"We did a complete inventory of weapons." The sergeant exhaled. "All of them damaged. Every grenade, handgun and automatic weapon is ruined."

"Fuck," the Lt. said. "We're several miles from town with no transportation and nothing to protect ourselves, except a few knives." Lt. Mathews chewed the side of his lip. "Take a party of five to walk back to town and report our status to base camp."

Within an hour, the sergeant left with five soldiers down the BLM road. The men walked ten miles and caught a ride with a park ranger on patrol. He drove them back to base, and the staff sergeant filed his report. Colonel Baker sent two replacement vehicles with reinforcements and every weapon he could spare.

A few hours later, the trucks arrived. Lt. Mathews shook his head. "Store the weapons in the tent."

After lunch, he issued everyone a new weapon and stood at attention. "Stand down if you encounter any aircraft or spheres. I'll have no repeat of the last encounter." The troops drew in a deep breath and exhaled. Lt. Mathews bobbed his head. "That's right, no engagement with the enemy."

The following day, Wyatt and Colonel Claire Turner rode into the camp with all the others. Brandon and Wayne tended the horses and mules. Colonel Turner called a meeting with the team from special operations. She glanced over at Lt. Mathews. "We'll meet in your office, lieutenant."

Everyone filed in and sat down. Colonel Turner turned to Lt. Mathews. "I understand your troops had your own encounter." Lt. Mathews nodded and described their encounter with the crafts. Afterward, he handed Colonel Turner an intelligence report from Colonel Baker.

Turner skimmed the report and raised her chin. "According to the report, all communication systems were knocked out on 04-20-25. Satellites, Space Command, and missile defense systems were completely disabled. The report divulged that the military immediately suspected an alien attack because of the technology involved. They estimated they lost two-thirds of their soldiers, but the cause at the time was unknown."

Turner plopped the report on the table.

"We need to coordinate what we've learned from our mission with the previous information from the experts." She grabbed a marker and a flex board and wrote down two categories—Known Information and Unknown. Under the first category she listed—*Two-thirds of the population disappeared because of blood type with only negatives surviving.* The second item—*Advanced technology disabled all electric, nuclear, and military facilities.* The third item—learned from our observations and evidential facts—*Aliens have advanced technology with superior capabilities and took out every weapon and form of transportation in the military.*

Justin piped up. "As a test pilot and aeronautical engineer, I know for a fact that our military does not have the technology to match the aliens' capabilities." He wrinkled his forehead. "They make our space fleet and strategic defense systems look like we're in our infancy."

Colonel Turner pointed to the second category on the flex board—Unknown. She wrote the question, "What do the aliens want?" on the board. She turned around. "Let's list the possibilities."

Kent scrunched his face. "Possession of the planet."

Turner wrote it down.

Justin bent forward. "Use us for something."

Turner printed the statement on the flex board and folded her arms.

"The question remains," Kent said. "Use us for what?" He gaped at Charley. "Charley, it's time to tell us what you think."

Charley sipped water from his water bottle and swallowed hard. Amber peered over at Justin and bit her lip. Justin sat up and drew in a deep breath.

Charley leaned back. "I've practiced psychiatry for over thirty years. My specialty is hypnosis. Over thirty years, I've treated patients that claimed to be abducted by aliens. One of my patients and his family had either witnessed saucers or been abducted since the 1940s." Charley cleared his throat. "I believe that the aliens began scouting the planet in 1940. They've monitored our technology and military as early as the fifties. In the sixties, they began testing our species for compatibility. I think the early abductions were to retrieve samples of human sperm and eggs. In the seventies to the nineties it was for the successful production of hybrids.

"I treated a couple named Jim and Susan. I started working with them right after they were married and continued for many years. Jim revealed that his father had witnessed UFOs in the 1940s at their farm in rural Idaho, but it wasn't until Jim was a teenager that he encountered his first UFO." Charley lifted the water bottle, sipped his water and recounted Jim's story...

"Jim and Susan were on their way home from the movies. They decided to take the long way home on the back roads. Seventeen-year-old Jim planned to find an isolated spot to stop and hoped this would be his night to get lucky. The two had dated for nearly a year, and he wanted to move the relationship to another level.

"Jim was passing through a section of pines, when Susan pointed to a bright light in the sky. She asked him if it could be the moonlight. Jim stared at the sky, saw the quarter moon and steered Susan's attention to it. The light grew bigger and brighter until it was right over the top of them. The car stalled, and the light hovered above them. Susan scooted next to Jim. He rolled down the window and examined the blinding light. The car shook, and Jim held firmly onto the wheel. The next thing he remembered was the car running, and his hands were down at his side and felt like rubber. Susan was lying on the front seat with her head next to the passenger car door. Jim's window was rolled up, and the clock on the dash read four in the morning. The two were missing time. Jim woke sixteen-year-old Susan and helped her sit up. He drove a confused Susan home in silence and discovered two very angry parents. The two claimed they'd had car trouble."

Charley sat his empty water bottle down. "The couple came to me in their fifth year of marriage to try to recover those several hours of lost time. I hypnotized the couple one at a time and discovered that they had been abducted and each imparted the same traumatic story." Charley adjusted his seat and related Jim's experience.

"The car door opened and two aliens pulled Jim out. Jim tried to get control of his body, but found himself unable to move. A beam of light surrounded the three of them and teleported them to the craft. The aliens took his clothes off and put him on a clear table. Jim was paralyzed with fear and tried to scream, but nothing came out. One alien moved close to his face and asked him to relax. The only thing Jim could move was his eyes. The room was bright. Heat from the light made sweat pour from his forehead. He blinked his eyes as drops of his sweat hit the sockets. A metallic sphere hovered above him, and a blue light scanned his body. Sexual images of Susan filled his mind. His penis grew erect and completely out of his control. A small instrument came out of the sphere and surrounded the head of his erect penis. Jim felt something inserted inside and suction withdrew samples of his semen. Once that was accomplished, the instrument retreated back to the sphere, and Jim heard a spinning sound. His eyes grew heavy, and he lost consciousness. Jim awakened, and once again sexual images of Susan filled his mind and more samples were taken. Jim recounted that it happened three times before he was returned to his car."

Charley pressed back in his chair. "Jim suffered PTSD. The hypnosis uncovered that the aliens had abducted Jim several times from 1975 to 1995. They didn't always take semen samples, but definitely monitored him. Susan's experience was similar, but of course more intrusive." Charley drew in a deep breath and retold her story.

"Susan woke on the table drowsy, with her legs spread apart. She felt the pressure of something inside her and a twinge of pain in her ovaries. She tried to move her head but couldn't. She moved her eyes in a desperate search to make meaning of her surroundings but could see only forms and shadows in the distance. Tears ran down her cheeks. She could hear spinning sounds but fell into blackness. Susan woke up in the car hearing Jim's voice and felt his hand helping her sit up. A confused Susan bled for quite a few days and suffered cramps for several menstrual cycles."

"I also diagnosed Susan with PTSD," Charley said. "Susan reported three different abductions during hypnosis with her last encounter the most memorable for her. On her last abduction in 1997, she reported the following.

"Susan saw a familiar light shine in her bedroom window. And once again, she found herself teleported to the alien craft. But this time, there were several aliens walking around. One of the aliens walked up and held out her hand to shake hands. Without words, the young lady informed her that she was Susan's daughter. She appeared to be a young adult with dark eyes and no hair, but Susan knew she was part human. The young girl avowed that it was a pleasure to meet her, and she hoped one day to see Susan again. Susan described her as tall, thin and pale, but thought she was healthy. The young girl thanked Susan for her contribution and walked away. Susan asked her what her name was. The young girl turned and said, 'I chose Suz.' Susan smiled back at her and said, 'A pleasure to meet you, Suz.' Susan walked around the craft without restraint. She said several aliens nodded as they passed by her. Another alien came up to her and thanked her for coming. Then, within seconds, Susan found herself back in bed confused, and left contemplating her own reality.

"Susan and Jim stayed in counseling for a few more years," Charley said. "Later, they joined MUFON to help other abductees."

Justin's mouth twitched. "How many patients have you had like Jim and Susan?"

Charley stared at Justin. "Too many."

Justin squirmed. "Hybrids and what?"

Wyatt groaned. "It's the what I'm worried about."

Amber hitched her shoulders. "Harvest?"

"They are keeping us for something," Charley said. "Blood host, maybe?"

Justin scowled. "They probably need a continuous supply of negative blood?"

"Makes sense," Wyatt said. "Why else would they keep us around?"

"Living blood donors," Colonel Turner said. "Is that our consensus for the debriefing?"

"Yes," Wyatt said. "It's as good of a theory as any."

Justin and Brandon nodded. Colonel Turner finished the flex board and jotted down her notes on a tablet. Then the group packed up and headed for base camp to debrief Colonel Baker.

Colonel Turner submitted the group's intelligence report. Colonel Baker bent forward and placed his hands on the desk. "Are you telling me we are out of options?" The colonel stood up and shoved his chair back. "Get out there and find me some!"

"Yes sir," Lt. Colonel Turner said. She motioned for the group to follow her. The group left the officer's tent and congregated outside. Lt. Colonel Turner flared her nostrils. "We meet in one hour in my tent."

Justin clasped Amber's hand and pulled her aside. "Meet me in fifteen minutes at the same truck we rode in on." Amber tracked down her father and informed him she would see him at the meeting. She jumped on the hood of the truck and waited. Justin snuck around the side of the truck and grabbed her ankle. A surprised Amber gently kicked him and knocked him backward. Justin approached her, pushed Amber's knees apart and slid in between them. He grasped her waist, pulled Amber close to him and kissed her. She wrapped her fingers around the back of Justin's neck and returned his kiss. Justin reached around, nibbled her earlobe and whispered, "Can I see you after the meeting?"

"I'll try to get away," Amber said. "Where?"

"I'm going to set up a tent," he said. "I'll meet you here around midnight." Justin pressed his lips on hers, and the two headed for the Lt. Colonel's tent. Justin and Amber sat next to each other. Charley glanced over at his daughter and raised his eyebrows. Amber nodded and flashed her father a sly smile.

Colonel Turner sat down. "I need options, people." She laced her fingers together and placed them on the table. "Colonel Baker demands options, so let's give him some."

Wyatt shook his head. "Military options are off the table."

"We still need to find out why they didn't eliminate us," Justin said. "Find out why they still need us. All we have now is speculation, not fact."

Kent smirked. "How are you going to find that out?"

"Ask them," Justin said. "First contact."

"So, you're going back up there?" Wyatt said. "Just knock on the door?"

"We are," Justin said. "You, me and Brandon."

"We're riding up on our horses." Wyatt sneered. "Right into enemy hands."

"Yes," Justin said. "They'll open the door or ignore us."

"That's a ballsy move, Justin." Wyatt snarked.

"We need answers," Justin said. "I see no other way." He wrinkled his brow. "We're no threat to them. So why not?"

"Okay then," Wyatt said. "We ride back out." He dipped his chin at Colonel Turner.

"Okay," Colonel Turner said. "I asked you to find an option. And gathering more intel is an option." She pointed to the door. "Go find us that option!"

Kent spun around. "Wyatt, do you want us on this trip?"

"We need to ride hard and fast this time," Wyatt said. "But come find us if we're not back in six days." Kent and Levi bobbed their heads.

Colonel Turner turned to Kent and Levi. "You two can wait at the BLM camp and accompany a recovery team if needed."

Kent nodded and pat Levi on the back. "BLM, here we come."

They all agreed, and Justin left to set up his tent.

Amber and her father headed for their RV. At midnight, Amber kissed her father on the cheek. "I'll see you in the morning." Charley started to protest, but Amber shook her head. "I'm a grown woman."

Charley held his breath and released it slowly. "Be safe."

"I'll be in safe hands." Amber shut the door of the RV and sauntered across the camp. She hopped on the hood of the truck and, five minutes later, Justin grabbed her hand and the two walked over to Justin's tent.

The light of the lantern revealed a double sleeping bag and a bottle of wine. Justin opened the wine and poured the deep red liquid into two tin cups. He smiled and sipped the merlot. She lifted the cup to her lips, tasted the nectar and softly moaned. Amber rolled the cup between her hands and peeked up.

Justin grasped her cup and put both tins beside the sleeping bag. He dimmed the lantern and unbuttoned her blouse. She took it off and tossed it aside. Justin unfastened her bra and eased it off. He removed his shirt. He kicked off his boots and she hers. She unsnapped his pants and unzipped his fly. He reciprocated. Justin kissed her lips, slipped off Amber's panties, opened the sleeping bag, and the two climbed inside.

Amber kissed Justin and moved on top of him. She kissed his neck, snatched his earlobe in her mouth and used her tongue to caress it. Justin shivered in response, and his manhood throbbed in anticipation. Amber positioned Justin inside her, and he cupped her breasts. He moved his pelvis in response to the rhythm of her movements. The full force of their passion erupted, and the two cuddled for the night.

The next morning, Justin dressed, slipped out of his tent with the tin cups, and came back with coffee. He undressed and crawled back into the sleeping bag. He stroked Amber's bare back. She opened her eyes and sat up. The two finished their coffee, and Justin seized the empty cups, put them down and passionately kissed Amber. This time, Justin moved on top of her and like the night before, the two achieved a deep mutual satisfaction.

After fulfillment, they lay together in the early morning hours until the rustle and bustle of the camp reminded them they were no longer alone. Amber stroked Justin's dark skin and ran her fingers through his short, tight curly hair. She stared into his dark chocolate brown eyes. "I don't want you to go back there."

"I have to," Justin said. "We need answers."

"But you don't need to," Amber said. "Wyatt and Brandon can go."

"I'm the aeronautical engineer," Justin said. "I understand the technology terms. If we do talk to them and get inside, I'll understand what we see."

"Don't get yourself killed."

"I got close once. I won't do it again." Justin kissed her cheek and hugged her tight. "I promise I'll be careful."

Chapter Ten

Resources Dwindle

Denver

On a sunny day in Spring, Kellan tossed the last bale of hay for the horses and scraped every scrap of loose straw from the barn floor in a pile. Kami raced into the barn and raced up the ladder to the loft. Kellan threw down his pitchfork. "What's wrong?"

Kami clutched two cages and threw them over the side. "I'm going to hide the cages."

Kellan climbed the ladder and put his hand on her shoulder. "What's happened?"

Kami whispered, "Dad told me to come here and help you turn out the animals." She drew in a deep breath. "He'll meet us at the grove of trees."

"Why?"

"The men." Kami pointed her finger at the road.

"What men?"

"Looters," Kami said. "They're coming."

"How many?"

"Fifty," she said. "Maybe more."

"Wait here." Kellan rushed down the ladder, opened the horse stalls, let out all the horses and hit them with a rope to get them to run. Kellan opened the chicken coops and waved his arms in the air. He rushed outside to the pig stalls, unlatched the gate and shooed them. Then he crawled back up to the loft and peeked out the window at their house down the hill. He seized his sister's hand.

"We need to leave the barn right now and head for Nick and Paige's."

Kami climbed down the ladder behind Kellan and picked up the cages. He grabbed a box of matches next to the lantern and tossed lit matches into the loose pile of hay he'd raked.

Suddenly, gunshots rang out and loud voices echoed up the hill. Kellan captured a cage with one hand and his sister's hand with the other. Kami snatched the second cage, and they sped for the trees.

The barn burned and gunfire boomed from their father's house. The looters returned rounds of gunfire. The raiders stormed the house, drug their dead father from the residence and tossed his limp body on the ground.

Kellan's chest tightened, and his face blazed. Kami pumped her fists and started to stand, but Kellan seized her arm and pushed her back down. He glared at her and whispered. "Stay down."

The men packed out items from the house and loaded them in their trucks. They rummaged through the rest of the property for goods to steal and searched for any signs of survivors. The looters confiscated everything of value and scrounged a few chickens and pigs that had wandered back on the property.

Kellan and Kami eyed the burning barn from a distance, hidden in the ground cover in a grove of trees. After the men left, the two siblings rounded up their chickens, pigs and missing horses that had evaded capture by the looters. Kellan searched the ranch. All their four-wheelers, trucks and trailers were gone. He trekked back to the house and covered his father's dead body.

Kellan grabbed two ratty blankets, and the two spent the night on the hill.

The next morning, at sunrise, they buried their dead father and placed flowers on his grave.

Kami gathered the wandering chickens and stuck them in cages. She tapped the cage. "We'll come back for you." She put the pigs in a makeshift stall they made from scrap lumber from the dismantled pig pen and hid them on the hill.

Kellan gathered the four horses and haltered them with rope. Kami and Kellan mounted the horses bareback and led the two other horses behind them. They headed for Nick's on the back roads.

Kellan spotted two four-wheelers approaching and kicked his horse into a full run with Kami close behind. He headed for the river. Kami kept pace. The four-wheelers gained on them and fired two shots. Kellan ducked down, turned his horse hard right and proceeded straight onto a narrow horse trail that had thick brush on both sides. Kami followed single file. The two headed to the river's edge.

They rode along the bank and spied a shallow passage. Kellan led the horses in the water with Kami behind. The two crossed the river and left the four-wheelers stuck on the other side of the bank, deep in the briar patch. They rode a safe distance from the snipers' bullets, and Kellan stopped his horse. Kami raced up behind him. Kellan jumped off and inspected the horses. He peered up at Kami's leg and spotted blood on her pants. He hurried over and examined her calf. Kami lifted her pant leg and eyeballed her bullet wound.

"Must have caught a bullet. Looks like it just grazed it." She squeezed her finger through the hole where the bullet had passed through her pant leg. "Got lucky, I guess."

Kellen frowned and ripped two pieces of fabric from his t-shirt, soaked up the blood with one piece and crafted a bandage with the other. Nightfall crept forth, so the two proceeded onward under the cover of darkness. They doubled back and crossed the river and rode straight to Paige's.

Kami and Kellan dismounted and strolled up to the gate. Kellan exhaled. "Name's Kellan. Nick told us to come here if we ran into trouble with looters." Colt opened the gate, and the two tied their horses to the garden fence. Kellan knocked on the front door.

Paige opened. "What's happened?" She glanced down at Kami's leg. "You two come in and sit down. Nick's on watch right now. His shift ends in a few hours."

Paige replaced Kami's bandage, and Kami recited the entire event. Paige handed them a platter of bread and cheese and tossed them sleeping bags from the hall closet. "I'll have you sleep on the couch tonight and we'll fix something more permanent later." Kami rolled out her bag on the couch, and Kellan flopped down on the floor beside her.

The next day, Nick and Kellan drove back to his family ranch, fully armed. They loaded the chickens and pigs into two trucks and brought them back to Paige's. Paige and Kami placed the chickens in Paige's coop and the pigs in a makeshift stall they quickly constructed. Nick and Kellan tended the horses, jumped in Nick's trucks and returned to Kellan's. They packed up any items the looters had left behind and hauled them to Paige's.

Paige escorted the siblings to Nick's old room. "Please make yourself at home. I'm so glad you two are here. We can use the help."

Paige dipped her spoon in the chili beans and sipped the juice. "Needs a little more spice." Kami tossed in a teaspoon of red pepper flakes. Paige stirred and sipped. "That's more like it." She rinsed her spoon, dipped it in the pot, and fed Kami.

Kami bobbed her head. "That should fire the engines."

Paige giggled and plated the hot biscuits. Red-hot chili, coffee and apple crisp rounded out the evening.

Seth laid his fork down on his plate. "That crisp sure hit the spot, ladies." He glanced at Kellan. "I'm sure glad you kids made it here safe. Looks like those bastards are hitting every piece of property in their path." He turned to Nick. "I think we should patrol the area and assess the damage caused by the looters. Sounds like it's time to expand the compound and reach out to law enforcement and other neighbors in trouble."

The next morning, Nick, Kellan, Colt and Seth piled in the military truck and hit the road. In a thirty-mile area, looters had ravaged small farms and ranches. Nick shifted down to assess the wreckage. Shattered windows and open doors revealed the carnage. Lifeless bodies covered in blood littered driveways and doorways.

Two miles down the road, Nick pulled into one of the larger ranches and eyeballed armed ranch hands at the gate. He leaned out the window. "Just letting our neighbors know that we have a compound up the road if you run into trouble. We're stronger in numbers."

A tall, rugged gent shifted his rifle and lifted the latch. He marched up to the truck and rubbernecked the men. "Thanks for the invitation, but we'll hold out here for as long as we can."

"Understood," Nick said. "Just know you're welcome if it comes to it." Nick held out his hand. "Name's Nick. We're headed in town to see the sheriff. Hoping to work with him on the looting." They shook hands. "Maybe we can all work together. Looks like it's getting bad out there."

The man tipped his hat. "Friends call me Glen. Let me know how it goes in town."

Nick nodded and shifted gears.

Nick and the others parked the truck at the police station. The gang waltzed in, and Nick placed his hands on the counter. "We'd like to speak to the sheriff?"

The officer pointed his finger to an office across the hall. "Acting sheriff is over there. Our sheriff disappeared during the sighting. You'll have to talk to Acting Sheriff Lopez."

Nick stood in the doorway and knocked. Sheriff Lopez waved them in, and the group filled the sheriff in. Lopez leaned against his desk. "With the help of the National Guard, we've managed to keep a lid on the city, but looters have taken over outside the city limits. They have a compound at the airport."

"Can we combine resources and take out the marauders?" Nick said. "With all the military, surrounding neighbors and law enforcement, we should be able to neutralize the problem."

"I could spare some men," the sheriff said. "But I need to keep several in town, patrolling."

Nick conveyed that he understood, but would appreciate any he could spare or recruit.

Sheriff Lopez stood up. "I'll see what I can do." He introduced his deputy, Dylan Winters. "My deputy will help you out."

Nick shook hands with Deputy Winters, and the two formed a plan. Colt, Seth, Kellan, Nick and Dylan all sat in the sheriff's office and checked the rosters and schedules. They formed a list of ten revolving officers they could rotate on patrol with Nick's group. Deputy Dylan Winters planned to lead their group of recruitments. Nick's crew and the deputy agreed to patrol together three days a week, split the area into quadrants and patrol a new quadrant every week.

Dylan cleared his throat. "We'll have to take out the group one at a time, instead of hitting their compound at the airport. We don't have enough men to take them out, but can eliminate the marauders one at a time or one truck at a time." Dylan pressed back in his chair. "Let's start patrol on Monday."

"Sounds good," Nick said. "We can patrol using our two military trucks. Each with five men."

Dylan reached his hand out, shook their hands and escorted them out.

The next day, Kami took a revolver that Nick gave Kellan and strode out in the field. Airman Colt Walker trailed behind. "How's your leg? Need any help?"

"My leg is fine," Kami said. "It's just a scratch."

Colt raised his eyebrows. *I wonder if her leg is really fine?* He smiled and sat down on the grass. *Hope she can handle a revolver.*

Kami put up a tin can from the garbage on a fallen branch and stepped back, ready to aim. Colt cringed. "I can show you how to hold it."

She turned and stretched it out. He jumped up and stood behind her. Colt placed her hands in the proper position. "You're going to squeeze the trigger."

Kami squeezed, jerked, and missed the can just above the target.

Colt positioned her hands once again. "Take a breath, hold it and squeeze the trigger."

Kami fired, hit the can and knocked it off the branch. She lowered the revolver, put the can back up, stepped back further and shot the tin can. Kami backed up a few more steps and shot again. She repeated the process until she was out of range.

Kami flopped down next to Colt and laid the gun on the ground. "Can I shoot your sniper rifle?"

Colt pulled up a blade of tall grass. "Why a sniper rifle?" He stuffed the end in his mouth and chewed.

"If I had a sniper rifle," Kami said. "I could have killed the men who shot my dad."

"They would have hunted you down and killed both of you," Colt said. "Kellan did the right thing. I'm glad he didn't have a weapon with him. Both of you were outnumbered."

"I never want to feel that way again."

"There's a time to stand and fight, but there is also a time to fight another day," Colt said. "If you're sure, Kami, I'll teach you."

Kami pursed her lips and nodded. He jogged back to the house, grabbed his sniper rifle, and the two headed to the practice range.

Colt set up a few targets downrange at a variety of distances. He lifted his unloaded rifle and demonstrated how to operate it. He pointed to the ground. "Lie on your stomach." She dropped down and peered up. He knelt down. "I want you to visualize and focus on your target." Colt touched the small of her back. "Relax, balance and aim at your target." He lay beside her with his hand flat on her back. "Hold your breath, and I'll count to three. Exhale and slowly pull the trigger."

They practiced Kami's rhythm and worked on using the scope. Colt loaded the gun. He counted a three count and lifted his binoculars to score the hit. He adjusted for recoil, and she hit the closest target.

The sun sunk behind the hill. Colt threw his hands in the air. "Getting too dark to see."

Kami wrinkled her forehead. "It was just getting good."

He cracked a smile. "If you want, we can come back later this week."

Kami agreed, and they packed up their things and headed back to the compound.

On the way back, Colt squinted. "How old are you?"

Kami fingered her short hair. "I turn twenty in a few months." She guffawed. "My short hair makes me look young, kinda like a boy."

Yeah, confuses many a suitor, I bet. Colt glimpsed over at her and mumbled, "Thank God you're over eighteen."

She rubbernecked him. "What?"

"Oh, nothing." He grew a snide smile and ogled. *She's cute and bubbly. She's going to be taken really fast around this bunch of horn-dogs.*

Saturday morning at the practice range, Kami eyed Colt. *He's so confident. I'll bet he's had extensive training and experience with weapons.* His tanned and toned arms rippled with every movement. He fingered his dark chestnut hair out of his eyes. She cast her eyes down at the ground. *Obviously, no barber to speak of at the base. Probably all of them have to cut their own hair. They'll wait until they can't stand it before they'll whack it off.* She peeked up and tilted her head for a better view.

Colt drew closer to the gun's scope. His light green eyes focused on the target ahead. The twenty-four-year-old stuck his finger in the air to test wind direction and squeezed the trigger. He lifted his head, adjusted his rifle and fired. Colt eyeballed the target and flashed a mischievous grin.

Kami licked her lips. *I wish I knew the secret behind his grin.* She closed her eyes. Images of him kissing her flashed through her mind. She opened them.

Colt reached out his hand. Kami placed her hand in his, and he pulled her up. She steadied her feet. "Time to go?"

"Yup, need to get back before dark," he said. "We can come back next Saturday."

"Sounds good to me." She moved in closer. "Thanks for teaching me."

He cracked a wily grin. "'Tis my pleasure."

The next morning, Paige placed Grace in the carrier and packed her out to the garden. She put on her gloves and helped Kami, Nick and Kellan add compost. Afterward, they toiled the soil to plant the garden. Grace squealed. Kami crept over on her hands and knees, puckered her lips and blew on Grace's legs. Grace giggled and kicked. Kami laid out the seed packets ready to plant, wrote on the reusable planting sticks and stuck them out near the seed packets.

Afterward, she skulked towards Grace and popped her head up. "Boo." A wide-eyed Grace jumped and shrilled with laughter.

Paige glance at Grace and Kami, chortled, and snatched the seeds and planting sticks. The group planted each row and stuck the labeled sticks in the ground. Paige planted the tomato and pepper plants she'd grown earlier in her makeshift greenhouse. They put in the seeded potatoes from the cellar and finished with several varieties of squash. Nick doubled the garden space from last year with the help of the soldiers—they needed to increase their yield with the compound's expansion. Colt and Seth made their way out to the garden after guard duty and helped finish all the planting and watering.

The following Monday, Colt, Seth, Kellan and Nick loaded up the military truck. Nick recruited Airman Tyler Steele and Kyle Hill from the compound to join them on patrol. They met Deputy Winters just outside the compound. Both trucks took off to patrol the first arranged quadrant—Deputy Winters had reports that two trucks were in the area.

Around noon, gunfire rang out in the distance. Seth lifted up his binoculars. "Four trucks loaded with men and weapons."

Nick leaned out the window and glanced over at Deputy Winters. "Let's hit them during their exit. We'll wait until the last truck departs fully loaded with loot."

Deputy Winters and Nick positioned their trucks just past an intersection. Nick blocked the road, and Winters hit the last truck from the rear. A few men fired off rounds from their truck until they ran out of ammunition. Guns flew out the windows and truck bed. They raised their arms above their heads and climbed out.

Deputy Winters and his men lined up the seven men on the roadside. Winters waved his pistol at the looters. "On your knees." The looters gazed at each other. Winters aimed his revolver at them. "Down!" They bent their knees and slowly knelt down. He paced behind the looters. "Any last words?"

The looters leader turned toward Deputy Winters. "In this world, it's either kill or be killed. We chose the first."

Winters scoffed at him. A young man kneeling next to their leader shrieked and wet himself.

Winters glanced down at his wet, urine-soaked pants and raised his voice. "Deputies take aim." A looter jumped up and ran. Deputy Winters aimed and fired. The runner dropped.

Their leader glared at Winters and yelled. "Fuck you!"

A steely-eyed Winters fired his gun and motioned his deputies to take the position. Each deputy stood behind the remaining perps and raised their weapons. Deputy Winters clicked back the hammer.

"On three. One, two, three."

On the third count, the deputies shot each looter in the back of the head, and Winters fired two shots in succession. The men dropped forward from impact. Nick grimaced and glanced at the airman. Winters men heaved the seven dead bodies in the back of the police truck.

Winters motioned to his men. "We'll take them to the morgue for cremation in the morning." Winters eyed Nick's men. "We don't have a court system or the manpower to house them in our jails." Deputy Winters held his stare. "Justice must be swift and without mercy."

"I'm good." Kellan glared at the dead bodies in the back of the truck. "You can bet one of them killed my father."

Every man nodded and loaded the stolen guns, ammo, and food items they'd confiscated from the looters into Nick's military truck. Winters tapped a deputy on the shoulder. "Drive the looters' pickup to impound for storage. We'll follow." The officer dipped his chin and jumped in the pickup.

Nick and the others checked the victims' house for survivors. Two bloody, lifeless bodies lay on the floor. Nick threw a blanket over the dead. "We'll come back and bury them in the morning." He pointed to the door. "We need to leave. The three other trucks might come back to find the missing truck, and we'll be outgunned."

They returned home and unloaded the items confiscated from the thieves. Nick eyeballed the group. "One truck down and three to go."

The next day, Nick and the group returned to the previous carnage and buried their bodies. On the way home, they stopped at two houses, warned them about the nefarious looters in the area and invited them to join their compound. The two young families agreed.

On the road home, Nick glanced over at Colt. "We're going to have to expand the compound. We're getting pretty full, and I bet we'll have more coming."

The rest of the week, they gathered building materials and worked on the expansion. By week's end, the two young families joined the compound with toddlers in tow. The camp now had four little ones, counting Grace.

The next Monday, Nick's group met Deputy Winters and searched for insurgents in the next quadrant. Nick brought two new recruits from the neighborhood. Each brandished his own firearm and ammunition, ready for vengeance on the people who'd murdered their friends and neighbors.

By the end of the night, Nick and Deputy Winters had located their enemy in the act of committing their crimes. The groups split up and positioned themselves on higher ground. Colt procured a rocket launcher from the military truck. He aimed at the truck transporting the men, but waited until the last truck was fully loaded with goods. The driver hopped in and started the engine. Colt counted to three, launched, and took out the transport truck. The supply truck raced away. Deputy Winters intercepted and ended their getaway. The remaining truck turned and headed for town. Nick's group fired at them and killed several in the back of the pickup, but the damaged truck limped away.

Nick checked the burning truck for survivors. "They're all dead. Probably died instantly." Nick shrugged. "Just let it burn. That way we don't have to worry about burying these thieves and murderers."

Seth and Colt combed the area for any victims that may have survived, but only found dead bodies. They covered the victims and placed them aside for burial.

Deputy Winters inspected the truck he'd taken out and loaded the dead bodies in his police truck. He drove over to the burning truck Colt had destroyed and threw their bodies in the burning truck. "Saves us a cremation." The flames were dwindling, so he grabbed a can of diesel out of his police vehicle and poured it on the truck. "That should dispose of the bodies completely."

After completion, they searched for any living victims. With no survivors and their mission complete, the group headed home.

Two days later, a young couple spotted marauders coming down Kat Levine's drive. Neil Stevens, an intern, and his girlfriend Jamie Levine, a registered nurse, finished their shift at the local clinic and pulled into Jamie's sister's home. The two rushed inside, threw together a few items, grabbed Kat and jumped in Neil's four-wheel-drive. The three drove off-road to Nick's compound.

Paige invited the three inside and gave them a bite to eat. After they'd finished eating and had relaxed a bit, Paige took them out back to one of the buildings in the compound. "You're welcome to stay here."

Neil wrapped his arm around Jamie. "No, thank you. Jamie and I have a small apartment next to the medical clinic. It's safe there." He glanced over at Kat. "Kat's place is isolated and not safe at all. Kat, you should stay."

Kat sat on the mattress. "Thank you, Paige. I'll stay. There's probably nothing left at my house, anyway."

A few days later, Seth and Kat drove to Kat's house. Empty drawers littered the floor. Busted cabinets revealed little but shattered glass and broken plates. Clothes carpeted the hard wood floors.

Kat eyed her ripped luggage. "Why the luggage?"

"Looking for hidden cash," Seth said. "You'd be surprised how many people hide it there."

Kat ambled into the kitchen and retrieved trash bags from under the sink. She picked up dirty sheets, blankets, blouses, t-shirts, underclothes and jeans off the floor and stuffed them in her scented trash bags. She pulled a stool up to the closet, snatched her photo album and a tin can. Kat flopped down on the floor and turned the pages of her photo album. She tore the seal back and lifted her graduation picture off the cardboard. Kat plucked three one-hundred-dollar bills off the backing and waved them in the air. "The fuckers weren't that smart." Seth shook his head and laughed.

Kat shoved three dresser drawers back in the dresser and held up a broken one. "I think I can fix it."

Seth bobbed his head and loaded it in the truck. Kat grabbed the tin can and a shovel. She dug a hole, placed the tin can inside and buried it. "Rest in peace, Kitcat."

Seth dipped his chin, and they loaded the rest of the salvageable items and returned to the compound.

Kat lugged her trash bags of dirty clothes into her room and placed it next to the broken drawer. She folded the few clean clothes they'd recovered and placed them in her dresser. Kat lifted her kitty cat knick-knacks out of her plastic container, kissed each one and placed them on top of the dresser. She placed her only clean sheet, semi-clean comforter and uncased pillow on her assigned bed. Kat fluffed her pillow, flipped through her photo album and stopped at pictures of her beloved Bombay cat, Kitcat. She hugged the album to her chest. "At least I saved my precious photos."

A week later, they finished the new building on the compound. One wing held six women and the other wing held six men. They shared a kitchen in the center. There were two bathrooms in each wing.

Kat moved into the new building and shared a wing with five other residents—two soldiers and three civilians. Six single men moved into the adjacent wing.

Kat set her things down. "It's great to have company. I was the only woman in the other building. I'm Kat."

Anna stretched out her hand. "Anna." She scanned the room. "Wow, this is nice. I'm glad they posted me here." Anna stuck her military sidearm in the drawer.

"Can you show me how to shoot?" Kat said. "I need to learn."

Anna closed the drawer. "Absolutely. Let's start tomorrow."

The next morning, Anna and Kat headed for the shooting range, and for the next two weeks, Kat spent hours learning how to shoot every weapon.

At the end of her training, Kat joined Nick's patrol with Airman Anna Wagner, Lance Corporal Morgan Wriggs and Kami. He'd recruited additional men and added more trucks to the patrol. As the casualties had mounted in the area, the compound had grown. Civilians in the suburbs were forced to make choices out of necessity as their resources dwindled. They either became marauders or joined groups like Nick's to survive.

Monday night, Nick's patrol met Deputy Winters at their normal rendezvous point. Winters rolled down his window. "The marauders have increased in numbers and are out in full force."

Nick dipped his chin. "Then it's going to be a busy night."

Winters motioned to move, and the caravan drove off to patrol with Seth and Tyler at point position. A few miles down the road, looters pulled out in front of them in two separate vehicles and boxed Seth and Tyler in. The marauders detonated a roadside bomb and disabled Seth's vehicle.

After the explosion, the enemy's trucks fled. Snipers positioned on the hill fired and pinned Seth and Colt down. The blast killed three soldiers riding in the back of Seth's truck and injured three others. Dark smoke rolled from the blast. Seth and Tyler dragged the injured to safety under the cover of blackness and held their ground with a side arm and an M-16.

Colt turned his military vehicle to the right and headed above the blast to higher ground. Lance Corporal Morgan Wriggs drove the third truck and chased a fleeing truck leaving the scene. Colt stopped on the hill and retrieved the rocket launcher out of the back. With cover from their truck, Kyle and Colt set up the launcher, took aim on one of the moving trucks and fired.

Kyle pumped his fist and threw it up in the air. "Direct hit." Kyle reloaded, and Colt fired again and disabled the second truck.

Lance Corporal Wriggs stopped, neutralized survivors from the disabled truck, and headed back to the blast site to offer cover from the snipers. Colt put the rocket launcher in the back and picked up Seth, Tyler, and the other three injured soldiers with cover from Nick and Morgan.

One of the soldiers they'd loaded onto Colt's truck clasped his leg and moaned. Blood gushed from a deep gash on his calf. A sliver of shrapnel protruded from the wound.

Kat grabbed the first aid kit out of Lance Corporal Wriggs's truck and jumped in the back of Colt's truck. "Colt let's go!" Colt punched the gas pedal and headed for the hospital.

Kat opened the kit, removed a pressure gauze and slapped it on the gaping wound. She glimpsed at the other two battered soldiers. "Where are you injured?" They showed her their wounds. Kat threw Kyle a roll of gauze, and he wrapped their wounds.

Colt pulled into a makeshift ER, and the emergency staff unloaded the wounded. Colt, Kyle, and Kat sat in the waiting room.

Kyle glimpsed over at Kat. "Where did you learn first aid?"

"I used to be a paramedic," Kat said. "Runs in the family."

"Why did you quit?"

"No working vehicles after the sightings," Kat said. "No more job."

"Why not work at the hospital?"

"I filled in when they needed help, but I lived too far out," Kat said. "I had no transportation."

"We need you at the compound," Kyle said. "Lucky for us that you live there."

"Yeah," Kat said. "We are lucky to have a compound."

Nick circled back, checked for snipers and secured the area. He picked up their casualties and transported them back to the compound. Deputy Winters, Lance Corporal Wriggs, and two other military trucks finished patrol in the area and headed back just after sunrise.

Nick handed Winters a cup of hot coffee. "Lost three soldiers, but we took out two enemy trucks and several snipers. Colt brought home two injured soldiers who were treated and released. Airman Warren is still in the hospital with serious injuries to his right leg. He had surgery to remove the shrapnel, repair shredded muscle and set a broken femur. The doctors put him in traction until the swelling goes down and they can cast it. Warren also has stitches in his side and right arm from small shards of shrapnel. What a night."

In the afternoon, Nick and Colt checked on Airman Warren. The doctor pulled them aside. "He'll need to remain here for at least another week."

"Thanks, doc." Nick shook his hand and motioned to leave.

Nick and Colt left the hospital and stopped by the sheriff's office to see Deputy Winters. He sat on the edge of Winters' desk. "We need to run surveillance and find out the status of the enemy compound at the airport."

Winters folded his arms. "We only have a rough estimate of the total number of membership or weapons. I fear the numbers we have are low."

"We'll need at least two scouts to find out more information," Nick said. "I want to recruit two intelligence officers from Wyatt's squad. We need a light footprint, in and out without detection. I'll ask Seth to go to the military camp outside Denver and request two officers from Wyatt's squadron. Wyatt left one of his officers in charge of the camp. Seth has served under both of them." Deputy Winters agreed, and Nick and Colt headed home.

The next day, Nick sent Seth to ask Major Quinn for surveillance reinforcements.

Seth and Colt traveled to the military camp and met with Major Quinn. Major Quinn shuffled his papers. "I'll have First Lt. Gerald Farns and First Lt. Cooper Adams run a special mission to gather intelligence for Nick's group and the Sheriff's Department. First Lt. Adams is in charge of the mission." Major Quinn ordered his sergeant to brief Adams and Farns.

Fifteen minutes later, Adams marched in and saluted. Major Quinn returned the salute. "Has the sergeant filled you in?" Adams responded and Major Quinn stood. "Cooperate with Deputy Winters as much as the mission allows."

Lt. Adams stiffened and saluted. "Yes, sir. I'll try not to step on anyone's toes."

The major shot him a sly grin. "Evaluate the need for more military support in the area and include it in your intelligence report." Adams agreed, and the four men collected the necessary weapons and surveillance gear to complete their mission. Farns and Adams headed for the compound with a Special Forces Team to run an ISR—Intelligence, Surveillance and Reconnaissance mission—and Colt and Seth followed.

The next day, Lt. Adams led his team and took their positions surrounding the airport. He set up their night vision pocket scopes and thermal image cameras and scanned the area at night. In the day, they surveyed through telescopic lenses and recorded all activity coming and going. Special Forces infiltrated the looters' limited security, inventoried their food and fuel supplies and weapons cache.

Within three days, Lt. Adams and his troops knew the number of looters, weapons, and equipment involved in the enemy compound at the airport. The team headed back to Nick's compound and issued their report to Nick and Deputy Winters.

Lt. Adams offered Nick and Deputy Winters more ground support, and the three made a plan to submit to Major Quinn. Lt. Adams presented his report and the group's request. Major Quinn granted the request and sent four platoons for military support under the command of Lt. Adams.

Lt. Adams met Nick's group and Winters's deputies outside the city just before five p.m.

Adams leaned against his truck. "I've posted surveillance to follow the looters on their departure from the airport. After they leave, we move in." Nick and Winters confirmed.

After the looters left, Lt. Adams surrounded the airport with snipers. On his count, they moved in silently with two squads and neutralized the marauders' security personnel.

Lt. Farns divided his squadron into three sections. Section one took care of fuel and transport; section two—weapons; section three—snipers and explosives. Three men secured the fuel storage area to back up the snipers and aided Nick's men in stealing and transporting stolen fuel back to the compound.

Four other men confiscated weapons from a locked facility and transported the items back to Nick's. A team of five soldiers with two snipers set up in the transportation storage yard to take out three posted guards. The snipers calculated and adjusted the scopes on their rifles and dropped three guards. The five soldiers took explosive devices out of their bags, planted, and secured their devices on each of the vehicles. The sergeant radioed into the lieutenant and checked on the status of fuel and weapons retrieval and transport. Then, on confirmation from the lieutenant, he set the timers, detonated the devices, and disabled all the vehicles in the yard.

Deputy Winters moved in and helped the remaining troops search the entire airport above and below ground. They flushed out several residents living throughout the terminal. Deputy Winters ordered the women and children to pack up all their supplies and board a military truck. Once the groups were loaded, he transported them to shelters throughout the city. He arrested all the men with military-style weapons in their possession or who were suspected of previous criminal looting. He confiscated all the weapons, detonated explosive devices and destroyed the entire looters' camp.

Deputy Winters ordered the men he arrested to line up in single file. He turned to the deputies. "Have you witnessed any of these men on patrol with the looters or witnessed them looting?"

The deputies pulled out twenty known members of the looters' compound and separated them into four groups of five. Next, they pulled out one group at a time and forced them to their knees. The deputies stood behind them and, on the count of three, executed them on the spot.

The remaining arrested men stood in line. Winters walked the line twice and stared at each man. He stopped in the middle. "If I ever see any of you looting or back in this compound, you'll receive the same justice. Now start walking!"

With the airport secured, Lt. Adams radioed his surveillance team and ordered his troops to join the reconnaissance team. All the troops intercepted the patrolling marauders, and within a few hours, the marauders were outnumbered, outgunned, and taken out with no survivors. The teams reported back to Nick's compound to debrief on the ISR mission and inventory all the items confiscated from the mission. Lt. Adams and Farns returned to camp, and Adams filed his report.

Chapter Eleven

Revelation

Denver

Paige trod up the stairs and stopped in the doorway. Charge peeked his head over the blanket. "Peek-a-boo." Grace babbled and giggled. Charge glanced over at Paige. "Good day."

Paige leaned against the doorframe. "Good day to you too."

Charge sat down in the rocker by the crib. "It's time, Paige."

"Time for what?"

Charge grasped the arms of the chair and rocked. "To decide."

Paige sat down on the bed. "What do I have to decide?"

"If you want me to take her now?" Charge said. "Or leave her here?"

"Leave her!" Paige creased her forehead and flailed her hands in the air. "We love Grace. She's our family."

"I can leave her, but I must explain the rules." Charge displayed a large hologram of a planetary system in the middle of the bedroom. Paige laced her fingers, took a deep breath and slowly released it. Charge bowed his head and, without words, narrated, "This is a 3D portrayal of my ancestors' solar system. Our scouting ship left in search of a new planet to seed. They arrived at Earth in the 1200s in Europe. Their medical personnel removed the Rh protein from the genome in several human embryos and planted or seeded them back into the population for future Rh-negative compatibility."

Paige scrunched her face. "Is that how Rh-negative blood was created?"

"It's the nature of evolution," Charge said. "They just helped it along a little faster."

The next image displayed a close-up of a planet. "This was my ancestors' planet, Nustu. Over time, the sun grew in size until it devoured every living thing. They evacuated to the mothership and traveled to Earth's solar system to begin adaptation and integration." He tapped on the arm of the rocker. "My ancestors arrived in the early 1940s and conducted tests on the planet and the inhabitants. They performed genetic experiments and nurtured hybrids in synthetic incubators and made modifications along the way."

A picture of Charge's human mother emerged. Charge pointed at the 3D image. "They used a genetic modification of my alien father's frozen sperm that had been preserved for generations. The infertile aliens lost the ability to conceive. The hostile environment of a dying planet had taken a toll on their species. Frozen eggs and sperm were their only hope to prevent extinction." Depictions of his human mother's European family history appeared. A map of her genetic DNA popped up and revealed an Rh-Negative dominance. Charge stood and sat beside Paige. "Not all Rh-negatives can be traced back to European roots. However, your roots do trace back to a European heritage."

Grace and her mother, Renee, appeared. Renee's genetic compatibility to the aliens and all the hybrids related to Grace displayed on the 3D screen. Aunts and uncles from the eggs of Grace's great grandmother and her mother unfolded. Paige viewed a rendering of Renee's remaining frozen eggs preserved for future insemination. The hologram displayed Grace's genetic map and emphasized the potential with her Rh-Negative dominance.

Paige narrowed her eyes. "Is all of this because Grace has Rh-Negative dominance?"

"Yes," Charge said. "She is very important to our survival."

Paige pursed her lips. "So, what does all this mean?"

"When Grace comes of age, I must collect some of her eggs." Paige's eyes grew wide. Charge tilted his head. "I assure you Paige, no harm will come to her, and she will have the choice to be involved with any offspring produced." He cracked a hint of a smile. "I know what you're thinking." Paige hitched her shoulders, and he dipped his chin. "She'll have plenty of eggs for her own reproduction." Charge bent forward and placed his hand over his heart. "I am in charge of Grace until egg retrieval and will be happy to work with you. The aliens prefer that their subjects remain with the parents or bonding couple, because the children thrive under such care." He rose from the chair. "You must agree to those conditions to keep Grace."

Paige peered at Grace in the crib, then turned to Charge. "I agree to your terms." She held her stare. "Why kill everyone just for Rh incompatibility?"

Charge pointed back to the middle of the room and displayed Earth and the sun in a hologram. Their mothership entered Earth's orbit. The mothership resembled a rotating, round, metallic planet, or moon. A section at the top and bottom retracted to a thin rim and opened up at the poles. Large saucer-shaped ships emerged from the top and bottom of the mothership. They dispersed, entered Earth's atmosphere and assumed their position above every continent on Earth.

Several large spheres assumed positions between the sun and Earth. They rotated and revolved in a circular pattern, spinning and gyrating faster and faster until an energy field appeared in the shape of a funnel. The narrow end of the funnel pointed at the Earth, and the larger end aimed at the sun. The larger end of the funnel expanded until it dwarfed the size of Earth.

The mothership rotated on its side and positioned itself in front of the small end of the funnel. It separated at the center, split into two separate halves and stopped, leaving behind a large gap in between. Electric waves emerged in the chasm.

Suddenly, a close-up of the sun eclipsed the hologram. A huge solar flare exploded from the sun, and solar particles raced toward Earth. The funnel captured the radiation from the solar flare like a vacuum shielding the Earth from the assault. The funnel absorbed the fatal onslaught and transformed the radiation particles into a swirling energy.

Charge displayed the crop circles, and the millions of people at the sightings. 3D images depicted large saucer-shaped spaceships positioned in the skies above cities. Beams of green light scanned the crowds and teleported people deep inside motherships' chasms. Then, in microseconds, billions were thrust into a swirling tunnel of death.

Paige grimaced as a steady beam of emerald green light teleported Earth's innocent souls into a swirling radiation field and vaporized. She cupped her hands over her eyes. "Why?"

Charge clasped her hands and un-cupped them. "Look and see Earth's tragic history." Images of industrial pollution poured into the air from coal and other fossil fuels. Earth's ozone depleted, surrounded by a choking atmosphere. Garbage dumped into the rivers and oceans with dead fish and mammals surfaced, blanketing the fragile planet. Views of every extinct and threatened species flashed in rapid secession. Nuclear waste from power plants, and its fatal impact on humanity projected. Atomic and nuclear bombs blasted, revealing their destruction across the world. Overpopulation and an exhausted Earth, with resources depleted and destroyed, emerged. Endless desert and dust bowls appeared. Every war fought throughout Earth's history scrolled by, showcasing dead bodies, animal carcasses and the environmental carnage left behind in its wake.

"The planet reached the tipping point in 2015," Charge said. "With overpopulation, half of all the animals gone, and the Earth choking on mankind's poison, Earth had reached the point of no return. It became unsustainable for both humans and aliens. At that moment, the aliens had to make a difficult choice. They could choose to abandon Earth and let the solar flare take it or save both of them. They chose to save both. They believed the only way to preserve all living things on the planet and ensure that humans and aliens would survive was to save the most compatible humans, reducing the population to a sustainable impact on the planet. The aliens believed they made the only logical choice for Earth's recovery and survival."

Paige's forehead etched. "How many solar flares have you captured so far?"

"We have captured three fatal flares since the main event."

She threw up three fingers. "So, you saved Earth three times?"

"That's correct," Charge said. "I'm going to show you one final hologram. It depicts the possibilities."

A simulation of a community of hybrids and humans living together appeared. Dome-shaped houses and green gardens painted the landscape. Endless pastures with free-range animals roamed the valleys. Walking trails lined the area around the community. Bicycles, covered carts and scooters darted around on rock-paved ground. Triangular aircraft flew in the clear blue sky. Children frolicked along the trails and foliage, unencumbered.

"I don't see any fancy cars, houses, sparkling jewelry or designer clothing in this community," Paige said. "Everyone lives and possesses the same materials."

"Balance of resources." Charge cracked a thin-lipped smile. "Society can only exist with a shared balance. And that means equality and balance for all living things." He raised his hand and pointed. "There is only peace through justice, so please remember that justice and equality for all is only attained through the rule of law."

Paige exhaled. "A rule of law that ensures justice must be balanced and equal."

Charge bowed. "Yes."

She lifted Grace out of her crib. "How many hybrids are going to integrate?"

"Currently we have a population of less than one million," Charge said. "Slowly the numbers will increase, but Earth's population must never exceed 1.5 billion."

"Sustainability," Paige said. "What is our current population on Earth?"

"We currently have six hundred and fifty million humans and hybrids."

Paige jiggled Grace's foot. "How do we control population?"

"We all work together." Charge bent forward and raised his hand. "Paige, I have one more rule to discuss with you."

She furrowed her brow. "Okay."

"You must not tell Nick about us until June seventeenth, 2026."

Distrust laced her voice. "Why?"

"I will explain in time."

Paige slanted her head to the right. "Trust you?"

"Yes," Charge said. "It is important to ensure Grace's welfare."

"Agreed," Paige said. "But please tell me how you knew about the solar flare, and that I would get Grace, and… the shot you gave me?"

"I can tell you we have a limited view of the future and time-shift ability."

Paige scowled. "Explain it to me someday?"

"Someday." Charge grew a slight grin. "When the time is right." He waved goodbye and faded away.

Paige peered out the window and spied the growing garden. "April showers and warm temperatures in May enticed you to grow." She held Grace up to the window. "It's going to be a productive harvest this year." Paige kissed Grace's chubby cheek. "I wonder what will happen after June seventeenth." She bounced Grace on her hip. "All I know is that we have a secret, and you, little girl, are the most important person in the world to me. Nick will understand."

"What will Nick understand?" Nick leaned up against the door.

A wide-eyed Paige swallowed hard. "How important our little girl is?"

"How important both my girls are." Nick strutted over and kissed his girls.

"See there, little one." Paige handed Grace to Nick and picked up a diaper. "Your turn. She left you a little gift."

Nick grinned and peeked inside the back of her dirty diaper. "Not so little. Just like your dad, huh?" He lifted her up in the air. "If you do something big, do it right. Besides, we're both full of shit."

"I heard that, Nick," Paige said. "You are, definitely."

"Truth be known, this whole family is," Nick whispered to Grace with a chuckle and changed her.

Nick escorted a freshly diapered Grace downstairs and plunked her on the table in her carrier. Paige sliced meat and potatoes for stew and scooped them in her soup pot. He flopped down at the table and jiggled Grace's toes, initiating a giggle. Paige glanced at both and smiled.

Nick jumped up, put his arms around Paige's waist and pulled her close. "I understand how important Grace is to you. She's important to both of us."

"I know."

He drew his head back. "Everything okay?"

"Absolutely."

"I love you and Grace," Nick said and kissed Paige.

"I love you more."

Nick grabbed her ass firmly with both hands. "Good, then tonight you can show me."

"Behave yourself." Paige laughed and struggled to get free. "Grace might get the wrong idea."

"Grace is four months old, she thinks we're playing around," Nick said. "Oh well, we better save your energy for later."

"Good idea. Or…" Paige giggled. "Is it 'Not tonight dear. I'm too tired?'"

Nick stopped his horseplay. "I'll behave." He snatched a piece of raw potato and popped it in his mouth. "I need to go out and check the horses before dinner, anyway."

Paige smirked. "That was just too easy."

"Hey, I know a winning hand," Nick said. "I'll collect my winnings later." Nick flashed a wily smile, pointed his finger at her and dashed out the door.

"Know when to fold 'em and when to hold 'em." Paige smooched Grace. "Your daddy's a smart gambler."

A few hours later, Nick and Kellan walked in the house and sniffed the aroma of meaty stew and fresh bread. Kellan's stomach grumbled. Paige placed the last bowl of steamy stew down, and Kami took her seat. Nick and Kellan washed their hands, pulled out their chairs and joined Kami, Grace, and Paige at the table. A contented Grace kicked her legs in her carrier next to Paige.

Paige passed the hot bread to Nick. He tore off a piece of bread, dipped it in the stew and popped it in his mouth. "Delicious."

Paige pointed to Kami. "World's best baker."

Kami flushed crimson. "It was Paige's recipe."

"Kami," Nick said. "She stole the recipe from me."

Kami choked back a giggle. "Then thank yourself, Nick."

"Thank you, Nick." Nick patted himself on the back. "Delicious bread."

Kami laughed and threw a piece of her bread across the table at him. Nick sat up straight. "Okay girl, we're on." He tore a piece of his bread off and threw it back at her. The two threw several pieces of their bread at each other. Kellan cast his eyes down and kept eating his stew. Paige shook her head at both of them and dipped her spoon. Grace's eyes grew big with all the ruckus. Nick started to grab another slice of bread, but Paige grabbed the plate and moved it out of his reach.

Nick raised his hands in the air. "I give up."

Paige slowly passed the plate of bread to him, and Nick snatched a slice of bread off the plate. He tore a piece off, glanced at Kami and paused for a moment, but instead of tossing it, he dipped it in his stew and put it in his mouth. Then he tore off another piece of bread and squinted at Paige. Paige glared at him, so he smiled at Kami, dipped it once again and stuck it in his mouth. Kami stared at Nick, raised her shoulders, and wiped her hands with a victorious smile. Nick grinned at her, finished his stew and reached for seconds.

Paige threw Kellan a grin and pushed her chair back. "Let's let these two clean up after all the fun."

Kellan slid out of his seat. "Sounds good to me." Then he strode off and left his empty bowl on the table.

Nick and Kami smirked at each other. Nick winked and chuckled. "KP Duty."

Kami snorted. "What is KP Duty?"

"It means Kitchen Patrol Duty," Nick said. "The dreaded shit duty for bad behavior, or conduct unbecoming of an officer."

"Was it worth it, bad boy?"

"Hell yes," Nick said. "What's life without a little misbehaving?"

"You might be in the doghouse, Nick."

"Keeping it spicy, Kami." Nick winked. "Interesting and never boring."

Kami tossed her napkin on the table. "Boring, you're not."

The two cleared off the table, swept the floor and did the dishes.

Later, Nick leaped upstairs and jumped in the shower. Paige tucked a sleeping Grace in her crib, slipped on her nightshirt and climbed into bed. Nick brushed his teeth, shaved a day's stubble and snapped off the gas lamp. He lifted the covers and crawled into bed naked next to Paige. He rubbed her back and snuck his hand under her nightshirt. Paige turned to face him, and he pulled off her shirt and panties. Nick kissed her with long slow kisses, lightly touching his tongue to hers. He nuzzled her neck, caressed her breasts and flicked his tongue to stimulate her nipples. He used his finger to arouse her sweet spot. Nick opened her legs, entered her with gentle precision and moved in a steady rhythm. Paige clutched the bottom sheet with her fingers and softly moaned. He held steady until they both reached their summit. Nick released himself and cuddled next to Paige's naked body. He put his lips to her ear. "You're the love of my life."

Paige squeezed his hand. "And you are mine."

The next day, in the early morning hours, Nick rifled through Paige's jewelry box and snatched one of her rings. He drove into town on a special mission.

Nick stopped at his third jewelry store. "Dammit, another one looted and empty." He hopped in his truck, drove around and spotted an old abandoned antique store. "Well now. What do we have here?" He pulled in and parked.

Nick broke the lock, slipped inside and flipped on his flashlight. He ambled into a back room and stopped at one of the glass counters. He slid opened the sliding glass panel and removed a small selection of old diamond rings, carefully positioned in a velvet ring holder. Nick took Paige's ring out of his pocket and put it on his little finger to size it. He chose three antique wedding rings and tested each size on his little finger. Only one fit. Nick compared Paige's ring with the antique. He held it up. "My little friend. You just might do." He placed Paige's ring back in his pocket and headed outside.

Nick held the 14-carat diamond ring in the sunlight and examined the doubled-banded white gold ring for quality. "You're a little dirty from neglect, but otherwise in excellent shape. Hmm, white gold bands." He drew it closer. "Okay little buddy, your engagement ring has a nice-sized diamond, and the attached wedding band is just plain white gold. But that's okay." Nick rubbed his finger along the band. "I could detach the engagement ring and give it to Paige first. Then reattach the wedding band after our wedding. I just need a few jewelers tools to use with the tools I already have in the shop at home."

Nick stuffed the new ring in his pocket and drove back to one of the looted jewelry stores. He dashed in the store and collected jewelers tools from the back room. Nick brought his bounty back home, parked his truck, and headed for the shop. He set out the jewelers tools that he'd collected, dug through all the tools in the shop and pulled out the necessary ones. He removed the diamond, grabbed the soldering iron and lit the butane micro torch. He stuck the ring in his improvised vice grip, thinned the flame and heated the white gold. He separated the bands and let them cool.

After they'd cooled, Nick grasped a piece of fine steel wool, then sanded and buffed the bands. He rubbed his finger across the smooth metal. "Smooth as a baby's butt." He used a polisher, cleaned the bands with ring cleaner and wiped off the white gold with a piece of gauze.

Nick cleaned and replaced the diamond. He attempted to wiggle the setting. "Secure, you're not moving." He rubbed his fingers across the bands. "Good deal. You look brand new." He kissed his future. "Little buddy, I'm counting on you to make my dreams come true. I hope she loves you." Nick wrapped the rings in cheesecloth, placed them in a velvet bag with an old antique pocket watch and placed the bag in his top drawer. He returned Paige's ring back to her jewelry box, headed downstairs for dinner and ate without divulging the day's special mission to a soul.

Chapter Twelve

Contact

The Nevada Desert

Wyatt stuffed his rifle in its scabbard, climbed on his horse, and joined Brandon and Justin on the trail back to the alien site. He tightened his reins. "We'll need to travel fast and light." He kicked his horse and spun around. "With only the essentials."

Brandon scowled, dropped his bundle of firewood, and kicked his horse. Justin snickered and galloped behind him.

After a day's ride, the three dismounted and led their horses to a trickling stream. Wyatt marched upstream and dipped his canteen in the water. He popped in a purification tablet and shook it. He flopped down on his bedroll and pulled out dry jerky and energy bars for dinner. Wyatt chomped on a piece of jerky and grew a devious smirk across his face. "Too bad there's no wood for a fire tonight. It could get nippy."

Justin turned toward Brandon and curled up his nose. "It just might." Brandon sneered. Justin cackled, laid out his bedroll and folded his jacket to use as a pillow. He gazed up at a silver-studded sky. "Maybe no cozy fire, but the stars are really visible this time of year. I guess that's our only comfort tonight." Justin stretched back and tucked his hands behind his head. "I wonder how many civilizations have passed by Earth on their journeys through space. Why, out of all the galaxies and stars in the sky, did these aliens choose our sun and Earth?" He glanced over at Brandon. "Do you think we're the only planet that can support their life?"

"Maybe," Brandon said. "Or the easiest to take."

"They have better technology," Justin said. "Right place, right time in evolution."

"Get some sleep." Wyatt groaned, turned over and closed his eyes. "We can contemplate motives later."

The next morning, the group stretched their sore and stiff muscles and rode off for another grueling day in the saddle. By late afternoon, the sun exacted its punishment. Justin wiped the dripping sweat off his forehead with his t-shirt and sipped from his canteen. He removed an electrolyte tab out of his saddle bag and popped it into his mouth. Wyatt tossed him his wide-brimmed hat. Justin plopped on Wyatt's fedora and glimpsed back at Brandon. He leered, dropped back beside Brandon and whispered, "Wyatt wouldn't stop for anyone's discomfort."

Brandon tilted his head toward Justin and lowered his voice. "The man is as tough as nails." He snorted and swiped a trickle of sweat. "He wouldn't stop even if we were dying."

The sun's light dipped behind the horizon, so the three men dismounted for the night. Justin tied up his horse and threw Wyatt's hat at him. "Thanks, old man. Once again, you saved my black ass."

"Yeah, yeah, I just saved us time was all," Wyatt said. "We didn't have time to stop and coddle you. Get your beauty sleep. Tomorrow we press on."

"Beauty sleep, huh?" Justin batted his eyes. "Does that mean you think I'm pretty?"

Wyatt threw his hat back. "You're butt ugly and you know it."

"Long as the ladies like me, that's okay." Justin threw Wyatt's hat back. "Besides, we stay out here much longer and even Brandon might start to look good."

Brandon scrunched his face. "Time to go home."

After all the banter, the guys drifted off and snored in unison all night.

In the morning, the sun's rays pierced through the clouds. Wyatt covered his eyes and leaped to his feet. He shook out his blanket and kicked his comrade's boots. "Time to get up, dandies."

Brandon jumped up, ready to strike. Justin laughed. "Go get 'em, Brandon."

Brandon scoped out the empty area and thrust his middle finger. "Fuck you, Justin."

Justin smirked, collected his things and walked towards his horse. Brandon threw a stick and Justin ducked. Justin spun around with fists drawn. Wyatt mounted his horse and held up his hand.

"Knock it off, you two. Save it for the enemy." Brandon saddled and mounted his horse. He jerked the reins hard right, kicked his horse and fell in behind Wyatt. Justin stuffed a blade of dry grass in his mouth and brought up the rear.

After two hours of hard riding, the weary scouting party arrived at Wayne's designated stopping point. They tied up their horses and left their side arms and rifles at camp. The three men hiked to the same observation point at the alien compound.

Wyatt, Justin and Brandon walked up to the alien site, stood and waited. Within a few minutes, a sphere appeared and hovered above his head. The three stood without moving, and the sphere scanned each one of them.

Wyatt stared directly at the sphere. "I'd like to speak to the alien in charge." It moved in closer to Wyatt. Two more spheres emerged and positioned right in front of Brandon and Justin. It instantly perused them with blue light. Brandon and Justin repeated Wyatt's words. The three men waited for a response. The spheres darted back to the alien compound.

A small slit opened at their compound and Charge walked out to meet the three men. Charge turned to Wyatt. "Hello, Wyatt."

Wyatt glanced at Brandon and Justin, then back to Charge. "How do you know my name?"

"I know who and what you are," Charge said. "Captain Wyatt Reynolds, and Lieutenants Justin Jones and Brandon Jackson. What can I do for you?"

Wyatt narrowed his eyes. "We are here to gather information and make contact."

Charge tilted his head. "Assess the enemy and negotiate?"

Wyatt held his gaze. "Something like that."

"Well then, let's go inside," Charge said. "All three of you or just the captain?"

Wyatt glimpsed over at Brandon and Justin. They nodded. He dipped his chin at Charge. "All three."

"Very well," Charge said and led the way.

The group entered the compound. Charge showed them the docking stations and the ships. Justin scanned the outside of the crafts. *The structures are amazing. I wonder what the payload and propulsion systems are?*

Charge glanced at Justin and grinned. "Want to look inside?"

Justin turned his head wide-eyed. "Of course."

Charge opened the craft, and the men stepped inside. A single seat sat in front of a shiny panel. Charge pointed to the seat. "Justin, it's all yours. Please set in the seat." Justin climbed in the seat, and it instantly sealed to his body like a magnet. Justin took a deep breath and held it. A 3D hologram appeared with an instrumentation panel and a navigation system. The shiny panel cleared and revealed the outside docking station. Charge said, "Engage." The craft lit up and asked for coordinates. Charge ordered perimeter patrol and guided Wyatt and Brandon out of the craft.

Justin exhaled and studied its guidance system. The craft released from the docking station and proceeded out of the compound to patrol a two-mile perimeter around the area. He whispered, "I wonder if I could fly this to base camp."

A voice answered, "Access and request denied. Interface with the computer is prohibited."

Justin clenched his jaw. "Understood." After a few minutes, the craft slowed and stopped over their campsite above the horses. A sphere released from the craft and scanned the animals. The scan displayed on a hologram in front of Jason.

Voice command stated, "Two-year-old equines. Purpose—a form of human travel and herbivore. No threat." The sphere scanned the items left in camp and displayed holograms of each item. Justin swallowed hard. 45 caliber revolvers and the hunting rifles appeared. Voice command said, "No threat."

Justin's jaw relaxed. The sphere docked back onto the craft, and the spacecraft resumed flight back to the compound. Justin's seat released, and he stood up. "Thanks for the flight."

Voice command responded, "Perimeter complete, secure. No reported threats."

Justin saluted. "Good to know." He strode over to the exit area and stopped. "I know this is where we came in." He stuck his hand out and rubbed the strange metal. A seamless door opened. He jumped back and eyeballed the opening. "Well, that's fucking cool." Justin stepped out and joined the others on the other side of the docking station.

Charged dipped his head. "Did it answer your questions?"

"Not really," Justin said. "It left me with even more questions than answers, but very, very, cool."

"Let's continue and answer a few more of those questions." Charge thrust his hand out. "I'll show you the control center."

The group passed by a few hybrid pilots. The pilots glanced up, dipped their chins and marched forward. The three visitors entered the command center. The aliens eyed them from their seats but continued working at their holographic panels.

Justin held his gaze. The aliens interacted with each other without uttering a single word. The hybrids pointed their long fingers at unfamiliar holographic symbols, algorisms and formulas. Justin bent forward and squinted. *They communicate with each other with unmistakable recognition. They interface directly with the computer and with each other, using wordless thoughts.* Justin shook his head. *Damn, how do they do that?*

Charge waved his hand over an empty seat. A hologram translated the images in a formula that Justin understood. Justin studied the formulas. "I've never seen this propulsion system before. Is this a fusion technology?"

"A little more advanced than your simple definition of fusion," Charge said. "We use a quantum propulsion system to utilize solar particles, collect and convert hydrogen and oxygen from asteroids and planets, and harness dark energy from deep space." He displayed the schematic of a quantum computer and quantum algorisms with detailed formulas captured in some kind of code.

Justin studied the images. "Do you have time travel technology?"

"Only limited," Charge said. "We use quantum technology for teleport or to transport, but mostly for energy production and fuel." A hologram displayed an image of a rim of spheres in the sun's orbit that captured solar eruptions from the surface. Each sphere spun into a vortex that absorbed, converted, transformed and stored energy. After absorption, the spheres slowed rotation and disengaged their small funnels. They assumed a lined formation and headed back to the large ship designed for energy storage in their fleet of space crafts.

Charge's hologram displayed the schematics of the mothership and the large ships docked inside for space travel. It showcased prints for the triangular crafts that were stored within the perimeter of the large crafts. Suddenly, the fleet appeared in the hologram and departed their solar system at unbelievable speeds through space. Spheres from the storage craft emerged and created wormholes to transport or teleport them through solar systems effortlessly.

Charge showed Justin, Brandon, and Wyatt the same holograms he'd shared with Paige. He revealed their planet's destruction, their journey to Earth, their arrival, testing and experimentation, and the successful evolution of the hybrids. He projected images of the solar flare and explained their difficult choice to save Earth on April 20 2025. He exposed the damage the Earth had endured under human stewardship. Charge flashed Earth's progression and froze the last image presented. He pointed at Earth's ozone layer. "The planet reached the tipping point and is beyond the point of no return."

Charge displayed the rules for survival and the final stage on August 21, 2026. He flashed in big bold letters the word NO and exhibited pictures of dirty energy. Nuclear, coal and natural gas power plants streamed across a holographic screen. Factories pouring pollutants and dumping waste into the waterways flashed in front of them. Gas and diesel-powered vehicles dispensing carbon into the air emerged. Nuclear weapons, weapons of mass destruction, military drones, subs, carriers and aircrafts scrolled by. Images of items requiring dirty energy to operate it raced past with the word NO in big bold letters, strobing across each one to clarify the message. The hologram ended with clean energy technology and the schematics to accomplish every one of them with the date August 21, 2026.

Justin stared at Wyatt and Brandon. "This technology is incredible." He turned around and peered at Charge. "You're going to give this to us?"

"Yes," Charge said. "If you agree to the terms."

"No use of dirty energy." Wyatt held his stare. "We understand."

Charge dipped his chin. "If you comply, we'll aid you in future technology and clean up."

Justin exhaled. "How can you clean up this mess?"

"Just know we can," Charge said and led them out of the control room. He escorted them to the second compound and stepped inside.

Charge guided them to an empty room on the bottom level. "This is our pilot's quarters." He waved his hand, and a bed, a sink, a shower, and a strange toilet shaped like an egg emerged.

Justin snickered. "Just like all those sci-fi movies I used to watch. Press a button, wave your hand, voice command or just think it, and whatever you imagine or wish for magically appears."

A recliner with a retractable table top and a holographic screen appeared. The screen displayed old movies from Justin's childhood. Justin shook his head. "How?" Charge slipped Justin a sly grin and brought them in the food area.

Round tables with seats that seemed like something you would see on the deck of a starship blanketed the area. Justin remembered that they'd watched this dome invert and dock a few weeks earlier. Charge ogled at Justin's puzzled expression and said, "They can appear right side up or upside down, it doesn't matter. It will adjust to what you need or any position the ship is in."

Justin slipped a glance at Charge. *Does he read my mind?*

Charge grinned at Justin with his narrow lips and answered, mind to mind, "Yes."

Justin gawked. "Shit."

"No shit," Charge answered back out loud.

Wyatt and Brandon turned and gaped at Charge.

"They materialize easily with thought command," Charge restated.

Justin gazed at Charge and smiled at their little secret.

Charge strolled up to the wall and waved his hand. A holographic menu popped down with unrecognizable symbols and words in English translated beside them. Charge selected coffee and energy bars off the list. A dispenser opened and coffee in metal containers with three energy bars came out on a shelf that popped out. Charge handed them a coffee and a bar each.

Then he walked over to an empty area and waved his hand above a circle with six triangle designs imprinted on the floor. The circle replicated a table with four chairs attached.

Justin gaped at Charge. "Easy." Charge nodded his head, and the four sat down at the table. Justin bit off a piece of his energy bar and chewed slowly. "Yum, coconut, and chocolate." He sipped his black coffee. "Just as good as the coffee shop on the corner of any city."

Brandon sipped his and closed his eyes. "Wish you made coffee like this, Justin."

Justin chuckled. "Me too."

Charge lowered his chin. "Glad you like it."

Brandon bobbed his head at Charge and held his gaze. *Is this guy human too?*

Charge eyed Brandon and mind to mind said, *Hybrid. I'm part human.*

"Thought so. Like Spock." Brandon stopped and stared at Charge. "Wait, what just happened?"

Charge stared at Brandon and mind-to-mind said, *"The half-human Vulcan on TV?"*

Brandon cackled. "Exactly." A mystified Wyatt wrinkled his brow and eyeballed Brandon. Justin shot Brandon a wily smile. Brandon shrugged his shoulders. "What a mind fuck."

Charge grinned. "Indeed." A lost Wyatt glowered at all three. Charge stood. "Shall we?" He strolled over toward the wall and placed his metal coffee container in a receptacle that opened when he approached it. Wyatt, Justin, and Brandon grew wide-eyed and did the same.

Justin turned to Charge. "How does all this work?"

"We restructure or fabricate particles in the replicator," Charge said. "We do the same when we recycle the items in the receptacle." Charge escorted them to the upper level. The area resembled the control center, with hybrids busy in their seating areas. Charge extended his hand. "This area is for work and education." He stopped by an empty station and waved his hand. "I must show you one more thing before we end the tour." A holographic image of a military operation in full combat appeared. One of the aliens' large disc-shaped aircraft hovered above the military with their force field engaged. Their spheres emerged and, within seconds, a yellow-orange beam of light evaporated every military threat, leaving nothing behind. Every trace of weapon, vehicle, and human being were all gone. Not a bolt, a hair, or a speck of dust from debris remained.

Wyatt pursed his lips. "Comply or gone."

Charge nodded. "Exactly."

"Defiance is futile," Justin said. "Now, how do we convince the military?"

"I have no doubt that seeing is believing," Charge said. "But an intelligence report is a good start."

Brandon scowled. "You think they'll have to see the evidence firsthand, don't you?"

"I'm afraid so," Charge said. "That seems to be our experience on this planet. We observed and concluded that humans seem to try everything else first, but eventually they relent and do the right thing in the end."

"Whether it's Winston Churchill or Abba Eban," Brandon said. "The sentiment's the same. Humans will exhaust all the possibilities or alternatives before they'll do the right thing."

"So true," Charge said. "This time let's hope they have examined and exhausted the alternatives already."

"Why didn't you intervene afterwards?" Justin glowered. "Before resources dwindled and violence erupted?"

"We knew the strongest and the smartest would survive," Charge said. "We've protected some. We estimated there were enough resources for everyone before implementation on August twenty-first." He pressed his lips together. "Living in balance is the greatest human challenge. Some areas in the world are doing very well helping each other and integrating equally. Unfortunately, some countries are not."

Brandon lifted his shoulders to his earlobes. "A shared balance."

"That means sharing and balancing resources equally and wisely." Charge wagged his long slender finger. "That applies to all living things."

Wyatt scoffed. "Most of the time we have to be forced."

"It looks that way," Charge said. "This time we hope it's voluntary."

"One more thing." Justin folded his arms and slanted his head to the side. "How did you determine who was Rh positive or negative?"

Charge lifted his hand. "Rh positives have a genetic marker that our scans detect easily."

Justin arched a brow. "The blue scan?"

"Blue," Charge said. "Also, bright white light and infrared scan."

"So," Justin uncrossed his arms. "You can penetrate anything?"

Charge drew in a long, slow breath. "Yes."

Wyatt pressed his lips together and bobbed his head. "Okay, we'll do our best to convince others."

Charge grew a lopsided smile. "That's all we can ask."

Wyatt etched his forehead and rubbed his chin. "You said we. Is we the aliens and hybrids?"

"Yes," Charge said. "I speak for both."

Wyatt rubbed his hands together. "When do we meet the aliens?"

"After implementation," Charge said. "They'll wait until then."

Justin cocked his head. "Where are they?"

"Orbiting Earth," Charge said. "They need a different environment and must remain in their own. They will meet your leaders when Earth is stable."

"A different environment?" Justin said. "What do you mean?"

"Cleaner," Charge said. "Hybrids are acclimated to Earth, and they are not. Not for long-term exposure."

Justin snickered. "Long-term exposure is dangerous for all of us under Earth's current conditions."

"We can clean it up," Charge said. "Do you have any other questions or concerns?"

Justin furrowed his brow. "Why create hybrids?"

"The aliens, or the Nustu, exhausted their genetic code over generations and they could no longer propagate or survive," Charge said. "They faced extinction."

"Eventually," Justin said. "We would as well."

"No," Charge said. "Your species would have all expired on April twentieth, 2025."

"Whoa." Justin squirmed and snorted. "I'm glad you saved our species." He pointed his finger at Charge. "You're part human too."

"Indeed," Charge said. "The only logical choice for both." He stretched out his hand. "This way, gentlemen. I'll escort you back to the border." He walked the three men back to the border's edge and shook their hands. "Good luck with your new mission."

Wyatt bobbed. "You've given us a difficult one."

"One last thing, Wyatt," Charge said. "It is imperative that you return to Denver by June seventeenth, 2026. Your troops and family depend on it."

Wyatt jutted out his jaw. "What do you mean troops and family?"

"Logan's family," Charge said. "And the troops you left in charge."

Wyatt furrowed his brow. "Are they in danger?"

"Yes," Charge said. "You and Justin must be there."

Wyatt bent forward. "If I'm there, they'll survive?"

"Yes," Charge said. "They need your information. If they don't have it, some will perish."

"All right," Wyatt said. "I'll make sure Justin and I are home."

"Remember," Charge said. "By June seventeenth." He spun around and marched back to his compound.

With the evening sun fading, the men returned to their horses and camped for the night. Wyatt glanced over at Justin. "Back by the seventeenth. We have our work cut out for us."

"Yes, we do," Justin said. "And very little time." He stretched out on his bedroll and peered up at the twinkling stars. *I wonder how many suns supporting planets with life are among those stars. Right now, two species are going to share our sun and this planet.* Justin folded his arms across his chest and drew in a long, slow breath. *Charge is going to share their advanced technology. He'll share everything they've learned from space travel. I hope I can explore space with the hybrids in the future. Is it really so bad to share the planet between two different worlds?* Images of possible battles and the annihilation of his brothers and sisters in arms from Charge's hologram flashed before him. Justin's chest tightened and his eyes watered. He stared at the stars and searched for the words to convince ranking bureaucrats of a losing battle. He swallowed hard and whispered, "Fuck, we're all going down."

The next morning, a soft haze from the sun peeked through the clouds. A sprinkle from dark rain clouds off in the distance threatened their speedy return. The three men packed up their gear and headed out.

By mid-afternoon, the group had removed their rain ponchos from their saddle bags and put them on. The sun disappeared behind storm clouds and rain-drenched the wrapped horseman.

Wyatt jerked his reins. "We'll head off-trail to avoid a flash flood. This is going to add more travel time to our trip back, but I'd rather be safe than sorry." The scouts plodded through the muddy terrain until dusk forced them to camp for the night. They snatched their thermal blankets from their bedroll, wrapped up tight like a burrito, and stretched their ponchos over the top.

After a long night with limited sleep, the sunrise revealed blue skies and spared the travelers from another day of misery. The group shook out their wet ponchos and put them on to dry out in the sun. They packed up, mounted their horses with their damp ponchos on, and pushed on. Around noon, the group stuffed their ponchos and shirts in their saddlebags and resumed the original trail in their t-shirts.

The day ended long after dark. They watered the horses and let them graze through the night. The group hit their makeshift pillows and snored all night.

The next day, a rested crew resumed their journey refreshed and rode hard. That night, they made camp, passed out dried jerky and protein bars, and unscrewed the caps on their canteens. Justin took a swig from his canteen and glanced over at Wyatt. "We'll be there tomorrow. What are you going to tell the colonels?"

"We're going to sit down and write out our report before we take it to them," Wyatt said. "Then we'll carefully present the evidence."

Brandon scoffed. "What if they won't listen?"

"We'll have to keep talking until they see." Justin flared his nostrils and threw a rock. "Remember, we're on a fucking timetable."

"All we can do is give them the information," Wyatt said. "I'm going to tell the colonel we have to present the evidence to others as well.

Justin, you and I will take off and do just that, starting with Denver."

"Charge thinks he may have to show them," Justin said. "A forceful demonstration perhaps." He squinted his eyes and popped in a chunk of jerky. "I have no doubt he'll give them quite a show."

"We'll leave that to him," Wyatt said. "In the meantime, Brandon can stay and reinforce whatever Charge has in store for the military here." He pointed his index finger at Justin. "You and I have another mission in Denver."

"Okay Wyatt," Justin said. "Sounds like you have it covered." He laid out his bedroll and turned in for the night.

At sunrise, the three rode at a steady pace and arrived at Lt. Colonel Turner's outpost on the BLM road around noon. Wyatt, Justin and Brandon sat down with Lt. Col. Turner and mapped out the evidence to present. Lt. Col. Turner slid her chair back. "After witnessing the capabilities of the aliens' warfare firsthand, I agree with your analysis. Wyatt and Justin, you have my full support to brief the other bases, starting with Denver, but I want Brandon to accompany me to Edwards AFB in California. I'll give any informational reinforcement I can, but my outpost and Colonel Baker's camp in town aren't the problem. We have already experienced the evidence."

"I agree," Wyatt said. "Justin and I will get ready to leave after our briefing with Colonel Baker in the morning."

The group split up the evidence and each wrote their section of the report. By four in the morning, they put it all together and grabbed a few hours of sleep.

The next morning, Lt. Colonel Claire Turner, Wyatt, Justin, and Brandon met with Colonel Baker and presented the evidence. Colonel Baker listened and read their comprehensive reports. He shuffled the pages and exhaled. "Well, it is what it is. Let's get to work convincing the others. Pack your gear. You and the second lieutenant head out in three days."

Wyatt and Justin met with Kent, Charley, Amber, and Levi in Kent's tent. Kent tapped his makeshift table. "Levi and I are going home too."

Amber spun around. "Me too."

Justin grasped her forearm. "Amber, this could get very dangerous. I have no idea what we are walking into in Denver. Charge warned us that lives depend on our return. You are much safer here."

"If you go, I may never see you again." Amber grabbed his shirt and pulled him close. "I don't care if it's dangerous. I would rather be with you than without you. I go with or I follow you."

Justin put his forehead on hers. "You are stubborn enough to follow us, aren't you?"

"Yes, I will."

"All right." Justin whispered, "But your father is not going to like it."

"You leave him to me," Amber said.

After the meeting, she cornered her father.

Thirty minutes later, Charley reluctantly agreed. "I know it's time to let you go live your own life. I have to let you grow up. Lt. Col. Turner has asked me to go with her and Brandon. They need me now." He hugged his daughter and whispered, "You stay safe."

Amber pressed her lips up to his ear. "I'll be fine with Justin, Dad. You stay safe too. I'll see you before you know it."

Charley lifted the flap on Justin's tent, popped in and stood nose to nose with him. "Take care of my daughter. I know I can't change her mind."

Justin placed both hands on Charley's shoulders. "I give you my word. I'll do everything in my power to keep her safe. I love her and would give my life to protect her."

Charley swallowed hard. "I believe you would. Bring her back to me." Justin nodded.

Three days later, Charley, Lt. Colonel Turner and Brandon packed up supplies and headed south.

Chapter Thirteen

Return

On a sultry summer night

On June 14, around ten in the evening, Wyatt pulled into an empty rest stop to fuel and switch drivers. Amber snuck behind the building to use the bathroom. Justin opened his eyes from his nap and caught sight of her dip around the side of the building. "Damn it, Amber." He jumped out, dashed to catch her and stared down at her. "Never go without me." Justin tapped on the holstered gun strapped on his side. "It's far too dangerous alone."

Amber eyed his hand on the gun. "Sorry, I didn't want to wake you." She wiped, pulled her jeans halfway up and leaned against the building. "Interested?" Justin strolled up to her and kissed her. Amber put her hand down and touched the front of Justin's pants. "Looks like you're happy to see me after all."

"Always happy to see you." He cupped her bare bottom and drew her close. He unfastened his jeans. Amber slipped out of her jeans and panties. Justin lifted her leg and placed it around him. He entered her, and she met him thrust for thrust. After their fiery encounter, he caught his breath and gazed at her. "Promise me, no more sneaking to pee alone. You wake me."

Amber saluted. "Yes, sir. Only if you promise to make it worth my while again."

"Happy to." Justin chuckled. "Always happy to sneak away and see you."

Amber giggled. "Okay, Justin. Next pee break." Justin smirked. Amber slid her panties and jeans on and raced for the truck. Justin peed and buttoned his jeans.

Wyatt filled the tank with fuel and huffed. "Justin, let's go." Justin sprinted to the truck and climbed in. He turned and winked at Amber on the passenger side. Wyatt crawled in the back with Kent and Levi. Justin glanced at the men in the back seat in his rearview mirror and grinned. Kent eyed him and shook his head. Amber put her head on the passenger window, closed her eyes and grew a sly smile.

Justin pulled into Fort Hill Air Force Base at two in the morning and replaced all the empty diesel fuel cans. Wyatt met with the commander and filled him in. The group claimed a bunk in the barracks for a few hours of sleep. The commander assigned Amber a private bunk in an officer's room. After lights out, Justin snuck in Amber's room. Wyatt glanced at Justin's empty bunk and shook his head. "That lucky bastard."

The next morning, they left for Denver with Levi at the wheel. Justin wrapped his arm around Amber and cuddled close to make more room for Kent. Wyatt sat in the passenger seat, ready to take the second shift.

They stopped just before Laramie, Wyoming to eat a late lunch and switched drivers.

Wyatt drove a few miles with Justin in the passenger side. Suddenly, a loud pop. The wheel shook. Wyatt pulled over and scowled. "We blew out a tire." Justin grabbed a spare out of the back.

Wyatt checked all the tires. "This one's threadbare. Let's do both." Wyatt stared at the sunset. "We should eat a bite first before we head out." After dinner, the group hit the road and headed for the Colorado border.

Wyatt rounded a corner and Justin pointed to a roadblock a few miles from the border. Two trucks facing each other blocked the road in a narrow section of the highway. Wyatt stopped the truck and peered through his night vision pocket scope. "Get your automatic rifles. Lock and load."

He backed up the truck, but spied a semi-truck that pulled out from an intersection and blocked their back route. "Kent, take the wheel." Wyatt and Justin climbed in the back of the truck with their sniper rifles, and Justin seized the rocket launcher and loaded it. Kent moved the truck ahead.

The assassins revealed their location with several shots. Justin and Wyatt viewed two snipers on a hilltop through their night vision scopes and took aim from the semi-truck. Justin and Wyatt fired and hit their target. They scoped the rest of the area. Two other snipers moved in closer from the other direction and took aim, targeting Kent.

Wyatt said, "Kent, drop down." Kent ducked and crawled in the back seat with his gun. Justin aimed, confirmed a position of one click away and shot one of the assassins. Wyatt searched for the remaining sniper, but the gunmen fired several rounds into the driver's side of the truck. Wyatt and Kent shot above the sniper's head to distract him. Justin slid out of the truck with his sniper rifle.

Wyatt handed him the rocket launcher. "Justin, watch your six."

Justin spun around. "You too." He dropped back into the cover of darkness and laid the launcher down. He assumed a position lying on his stomach and aimed his sniper rifle at the gunmen. The sniper shifted his position to fire back at Wyatt. Justin aimed and clipped the assassin. The sniper fell back right into Wyatt's sight. He marked and captured the final shot and dropped him.

Three killers with automatic weapons moved in front of the trucks. Justin grabbed the SMAW rocket launcher, used the starlight scope, discharged his rocket, and blew up both trucks. All three killers perished in the carnage.

Justin and Wyatt jumped in the back. Kent leaped back into the driver's seat and plowed through the fiery blockade. Justin and Wyatt scanned the area for the enemy from the back of their truck, and Kent sped off. Levi and Amber stayed in the back seat and watched out the windows with their weapons drawn.

Kent drove the truck down the road, and Wyatt and Justin scoped the terrain to make sure no one was following. Wyatt turned toward Kent. "Kent, stop the truck two klicks down the road, and we'll check on any damage from the battle."

After they stopped, Justin checked the door, dash, electronics and the engine for destruction. "Doesn't look like there's any lasting damage." He peered back at Amber. "Are you bleeding?"

He rushed to the back door, opened it, and grabbed her arm. Amber groaned in pain. Justin pulled back his hand and rubbed the red wet blood on his fingertips. He ripped the sleeve of her shirt and revealed a bullet wound. He fingered her torn skin and exhaled. "Looks like the bullet just grazed you." He spotted the bullet hole lodged in the seat behind her. Justin tore her shirt sleeve into three pieces and wiped the blood off her arm. Wyatt handed him the first aid kit. Justin opened the kit, took out the Betadine, cleaned the wound and bandaged it. After he'd finished, he sat back in the seat next to Amber and put his arm around her. He pulled Amber close and kissed the top of her head. "You're all right, babe."

Levi climbed in the driver's seat. Wyatt put his head on the passenger window and closed his eyes. Kent sat next to Justin and put his hand on Justin's knee. "Everyone's all right now. Relax."

Justin glimpsed over at Kent. "I'm just glad those guys were terrible shots. They had the high ground and definitely were not soldiers."

"Just thieves," Kent said. "Lucky for us, not very good at it."

Amber cleared her throat and raised her arm. "Good enough to hit one of us."

"They had the chance to make several fatal shots." Justin scooched her closer. "They had us pinned down, trapped."

Amber flashed a wide grin. "They didn't know who they were messing with."

"Tough, aren't you?" Justin said.

"You bet," Amber said. "I better be if I ride with you guys."

Justin tilted his head. "Are you saying we're a rough group?"

Amber poked her finger in his side. "The tough get rough."

Justin flinched. "Rough when I need to." He leaned in and whispered, "But gentle when I don't. I can show you later."

"Yes." Amber lowered her voice. "A very gentle touch."

Justin whispered, "Gentle touch, huh?" He pressed his lips against her ear. "Just the way you like it."

Amber nuzzled in close. "Perfect touch."

Levi pulled into Buckley Air Force Base around four in the morning. Justin removed his arm without waking Amber. He accompanied Wyatt inside and met with their commanding officer, Lt. General Sloan. Wyatt and Justin presented their intelligence report and final assessment.

The Lt. General stood. "Report to Fort Carson in two weeks and present your assessment to the commanders of Schrivener, Cheyenne, and Peterson AFBs. I can get the word out and have all the commanders assembled by then." Wyatt and Justin saluted and prepared for departure.

Justin fueled the truck, replaced the empty cans and grabbed a few more supplies, and the group headed for the other side of Denver. They pulled into Paige's around seven in the morning. Justin glanced over at Wyatt. "This is an impressive compound." He rolled down the window and yelled at Colt, who was standing guard.

Colt walked up to Justin fully armed. "It's about time you guys got back."

Justin jumped out of the truck and hugged Colt. "You've done a lot of work around here."

"You have no idea." Colt strutted over to the passenger side and saluted Wyatt. Wyatt opened his truck, returned salute, and hugged his friend. Colt leaned inside the truck and gawked at Levi and Kent. "Hey, you two look like hell." Kent raised his middle finger and Levi followed suit.

Justin opened the truck door and introduced Amber. Amber climbed out and shook his hand. Colt glanced at Amber's arm. "Trouble on the road?"

"You could say that," Amber said. "Ran into looters the other side of Laramie."

Colt pressed his lips together and dipped his chin. "We've had our share of looters here too."

Wyatt waved his hand. "That's the reason for the compound?"

"Yes, sir. Some difficult battles at times," Colt said. "We finally got it under control."

Wyatt narrowed his eyes. "Any sightings here yet?"

Colt arched his brow. "Spaceships?"

"Flying saucers or triangular crafts?" Justin folded his arms and leaned against the truck.

Colt shook his head. "None."

"There will be soon," Wyatt said. "We need to talk about that."

"Shit, sir," Colt said. "The looters were bad enough."

"Buckle up," Wyatt said. "It could be a bumpy ride, if they don't listen."

Colt scowled. "The aliens or us?"

"Our military," Justin said. "We have a lot to tell you."

"So do we," Colt said. "A lot has happened, and not good either." He cast his eyes down at the ground. "You need to go in and talk to Paige and Nick."

Justin stared at the house. "Are they up yet?"

"Should be soon," Colt said. "Babies get you up early." He thrust his hand forward. "Go on in."

"Babies?" Wyatt wrinkled his forehead. "Whose?"

Colt pointed at the house. "Go find out."

Wyatt strolled up to the door and knocked. Paige opened the door with Grace in her arms. "Come in and meet your niece, Grace." Wyatt sat next to Paige, and she explained the loss of Logan and Renee. Wyatt stared at the floor and wiped the tears from his cheeks. Paige placed her hand on his knee. "Wyatt, we love Grace very much. I love her like my own."

Wyatt gazed up with red eyes. "Paige, what should I do?"

"Nick and I want to raise her, but you need to be a part of her life." Paige handed Grace to him. "Just love her. Grace is the best part of Logan."

Wyatt smiled at Grace. "She looks like Logan."

"She has his smile." Paige tickled Grace's feet. Grace laughed and squirmed around. Paige grasped her foot. "Grace, this is Uncle Wyatt."

Wyatt lifted her up on her feet. "Nice to meet you, little Grace." Grace grabbed his nose. Paige giggled as Wyatt tried to break free of Grace's firm grip.

Nick ambled into the room. "I see you met the little lady of the house. This charmer rules the roost around here."

"I see that. She is a charmer all right," Wyatt said. "It looks like she's in good hands."

"The best," Nick said. "There is no better mother."

Wyatt smiled at Paige. "Of that I have no doubt." He nodded at Nick. "Looks like she has a daddy who thinks she's pretty special."

"Those are my girls," Nick said. "Nothing I won't do for them."

"I see that," Wyatt said. "Let me know if I can do anything."

"Be there for our little lady," Nick said. "A kid can't have enough people who love her." Nick thrust his finger forward. "Uncle Wyatt, your family."

"Thanks for that," Wyatt said. "I will, every spare minute."

Nick pulled back the curtain and stared out the window at Justin, Kent, and Levi. "I'm glad you guys are back. A lot of changes around here."

"More coming, I'm afraid," Wyatt said. "We can talk about that later. Go out and give those guys hell will yah. They need someone else to give them shit." Wyatt grimaced. "Sorry, she's probably picking up words now."

Paige peeked at Grace. "Yes, we don't want her first words to be s. h. i. t."

Nick laughed and opened the front door. "Or a few other choice words. I'm afraid all of us have been contributing to that list." Nick shut the door and raised his arms in the air. "Look what the cat dragged in." Justin spun around and hugged Nick. Kent and Levi joined the welcome line. Justin introduced Amber to Nick. Nick cocked his head to the side and grabbed Justin's cheeks. "Good to know someone can love his ugly mug."

Amber grinned. "Someone has to do it."

Nick chuckled. "Oh, I like this girl, Justin. She'll keep you on your toes." He wrapped his arm around her shoulders. "Welcome to our little compound." Nick opened the front door. "Come on you guys and meet the new addition to the family."

After dinner, Seth and Colt joined their meeting. Wyatt and Justin shared everything they learned on their recon mission, and Nick filled Wyatt in on the events that transpired in their absence. Wyatt sipped his coffee. "Justin and I leave for Fort Carson at the end of the month, but we should return shortly afterward." After everyone went to bed, Wyatt sat on the porch alone. His heart raced and his stomach fluttered. "What happens tomorrow and why in the hell is it so important?"

Chapter Fourteen

6-17-2026

The sun's rays hit Wyatt's face from a crack in the closed curtain. He turned and glanced at the wind-up grandfather clock in the living room. "Six o'clock." Wyatt sat up, pulled back the curtain and gazed out the window at clear blue skies. He scanned around the room and spotted Logan's wooden bat in the corner. Memories of him playing baseball on warm summer days flooded his mind. His chest tightened and tears streamed down his cheek. An eerie silence awarded him the space to release emotions he'd suppressed for hours.

After several minutes of liberation, Wyatt headed to the downstairs bathroom. The patter of footsteps upstairs signaled an end to his cherished tranquility. Wyatt emptied his bladder and flushed the toilet. He washed his hands, splashed water on his face and peered in the mirror. The black rings under his red swollen eyes uncovered the story of a restless night.

He emerged from the bathroom and spied Kent and Levi sitting at the table. Nick brewed coffee, cracked eggs in the cast-iron skillet, and poured pancake batter on the griddle. Wyatt pat Kent on the back. "It's been a while since we had a real breakfast."

Kent nodded. "It's good to be home."

Wyatt scooted up a chair. "It looks like they have a full house."

Nick turned around. "We have to get you a room, Wyatt. We'll have it figured out when you get back from Fort Carson." He poured Wyatt a cup of coffee and sat it down in front of him.

"I was fine on the couch." Wyatt lifted the cup and blew on the black java.

Nick flipped a pancake. "Not good enough, Uncle Wyatt."

"Levi and I might take one of those rooms in the compound," Kent said. "I hear you have some single ladies there."

"We'll work it out later," Nick said. "Besides, those ladies can kick your butt."

Kent grew a wily smile. "Just the kind I like."

"Well now," Nick said. "We meet the real Kent."

Paige and Grace waltzed in. "Freshly bathed, fed and changed." She handed Grace to Wyatt. "She's all yours, Uncle Wyatt." She grabbed a stack of plates and silverware and placed them on the table. Nick laid a platter of eggs and a stack of pancakes down and flopped down in his seat.

Colt rushed in. "You guys need to see this." The group grabbed their guns and ran outside. Colt and Seth pointed to the sky. Wyatt peered up and witnessed once again the saucer-shaped craft, but this time over Denver instead of the Nevada desert. Triangular crafts emerged from the ship and began patrol.

Wyatt laid down his gun. "Stand down, now!"

Nick glanced over at Wyatt. "Fuck that, Wyatt."

"Put it down, Nick. I mean it!" Justin said. "I'll come over there and take it from you."

Colt and Seth studied all three of them. Wyatt glared at them. "Stand down!"

Colt and Seth dropped their automatic weapons. "Yes sir." Seth turned around and ordered all the soldiers in the compound to stand down. Colt eyeballed Kat and Kami and motioned them to drop their weapons. All the other soldiers complied.

"Nick, put it down," Wyatt said. "If you want to be alive for your girls."

"Put it down Nick, please," Paige pleaded and held tightly onto Grace.

Nick dropped his weapon. "Fuck!"

"Don't move." Wyatt said, "They're just scanning."

The triangular crafts dispersed the spheres. The spheres perused everyone in blue light. They stopped at Grace and scanned her once again, but with white light. Nick eyed Grace and slowly leaned down to grab his weapon.

"You grab it, you're dead, Nick," Wyatt said. "Stand up slowly and put your hands in front of you."

"Do it, Nick!" Justin said. "I've been there and almost died."

Nick slowly stood back up and raised his hands. One of the spheres darted back and scrutinized him once again.

Paige eyed the sphere. "Charge, you promised!"

The sphere finished scanning Grace. Paige stopped. Charge's voice echoed mind to mind. "They only examined her. It's okay."

The spheres retreated back to the triangular craft and flew off to patrol.

Wyatt exhaled, took a deep breath and stood next to Justin. "That's why Charge insisted we get back here. Nick's a wild card." He glimpsed over at Nick. "Next time, if you don't listen, I swear I will kick the shit out of you."

"I get it, Wyatt," Nick said. "There won't be a next time."

"There better not be." Justin grabbed his weapon and marched back inside the house.

Paige strolled over to Nick and hugged him. "Listen to Wyatt, Nick."

Nick picked up his gun and ambled back inside. They all sat down at the table and ate without a word. Paige refilled all the coffee cups.

Nick broke the silence. "I'm sorry, I just wasn't going to let them take Grace."

"They're not going to take Grace," Paige said. "Charge told me they wouldn't take her from the people who love her."

Nick frowned. "Who the hell is Charge?"

Paige cast her eyes down. "Shit." She bit the side of her lip. "He's one of them." She disclosed how she knew Charge. Paige laced her fingers together. "I promised not to tell anyone until June seventeenth. "

Justin interrupted and clarified their experience with Charge.

Wyatt narrowed his eyes. "Nick, Charge must want you in the picture or he wouldn't have gone to all this trouble to save you."

Nick sat back and put his hands on his head. "I'm such an ass." He pushed his chair out, stood up and walked outside. Paige handed Grace to Wyatt and followed Nick.

Nick turned to Paige. "Why didn't you tell me?"

"I couldn't tell you until today. We would have lost Grace," Paige said. "The white light you saw is a scan. They would have taken her if not for Charge."

"What the fuck, Paige?" Nick said. "You made some kind of deal with these freaks?"

"Charge saved Grace from the fire!" Paige said. "And Charge saved you and our family. I would do anything to keep both of you."

Nick glared. "Don't lie to me again, Paige."

"I never lied to you."

Nick clenched his jaw. "Omission is the same thing as a lie."

"I would lie to save you, Nick," Paige said. "And you would to save me."

"I won't ever lie to you," Nick said. "So, don't lie to me, Paige."

Paige dropped her head. "I promise, no more omissions." She glanced up and thrust her hands on her hips. "By the way, I have never lied to you." She stomped her foot. "You're not an ass, Nick. You're a stubborn ass!"

"I stand corrected." Nick cocked his head. "A stubborn ass." He put his arm around her and leaned in. "But you love this stubborn ass."

"I do," Paige whispered. He pulled her close, and the two walked back in the house.

Nick sat back down at a full table. "I'm sorry I endangered everyone. Won't happen again."

Everyone nodded, and Wyatt pointed his finger. "It better not. I can't afford to lose you."

That afternoon, Nick and the others all drove to town to meet with Deputy Winters. Paige, Kami and Amber headed out to water the garden and pull weeds. Paige placed Grace in the shade next to Amber and trudged to the shed to get the tools. She stuck her hand on the door handle and stopped. Two soldiers were discussing the blood supply at Bunker's storage. She pressed her ear to the wooden door. One was hatching a plan to use the blood as a weapon against the aliens. They planned to leave in the morning after their night shift. The handle clicked and Paige darted to the side of the shed.

After they left, she grabbed the garden tools and headed back to the garden. Paige set her tools down and stared at Kami and Amber. "Could you two watch Grace for a while? Kat and I need to check on the project at Bunker's." The girls agreed, and Paige dashed to the barracks.

"Kat, we need to go to Bunker's." She explained her relationship with Charge and that she didn't want to endanger his life or lose Grace.

The two gathered supplies from weapons storage and hatched their plan to destroy the blood supply that night. Kat seized blasting caps out of storage and wire cutters from the toolbox. She gathered lighter fluid and matches and put them in her backpack. Paige grabbed a flashlight off the shelf, a quiver full of arrows and a crossbow, and threw them in the truck. The two drove up to Bunker's house and hiked out to the storage area in the dark.

Paige examined the propane tank with her flashlight. "Good. Half full." Paige opened the storage area, spotted the hose to the refrigeration unit and unhooked the gas connection. She smelled the propane filling the storage unit. Paige closed the unit and exited the underground storage compartment. Kat and Paige moved back a safe distance, and Kat loaded an arrow in the crossbow.

They waited fifteen minutes to let the gas fill the unit, then Paige squirted lighter fluid on the end of the arrow and lit it. Kat aimed the crossbow and shot the arrow at the entrance, but nothing happened. Kat loaded another, and Paige added more lighter fluid on the arrow and tried again. Once again nothing happened.

Paige jumped up. "Kat, I have to check it. Maybe the gas automatically shut off."

Kat yelled, "It's too dangerous."

Nick, Wyatt and Justin pulled into Bunker's. Nick ran up to Kat. "Where's Paige?" Kat pointed to Paige, who was at the entrance of the unit.

Nick turned and started to run towards Paige, but Justin grabbed him. A blast rang out. Everyone dropped to the ground from the first impact. Another shock wave hit from the second explosion. Debris flew in every direction. Fire and smoke permeated the area.

Nick stood and screamed, "No, baby, no!" Justin held him back. Wyatt hopped off the top of Kat and helped hold Nick down. Suddenly, out of the smoke, two figures emerged from the chaos. Justin hit Nick on the back and pointed to the figures coming out of the flames. Black smoke billowed around them. Nick rubbed his eyes and spied a tall slender image shielding Paige with his arm around her.

"Charge!" Justin shouted. "It's Charge." Nick rushed towards Paige. Justin grabbed him. "Let them come to us. It could still be dangerous."

Justin pulled Nick back, and Wyatt snatched Kat's hand and pulled her back to the safe zone. Charge and Paige walked together. Nick studied the energy field that surrounded the two of them. As Charge and Paige reached Nick, the energy field dispersed. Nick scooped Paige in his arms and gaped at Charge.

"Hello, Nick," Charge said. "I've heard a lot about you."

A befuddled Nick stopped and gawped. "Thank you. I don't know what happened but thank you."

Paige stared at Nick. "He appeared a second before the blast and covered me with his force field. Oh my God, I was right in the center of it all and felt absolutely nothing."

"Please don't risk your life again," Charge said. "You guys are keeping me very busy."

Justin arched his sooty brow. "Earning your money, aren't you?"

"No money." Charge rubbed his bald head. "But gray hair, if I had any." He finished with a thin-lipped grin.

Paige hugged Charge. "Thank you for everything."

"You risked your life to save me." Charge leaned over. "You also saved everyone else, Paige. They viewed the blood supply as a threat if humans attempted to use it against us. It revealed a nefarious intent."

"You knew the blood was there, didn't you?" Paige held her stare.

"The scanners picked up the protein," Charge said. "The protein is of no real threat to hybrids, but for a human Rh-positive fetus it is lethal. They would not survive. It is our antibodies to the protein that are fatal for humans."

Paige scrunched her face. "So, this is all about compatibility?"

"Yes, hybrids thrive with human Rh negatives," Charge said. "Grace's children will be completely resistant to any infection or cancer. Their life span will be twice as long as a human's."

"So," Paige said. "The protein is not a threat at all to hybrids, but it is your antibodies to the protein that threaten an Rh-positive baby in utero and therefore can't survive?"

"Yes, Rh-positives are not compatible," Charge said. "Even blood transfusions to Rh-positive human adults would be fatal. We chose the most compatible humans, so both species could thrive."

"How did you know I was here?" Paige said. "Is this one of your time rifts?"

"For your first question, I watch over you and Grace," Charge said. "The answer to your second question—maybe."

"I knew it," Paige said. "You still have to explain it someday."

"Someday," Charge said. "But for now, duty calls. I have to go." Charge waved and teleported back to the alien compound.

Nick grabbed Paige's hand. "What is he talking about?"

"Time shifts or rifts. I think it is time travel of some kind," Paige said. "They know events before they happen."

Nick stared at Justin. "You guys know about this too?"

"A little," Justin said. "I asked Charge, and he said they had limited ability." Justin shrugged. "We still have a lot more to learn."

Nick glared at Paige. She wagged her finger. "Wait, a minute. Before you yell at me again, Kat and I found out about the plan to use the blood supply a few hours ago. They were going to get it and use it in the morning. We didn't have time to tell anyone. They put all of our lives at risk."

Nick shook his head. "Okay, you heard Charge. No more risking your life. You and Kat stay away from explosives."

Kat threw up her hands. "No problem."

"Paige, no more." Nick grabbed Paige and looked at her eye to eye.

"Okay," Paige said. "No more explosives, or gas bombs."

"Good." Nick drew her close and escorted Paige back to the truck.

Kat picked up her crossbow, quiver with arrows, and backpack. Wyatt noticed blasting caps inside the open backpack. He stopped Kat and pointed to the caps. "Were you going to use those?"

Kat eyed the caps. "Maybe, if the arrows didn't work."

Wyatt wrinkled his forehead. "Have you ever used detonators before?"

Kat smirked. "No." Wyatt stared at Kat until she squirmed in discomfort. Kat held his gaze. "What?"

"Do you have any idea how dangerous those are?" Wyatt said. "You could have blown you and Paige up."

"No risk, no glory." Kat strutted to the truck.

Wyatt scoffed. "No guts, no glory." He trailed behind her and stopped at the driver's door. Kat shot him a dirty look. Wyatt grabbed the door handle. "What do you think you're doing?"

Kat swiped his hand. Wyatt held firm. Kat glared at Wyatt. "I'm going to drive my truck home."

Wyatt gaped. "Is this your truck or the military's?"

"Fine." Kat folded her arms. Wyatt opened the door, and she jumped in the back seat.

Justin glanced down at the floorboard of the truck and smirked. Wyatt hopped in the driver's side. He started the truck and drove silently back to Nick's compound.

Kat hopped out with her things, slammed the truck door and whispered, "Fuck you, Wyatt." She shot him her middle finger. "Asshole."

Wyatt gawped at Justin. "She's a real spitfire, isn't she?"

Justin patted Wyatt on the back. "Just your type, Wyatt."

Wyatt laughed. "We'd probably kill each other."

"Wouldn't ever be a dull moment." Justin opened the truck door and leaned in. "I wonder who's on top?"

Wyatt shrugged his shoulders. "Who cares?"

"It has been a while, hasn't it?" Justin chortled.

Wyatt jumped out of the truck. "Too damn long."

Justin got a drink of water in the kitchen, and Wyatt flopped down beside Paige and Grace on the couch. Paige turned to Wyatt. "Where's Kat?"

Justin snickered. Wyatt spun around and glared at Justin. "She went to the bunkhouse."

Justin put down his glass. "Kat flipped Wyatt off because of his winning personality."

Paige giggled. "What did Wyatt do to deserve the finger?"

"Wyatt told her he was driving the truck home," Justin said. Paige glanced at Justin, holding in a laugh. Justin burst out laughing. "A lover's quarrel."

A puzzled Paige sat back against the couch. "When did that happen?"

"Nothing happened," Wyatt said. "It's Justin's imagination."

Paige grinned. "You interested, Wyatt?"

Wyatt furrowed his brow. "I don't know."

"If you don't know, Wyatt, who does?" Nick popped in from the kitchen. "Let Kat know when you figure it out."

"Yeah, yeah, the girl flipped me off and told me to fuck off," Wyatt said. "That's not a good start to a relationship."

"Just means there's passion." Justin sipped his water.

"Paige and I started out with a fire between us," Nick said. "We did just fine."

Paige sneered. "Nick had the fire."

"That's true, I wasn't giving up," Nick said. "You going to give up, Wyatt?"

"I don't even know if I want it." Wyatt crossed his arms.

"I wouldn't wait too long to figure it out around here. There are more soldiers coming in every day," Nick said. "You snooze, you lose."

"Better go apologize and turn on the charm." Paige snuggled a sleeping Grace.

Justin leaned back in his chair. "Dig deep for that charm."

Wyatt glanced over at Justin. "Charm's not going to do it with Kat."

"Let the uniform speak for you, Captain," Justin said. "You outrank everybody here, except Nick."

"That sure as hell won't do it," Wyatt said. "The woman is not going to let anybody tell her anything."

"Well, a wimp isn't going to do it either," Paige said. "An officer's charm might. Go give it a try."

Justin thrust out his hand. "Go!"

Wyatt stood up. "Okay, what the hell."

He marched over to the compound and rapped on her door. Kat cracked the door open. Wyatt stared. "I'm sorry for being so rude. Please accept my apology." Kat stood silent and slowly opened the door. Wyatt swallowed hard. "I treated you like one of my soldiers, and that isn't fair." Kat waved him in, and the two talked until late in the night.

Wyatt crept back to Paige's and flopped on the couch. *Kat's beautiful, smart and curvy.* He tossed and turned in his soaking wet t-shirt. Wyatt slammed his fist down on the couch. "Only one thing that cools this itch, and I probably blew that with Kat." He ripped off his sweaty t-shirt and headed for a cold shower.

At the end of the month, Wyatt and Justin headed for Fort Carson. In an hour and a half, they marched into the conference room and presented a long and extensive intelligence report to the commanders. Then Wyatt and Justin strode out.

Wyatt scrunched his face. "That meeting wasn't promising at all. Completely unresolved, with no consensus. I have very little hope of any cooperation."

Justin shrugged his shoulders. The two jumped in the truck and drove back to Nick's compound.

Justin headed to the barracks, and Wyatt strolled into Paige's and sniffed. "Something smells good." He peeked around the corner and stopped. His eyes grew wide. Kat whipped her head around and grinned.

Wyatt sat down across the table from her. "Joining us for dinner I see."

She raised her eyebrows and cocked her head to the side. "Is that all right with you?"

Wyatt flashed a sly grin. "It's all right with me."

She flipped the hair out of her green eyes and threw back a laugh. "Good, because I would anyway." He shot her a lopsided grin. She laced her fingers together, cast her eyes over at Paige and expounded on the latest compound gossip.

Wyatt's gaze wandered to her neck and breasts. He snuck in glances to escape detection. He discreetly scoped every inch of her body with his eyes. Wyatt feigned attention to their conversation and maintained eye contact when called upon. Thoughts of intimacy with Kat flooded his mind. Every time she said his name, his knees knocked and his heart raced.

Around midnight, Wyatt walked her to the bunkhouse. When they reached the door, Wyatt cast his eyes down at his feet and struggled to find the right words. Kat rolled her eyes, pulled his chin up, leaned in and kissed him. Wyatt grabbed her around the waist and pressed his lips firmly against hers. Kat wrapped her arms around his neck, stroked her fingers through his hair and lightly touched the tip of her tongue on his. Wyatt slipped his hands down to her firm bottom and drew her close to his engorged member.

Kat threw him a Cheshire grin. "Care to spend the night?" She snuggled to his ear. "I have too many roommates here, but I bet we could come up with something."

Wyatt sneered. "Give me ten minutes and meet me by the garden."

He rushed out, procured a sleeping bag and met Kat in a quiet secluded area next to the garden. Wyatt kissed her lips under the moonlight and pulled her down to the sleeping bag. She unbuttoned her shirt, unhooked her bra and dropped it on the ground. Wyatt removed his clothes and helped Kat with her pants and panties. He peered into her green eyes and slowly eyed up and down her body. Wyatt cupped her pert breasts, leaned in, and put his mouth over Kat's aroused nipple. After tantalizing her nipples to erection, he turned her over and trailed his lips down her back. He continued his pursuit and explored every inch of her body. Fire raged in his loins and could no longer be contained. Wyatt drew her closer and entered her. Kat clasped her hands on his firm buttocks and set the pace.

By the end of the night, Wyatt had satisfied every suppressed desire and uncovered the answer to Justin's question—who's on top? Under the glimmer of moonlight, and after a few rounds of pleasure, Wyatt and Kat had equally shared the leadership experience.

The next morning, Wyatt climbed out of the sleeping bag and put his pants on. He sat beside Kat with his shirt off. Kat put her hand on his back, and Wyatt flinched. She sat up and gently swiped the yellowed black and blue bruises on his upper back and shoulder. "Do those bruises still hurt? I hope we weren't too rough last night."

"No, I felt no pain last night," Wyatt said. He snatched his shirt and placed it over Kat's shoulders, covering her breasts.

"Always protecting me, aren't you?" Kat said. "You got those bruises protecting me from the explosion, didn't you?"

"Yes," Wyatt said. "I love looking at your breasts, but I sure don't want everyone else getting the view."

"Protecting my virtue?" Kat licked her lips and smiled. "Meet me at the tool shed in an hour."

Wyatt flashed a devious grin. "See you at ten." Kat slipped her shirt and pants on under the sleeping bag. After she'd finished, Wyatt rolled up the sleeping bag, slipped his shirt on and strutted inside the house and showered. Paige had left him a plate of food in the oven from breakfast.

Justin glanced at Wyatt eating breakfast. He strolled over to Nick, raised his arm and high-fived over Wyatt's accomplishment.

Nick poured a cup of coffee and sat it down in front of Wyatt. "Need a little bump after an active night, Wyatt?"

Wyatt smirked. "Maybe."

"Missed you at breakfast." Justin sat down at the table. "Better refuel and keep your strength up. I think you are going to need it with Kat."

Wyatt took another bite. "Hope so."

Nick patted Wyatt on the head. "You do me proud, son."

Justin winked at Nick. "Our work is done here."

Wyatt rinsed his plate off and checked the clock. "Shit, a quarter to ten." He brushed his teeth and dashed to the tool shed.

He stepped over several garden tools outside on the step. Wyatt sneered. "Smart girl. No interruptions." Wyatt stepped inside the tool shed and locked the door. Kat unbuttoned his shirt, removed it and laid it flat on the counter. Wyatt lifted Kat and sat her down on his shirt. He slipped Kat's shirt off and kissed her. Wyatt smelled Kat's freshly shampooed hair and kissed her neck and bare breasts. His heart raced and loins burned. Kat unfastened Wyatt's pants and released the engorged prisoner. Wyatt slipped her shorts off and drew her close to him. Kat leaned back and grabbed the edge of the counter as Wyatt's steady thrusts brought her closer to arrival. She moaned and closed her eyes until completion. Wyatt erupted and pulled her close. Kat wrapped her arms around Wyatt's neck and fingered his hair. He leaned in. "I can't get enough of you."

"I think both of us can't get enough," she said. "We're making up for lost time."

Wyatt stroked her cheek. "It'll be fun getting caught up."

After an hour, the two emerged from the shed. Kent and Levi passed by the couple and stopped. "Hold on, Wyatt." He backed up and handed Wyatt one of his two boxes. "Follow me."

Wyatt spun around with the box, kissed Kat goodbye on the cheek and tailed him.

Kent slanted his head. "Now you don't have to meet in the toolshed." He shifted his box. "Take our old room and move Kat in with you. The flush on her cheeks reveals a woman very interested."

Wyatt raised his eyebrows. "Nothing's wrong with the tool shed."

"It's okay after midnight, but too many people use it in the day," Kent said. "You can't keep setting the tools outside every time."

Wyatt lowered his chin. "You needed tools from the shed this morning?"

Kent arched his brow. "Yup, I needed the hoe, but I didn't want to interrupt."

Wyatt smiled. "Thanks for that."

"I'm happy for you, Wyatt," Kent said. "But you better move her in soon."

"Thanks, old friend," Wyatt said. "You're probably right. She's not going to put up with a roll in a toolshed for long."

"Women like Kat don't wait forever."

"I know," Wyatt said. "I'll bet Claire comes with Charley after this is over."

"Think so?"

"Charley gave Amber some space at her insistence, but he won't stay away for long," Wyatt said. "I think Claire will come with him. If not, go find her. There's chemistry there Kent."

"Maybe I will," Kent said. "I hope Levi finds someone."

"Levi lost his partner," Wyatt said. "He will when he's ready."

"Levi's a good-looking man," Kent said. "I see guys looking at him. But you're right, he will when he's ready."

Wyatt and Kent moved the bunk beds to the barracks for Kent and Levi. Afterward, Wyatt packed his things in Kent and Levi's old room. Nick confiscated a queen-size mattress and a frame from the storage room and rounded up sheets, pillows, and blankets. Nick slipped on two pillowcases and tossed them on the bed. "Perfect bed for two. When's

Kat moving in?"

"She probably will sometime," Wyatt said. "But I want to take it slow."

"Slow is good," Nick said. "But not too slow." Wyatt nodded, and the two joined Justin downstairs. Nick popped the tabs on two cans of brew and handed one to Wyatt.

"We need to acquire a few electric cars. According to Charge, after August twenty-first, gas and diesel vehicles won't work anymore. That gives us around seven weeks to get ready."

"Conversion will be easier with Charge's technology," Justin said. "I want to get my hands on several pickup trucks and use the beds and axels to convert into wagons. We can pull them with horses. Hard telling what life's going to be like after integration. Don't want to be caught with our pants down."

A few days later, Wyatt's commanding officer sent an officer to retrieve Justin and Wyatt. They traveled to Buckley AFB and met with Lt. Gen. Sloan. Sloan bent forward. "Couldn't convince Fort Carson to stand down, but I managed to talk the other commanders in the neighboring bases to avoid confrontation. Just hold tight at Nick's compound until further notice. There's nothing more anyone can do."

"Too bad, General," Wyatt said. "We're going to get ready at the compound, and I encourage you to do the same on the base. I would put all the weapons and military vehicles in one area and stay clear on August twenty-first."

The general shook his head. "We need something to distract us from all the chaos." He glanced over at his signed baseball and snatched it off the shelf. "What about baseball? It's the great American sport."

Wyatt smiled. "That is a damn good idea. Have a tournament all week with all the different military bases, play the finals, and have a championship game that night. Who knows, maybe Fort Carson will change their mind and join us."

"Maybe so," Lt. Gen. Sloan said. "Get your team ready."

Justin bobbed his head. "We'll be there."

Justin and Wyatt drove back to Nick's compound. Wyatt posted a sign-up sheet for intermural baseball, and Wyatt, Nick and Justin hit abandoned sports stores, schools and gyms to collect supplies for the team.

The next day, the group designed a practice field and began practice. Justin and the others worked on vehicle conversion during the day, and the team practiced baseball after five.

One night after baseball practice, Nick grabbed Ella, Trudy and their guitar stands, and headed back to the baseball field. He sat down on a chunk of wood and reached for the double-necked electric guitar that he named Trudy. Nick popped the glass guitar slide on his pinky finger and slid his fingers across Trudy's double neck.

"Good ole, Trudy." Nick stopped playing and closed his eyes. An image of Trudy—the lunch lady from his junior high school that the football team fondly called double-neck Trudy, flashed through his mind. Trudy was a big strong woman who'd had a thick neck like an NFL linebacker. Her deep voice made the team's spines quake with every spoken word. She wore a hair net that emphasized an unplucked unibrow that stretched across her forehead.

Every day, Trudy stood at the lunch counter and, in a low baritone voice, barked "Peas or corn?" The boys swore, if they refused the peas or corn, Trudy would reach across the counter and snap their scrawny little necks, so, day after day, the boys pointed at one of the choices, smiled politely, and said, "Please." With each proper response, Trudy stared across the counter with one raised brow, shot them a triumphant grin, and slammed the chosen veggie down on the plate.

Nick chortled and opened his eyes. "Just for you, Trudy." He strummed his guitar and made up a song on the spot called, "Peas, please."

Nick stopped, put Trudy back in the guitar stand and strolled to the shop. He grabbed his converted solar-powered generator and modified amplifiers, and positioned the solar panels directly in the sunlight right out in the middle of the baseball field. Once ready, Nick plugged in, sat down on his chunk of wood, and played renditions of songs from the seventies on Trudy. He played special cords and riffs on his double-neck guitar, and within minutes, people gathered around to witness Nick's concert.

Before Nick finished the first song, Justin, and Kent set up the drum set and hooked up the microphone for Nick. Justin snatched the drumsticks, banged out a beat and turned toward Nick. "This is the best set I've ever played on. I had a cheap set of drums in high school, but this beauty is so much better."

Kellan grabbed the Gibson electric, Colt retrieved the bass and acoustic guitars from Nick's closet, and they hauled them down to the field.

Kellan spun around to Nick. "Looks like all those sleepless nights Colt and I spent sharing cords and riffs and learning those older songs of yours just might pay off, old man."

After everyone had finished setting up, Kent pulled out his harmonica, Levi his flute, and Seth his banjo, and the seven impressed their gathering audience to several songs from the 70s, 80s, 90s, 2000s and a few of the group's current familiar favorites.

The six sat in the field on chunks of firewood and gave the people a concert until the last ray of sunlight shut it down. Paige kissed Nick goodnight and took a sleeping Grace back to the house. Kent built a fire in Levi's outdoor fireplace, and a small group of leftovers from the concert moved around the warmth and light of the fire. After Nick, Colt and Justin had put away their drums and electric instruments, they gathered around the fire with the acoustic guitars, Justin's drumsticks, a plastic bucket, Kent's harmonica and Levi's flute. Seth plucked the banjo, and Kat joined Nick with vocals on the songs she knew. Levi broke open a bottle of Grey Goose and passed it around to the remaining stragglers. Around two in the morning, Kent snuffed out the last ember and tossed out two empty bottles of Grey Goose.

The next morning, Nick's band woke up with hangovers and throbbing headaches. An unsympathetic Paige threw back the curtains and revealed the bright sunlight. "Wake up sunshine, your fans await your presence." Paige put Grace on the bed beside Nick. Grace climbed on top of his back.

Nick opened one eye. "I beg you, Paige, please put me out of my misery."

"Hey, rock star," Paige said. "You play, you pay."

"Shit," Nick said. "No mercy here."

"None."

Nick scowled. "You're a hard woman."

Paige giggled. "Hard-hearted woman." She pulled the blankets off Nick. "Poor baby." He slowly turned over and covered his eyes. Paige picked up Grace and tickled Nick's bare feet. He moaned and groaned. She hummed and strutted to the door. "Your adoring fans await, rock star."

He hoisted the covers over his head. "Fuck my fans."

Nick made his way downstairs around noon and glanced over on the couch. He blinked twice. "Declan?"

"Hey, old man," Declan said. "Looks like you need the hair of the dog."

Nick wrinkled his brow. "You missed a hell of a concert last night."

"Paige told me about it," Declan said. "Too old to hang one on, old man?"

"Yeah, no hair of the dog for me," Nick said. "You're out of luck. The party's over."

"Story of my life." Declan stood up and hugged Nick.

"What I wouldn't give for a strong cup of coffee," Nick said. "I ran out last month." He turned, eyeballed the kitchen and sniffed the air. The smell of freshly perked coffee hit him. Nick stared at Paige.

She held up her coffee cup and pointed to Declan's cup on the coffee table. "Saved some for a special occasion."

Nick walked over to the coffee pot, grabbed the package of course ground coffee off the shelf and kissed it. Then he poured a cup of coffee, closed his eyes, and drew in the aroma. He opened his eyes, put his hands together in prayer, pointed to Paige, then up in the air, and said, "God I love that woman."

Nick took his cup of coffee and sat down at the table. Declan joined him. After they finished their first cup, Nick stared at Declan. "What brings you back this way?"

"I made it back to Portland, only to find out that my brother and mother disappeared the day of the sighting," Declan said. "A few months later, Dad was killed in a home burglary and our house was destroyed. My friends from Denver University went on to Seattle, so I stayed with old friends from Portland until a group of looters robbed them. Only two of us made it out alive. We decided to come to Colorado." Declan pointed to Nick. "There are good people in Colorado."

"Damn straight," Nick said. "Even if we're implants."

Paige kissed Grace on her chubby cheeks. "Some of us aren't, huh, sweet girl?"

Declan cast his eyes down. "I lost my friend on the way back to Colorado on a gas robbery when we stopped to siphon gas. I think the man snuck up behind my friend and slit his throat before he had a chance to draw his weapon." Declan lifted his chin. "They killed him for a fucking revolver and two gas cans." He shook his head. "We always went out one at a time to collect gas, leaving one of us to guard the truck. I found my friend dead in a pile of his own blood when he didn't return. I searched everywhere for the bastard who murdered him but couldn't find a trace."

Declan wiped his cheek. "After my friend died, I traveled until my truck broke down on the Wyoming-Idaho border." He swallowed hard and cleared his throat. "Fortunately, I had my old Kawasaki trail bike and an extra battery in the back of the truck." He stared straight at Nick. "Nick, I'm so glad I paid attention to your install while I was here at Logan's. Thank God you gave me weapons training."

Nick patted Declan on the shoulder. "Declan, those were good choices in very difficult times." He poured the two another cup of coffee. "It sounds like you've been to hell and back."

"I wouldn't have survived any of this if you hadn't taught me."

"Welcome home Declan." Nick raised his cup. "Let's eat breakfast."

Declan smirked. "It's lunchtime."

"Well, let's have lunch then." Nick shot him a wide smile. "Hey, do you play baseball?"

"I do," Declan said. "I hear you need someone."

"Did you now?" Nick glimpsed over at Paige and raised his brow. "Yes, I do." He grabbed the coffee pot and emptied it. "You interested?"

"Yeah," Declan said. "Get ready to take home the trophy."

"I like the way you think." Nick flinched in pain from another stark reminder of overindulgence the night before. He threw back his last sip of coffee and made sandwiches for the three of them using Paige's freshly baked bread from the oven. After lunch, Nick popped an aspirin, and the three spent the rest of the afternoon sharing war stories.

A few weeks later, Nick gathered his band mates on the field after baseball practice. "We are invited to play after the tournament from nine to midnight. Two other bands from the surrounding Air Force Bases have also agreed to play." They nodded. He held up a power cube. "Thanks to Charge, we can continue practice after dark. This is a power cube. I've modified the generators using one of these trusty cubes so we can use it when the sun goes down. With enough cubed generators we can power lights, electrical equipment and amplifiers for all the bands during the concert after the game." Nick arched both brows. "We're set. Let's practice."

Kat practiced with Nick on lead vocals. After they finished the first set, she turned toward Nick. "A fiddle or violin would sound good with the last number."

Nick bobbed. "I wish we had someone."

"I play," Kat said. "I lost mine in a robbery a few years ago."

Nick's eyes sparkled. He raised his hands in the air. "Kat, I found a Stradivarius violin in an abandoned house on one of our searches."

"Stradivarius!" Kat screeched. "They're very rare."

"I know it is," Nick said. "My dad always wanted one."

"Can I play it?" Kat jumped up and crouched down. "I'd love to play it." She rubbed her hands together. "I promise to be careful."

Nick grinned like a Cheshire cat. "I want you to have it."

Kat jumped up and wrapped her arms around him. Nick grasped her shoulders and laughed. "It's in my bedroom closet."

Kat raced to the house, and Paige lifted it off the top shelf and handed it to her. Kat squealed and dashed back to practice, gently removed the Stradivarius out of its leather case and stroked the handcrafted instrument. She tuned it and directed the bow to reveal its clear silky sound. The men gawked at each other. She stopped. "What?"

The men shrugged their shoulders and resumed practice. After they finished rehearsal, Nick dragged Kat aside. "Aren't you full of surprises? You play beautifully."

"It feels good to play again," Kat said. "It's been too long."

"Maybe you should do a solo during the concert," Nick said. Kat cast her eyes down and shook her head.

"Kat, two-thirds of the soldiers are men," Nick said. "They would love to see a girl on the stage."

"A duet?" Kat sneered. "A sexy song together?"

Nick raised his eyebrows. "That would raise some temperatures." He stared straight at her. "Raise Wyatt's temperature. He would kill both of us. Not to mention Paige. I would lose a few body parts."

"I know, there is no way I would prance around half-naked, acting sexy, and sing on stage anyway," Kat said. "What did you have in mind?"

"Something upbeat with your fiddle?"

Kat scrunched up her nose. "You can't call a Stradivarius a fiddle." She tucked her hair behind her ear and bit the side of her lip. "I know several songs, but I prefer to do a duet so I don't have to sing alone."

Kat listed several songs she knew, and Nick raised his finger on the sixth one. "That's the one. I can play double-neck Trudy on that one and sing backup." He grew a wily grin. "I've got something else too, but it will mean you and Amber running around on the stage. Not half-naked, but more with an athletic flavor. We'll have you two guide the audience clapping and shouting."

"Yeah," Kat said. "Sounds fun. Amber might do it." The two practiced Kat's duet until she felt comfortable with their own rendition.

The next morning over coffee with Nick, Wyatt shot Nick a nod. "Kat loved the violin. Thank you for such a generous gift."

Nick dipped his chin. "She's welcome. It deserves to be played by someone who really loves such a fine instrument." He slapped his hands together. "Wyatt, wanna play chess?"

Wyatt stood and waved him on. Nick set up the chess set on the front porch and clasped his hands on the arm of his chair. He thrust his head forward and held his stare. "About time you took me on. I was beginning to think you too scared." He narrowed his eyes. "Let's find out who should be crowned chess master."

Wyatt scooted up in his chair, squinted at Nick and sneered. "You're going down, son."

Nick shot back a grin. "Bring it on." An hour and a half later, Nick smirked and slid his last piece. "Checkmate."

Wyatt exhaled. "Why is it that you look like the cat that just pounced on the mouse he's been toying with for the last hour?"

Nick cracked a sly grin. "Whatever do you mean?"

Wyatt flopped back in the chair. "Nick, you and I both know you could have pinned me down several moves ago."

"What's the fun in that?"

Wyatt gaped at him. "Okay, smart ass. It's a good thing I like you or I'd kick your ass."

"You could do it too."

"Probably not." Wyatt grinned. "But I'd give it a hell of a try." He pulled Nick's shirt sleeve up and touched his snow leopard tattoo. "I knew a one-eyed lieutenant named Vance who had one of those."

Nick flashed a devious grin. "Did you now?"

"Vance disappeared after the sighting," Wyatt said. "He was in Special Forces in the military and had the same tattoo. One of the members of his team was an engineer they called Tinman. Vance retired after he lost an eye on one of his missions. His helicopter crashed just over the Iraqi border on a rescue mission. They lost five members of their team in the crash and four from the helicopter crew. Two of the members from Special Forces escaped with injuries. One was Vance with an eye, and the other was Tinman with a broken leg." Wyatt stared straight at

Nick. "Sound familiar, Tinman?"

Nick unbuttoned the top buttons of his shirt and showed him his Tinman tattoo. "Too familiar."

Wyatt narrowed his eyes and pointed his finger at Nick. "I thought so."

"After the crash, we both recovered at the VA and retired from the military." Nick scowled. "I lost my best friend, Dekker, in the helicopter crash. Dekker was one of the nine that died."

"Same Dekker you played guitar within the service?" Wyatt slanted his head. "He teach you the tunes you play frequently?"

"Yup, the one and only," Nick said. "He gave me the nickname Tinman after one of the songs."

Wyatt nodded. "What about your early military service?

"I started off with the Corp of Engineers and ended up in tactical operations," Nick said. "Served two tours in Special Forces. After Special Forces, I was lost for a while. Mourning Dekker, I suffered survivor's guilt. I felt anxious and restless, and eventually missed the adrenaline rush of active duty." He clenched his jaw. "You know as well as I do, Wyatt, that you never feel more alive than when you're in the heat of a mission. It's addicting." His eyes glazed over. "A mission gives you purpose, and I missed that purpose after I left the military." Nick cleared his throat. "You also know that you never feel more connected than when you are with your brothers-in-arms. I missed the camaraderie."

Wyatt pressed his lips together and concurred. Nick shuffled in his chair. "Transition back into the ordinary world is dicey. I should've taken more time to decompress. I didn't take enough time to grieve the loss of Dekker. It nearly destroyed me." Nick folded his arms. "I drank and fucked too much for a while. I banged any woman with a pulse and slammed too many shooters in the local bar. All I wanted to do was numb the pain." Nick leaned back in his chair. "All that changed one day when my business partner dragged me out of the bar drunk one night, sat me down, and gave me an ultimatum. My partner told me to turn all my pain into power and focus on what's important or end our partnership." Nick drew in a long slow breath. "I chose the first one and went into group counseling at the VA. It was the best thing I ever did. In the group, I met a man who gave me the advice that changed my life. He said it isn't just what you do on the battlefield that's important. It's what you do with it once you get home. This wise man suggested I take time to heal my emotional wounds and find a new mission—a mission that helped me instead of hurting me. After he'd imparted those sage words, I got the help I needed, and it changed my life. And after that help, I poured everything I had into our engineering company, and it resulted in a very successful business."

Nick rubbed his chin. "My business partner married a lady from Paris and moved there, so we sold our business in New York. Made a healthy profit too." His eyes sparkled, and he grew a wide smile. "That's when Paige and Kent walked into my life, and right at the perfect time. It was just a few months after the sale of my business. I was looking for a change. Wyatt, you know the rest."

Wyatt stared straight at Nick. "How much profit?"

Nick raised his brow and flashed a crooked grin. "A few million. All gone after the sighting and the collapse of the banks."

Wyatt shook his head. "A millionaire? No shit!"

Nick scoffed. "Was another lifetime."

Wyatt nodded. "Did you really hit *anything* that was fuckable?"

"At my low point and drunk enough I'd hit it. Teeth, no teeth, old, tall, short, large or small, married, it didn't matter." Nick snickered. "Through the lens of Kentucky bourbon at closing time, you're in love with all the ladies."

"Old and no teeth." Wyatt chuckled. "That's low, bro."

"I did." Nick chortled and held his stomach. "It's amazing what a round of drinks and twenty bucks can buy. At least a blow job."

"And you had to pay." Wyatt busted out with a belly laugh and took a deep breath to recover. "I feel bad laughing at your misery Nick, but you're one funny S.O.B." The two cackled for a while, finished their morning coffee, and scoped out over their expanding compound.

Wyatt waved his hand over the compound. "We need to round up more horses as another means of travel for our growing community."

Nick agreed, so that afternoon, Nick, Wyatt, Kellan, German Shepherd Bo and Declan took off to find horses and feed. Being a native of the area, Kellan drove and led the mission on the search for abandoned ranches. By the end of the day, the four men had discovered several abandoned barns full of hay, numerous stray horses and a few cattle that survived the winter.

Kellan pulled in and stopped at the last ranch at the end of the road— his family had known their family for many years. Wyatt, Bo and Nick hopped out of the truck and checked the seemingly abandoned house. Kellan and Declan checked the barn and the surrounding vicinity. Wyatt knocked on the door, but there was no answer. He opened the door, and the two were instantly hit with the stench of filth. Wyatt glanced at Nick. "Smells like you after your workout."

Nick shot Wyatt a shrewd grin. "Smells like the troops after a ten-day mission, huddled in a hut or on the chopper ride headed home."

Wyatt sniggered and scanned the room. "Someone's here. Either squatter or survivors." The two took out their 45s, separated, and searched the house room by room.

Nick slipped into one of the bedrooms upstairs and yelled, "Wyatt!"

Wyatt rushed upstairs. Nick pointed to the toys displayed on the floor. "We got some young ones here somewhere."

They searched every closet. After an intense search of the house, they came up empty. The two men checked the backyard. Nick pointed. "Port-a-potty's full." He spotted an unsanitary fecal dumping site a few yards from the house. They discovered freshly opened cans of fruit in the garbage. Nick rifled around and uncovered a cache of canned food and a four-wheeler hidden just off the property.

Kellan and Declan finished their search of the grounds and went into the barn. Declan shut the barn door. Strands of hay fell from the loft. He hit Kellan's arm and pointed to the falling strands and hay dust.

Kellan peered up at the loft. "Jake, Lacy are you in here?" Only silence answered back. Kellan yelled, "It's Kellan from down the road."

Thirteen-year-old Jake popped his head up out of the hay. "Kellan?" A soft voice squeaked from the corner. Declan tip-toed over and lifted up a wooden storage bin. Three small children huddled inside.

Declan smiled at the children. "Hi guys."

The kids peeked up at Declan. A little girl said, "Is Kellan here?"

Declan grinned. "He sure is." He stretched out his arms, and the four-year-old girl stood up. Declan grabbed her out of the dirty box and sit her on the floor. Lacy ran over to Kellan and jumped in his arms. Declan lifted eight-year-old twins, Carson and Carlin, out of the bin.

Kellan whispered, "Who might you two gentlemen be?"

Jake bellowed, "They're our cousins who live on the other side of the hill."

Kellan motioned for Jake to come down from the loft. "Where's your mom and dad?"

Jake climbed down from the loft and stood stoic in front of Kellan. "Gone."

Kellan pointed to the twins. "Where's your parents?"

The twins lowered their heads. "Same. Disappeared a year after the sighting."

"Kids, come with me," Kellan said. "We're going to find Nick and Wyatt. They're very good friends of mine." The six strolled up to Wyatt and Nick with the horses in the pasture.

Nick smiled. "Mystery solved."

Jake smiled back. "I did my best to take care of them."

Nick looked Jake in the eye. "You did a hell of a job son."

Jake grinned proudly. "Thanks."

"You go back to the house and pack some clothes for the kids for the night," Nick said. "We'll come back tomorrow to collect the rest of your things. You're going to the compound to live with Kellan and Kami." Nick winked at Jake. "Our little Grace would be very happy to have someone like Lacy to play with." The wrinkles in Jake's forehead disappeared, and a smile erupted.

Kellan swiped Jake on the arm. "Cool, dude. Let's go."

Kellan and Jake ran to the house, gathered up a few clothes for everyone, and picked up Lacy's favorite stuffed animal and her blanket. The kids climbed in the back of the truck with Kellan, Declan and Bo. Bo eased up to Jake and laid his head in his lap. Jake grew a slanted grin and patted him on the head. Bo nuzzled in for a second helping.

Nick pulled into the compound, rounded up the kids and introduced them to Paige and Grace. Paige eyeballed the dirty orphans, shifted Grace onto one hip, scooped up Lacy on the other and packed them upstairs. She ran a tub of water and stuck Lacy and Grace in the tub.

After their bath, she picked through the clothes Jake had packed in her backpack and huffed. "Not one clean stitch of clothing." Paige grabbed the smallest t-shirt she owned and put it on Lacy. "This is your new long nighty." Paige brought Grace and Lacy downstairs and handed them to Kellan and Nick. Then she turned toward the twin boys and crooked her finger. "You two, come with me."

They headed for the bathtub. Paige filled the tub and handed them soap. "Scrub." She shut the bathroom door and marched back downstairs. "Kellan, you oversee the twins' bath." She pointed to Jake. "You're next." Jake nodded between bites of his sandwich.

Kami laughed. "You better do a good job, Jake. Wash behind your ears or she'll send you right back up there." Kami glanced over at Paige and giggled. She squeezed Lacy on her lap and eyed Paige. "We got their beds ready at the bunkhouse."

Paige nodded, gathered up all their filthy clothes and put them in the wash. Kami handed Lacy to Declan, ran over to the bunkhouse and gathered t-shirts, socks and boxers from Levi's closet for the boys—Levi was the smallest man on the compound and was the closest fit. Kami returned with the goods.

The boys dressed for bed. Kellan and Kami escorted the kids to their sections and assigned them bunk beds. Kami tucked Lacy in her bed on the women's wing, handed Lacy her stuffed animal and dirty blanket and lay down beside her in case she woke up frightened. Kellan stayed with the boys until they fell asleep. Afterward, he returned to his wing on the other side.

The next day, Nick, and Kellan took Jake back to his house, and they collected the items Jake wanted to keep. Nick locked up the house, loaded Jake's four-wheeler and hauled everything back to the compound.

Over the next two weeks, Nick, and the others resumed their previous mission and rounded up all the horses and cattle they could find. They loaded flatbeds and horse trailers, and hauled stray horses, cows and hay to Nick's compound. The rest of the group doubled their existing barbwire fences and began building another barn for the horses and milk cows. They built a stockyard for the cattle and made makeshift buildings to store the collected hay for the winter.

The week before the tournament, Nick held a final practice for the concert. Amber handed Nick a slip of paper. "Can we add this old song to the list? It's for Justin's birthday. I was afraid we wouldn't have time to put it together before the tournament."

Nick lifted his chin. "Amber, this is a really sweet gift for him."

Amber smiled. "I think he will like it."

Nick put his arm around her shoulders. "If he doesn't, I'll kick his ass."

Amber wrapped her arms around Nick's waist and hugged him. "You won't have to because I will."

Nick laughed. "I believe you would, Amber."

Chapter Fifteen

Integration

On August 21, Wyatt, Nick and Justin stored the last of the weapons in a storage unit on the outskirts of the compound. They emptied their weapons cache stored in the basement of the house and parked all the military vehicles in the same location. After they'd finished, they held their last baseball practice before the tournament. They finished around nine in the evening and Coach Nick curfewed everyone to an early bedtime—the tournament started at eight in the morning.

At sunrise, they loaded up all the horse-drawn flatbeds and converted truck beds and traveled eight miles to attend the finals at the baseball tournament.

The finals started at eight sharp. Fort Carson had refused to participate in the tournament, but all the other bases required mandatory attendance at the event. Nick's Compound played the winning squad from Air Force Academy. Nick's team was eliminated, thrusting Air Force Academy to play in the final. Peterson Air Force Base played Cheyenne Mountain. The game ended with Peterson qualifying for the championship final.

At two in the afternoon, Air Force Academy and Peterson played for the championship. An hour into the game, spaceships flew overhead. The players stopped. All eyes focused on the spaceship's descent on the city of Denver. Suddenly, a flash of red-orange light in the distance signaled an invader's success. Fifteen minutes later, dead silence surrounded the stadium. The invasion ended, and spaceships departed.

The commanding officer stood in the awkward stillness and yelled, "Play ball." The two teams resumed.

The game ended around six, with a final championship trophy going to Air Force Academy. They held up a gold, spray-painted wooden bat with 2026 Tournament Champs carved on the side of it. Academy's team captain lifted the golden bat over his head in one hand and a signed baseball in the other hand—the four teams from the finals had previously signed the bat and ball upon arrival. All the tournament players cheered, stripped off their t-shirts, and pelleted the captain with their tees and leftover practice balls. After the presentation of the trophy, everyone filed out of the stadium and headed to the picnic area for a barbeque.

The bands set up their equipment for the concert in the center of the field on four flatbed wagons that served as a stage, then joined the barbeque. Around nine o'clock, the troops filed back into the stadium for the concert. Lt. General Sloan introduced the first band from the Air Force Academy. Several of the cadets played their band instruments. A small group of cadets stayed behind and did a bit of rap and hip hop to change things up. The second group from Cheyenne Mt. filed in and focused on country music and blues. Nick's Compound played last with a mixture of rock and country. They played songs from the 70s, 80s, 90s, and 2000s. Nick started with a song from the 70s, and by the third number, Amber and Kat had the audience on their feet. Most of the troops piled down on the field, singing along with the band. A sea of power fists and chants vibrated the stadium in unison.

Kat stood beside Nick with her violin, and the two performed a couple of duets together to slow things down. After their duets, Kellan, Seth and Colt played guitar—Kellan and Seth were on electric, and Colt played bass. Justin sat down at the drums again, and Amber joined him with her triangle. Kat grabbed her violin, and Kent played his harmonica and sat at the keyboards. Levi took his flute and stood at the mic to play and help with vocals. Once again, the group delivered a high-energy punch from one of their song selections.

For their final song, Nick removed his sweaty t-shirt, wiped off his face, and threw it down on the ground. He grabbed Trudy, his double-neck guitar, and grabbed the mic. "Ready to jump into the fire?" The crowd screamed. Nick held the mic close. "Here we go!"

Nick and Colt played their intro. Justin and the band joined in. The troops raised their hands in the air, jumped up and down to the beat, and clapped on command with Amber and Kat. Kellan and Seth stayed in sync with their electric guitars and assisted Nick on Trudy. Kent and Levi played and sang backup vocals with Colt on bass and Nick's impressive riffs on Trudy. The audience applauded for several minutes and demanded an encore. A spent Justin swiped the sweat from his forehead and cheeks, eyed Nick, and twirled his sticks.

After a rowdy standing ovation, Nick caught his breath and seized the mic. "I have a parting wish for all the gents and ladies here tonight." The stadium grew dead silent. Nick pointed his finger at the crowd and waved it around. "And also… for those beyond this arena."

The troops erupted. Nick lowered his mic and paced back and forth until they quieted down. He raised one hand in the air and lifted the mic to his lips. "And with all of you in mind, I'll leave you with this parting wish…May you find someone special." He paused a few seconds, drew the mic closer, leaned down towards the audience with his hand out, and in a slow deep voice said, "And…"

With the audience in the palm of his hand, Nick cocked his head to the side, and quickly shouted, "Give them every inch." Then he briefly paused for effect and said, "Every fuckin *inch!*" The crowd roared, raised their power fists back in the air and jumped up and down.

Nick stood up and started the intro to the song. The band slowly joined in. In the middle, Nick added a few riffs on Trudy. Justin did an impressive drum solo to match Nick's flair.

Towards the end of the song, Nick slowed things down, put his guitar slide back on his little finger, strummed on Trudy, and gazed out over the masses. "Yeah, find someone special and give them every inch of your—"

Nick stopped abruptly and cupped his ear for a response. He repeated his phrase and all at once the entire audience hollered, "Love," in unison. Nick nodded and played a quick riff on Trudy with the band. He grabbed his mic, fell to his knees and finished. "Love." The rest of the band resumed playing and finished with their final cords for a dramatic ending.

Wyatt and the Lt. General hid their grin and shook their lowered heads. The Lt. General cracked a smile, leaned over to Wyatt, and whispered, "It was a nice wish."

Wyatt nodded. "Only Nick would have the balls to say that in front of five commanders."

"Not active duty," the Lt. General said. "He's untouchable, can do and say whatever he pleases."

Wyatt stared straight at the Lt. General. "It wouldn't make a damn bit of difference, active duty or not."

Nick let the audience applaud. After about thirty seconds, he slowly raised his head, jumped up and waved. "Good night, everybody." Then he and the other band members left the stage.

It wasn't long before the audience wanted another encore. They screamed, "One more," and simultaneously jumped up and down in sync until the whole stadium thundered and roared.

After a few minutes, Nick gawked at his band mates. "They're getting too rowdy." The crowd's chants and stomps escalated into a contest on who was the loudest between sections. He stared at Justin. "They're wound up tight. Better go in and unwind them for the general."

Justin bowed his head. "You need us?"

Nick shook his head. "No, I think Amber, Kat and I got this." Nick bit his lip. "Give me a few minutes and send Amber and Kat out with her violin. Tell her we'll breakout the present early."

Justin cocked his head, mystified, furrowed his brow, and mumbled, "Will do."

Nick stopped and whispered in Amber's ear. She smiled and nodded. Nick strolled back out on stage and grabbed Trudy. He walked around, strummed his electric guitar, and increased his intensity and speed to get their attention.

Nick sauntered to one side of the stage, blasted a riff and promenaded back to the mic. "I'm back." The crowd slowly stopped their chant, clapped, and howled. Nick ambled to the other side of the stage, slammed more hard rock and hit the mic. "Stay with me." Nick moved around the stage and slowed his tempo to calm them down. After he held their full attention, he transitioned into his smooth intro for their final number.

Nick floated across the stage with his weeping guitar. He leaned into the mic. "There is nothing like flying." He paused, slowly cracked a grin and blurted, "Especially the latest design." He motioned for Kat and Amber to come out. Nick pressed his lips close to the mic and in his impish baritone voice said, "Airman love to fly. Isn't that right, earthbound rebels?" The crowd concurred. He pointed to the sky. "You're more at home twirling and rolling in the clouds in your hunk of metal and leaving your trail behind." The crowd responded again. Nick strummed Trudy and threw his hand in the air. "Right?" The crowd roared with a sea of fists up in the air.

Amber stood beside Nick with her mic. Kat grabbed her violin, walked out on the stage, snatched her mic stand, and put it on the other side of Nick. Kat peered at Nick, still strumming, pointed to her mic, and mouthed that she was going to speak. Nick nodded, so she put her lips up to her mic. "This goes out to all you renegades." The airmen cheered and whistled.

Kat pressed her lips up to the mic, turned around and glimpsed over at Justin. "I want to wish an early Happy Birthday to Airman Justin Jones. We love you."

Justin waved and nodded. Kat put her violin up to her chin and joined Nick with the soft sweet sound of her Stradivarius. She tenderly sang backup with Amber, and together they echoed the words, "My earthbound rebel." The three captured their audience with their haunting rendition and melodic riffs.

When they finished, Nick pointed to Kat and Amber and bowed. "Ladies and gentlemen, the beautiful Kat Levine and Amber Howard." The group cheered and clapped. Kat and Amber waved and left the stage. They went backstage, walked over to Justin, hugged him, and whispered, "Happy early birthday."

Justin smiled. "Did you guys plan that?"

Kat grinned. "We were supposed to sing it for you on your birthday next week, but obviously there was a quick change of plans. It fit well here tonight."

"Sure did," Justin said. "Thanks, it's quite a gift." He winked at Kat and glanced over at Amber. "I'll give Amber a proper thanks tonight."

Kat giggled. "I'm sure you will."

Nick pointed to Lt. General Sloan just off stage and raised the mic. "The general has a few words before we all leave tonight." He waved to the audience. "Thank you all, and goodnight everyone." Nick turned the stage over to Lt. General Sloan and exited off stage and stood beside Wyatt.

Wyatt snickered. "Man, you're fearless and one ballsy bastard."

Nick turned towards Wyatt with his back to everyone and grabbed his crotch. "Big balls, but no fuckin' brains."

"You're too smart for your own good, smart ass." Wyatt sneered. "Besides, that was a nice save at the end."

Nick grinned back. "Thank Kat."

"I sure will." Wyatt shot him a wide smile. "She has a thing for airmen."

Nick patted Wyatt on the back. "Only for one airman I know."

Wyatt puffed up his shoulders. "Lucky me."

Nick narrowed his eyes. "Lucky tonight too, I bet."

The general thanked everyone and issued his instructions to the troops. Afterward, Nick joined his bandmates. He grabbed a bottle of water out of the cooler, took a long drink and poured the rest over his head. Paige walked over and hugged him. She brushed the wet hair out of his eyes and off his forehead. "Quite the wish tonight."

Nick raised his brow and gave Paige his crooked smile. "What? Just spreading a little hope and love."

"Uh huh," Paige said. "Nick style, no filter."

Nick wrapped his arms around Paige, kissed her and smacked her on the butt. "Only way I know is totally unfiltered."

Paige smiled. "The audience got a bit out of control for a minute, but that was a great save with Kat and Amber."

"All in a day's work, babe." He flashed her a cunning grin. "Besides, pretty girls will get and keep a man's attention every time."

Paige nodded. "No doubt."

Nick pulled Paige close. "Pretty lady, you definitely keep this man's attention."

"Good to know," Paige said. "I intend on keeping it that way."

Nick and the others packed up and loaded their equipment back onto their converted flatbed wagons. They hitched and saddled their horses and rode home by moonlight.

Paige and Jake walked in the house and spotted Kami reading in the candlelight, with the twin boys sleeping soundly on the floor in sleeping bags. Grace and Lacy slumbered upstairs, Grace in her crib and Lacy on Paige's bed. Kami grabbed Lacy and the twins and headed for the bunkhouse. Paige slipped into her comfy bed.

Nick, Justin and Wyatt checked the weapons storage unit off site. They discovered military-style arms gone. The hunting rifles, .22 and .45 pistols, and bows with arrows remained untouched. They rushed out to the yard and encountered no military trucks. The three attempted to start all the other gas-powered engines, but no gas and diesel engines worked. Everything else on the compound was left unharmed.

Lt. General Sloan combed the parking area and discovered all their military trucks and weapons were gone—the general had previously designated a special area to park the military trucks off site before the tournament and ordered the troops to store all their weapons in those trucks by noon.

After the concert, the Lt. General and the other commanders loaded up their wagons and rode back to their temporary camp. The general and commanders feared all the bases may be completely destroyed during the invasion, so they had their troops set up tents, supplies and sanitation areas for a temporary camp as a precaution. After the tournament, the general sent two squads on horseback to the base to assist with the inspection of the base.

The following day, the two squads returned and reported that all weapons, aircraft, and military vehicles were missing, but structures were still intact. Lt. General Sloan made it back to Buckley AFB with the other commanders. The five commanders planned to disband their units and attempt to integrate their pilots with the hybrids. They agreed to combine all the bases into one air force, located at Buckley, with the possibility of an integration to learn advanced alien aeronautical technology, and turn the base into another Air Force Academy.

The next day, Charge appeared in Paige's living room. Justin glanced up and Wyatt pointed his finger at Charge. Nick set down his coffee cup and turned around.

Wyatt tapped his cup. "Care for a cup?" Charge sat down and Wyatt poured him a cup.

Charge sipped his brew. "I want to compliment you and the general on the creative invention of the games during implementation."

Wyatt lowered his chin. "How'd the other's fair?"

Charge removed a coin-sized disc from his uniform, placed it in the middle of the table and displayed a hologram that replayed the resistance at Fort Carson. "Two-thirds of the soldiers were evaporated. The soldiers that disobeyed orders and laid their weapons down as soon as the crafts arrived survived." The four viewed weapons and military vehicles disappear into thin air at Fort Carson. Then, after viewing the damage at the US base, Charge projected the extermination of other militaries around the world.

Wyatt stared at Charge. "Comply or gone."

"Yes. They simply refused to comply." Charge laced his long fingers together. "Now it's time for stage two: integration." Charge ended the hologram, replaced the disc and peered over at Justin. "Are you ready to meet the aliens or Nustu?"

Justin glanced over at Wyatt, and they both nodded. "Yes."

Charge stood, pushed in his chair and backed up. "Justin, Nick and Wyatt, please stand next to me." They glanced at each other and fell in line. Charge touched a metal circle on his suit, and the four teleported aboard the deck of Charge's orbiting ship. Justin gazed out the window on the deck of the ship. Floating robotic arms drilled and assembled flexible metal onto the frame of a spacecraft.

Charge pointed to the spaceship under construction. "This is our new starship. We designed the ship for space exploration." Charge turned to Justin. "Are you interested in exploring the next frontier? Discover different worlds and different suns?"

Justin bobbed his head. "Of course."

Charge smiled. "Are you interested in going with us on our starship, Solstice? She has the latest technology. No more storage ships and motherships. Solstice can generate her own wormholes to jump across the galaxy and even jump galaxies. We can travel the stars without the need for an escort. We are independent, self-sufficient, and unbound. No longer limited by borders or boundaries."

Charge waved his hand, and a hologram appeared. "Solstice is the first in a new fleet of starships." He flicked his finger and enlarged the images. "Solstice II and III will be in production in 2028 and 2030. The crew will be made of hybrids and humans from every continent." Charge displayed a distant solar system. "Solstice II and III will depart for exploration in late 2032 and explore new territory in search of habitable planets."

Justin stared at a hologram of Solstice. Images of his first day as an airman floated across his mind. A memory of sitting in the cockpit of his jet and dreaming of traveling among the stars flashed in front of him. "I dreamed of this so many times." He studied the hologram. "Is this real? Can it travel among the stars?" He dipped down close. "She's a beautiful starship and unbound?"

Justin turned to Charge. "Of course, when do we leave?"

Charge crooked his thin lips. "Soon. We leave 9-21-26." He dismissed his hologram and thrust his hand out. "I'd like you to meet our chief engineer, Oriess, and my first officer Enay. They will escort you and Nick through our engineering department and answer your questions. Wyatt and I must meet with the aliens or Nustu. They are very eager to meet with him. They selected Wyatt to represent Earth's final integration."

Wyatt wrinkled his forehead. "Why me?"

"We have always been impressed with your leadership and judgment," Charge said. "You convinced several military bases to comply and saved many lives. I agreed and recommended you."

Wyatt flashed a scowl. "I hope I live up to your expectations."

Charge handed Justin and Nick off to chief engineer Oriess and led Wyatt into the alien's chamber. A small frail alien encased in an atmospheric controlled bubble glimpsed up. The alien had black eyes, thin lips and a small nose. His smooth, hairless skin resembled the color of white chalk.

Mind to mind, the alien invited Wyatt to sit. Charge and Wyatt sat next to the bubble. The alien said, "I'm the last of my kind. I have fulfilled my mission after so many years. The Nustu's sole purpose is to ensure the propagation of our species. We must integrate with another compatible species to survive. This is true for humans as well. Someday Earth will face the sun's destruction and humans will have to find a new world for integration. The Nustu have collected, preserved, and stored genetic samples from several species on Earth in an interstellar arc to take with them at the time of Earth's evacuation. The arc will be safely preserved until departure. Your friends are looking at the new ship and are invited to explore the stars for the next planet to seed."

He coughed and drew in a long, slow breath. "My time has ended. I'm very old. It's time for a new generation to take the helm." He pointed to Charge. "I have chosen Charge and you to take control of the helm. I would like you to aide Charge in integrating our technology with the humans. They'll listen to you. Your commanders seem eager to learn, and I believe you can lead in the transition. Do you accept?"

Wyatt bowed. "I do."

"Excellent." The alien said and motioned to stop. Charge said his goodbyes and escorted Wyatt to the archives in the next chamber.

Hundreds of capsules containing cryogenically frozen aliens lined up against the walls of the chamber. Charge stretched his hands out. "These capsules contain generations of commanders in their quest through space in search of a new beginning. After integration is complete on Earth, this starship will be cast into the sun for what the Nustu or aliens call The Joining. Our customs and beliefs dictate that, after completion of our purpose, we must join with the source. The Nustu use the sun as their catalyst to join."

"A baptism by fire," Wyatt said.

Charge nodded. "We consider an impact with the sun a spiritual experience. The death of the humans chosen on 4-20-25 is an honorable and divine death." He lowered his head. "The aliens feel the humans' death on that day is one of reverence and respect to Earth's species."

Wyatt twisted his mouth. "When is The Joining?"

"Soon, if integration goes as planned," Charge said. "That is up to you and me."

"What is next?"

"We just need to implement the technology," Charge said. "We have to finish cleanup of the planet and set up sustainable energy systems. That means teaching and implementing our technology. We will teach our technology to you in stages, so as not to overwhelm or tempt you with unlimited power."

"Smart. Where do I fit in?"

"Presenting, convincing, and negotiating the deal with your commanders." Charge motioned to go.

"Done."

"Nick and Justin will also help with the transition," Charge said. "I will give them information to build and share."

Charge led Wyatt back to meet Justin and Nick, and they teleported back to Nick's kitchen. Charge handed Nick a cube and a smooth metal sphere. "This is a clean source of energy and can be used to power cars, houses or anything that requires power to operate. It is similar to the one I gave you to use for your band." He laid down a round crystal disc and waved Justin and Nick's hand over the top of it. "This has a biometric security system. The disc only answers to you. It will project a hologram explaining the cube's schematics and give you instructions on how to use the cube, the sphere and ways to utilize its energy system."

He flicked his finger over the disc and displayed an outline entitled The Phases. Charge stretched out his hand. "The plan consists of three phases. Phase One is conversion. It will convert the existing energy system and get you started until Phase Two is realized. Phase Two will help you learn an advanced design and build new energy systems. Phase Three will implement a cleanup and assist in recycling the old systems."

Charge passed Wyatt another crystal disc. "View the hologram and learn the contents of the proposal. Take it to Lt. General Sloan and present it to him for approval. The proposal consists of converting the bases into an academy. The academy will focus on education, design, and building new crafts. I believe that education is the key to any advanced society."

Wyatt nodded. "I'll take the proposal to the Lt. General."

Charge bowed. "Thank you, gentlemen. If you have no further questions or concerns, I need to meet with Paige." The two declined and Charge cornered Nick. "It's Paige's turn to get some answers to her questions. I'll return her soon." Nick nodded and walked with Charge to the garden.

Levi and Paige gazed up from weeding. Charge cast his eyes down at Paige. "Ready for some answers?"

Paige stood. "Absolutely." Levi hopped up and asked if he could go.

Charge stared at him. "Levi, you and I know that's not a good idea."

Levi shot Charge a puzzled look. "What do you mean?"

Charge scowled. "You formed a plot to destroy us."

Paige scoffed. "What are you talking about?"

"The blood supply. Levi told the two soldiers where to find it," Charge said. "He planned to destroy the beings that took his partner."

She scrunched her face. "You did this, Levi?"

Levi flared his nostrils. "They killed billions of people."

Nick rubbernecked Levi and narrowed his eyes. "You don't understand. They saved you and our planet." He glanced over at Charge. "Explain it to him."

Charge cleared his throat. "I'm going to let Paige do that after we meet aboard the ship."

Paige glared at Levi and spun around to Charge. "Then let's go."

Charge and Paige teleported aboard the deck of the starship. Paige turned to Charge. "Did Levi's plot endanger you?"

"We knew Levi's situation with the loss of his partner," Charge said. "Your attempts to correct the plot changed his fate."

Paige forced a smile. "What happens to children born with positive blood in the future?"

"The recessive Rh-positive gene has been neutralized. That protein will not appear with both Rh-negative dominant parents," Charge said. "Relax, Paige. You and Nick are Rh-negative dominant. Your children are safe."

Paige exhaled and peered out at the moon and stars beyond. "It's vast and beautiful." She spotted the ship under construction. "What's its name?"

"Solstice." He presented a hologram of the ship and briefly outlined Solstice's mission. "She'll serve us well." Charge clapped his hands. "Now, for some of those answers."

He waved his finger and displayed a computer system. "This is a quantum computer, called QC-4. We use algorithms to confirm our predictions. The hybrids network with the computer as one. QC-4 enhances our abilities to predict future events like the solar flare." Charge flicked his finger and projected an image of the spheres, creating an equatorial ring. He pointed at the ring. "It warps or bends time for limited time travel. We found a way to manipulate the central shift during the formation of the energy bubble to create a very limited time shift. That's how I was able to teleport and give you the shot." Charge cocked his head. "However, we rarely use it because it's dangerous and unstable."

He dismissed the hologram, led Paige into a chamber and introduced her to the alien in the bubble. Afterward, Charge escorted Paige to the cryogenic chamber and explained the source and The Joining Ceremony.

Paige gaped at Charge. "Is the source God?"

"Yes, the source is God," Charge said. "Isn't it interesting how we name or define God?"

She bobbed her head in response. "What do they think God is?"

Charge took a deep breath. "The source is unbound. It is defined as *everything*. We are all one and belong to the collective, and the collective returns to the source." Charge cracked a glimmer of a smile. "Even down to the smallest particle. Nothing dies or is wasted, only transformed, reunited, and joined."

"Joined and reborn again," Paige said. "Recycled back?"

"Perhaps to the humans," he said. "But not to the aliens or Nustu. They are only concerned with joining with the source. They want to remain joined."

She raised her brow. "No reincarnation?"

"No," he said. "Once is enough for them."

Paige sagged her shoulders. "That is true for some humans as well."

"They also believe that our purpose is simply to become, and after you fulfill your purpose, you take everything you've learned back to the collective." He put his hand up to his heart. "The Nustu believe that we must hold on to the sacred. To them sacred means knowledge. The sacred must never be forgotten and is forever expanding. We take the sacred back to the collective, so that we can reveal our wisdom to The

Divine and prove our worthiness."

"That's beautiful."

Charge lifted his long index finger. "Also, they believe that the source gives you everything you need, and it is up to you to use it wisely."

"Humans have not used it wisely."

He nodded and wrinkled his forehead. "No, humans have not." He held his gaze. "Are you ready to go back?"

"Yes," Paige said. "Thank you for showing me *everything.*"

He circled his arms in the air. "Yes, *everything.* Could you explain *everything* to Levi, please?"

"Yes," she said. "I will explain *everything*—the source, joining, and their purpose."

"Thank you," he said. "I would like to have Levi come to The Joining Ceremony. I believe if he understood, it would give him closure for his husband and partner."

"Of course," she said. "When is The Joining?"

"We have time," he said. "The planet must be cleaned up and integration complete."

Charge handed Paige a crystal disc. "I've programmed a hologram to explain the alien's history, journey to Earth, the solar flare, beliefs and The Joining." Charge tapped his insignia and teleported Paige back home.

Paige led Levi into the kitchen, laid the crystal disc on the table and waved her hand. After the presentation, Levi wiped his cheek. "I'm sorry for the trouble I have caused."

Paige rubbed his shoulder. "Do you understand now?"

"I do, but I still have so much anger," Levi said. "I wish my partner was Rh-negative."

"I wish my cameraman James was too, but he wasn't."

"I forgot," Levi said. "You have losses too."

"The aliens had to make hard choices," Paige said. "And I believe those choices weren't easy."

"I know," Levi said. "I'll be okay. No more plots."

"Charge wants you to go to The Joining," Paige said. "He thinks it can help you mourn your partner." She folded her hands. "During The Joining, the Nustu will also depart into the sun's solar flare just like James and your partner did."

"True," Levi said. "According to them, an honorable departure."

Paige hugged Levi, and they both joined Charge in the backyard.

Paige smiled at Charge, threw up two thumbs, and mouthed, "Everything, is okay."

Charge shot Paige a nod of understanding. "I hope both of you will join us for The Joining Ceremony." They both nodded.

Charge grasped Paige by the arm. "One more thing, Paige." He walked her over to a private corner. "We have a group of orphan children located at one of our stations and want to integrate them back into the community. They're doing very well. But I think it is safe enough to bring them back. I would appreciate any help Nick's compound can give us organizing their return."

Paige smiled. "Of course, whatever we can do." Her eyes grew wide. "It was your group that watched over Jake and the kids, wasn't it? He told me someone provided canned goods to them."

"Yes, it was us," Charge said. "We monitored them until Nick found them."

"Why didn't you tell me?" Paige said. "I could have gotten them?"

"I told Nick, or suggested it, when it was time to retrieve them."

"Mind to mind?" Paige said. "A telepathy?"

"Yes," Charge said. "I led Kellan, Declan, Wyatt, and Nick to their home when it was time." Charge crooked a side smile. "I had to wait until your group was ready. Also, Jake."

Paige cocked her head to the side. "Did you suggest that Nick and I stay in Denver instead of going to the desert with Wyatt and Justin?"

"Yes, I needed you here to save Grace." Charge seized her hand. "I needed Nick to build the compound."

"I thought so. Something kept telling me to stay," Paige said. "And Nick was so insistent that we stay. Come to think of it, so was Wyatt."

"I know, I had to plant that seed in you and Wyatt at the time I gave you the shot," Charge said. "Building the compound was all Nick. He was very determined to keep you safe, so I didn't need to intervene at all." Charge slanted his head to the side. "The reporter in you wanted to go. That urge was strong." Charge squeezed her hand. "Any regrets, Paige?"

"Not one," Paige said. "Grace is the love of our life."

"Good."

She rubbed the top of his hand. "How did you learn telepathy?"

"Humans only use a small percentage of their brains," Charge said. "We know how to access one-hundred percent of ours." Charge cocked his head to the side. "We also know how to access yours as well. We just turn all of yours on. It's temporary, but still very effective."

Paige shrugged her shoulders. "Ten percent, huh?"

"Yep." Charge winked. "I need to talk to Nick."

He ambled outside and sat beside Nick on the front porch with Bo. He leaned back in the chair. "Nick, you were my greatest challenge. I can't go on the next mission unless I know Grace and Paige are in good hands. Charge folded his arms. "Out of everyone, you were the toughest to convince. You are fiercely protective and have an innate instinct to fight and protect those you love. You and Justin both, but you, my friend, do not scare or trust easily." He leaned forward. "We just have one more issue to resolve." He held out his hand, teleported a journal in the palm of his hand and handed it to Nick. Charge tapped one of the metal discs on his uniform and activated a hologram. The corpses of the family Kent and Nick ran across on a supply mission emerged. Images of the mother who had killed herself and her two children displayed. Charge reached over and opened the journal. He pointed to the date: 3-5-25.

Nick read the entry. "She's deeply depressed. It looks like she'd contemplated suicide before the sightings." He wrinkled his forehead. "So her perception of a rapture was just an excuse to end their lives."

"I believe so," Charge said. "I know this weighed heavily on your mind, Nick. It has been hard for you to reconcile this. We used religious symbols in the crop circle because we thought it might give those humans with religious views peace. We believed it might give humanity a chance to express an attitude of cooperation and help each other. We hoped it would give humans an incentive and inspiration to work together and forge a new path for humanity and for the planet. I knew crop circles would ignite curiosity among UFO believers and hoped it would initiate contact, and the desire to help with integration."

Nick exhaled. "A smart strategy, Charge."

"Yes, it was," Charge said. "But... go ahead and ask it."

Nick held up the journal. "How did you know to get this journal?"

"I have monitored you, Paige, and Grace. You are important to me. Any time one of you are in distress, I come," Charge said. "That day your heart rate shot up, I felt your anger at her and those you believed caused the death. I knew I needed to explain, if at all possible, so I scanned the area and confiscated the journal right after you left the room. A crime scene investigation, if you like." He tapped the journal. "I kept the journal to use if your feelings had not resolved themselves in time. So, because of my impending departure soon, I'm afraid we've run out of time. Therefore, here I am with the journal for resolution." Charge smiled. "Has it helped?"

"Yes, my friend. It has," Nick said. "We're good."

"Good." Charge placed his hand on the journal. "Perhaps she can rest in peace now."

Nick shook his finger at Charge. "I'll make sure of it."

Charge stared at Nick. "Burn or bury it." He lifted his long thin finger. "That's a good idea. Maybe a few words over The Joining."

Nick shook his head. "You read my mind again, didn't you?" Charge dipped his chin. Nick clapped his hands together. "Burn it with the rest of her remains?"

Charge nodded. "Appropriate."

"I will do it soon," Nick said. Charge bequeathed Nick a sly grin and faded out.

Nick snatched the journal and slapped it with his hand. Bo perked up. Nick squinted at Bo. "Joining? What the fuck is The Joining?" Nick climbed up the stairs with Bo trailing close behind and slid the journal in the top drawer of his dresser.

Later that night, Nick and Justin poured coffee and prepared for a long night of study. They laid the crystal disc on the coffee table and waved their hands across the disc to activate it. A hologram projected the schematics and instructions for installing the cube and using the sphere. The two studied until three in the morning.

The next day, they installed the sphere on the rooftop to recharge from the sun's energy and synced up the cube. Nick chuckled. "Looks like a Rubik's cube, but each square has a removable energy chip instead of just a colored square. Very clever. The cube serves as a recharging unit." Nick removed one of the chips from the cube. "The chips work like a battery." He connected the chips to supply energy to the house. Then, the two connected the rest of the compound to their own grid using the chips.

After they'd finished the compound, the two converted the electric cars and SUVs they'd retrieved months before from the car lot. Using the instructions from the hologram, they used an energy chip in each car and noted that they had to exchange the chips every ninety days.

Wyatt packed his disc upstairs to his room, activated it and studied for his presentation. His presentation included Phase II and Integration.

He sat up straight and rubbed his hands together.

"Okay, integrations are separated into three stages." He thrust out his index finger. "Stage one consists of educating everyone with a tailored program specific to their abilities. Their abilities will determine their track, either pilot or engineer." He thrust his middle finger up. "Stage two, pilots learn to fly and engineers learn design." He tossed up his ring finger. "Stage three, the pilots fly and engineers build."

Kat peeked her head in Wyatt's room and handed him a cup of coffee. "Wyatt, take a break?"

Wyatt pulled her close. She straddled over him, sat on his lap, snatched his cup and set it down on a side table. Kat slid her top off, unhooked her bra and threw it on the floor. Then she unbuttoned his shirt and removed it. Wyatt unfastened the snap on her shorts and stripped them off her. Kat unsnapped and unzipped his pants. He stood up with Kat, carried her to the bed and kicked the door shut with his foot. He removed his pants and climbed on top of her. Wyatt kissed her slowly and teased her with his tongue. He lightly brushed the back of her neck with his lips and gazed into her eyes. Her pupils dilated as her hunger soared. She grabbed his hips and guided him inside her. Wyatt moved in gentle deliberate motions and Kat peaked. With their detonations close at hand, he increased his pace until both released.

Afterward, the two lingered in the moonlight. Wyatt caressed her and murmured, "I love you."

Kat kissed his cheek. "Love you more." She closed her eyes and slumbered, naked in Wyatt's arms.

Wyatt stared at the moon's rays shining down on Kat's breasts. He leaned over and stroked her cheek. "You're so beautiful." He peered up at the moon and stars. "What endless possibilities are out there for us babe?"

The next morning, Wyatt drove to Buckley AFB. He sat down with Lt. General Sloan and activated the disc. Wyatt displayed the hologram and went through Phase II-IV—Integration, Conversion and Cleanup. He disclosed the details of Integration, and the three stages for engineers. For engineers—he laid out the plans to educate, design, and build. Then he announced the stages for pilots—to educate, learn the designs, and fly. He impressed the general with a holographic instructor and laid out the program in full detail.

Wyatt pointed to the disc. "The crystal disc replaces all the computers. The program is individualized." The general viewed the program and eagerly agreed to convert the base to an academy. Wyatt stood. "I'll let Charge know we're good to go. General, I assure you that Justin and Nick will help convert the base and assist in an upgrade of the energy system."

Wyatt saluted, drove back home, contacted Charge and delivered the news from the general. Charge teleported a larger sphere and several cubes to convert the entire base, and Wyatt stored them in the storage unit.

On his way back from the storage unit, Wyatt spied Kent gawping at one of the SUVs in the driveway. He strode over and stood beside Kent. Kent folded his arms. "I'm going to drive to Winnemucca and see if Claire and Charley made it back there yet."

Wyatt leaned against the vehicle and crossed his arms. "That's a good idea."

"I asked Amber if she wanted to go, but she decided to stay with Justin until he leaves on Solstice," Kent said. "I asked Levi to go too, but Levi wants me to wait until after The Joining." He kicked the ground. "Do you know when The Joining is?"

Wyatt shrugged. "Could be a while."

"Should I wait?"

"You might give it some time," Wyatt said. "Claire may come here with Charley."

"She has no way to get here," Kent said. "No chips where she is."

"They're converting everywhere, not just here," Wyatt said. "We could ask Charge."

"Could you ask him?"

"Sure." Wyatt marched inside, activated his disc and contacted Charge. Charge appeared on a hologram. Wyatt curled his lip. "This is so cool."

Charge lowered his chin in response. "How can I help?"

"Can you locate Charley and Claire?"

Charge twisted his mouth. "I'll see what I can do."

Wyatt thanked him and signed off. He cracked the front door. "Charge is going to try to locate them." Kent thanked Wyatt and motioned for him to join him on the front porch. The two reminisced about the women in their lives and sipped sweet tea.

The next day, Kent headed to work in the garden and passed by the house. He glimpsed over and spotted Claire and Charley on the front porch next to Charge and Wyatt. Wyatt peered over at Kent. "Fast enough for you?"

Kent grinned from ear to ear. "How did you find them?"

Charge stood up. "One of the hybrids was working with them at Edward's AFB."

Claire jumped up. "I must go back in a few days to finish, but you can come with me if you like?"

Kent snorted. "How did you get here?"

"Teleporter," Claire said. "Charge can teleport us back in a few days. Charley wants to visit for a while."

Kent motioned for her to come out in the yard. Claire sauntered over to Kent. He leaned close. "Are you and Charley together?"

"No, no, he's helping us." Claire giggled. "He's good at it too. That man could convince anyone to do anything."

"Good, I'm glad you're not with him." Kent said. "Would you like me to go with you, when you head back?"

"Of course. I think we have something, don't you?"

"I do," Kent said. "But I wasn't sure if you did."

"I think you should come with me and find out." Claire kissed his cheek.

Wyatt strolled up to the couple. "Kent, why don't you show Claire around?"

Kent grasped Claire's hand and gave her a tour of the compound. The tour ended with the two alone in his room and spent the rest of the day canoodling.

Chapter Sixteen

Cleanup

After the solar event on April 20, 2025, Charge's cleanup mission began. Several of the hybrids' large spaceships hovered a quarter-mile above the ocean. Their scans revealed miles and miles of plastics, metal, glass, and cardboard floating in the ocean. The hybrids positioned the spheres a mile above the water and activated a vortex filled with swirling solar radiation particles. The spaceships scanned and used their tractor beams to lock onto debris they did not recycle and transported it directly into the swirling radiation field. The vortex scrambled the particles, and the spheres converted and stored them as energy.

After they'd completed the ocean cleanup, the hybrids targeted nuclear power plants and nuclear waste disposal sites deep within the ground. They destroyed waste from coal-powered plants, mining sites, oil refineries, and drilling sites. Tons of garbage in landfills and waste products in rivers and lakes disappeared. They recycled metals, glass, and paper, but scrambled toxic plastics and teleported them into the vortex for energy conversion.

Simultaneously, the hybrids strengthen Earth's weakened magnetic field. They slowly extracted carbon and toxic particles from the atmosphere mended the damaged ozone and reversed the effects of global warming. After reducing toxic carbon, they gently manipulated and gradually coaxed the water and air currents back into their original pathways. Water temperatures and weather patterns returned to normal. The hybrids initiated plans to replace the ice in the polar regions to minimize the impending threat of coastal flooding. Last of all, they scanned and removed pesticides and pollutants from the groundwater and soil.

By August 21, 2026, the hybrids had completed stage one. Afterward, Charge dispatched blueprints of stage two from Phase IV Cleanup. They unveiled replanting foliage on rooftops and replacing blacktop with plants. The plan designated areas to plant trees on hilltops and replace deforestation. Charge exhibited plans for a worldwide cleanup and included specific plans for the Denver area. On September 7, Wyatt presented the plans to Nick and the others and the deputy. Together, they forged a plan to harvest the seeds from pinecones and seedlings from deciduous trees in the area. The hybrids converted heavy operating equipment to run on clean energy to move topsoil and complete Phase IV.

After a long day of replanting seedlings, Wyatt flopped down on the couch next to Paige and Grace. He drew in a deep breath and slowly exhaled. "For the first time in ages, I feel the impossible is indeed possible. I understand that Charge's plans can't eliminate climate change all at once, but I'll bet they slow it, and we might be able to manage the damage already done. Perhaps the Earth can heal and cleanse herself, provided we don't contribute to any further damage."

Paige lifted her shoulders. "At least now we have a fighting chance." She slapped Wyatt on the knee. "Want some lemonade?" He nodded. Paige dashed into the kitchen, and Wyatt eyed Grace who was standing up using the edge of the coffee table. She let go. Her eyes opened wide.

Wyatt grinned. "Hey, sweetie, you're standing all by yourself." Grace turned, took her first step, and plopped down on her bottom. She crawled over to the table and pulled herself up once again. She let go, stepped twice, and plopped. Wyatt chuckled. "Baby steps, little one. At first, we all have to take baby steps. But sooner or later, we all succeed."

Chapter Seventeen

The Joining

Paige and Levi teleported to the mothership orbiting the Earth. Charge met them on deck. He stood rigid in a long, steel, blue gown with a silky headband, bejeweled with golden metallic symbols. Charge led them through two lines of hybrids paying tribute to the deceased one. The hybrids lined the wall on both sides of a long hallway to the alien's chamber. They lowered their heads and knelt down on one knee as Charge passed by them.

Charge, Paige, and Levi entered the chamber and spotted the alien's lifeless body laid out in his clear vault. Charge dropped down on one knee and lowered his head. "A purpose fulfilled and meaning realized. We honor all those who have returned to the source." Paige and Levi knelt and repeated the same prayer. The two finished, and Charge led the procession of aliens through the second chamber. Rows of ancient Nustu lined the walls of the huge chamber—each safely encased in their crypts.

After everyone filled the chamber, they all knelt, and in unison recited the same prayer. "A purpose fulfilled and meaning realized. We honor all those who have returned to the source."

Afterward, everyone filed out of the huge chamber in a beautiful procession and, two at a time, vanished. Charge cast his eyes down at Paige. "Relax, we're all teleporting back to the starship." Paige shot him a side smile. He dipped his chin, and the three teleported to the starship to escort the mothership on her last voyage to the sun.

An hour later, the starship stopped at the sun's boundary, and the hybrids stood at attention. They crossed their arms in the shape of an X across their chest and chanted as the mothership slowly vaporized into the sun. After the mothership melded as one, Charge lowered his head. "We are born of the stars, only to return once again, and come back to the source, to reunite, join, and forever remain."

The hybrids stood and in unison murmured, "To join and forever remain." Last, they bowed their heads in silence. After several minutes, the hybrids resumed their duties on the ship.

Within minutes, Paige tapped Levi on the shoulder. "We're back. Isn't she incredible?" She gazed upon Earth and drew in a deep breath. "How precious this beautiful blue marble in space is." Levi nodded. She turned to Charge. "We almost destroyed her, Charge. You did the right thing. Life on Earth is precious."

"It is." Charge glimpsed over at Levi. "Your partner would not have liked you joining at this time."

Levi gasped. "I know. It was only a fleeting thought."

Charge leaned forward. "I'm glad you changed your mind."

Paige eyed both men. "You two are always full of surprises." She put her arm around Levi. "Levi, don't you dare think of leaving us. We have too much work to do. Got it!"

Levi grinned. "Wouldn't dream of it."

She hugged Levi. "Good."

Charge thanked Levi and Paige for coming to the ceremony and teleported them back to the compound.

Paige turned to Levi. "Did you get any closure from the ceremony?"

"I think so. I like the idea that death is not the end and that we join or reunite," Levi said. "Someone once told me that God is like an ocean, and we are just merely a cup of God."

"Or maybe"—Paige raised her index finger—"we're merely a raindrop that fills a river and flows back to the ocean in a continuous cycle."

He lifted a brow. "Either way, eventually, we'll all join."

"Very true," Paige said. "But until then, my good man, let's enjoy the rain, the sun's warmth, and all Earth's rivers and oceans."

Levi bowed. "Let's."

Paige spied Nick sitting close by in a lawn chair with Grace standing up, holding on to one of Nick's knees and tugging on Bo's head in Nick's lap. She strolled over to Nick, leaned down and kissed his cheek and motioned for him to talk to Levi. She reached down, snatched Grace in her arms and headed back to the house.

Nick slapped the arm of his chair, popped up and put his arm around Levi. "How are you doing?"

"Better now."

"I heard a little of your conversation and I think I understand The Joining now," Nick said. "How was the ceremony?"

"Good," Levi said. "Peaceful. It gave me something to hold on to."

"We all need peace, Levi. Livin' can be a hard road to walk, especially alone," Nick said. "Remember, you're not alone. You're stuck with us." He squeezed Levi and lifted him off the ground. "That reminds me, I need to give a bit of peace to someone myself."

"Sounds like unfinished business." Levi wobbled from Nick's hug.

"You could say that." Nick said. "I made a promise to Kent before he and Claire left, and also to Charge, and I need to keep it." He patted Levi on the back. "Need to take care of business."

Nick ran upstairs, retrieved the journal out of the top drawer of his dresser and loaded Bo in the back of his converted truck. Bo and Nick pulled up to the home of the woman who'd killed herself and her children. He put the tailgate down and grabbed some old newspapers out of the king cab. He slapped his hands together. "Come, Bo."

They headed to the bedroom, and Nick placed the journal on top of the charred remains of the burned house. He crinkled up the newspapers, threw them in a pile and lit them. Nick placed the journal on top of the flames. The pages from her journal folded, crinkled, and burned to ash. The cover curled. He pressed his lips together and nodded.

"I hope you can find peace now, Miranda. I get it now. It isn't until you love deeply that you realize what you have to lose. If I lost Paige and Grace, I would feel the same desperation." He cleared his throat. "It is said that in death you are unbound, and if true, no longer bound to emotional or physical pain. It is also said that you shed all restraints of the physical world." Nick shuffled his feet. "I learned, that according to The Joining, that after death we are joined once again with the creator, and it is then that the soul is finally free." He smiled and drew his hands together. "Be free and go in peace."

Bo nuzzled his leg. Nick reached down and petted Bo's head. "Good boy. We've kept our promise. Time to go home." Nick put down his tailgate, loaded Bo and slammed it shut. "Promises kept."

Nick sat down on the front porch and slapped his legs. "Come, Bo." Bo put his head on his lap. Nick stared at the chess set displayed on the table. Suddenly, Charge appeared in the chair in front of him. Charge grew a slanted smile. "Care to play?"

Nick grinned. "Of course."

An hour into the game, Nick squinted at Charge. *Good ability. Damn, no weaknesses. Endgame is going to be tough to defeat.* Nick studied his final move. He put his hand to his chin, rubbed it, and glanced at Charge. Nick leaned back and tapped his finger on the arm of the chair. *Should I walk away in a draw or lose the game to win the best outcome?* He put his finger on his chess piece and sacrificed his king.

Charge smiled. "Checkmate, chess master."

Nick sneered. "Well played, mate."

Charge pursed his lips. "Very interesting move." He stared at Nick for a few moments. "You can strive to become the chess master, but remember that there is always the next challenge, and the challengers are never-ending."

"Sometimes you win when you lose," Nick said. "Especially if the best outcome is in the final judgment."

Charge held his stare. "How did I do in the final judgment?"

Nick gave him his clever grin. "Exceptional."

Charge lowered his chin. "I see that you have learned that sacrificing for the right outcome can be more beneficial than a victory at that moment."

Nick nodded. "A wise man will examine the character of a winner before rendering judgment." He gaped at Charge. "It is always best to look at the bigger picture."

"Nick," Charge said. "You are exactly as I expected. Exceptional as well." He put his hand on Nick's shoulder. "I'm glad you took care of the journal and returned it to its proper place."

"So am I," Nick said. Charge waved his finger in a salute and slowly faded away.

Nick gazed out over the landscape and peeked down at Bo. "It's time that Paige and I look at the bigger picture and join together as a family." He dashed upstairs, took the engagement ring out of the velvet bag and put it in his pocket.

Nick raced outside and spotted Paige playing with Grace in the yard. He lay down on the grass next to Paige. "Marry me, babe."

Paige glanced over at Nick. "Sure will."

Nick grabbed the ring out of his pocket and handed it to her.

Her eyes grew wide. "You're serious."

"I don't care when or where," he said. "Just marry me."

She squealed. "Where did you get this?"

"I found it at an antique store a while ago and refurbished it."

Paige leaped over Grace's toys and hugged him. "Yes, yes, yes!"

Nick snatched the ring and slid it on Paige's finger. "If you want me to jump over a broom, go to a church, or get married naked in a field of daisies, I will."

Paige giggled. "Here with all the people we love will be just fine."

He kissed her. "Let me know the time and place. Next week, next month, or next year, you decide."

She smiled. "I think we need to do it before Charge and the others leave."

Nick raised his brows. "Soon, then?"

She kissed her ring. "Soon."

He bent over and smooched the top of Grace's head. "Mom and Dad are tying the knot soon."

Paige stroked Grace's cheek. "Mommy will be Mrs. Nick Landon."

Nick snickered. "Really? You're going to take my name?"

"Yes," Paige said. "But little Ms. Grace will take her father and mother's name too. Grace Brody Reynolds Landon."

"What about Martin?"

"That's why I'm taking Landon, Paige said. "It will be less confusing."

"What's wrong with Grace Martin Brody Reynolds Landon?"

"I'm saving Martin for our son. We'll name our son Martin to honor my father."

"Oh, so we're having a son?"

"In due time," Paige said. "All in good time."

"Nicolas Martin Landon," Nick said. "I like that." He reached over and pulled her close. "Better get started on that."

Paige pushed his shoulder. "Better get married first."

"No harm in a little practice."

"You get plenty of that, Nick."

"Practice makes perfect," Nick said. "Making babies is hard work." He chuckled and picked up Grace. "Grace Brody Reynolds Landon, let's hope you don't marry a man with a long name. It might take all day to get through the ceremony."

Paige giggled. "Hopefully, she'll only do it once."

Nick laughed. "Save us money that way."

On September 16, a week before the group's scheduled departure on Solstice, everyone gathered around the front yard of Nick's compound to partake in the union of Paige and Nick. Charge stood in his silky blue ceremonial attire and pronounced the couple man and wife. Nick lifted Paige's wedding veil and slowly kissed his bride. He turned to the audience of friends, soldiers, hybrids, and police officers and shouted, "Let's eat cake, party, and celebrate the happiest day of my life."

Paige sliced a piece off their wedding cake and shoved a chunk in Nick's mouth, leaving frosting on his lips. She took her finger, scraped the goo from his lip and licked it off. Nick grabbed a slice of cake and held it up to Paige's lips. He paused, flashed a mischievous grin, and slowly popped it in her mouth. She smiled. "Sorely tempted to smear it on my face, huh?"

He grew a wily grin. "Not a chance. I want to get lucky tonight."

After everyone finished their cake, Nick tipped back a few shooters of Levi's Grey Goose and joined his bandmates on guitar to sing the couple's song. After Nick played their song, they said their goodbyes.

Nick winked, dipped his hand in his suit pocket and pulled out Paige's scarlet scarf. "I have a surprise for you."

Paige lifted her eyebrows. "What are you up to?"

He covered her eyes. "It's a very nice surprise." Nick nodded at Charge, and Charge teleported the bride and groom to Nick's first secret destination.

Nick turned a blindfolded Paige in the direction of the lake. "Guess where we are?"

Paige sniffed the air. "Outside somewhere in the trees around water."

He removed the blindfold. "Where I knew you were the only one I wanted."

She scanned the area. "The exact spot we swam naked together at Lake Perry."

He held her close and kissed her tenderly. "You still are the only one."

She gazed into his green eyes. "Thank you for not giving up on me here."

He squeezed her. "Never will."

The sun slid behind the horizon. Nick gathered firewood and started a fire. Paige rubbed her hands together. "Where are we going to sleep?"

Nick pointed to a section behind a stand of trees. Paige spied a dome-shaped pod hidden in the foliage. He grinned. "Charge set the pod up for our honeymoon."

Paige strolled over and opened the door of the pod. A fruit bowl with wine and cheese sat on display. An antique bed with luxurious silk bedding awaited. A long, white, laced negligée lay across the bed. She lifted it up to her bosom. "A perfect fit." Paige placed it back on the bed and poked her head out the door. She glanced over at Nick tending his fire. "This is beautiful." Paige joined Nick next to the fire and squeezed his knee. "I can't believe you did all this."

He leaned over and kissed her. "I wanted you to remember our wedding day."

She wrapped her arms around his neck. "And night, no doubt."

Nick pulled her close. "We'd take a dip, but it's too cold."

"I can think of a better way to consummate our marriage." She pointed to the pod. "Like on that beautiful bed."

Nick grasped her hand and pulled her up. Paige stopped. "Hold on there… not so fast. There is a very sexy white negligée in there, and I intend to wear it on our wedding night." She hopped up. "You stay here until I call you."

Paige slipped the gown on, fixed her hair and lay across the bed. "Nick."

He peeked in and crept over to the bed. He grasped her by the hand and pulled her into his arms. "You look beautiful, Mrs. Landon."

"Thank you, Mr. Landon." He kissed her and slowly peeled off the lace gown. He stripped off his shirt and pants and tossed them in the corner. He brushed her neck with his lips and lowered her to the bed. He caressed her breasts and tantalized her erect nipples. Paige ran her hands through his hair and urged him to return to her lips. He kissed her again. She snatched his earlobe into her mouth and nuzzled it. "Take me now." Nick entered her, and with slow, even thrusts the two achieved an equal release.

Paige gradually opened her eyes and witnessed the stars shining through the transparent roof of the pod. She pointed to the starlight. "Nick, look up."

Nick turned over on his back. "Amazing. Isn't it?"

"This whole night is amazing." She reached over and swiped the hair from his eyes. "I'm completely full."

"Then I've accomplished rule three."

Paige giggled. "Rules two and three."

Nick bit his lip. "What about rule one?"

Paige shot him a puzzled look. "How will you or I know if you've accomplished it?"

Nick gave her a clever grin. "Ah, rule one. Treat her right." Nick paused. "Well, babe, if I've done my job right, then I have created a space of trust. One safe place, where you feel loved, respected, and cherished. And if I've achieved all those, then rules two and three will thrive."

"Then indeed you have accomplished that rule as well." Paige caressed him.

Nick pulled her closer. "Good to know." The two cuddled and fell into a contented slumber.

The next morning, Nick checked the countdown timer that Charge gave him. "Oh shit, six minutes left before teleport." He slapped Paige on her bare bottom. "Hurry, Paige. We teleport in five minutes." Nick grabbed his clothes and fumbled. "Paige, let's go."

Paige jumped up and put her bra and panties on. She pulled her shirt over her head and shoved her foot through her pant leg. Suddenly, they both teleported to the next destination.

Paige struggled to get her other foot inside her pant leg. The two eyed each other and laughed. They scanned out over the riverbank. Paige slipped her pants on and spotted the fishing gear on the river's edge. Nick fastened his pants and grabbed the fishing gear. He passed a jacket to Paige. She zipped up her hoodie and slid on her socks and waders. Nick handed her a fly pole. She smiled. "Our favorite fishing hole."

Nick snickered. "No Cowbears this time." Paige threw a stick at him. The two waded into the stream and cast their lines. Paige caught the first fish and Nick netted it, cleaned it, and placed it in the cooler for teleporting back to Levi to smoke. The two fished until noon. Nick snatched a teleported picnic basket from under the tree and set it up for lunch.

Paige shook her head. "Charge again?" Nick nodded, and the two ate warm fried chicken and cold potato salad. She patted her tummy. "How on Earth did Charge do this?"

"Food replicator," Nick said. "He teleported it a few minutes before I retrieved it from under the tree." She spotted the pod off in the distance. Nick raised his hand. "The fruit and wine." He jumped up and retrieved them to add to their feast.

After lunch, they both resumed fly-fishing, but about two in the afternoon, Paige removed her waders, pants, and shirt. She stared at Nick, reeling in another fish. She snorted. "This is the perfect moment."

Paige waded barefooted in her bra and panties out toward Nick. He turned and spotted a half-naked Paige. Paige plopped down in the water and quickly jumped back up. Nick threw down his pole and rushed over and grabbed her. He peered down at her. "Paige, what the hell? It's freezing!"

Paige gasped and stuttered, "Body heat, babe."

Nick picked her up in his arms and waded back to the bank. He removed his waders and picked up a shivering Paige and carried her to the pod that Charge had teleported over from the lake. Nick frowned. "I'm glad I got to you as soon as I did."

Paige shivered. "Still need body heat."

Nick grinned and motioned for Paige's underwear. "Off with them." Paige shot him a triumphantly crafty grin and threw him her wet bra and panties. Nick drew in a deep breath, ripped off his shirt and pants. "Okay, babe, body heat."

They both climbed into their antique bed and used their body heat, skin on skin, to warm up. When Paige resumed a normal body temperature, the two spent the rest of the afternoon using Paige's scarlet scarf for a bit of kinky fun. Then, after their delicious consummation, Nick grilled fresh salmon with asparagus for dinner.

After dinner, Nick spied his lost fly pole stacked with the other fishing gear. "Hot damn! Charge saved my beloved pole." Suddenly, the pole and cooler disappeared. Nick smiled. "Thanks, Charge." Nick checked the timer. "Fifteen minutes." Two seconds before takeoff, Nick wrapped his arm around Paige, and they teleported to their final destination—Nick's favorite isolated beach.

Paige scanned the beach. "Hawaii?" Nick dipped his chin and pointed to their teleported pod. He popped inside, grabbed Paige's bikini off the bed and handed it to her. She threw the bikini back on the bed and stripped off her clothes. She waded out into the ocean and dived under.

Nick peeled off his clothes and swam up to her. He lifted her up and slowly lowered her down to his lips and kissed her passionately. Nick gazed into her blue eyes. "Glad you didn't turn away this time."

"Never again, Mr. Landon."

The two embraced the sunset, listened to the waves crash against distant rocks and made love under the stars.

The next morning, Nick and Paige teleported to their compound and began their newly married life together, forever joined in partnership

Chapter Eighteen

Departure

On September 21, Justin sipped his coffee and glimpsed over at Amber. She wiped a tear from her cheek. Nick bit his lip and cleared his throat. Wyatt took a bite of pancakes and struggled to swallow. Paige stood behind Justin's chair and reached her arms around his shoulders and gave him a hug. "I'm going to miss you, smartass."

"Right back at you, page-turner," Justin said. "Just write that great American novel when I'm gone, will yah." He eyed everyone closely. "I'll miss all of you."

Amber shot up and ran to the bathroom. Paige squeezed Justin and whispered, "She's not going to take this very well, Justin."

"I know, but I have to go."

"Are you sure you want to do this?" Paige twisted her head and kissed his cheek.

"Yes," Justin said. "As hard as it is to leave, I have to go."

Wyatt bobbed his head. "Justin, you're one brave son of a bitch."

Justin scoffed. "You could go too, Wyatt."

"And be gone for ten years?" Wyatt said. "Grace would be eleven."

Justin dipped his head. "True."

"It's tempting," Wyatt said. "But I would miss her growing up."

Paige raised her brows. "She'll understand, Wyatt, if you really want to go."

Justin folded his arms. "Wyatt, you've got fifteen minutes to change your mind before Charge gets here."

Paige tapped the table and stared at Wyatt. "Kat would go, if you go."

Wyatt stared at Kat. "I know."

"In a heartbeat," Kat said. "I've always wanted to be an astronaut."

Amber ambled back in and sat down at the table. Justin peered over at her and mouthed the words, "I'm sorry."

Charge teleported in the living room and strode over to the kitchen. Justin stood up and motioned Amber to come to him. Charge gazed at Amber. "Amber, are you going?"

Amber grew wide-eyed. "For real?" She wrinkled her forehead and stared at Justin. "I guess so."

Charge grinned. "Excellent."

Justin arched his brow and stared at Amber. "Really?" She nodded. He turned to Wyatt. "What about you?"

Charge scanned Kat and shook his head. "Wyatt can stay and help with integration and transition. Kat will not be joining us. They're going to be parents in about seven months."

Wyatt's knees buckled. Kat clutched her stomach. "Are you sure?"

Charge lowered his chin. "Definitely."

"Oh my God, Wyatt," Paige said. "You're going to be a father." She wrapped her arms around him.

Wyatt gaped at Kat. She shrugged her shoulders. "I guess that's it then."

Wyatt crowed, "Not this time, Justin." He puffed out his shoulders. "Looks like you're on your own."

Justin marched over and hugged Wyatt. "Congratulations, old man. Take care of your family."

Wyatt hugged him back and whispered, "Don't be a hero. Stand down when you're told to and come back to us alive."

Justin grew a wide smile. "Will do."

Wyatt squeezed him tight. "Watch your six."

"You too," Justin said. "Next time, we go together."

Wyatt pat Justin's shoulders. "Next time."

Justin and Amber hugged everyone and said their goodbyes. Charley sauntered over and stood beside Amber. "If she goes, I go."

Charge turned to Charley. "Good enough, we can use an expert on human behavior." He leaned in close to Paige's ear. "You're in charge of Grace now."

Paige moved her lips close to Charge and kissed his cheek. "I've got this, Charge. Come back to us."

"Will do." Charge grasped both of her shoulders. "Paige, how does your book end? *Is it the end or the beginning?*"

Paige's eyes grew wide. "I'm surprised you remembered I was working on a book. I finished everything but the last chapter. Hum, that's an interesting title—Is it the end or the beginning?" Paige flashed Charge a wide grin. "I think a new beginning." She gazed in his eager eyes. "What do you think?"

Charge pursed his lips. "Every end is a new beginning."

"The end of one way of life can be the beginning of another, and sometimes it turns out to be an even bigger and better life." Paige laid her hand on Charge's hand. "Or it's like doors closing and doors opening. You just have to have the courage to walk through the open door."

Charge bowed to Paige, turned to Nick and mind to mind privately said *I'm glad you're in Paige's and Grace's life. I trust no one else more.*

Nick nodded. "Don't worry, I'll take care of our girls."

Charge winked at Nick, then out loud said, "See you in ten." Charge hit the metal symbol on his suit. Charge, Justin, Amber and Charley teleported aboard the starship.

Once aboard Solstice, the group gazed out at the heavens. Justin pointed at the brightest star. "That star has my name on it."

Amber squeezed Justin's hand. "Our name."

Justin grinned at Amber. "Has *our* name on it." He turned around and spotted Brandon standing next to four other men.

Brandon gazed over at Justin and gawked at him. He marched over to Justin and threw his arms around him. "Glad you could make it."

A mystified Justin turned to Charge. "What the hell?"

"Brandon's joining us," Charge said. "Lt. Col. Claire Turner sent him along with two other pilots, First Lt. Jane Avery from Maine and Second Lt. Cassie Dorian from West Texas."

Brandon hit Justin's arm. "I've been training for the last year with Avery and Dorian to fly shuttle crafts at bases in California and Nevada."

Amber and Charley waltzed over and grabbed Brandon. After their brief reunion, the pilots resumed their positions near the engineering deck. Charley and Amber headed for the infirmary—father and daughter were assigned as the ship's counselors aboard Solstice. Charge escorted Justin to his seat, and Justin took his position as Second Officer on the bridge of the starship.

Charge directed the navigator to plot their course by using entangled particles to map and target locations. Once plotted and programed, Charge sat in the captain's chair and ordered the spheres dispersed to create an equatorial ring. The navigator complied. Charge eyed everyone on the bridge and turned on the ship's intercom. "We are on a scouting mission to find a potential planet and sun that can support life. The planet will be for future inhabitance and possible genome adaptation and evolution for both species."

The navigator spun around. "Equatorial ring has engaged, and the central shift and vacuum bubble are ready for departure."

Charge cleared his throat. "Prepare for final check."

The navigator complied and glanced back at Charge. "All systems are Go."

Charge scanned the bridge's crew. "Final approval?" Everyone verbally agreed. He clasped his side panel. "At the ready." He pointed his finger at the navigator. "Proceed." After his order, Charge smiled and sent a parting message by hologram to Grace. He drew in a deep breath and transmitted, "Bye-bye."

On September 21, Solstice departed into the abyss in a search for the next sun and a compatible planet to seed. At the moment of the ship's departure, Grace sat up straight in her highchair and waved at Charge's holographic image. "Bye-bye." And when Charge's image faded, Grace jumped up and down in an attempt to bring him back, but instead he disappeared completely. Grace suddenly stopped, and her bottom lip quivered. She waved her hands back and forth, peered over at Paige with watery eyes and babbled, "All gone."

Paige furrowed her brow and waved. "Bye-bye, Charge." She waggled her hands and said, "Yes Gracie, Charge's… all gone."

The end…or… is their adventure just beginning?

About the author

S. K. White is a lover of science fiction and enjoys inventing new worlds and situations for her characters to discover, grow, explore and fall in love in. She treasures writing in her journal and recording thoughts and ideas that flow from the experiences she sees and hears all around her. She uses many of those reflections to create the characters that appear in her novels, and in the poetry she writes. S. K. White resides in a small town in the west; she embraces glorious sunsets in the cool evening breeze, and savors the captivating western landscapes that surround her.

More Black Velvet Seductions titles

Their Lady Gloriana by Starla Kaye
Cowboys in Charge by Starla Kaye
Her Cowboy's Way by Starla Kaye
Punished by Richard Savage, Nadia Nautalia & Starla Kaye
Accidental Affair by Leslie McKelvey
Right Place, Right Time by Leslie McKelvey
Her Sister's Keeper by Leslie McKelvey
Playing for Keeps by Glenda Horsfall
Playing By His Rules by Glenda Horsfall
The Stir of Echo by Susan Gabriel
Rally Fever by Crea Jones
Behind The Clouds by Jan Selbourne
Trusting Love Again by Starla Kaye
Runaway Heart by Leslie McKelvey
The Otherling by Heather M. Walker
First Submission - Anthology
These Eyes So Green by Deborah Kelsey
Dark Awakening by Karlene Cameron
The Reclaiming of Charlotte Moss by Heather M. Walker
Ryann's Revenge by Rai Karr & Breanna Hayse
The Postman's Daughter by Sally Anne Palmer
Final Kill by Leslie McKelvey
Killer Secrets by Zia Westfield
Crossover, Texas by Freia Hooper-Bradford
The Caretaker by Carol Schoenig
The King's Blade by L.J. Dare
Uniform Desire - Anthology
Safe by Keren Hughes
Finishing the Game by M.K. Smith
Out of the Shadows by Gabriella Hewitt
A Woman's Secret by C.L. Koch
Her Lover's Face by Patricia Elliott
Naval Maneuvers by Dee S. Knight
Perilous Love by Jan Selbourne
Patrick by Callie Carmen
The Brute and I by Suzanne Smith
Home by Keren Hughes
Only A Good Man Will Do by Dee S. Knight

Secret Santa by Keren Hughes
Killer Lies by Zia Westfield
A Merman's Choice by Alice Renaud
All She Ever Needed by Lora Logan
Nicolas by Callie Carmen
Paging Dr. Turov by Gibby Campbell
Out of the Ashes by Keren Hughes
A Thread of Sand by Alan Souter
Stolen Beauty by Piper St. James
Mystic Desire - Anthology
Killer Deceptions by Zia Westfield
Edgeplay by Annabel Allan
Music for a Merman by Alice Renaud
Joseph by Callie Carmen
Not You Again! by Patricia Elliott
The Unveiling of Amber by Viola Russell
Husband Material by Keren Hughes
Never Have I Ever by Julia McBryant
Hard Limits by Annabel Allan
Anthony by Callie Carmen
Paper Hearts by Keren Hughes
The King's Spy by L.J. Dare
More Than Words by Keren Hughes & Jodie Harrold
Lessons on Seduction by Estelle Pettersen
Rigged by Annabel Allan
Desire Me Again - Anthology
Mermaids Marry in Green by Alice Renaud
Holy Matchmaker by Nancy Golinski
Joshua by Callie Carmen
Whiskey Lullaby by Keren Hughes
Forgiveness by Starla Kaye
When the White Knight Falls by Virginia Wallace
Cowboy Desire – Anthology
The Bookshop by Simone Francis
Secret Love by F. Burn
Mischief and Secrets by Starla Kaye
Be Patient With My Love by Keren Hughes
Michael by Callie Carmen
Rainbow Desire - Anthology

Our back catalog is being released on Kindle Unlimited
You can find us on:
Twitter: BVSBooks
Facebook: Black Velvet Seductions
See our bookshelf on Amazon now! Search "BVS Black Velvet
Seductions Publishing Company"

Made in the USA
Las Vegas, NV
28 December 2021

39705057R00146